The
Tanner Side
of
Town

To Dale & Ken —
I hope y'all love
getting to know the
"Tanners."

By
Pam Avery

Pam Avery

P

ISBN 978-1-0880-316-9-8
Shades Creek Press, LLC
Crossroads Enterprises, LLC

About the Author: Pam Avery

The author graduated from the University of Georgia in 1972 with a major in journalism (public relations) and a minor in business (marketing). Her experience in both professions for the last 40 years has included bank management training, advertising design and sales, owning and selling a restaurant, restoring and utilizing several old buildings on her property, teaching private dance and drama lessons for 20 years, free-lance writing for a national textile firm, self-publishing two children's books, ghost writing a book, and working as a reporter, photographer, and columnist for five weekly community newspapers. She also added advertising sales and design to the mix the last year she worked for the group.

Avery completed her graduate work via The University of Memphis online program in 2013 and received a master's in journalism, with a concentration in media writing. She taught media writing and public speaking at Columbus State University for five years before taking the next challenge – writing her first novel – "The Tanner Side of Town."

Creating this work has been my job since January 2020. Although a challenge, seeing the finished product is beyond rewarding. I look forward to turning out more."

Acknowledgments

Betsy Adams Dyches, Owner/ Consultant, Dyches' Consulting Services, Columbia, SC

Through the engrossingly fast-paced saga of the Tanners, Ms. Avery fosters an examination of the universal good, bad, and ugly often inherent in human nature. The story is one of determination and redemption which drips with life as familiar to Southerners as iced tea. Ms. Avery has exquisitely and skillfully crafted intriguing and complex characters who pique our compassion and give us hope in the age-old battle between the forces of good and evil. I was sad to "leave the Tanners" when the book concluded, but the ending leaves the door wide open for a sequel!

Betsy Dyches

Tom Barnes, Artist

The reason to head to The Tanner Side of Town is that there are both delightful and obnoxious people there who strive to be at peace or wreak havoc, depending. Seeing who triumphs in this small southern town tale is a satisfying read.

Tom Barnes

Brigitte Cutshall, Solutions Consultant & Founder, Gemini Media

My favorite book genre is Historical Fiction and found this book fascinating. When you live in a small town, everyone's business is on full display. This book demonstrates what can be accomplished when people work together, the strength to do the right thing, to overcome diversity and corruption.

Brigitte Cutshall

Tamara Pierce, Licensed Realtor, Pine Mountain Ga Living

Pam's novel was a great read; hard to put down! It spoke to me of the importance of protecting the things one cannot put a price tag on: home, family and relationships.

Amy Skinner, Retired Educator and Lover of Things Written

A relevant, grass roots, Southern American Gothic novel. Set in the early 1900's in rural Georgia, this novel encompasses social mores demanded of women, race inequity and environmental hurdles...issues persisting to this day. YeeeHA for the sheros of this story!

Jane McCoy, Freelance Editor and Gardener

This book captures the spirit of Lucy Tanner, who boldly confronts the cultural norms of rural Georgia. Viewing life from a different perspective presents challenges that can be daunting, and the story serves as a reminder that we all have personal strength if we choose to.

Alice Wade,

A masterfully written novel in which the voices are rich with courage and compassion. They speak plainly of greed, racism and sexism running rampant in a small southern town. Avery leaves the reader with a longing for front porch sitting, warm breezes, a cool lemonade...and just another page.

Alice Wade

Pete McCommons, Co-Publisher Flagpole Magazine

Pam Avery marshals the deep experience of her active and multi-faceted life to spin a story of courage vs. corruption and love vs. loss, while keeping us turning the pages and rooting for the good guys.

—Pete McCommons

The Tanner Side *of* Town

By: Pam Avery

First Edition
First Printing, 2022

Book Cover Credits:
Artist Painting by Betty Bauman
Final Design Production by Natasha Walsh
Contributing Cover Production by Christian Skinner

Initial Reader & Developmental Editor, Jane McCoy
Edited by Candice Lawrence, Athens, Georgia

ISBN 978-1-0880-316-9-8
Copyright 2022 by Crossroads Enterprises, LLC
Shades Creek Press, LLC
Printed in the United States of America

Disclaimer

This is a work of fiction. All the characters and plot situations are totally fiction and are not based in whole or in part on any known or related person(s), situations or circumstances. This work of fiction is an artistic creation of the author based on imagination and thought. Any similarities created are purely fiction.

Dedicated to
May Yon Dickey Freeman
...who planted the seed long ago.

Table of Contents

Acknowledgements

...a special thanks to Jane for two years of reading, editing, listening, and supporting.

And copious amounts of gratitude to Sage and Charlie, for making me their Mama.

CHAPTER One

Luke Tanner
1912

The only place Luke Tanner had ever lived was the Tennessee Home for Boys. He was a newborn when they found him on the porch of the orphanage, wrapped in a quilt and tucked in a wooden fruit crate.

He learned quickly that when a boy at the Home turned 14, they would be "adopted" — which was another word for working for room and board. So, when Mr. JJ Cooper came to Chattanooga, looking for a "son," Luke was determined to be the one he chose. The rumor was that whoever was lucky enough to catch his eye would be a lucky fella, because the Coopers were a very wealthy family.

Luke was a head taller than every boy his age, with broad shoulders and piercing blue eyes. There were about a dozen of them standing in a line in the dining hall, and Mr. Cooper slowly walked in front of them…staring at each one. Most of the boys were uneasy and bowed their heads or looked the other way. But not Luke. He held the man's stare and nodded. "Good day, Mr. Cooper," he said.

Mr. Cooper stopped. "What's your name, boy?"

"Luke Tanner, sir."

"Well, Luke Tanner, how'd you like to come to Kings County with me?"

"I'll be packed in five minutes."

***

Luke lived with several other hired hands in a bunk house behind the Cooper homeplace between Cantrell City

1

and Willow Creek. He was a natural mechanic and kept all the cars, trucks, and tractors in mint condition. Eventually, Mr. Cooper pegged him as his personal driver.

For four years, he chauffeured Mr. Cooper everywhere he went, and Luke quickly learned that his boss made his money in ways other than banking and farming. Like his father, Mr. Cooper had a monopoly on the moonshine trade in the Great Valley. That part of the job was exciting to Luke, but other incidents he was privy to were not. He saw way more than he wanted to see and had to keep secrets that haunted him when he closed his eyes at night.

Mr. Cooper liked women…especially black women. One of his favorite things to do was to "collect rent" from the Andrews women who lived out on the Valley Road, east of Willow Creek. Luke would sit in the truck while Mr. Cooper went inside the sharecropper house. There was always a little girl — no more than three or four — outside with an older woman. The two would sit under a tree, waiting for Mr. Cooper to finish his business and leave. If the little girl turned her head to look at Luke, the older woman would stop her.

Luke hated going there, except for that fact that he occasionally caught a glimpse of Genevieve Dobson, whose father owned the farm nearby. She was the prettiest thing he had ever seen, but when he commented on her looks to Mr. Cooper, his boss laughed out loud. "Well, you can forget that shit. Her ol' man is educated and a high brow. The last person he'd want around his daughter is a damn orphan. You better go looking on the other side of town, buddy."

Although Luke was grateful that he avoided living on the streets — like so many orphans did — he joined the Army when he turned 18…swearing never to return to Kings County. He wanted to forget the sordid secrets he knew.

But when WWI was over, Luke returned. He realized he had nowhere else to go. Mr. Cooper offered him his old job, but that was not an option for Luke. He told his former boss he had always wanted to be a farmer, so he got a job working for Mr. Joe Wisdom, who owned the land adjacent to the Dobson farm.

Not only was Luke very capable, he was smart and knew exactly what he was doing. Farmers helped one another by lending an extra hand and sharing laborers when needed. In time, he was confident that Genevieve's father would learn to respect him.

JJ Cooper was wrong. Being an orphan had nothing to do with becoming a man. That took courage and strength—something his old boss lacked.

Luke vowed never to be beholden to a Cooper again. He felt free for the first time in his life.

The Ridge
1925

One of the first things Josie Andrews taught her daughter Nettie was that climbing to the top of the ridge was as forbidden as eating an apple from "the tree of the knowledge of good and evil." If anyone dared to tempt the spirits, they would certainly be met with a fate worse than death: the ground would open and swallow them up alive.

When she told that story to her friend Nate Johnson and that she wouldn't go rabbit hunting with him because of the curse, he laughed and said he went up on the ridge all the time and he "ain't fell in no hole yet."

He told her she was a scaredy cat, but Nettie was anything but that. She said she wasn't afraid and that she would meet him up there after they got home from school. Both of them attended the Kings County School for Coloreds in Willow Creek. Most of the black children had to work, so there were only 15 students in the one-room schoolhouse. But both Nettie's mama and Nate's grandmama wanted them to have as much education as they could get.

Josie was in the garden, hoeing weeds when Nettie walked up the dirt drive. She told her she had choir practice at the church and would be home in time for supper. As always, her mother reminded her not to stop anywhere or speak to anyone.

Nettie Andrews learned at a very early age that colored girls weren't safe anywhere in Kings County.

She put two biscuits in a handkerchief, got the stick she always carried when she walked down the road, and told her mama goodbye. When she got to the end of the driveway, she turned around and crept, undetected, through the woods next to her house until she got to the base of the ridge. The land immediately went from flat to steep. Nettie stared at the dense forest in front of her. She was nervous but determined to show Nate she could do it. The incline went forever, with no end in sight, but, undaunted, she tied up her skirts and started her ascent.

***

Luke Tanner married Genevieve Dobson about a year after he returned form WWI and shortly after her father's death. He had the responsibility of supporting his wife and maintaining the farm that had been in her family for generations. Losing it was not an option, which was why he borrowed money to plant apple orchards. People in Kings County thought he was crazy, but Luke had a good mind for looking forward…most of the time. But not today.

He owed money to the First National Bank of Willow Creek, which weighed heavily on his heart. Like so many Georgia farmers during the early 1920's, he was struggling. Crashing cotton prices and the boll weevil had sent the agriculturally dependent South into a deeper Depression than what many parts of the country felt. He was in the minority of farmers who had not given up, lost their property, and moved to the city.

And he was determined to stay that way.

But he was late on his payment and had already gotten one extension from Mr. Cooper at the bank. Luke detested being beholden to him again, but he had no choice.

He used the Dobson farm as collateral to get the loan. And the greedy banker was all too eager to lend him whatever he wanted. Mr. Cooper had already foreclosed on a lot of land in Kings County and had no remorse for doing so.

Luke also felt the pressure of keeping the loan a secret from Genevieve. With a five-year-old and one on the way, she had all she could handle. Just making sure there was enough food to feed everyone — including Josie and Nettie Andrews — was a fulltime job.

Luke let out a sigh of fatigue and anxiety. He looked across the road but just did not have the strength to go home. Instead, he got his pistol and walked along the edge of the property, out of sight from prying eyes, and started up the steep incline to the ridge.

Without hesitation, he went straight to the massive poplar tree with an abandoned fox hole in it. He lit a match and held it at the opening just to make sure no critter was inhabiting it. He then reached inside the cavity, gripped the handle of an earthenware jug, put it to his lips, and took a sip. The relief was immediate.

Luke was careful not to make this an everyday habit. He had seen too many soldiers survive the war only to lose their lives to the bottle once they got home. And keeping it hidden from Gen was necessary. Like so many women he knew, she was a teetotaler and very active in the Temperance League. But he was pretty sure most of their husbands had their own poplar tree, too.

He continued up the path to the place he usually sat near one of the many creeks that flowed among the dense forests on the Ridge. Between the sound of the water spilling over the rocks and the effects of the liquor, he felt the tension ease up a bit. He took a few more swigs and closed his eyes, soaking up the forest sounds.

Suddenly, screaming shattered the serene silence. Luke jumped up, drew his pistol, and quietly crept toward the sound — with the finesse of a well-trained soldier. What he saw in the distance made him freeze with shock and revulsion: JJ Cooper was raping Nettie, who was just a young girl. Luke tried to think clearly. If he confronted him, the banker would surely foreclose on his land. If he did nothing, this image would haunt him forever.

Luke started to intervene, but Nettie was a fighter. She managed to squirm from underneath her overweight, drunk assailant and kick him before hightailing it down the path toward Luke. When she got close to him, he reached out, put his hand over her mouth gently, and pulled her down with him in the dense brush to hide. JJ stumbled down the path, yelling obscenities. As soon as they heard him drive away in his truck, Luke let Nettie go. She never looked back and ran away as fast as a jackrabbit.

When he stood up and brushed himself off, he looked down and saw blood on his pants—her blood. *I'll have to make up something to tell Gen*, he thought. *She won't know I'm lying. She never does.* He felt guilty for the deceit but justified it by telling himself he was protecting the farm.

At that moment, Luke Tanner made a promise—a promise that he would make sure Nettie Andrews was as well taken care of as his own.

***

When Nate got to the clearing where he and Nettie were supposed to meet that day, there was no one there. The circle of rock graves that folks said belonged to the Cherokees who once lived in the Great Valley was as silently strong as it always was.

Nate was afraid that Nettie wouldn't show up, but he had held out hope until now. He was a couple of years older than her and knew he wanted her to be more than just a hunting buddy, but he dared not tell her. She was too young and saying things like that would surely scare her away.

He sat down on a rock and took out his knife...*I might as well wait a little bit*, he thought. *Maybe she had a hard time getting away from her mama.*

He started whittling on a stick when he heard a noise. It sounded like someone was walking up the path from below. He hid in the thicket and watched, ready to jump out and scare Nettie.

But then he saw Mr. Luke Tanner come into the clearing. He was as pale as a ghost and had blood on his pants. His right arm dangled loosely by his side and in his hand was a pistol. It looked like the gun was almost too heavy for him to hold.

Nate watched Luke walk over to the largest grave and bend over. Luke picked up something and turned around. He continued down the mountain, holding a shovel in one hand and the gun in the other. When the clearing was empty again, Nate jumped up and ran down the trail on the top of the ridge until he got to the path that led to his house.

He didn't understand what had just happened, but he was pretty sure he wasn't supposed to. *It's a good thing Nettie didn't show up,* he thought. *I'll tell her my grandmama had chores for me to do and that I hope she didn't wait for me too long. She'll never know that I was there. No one ever will.*

The Garage
1960

Lucy Tanner always cleaned out the garage when she got rid of a man. "Shit," she said. "I'm 35 years old, and I feel as stupid as I did when Billy Joe dumped me in the damn creek 25 years ago."

"Who's Billy Joe, Mama and why did he dump you in the creek?"

Startled, Lucy looked up and saw her son, Hank, standing there. "Hey, buddy. You snuck up on me. Billy Joe is somebody I knew a long time ago. He dumped me in the creek behind the dairy barn because he and his brothers made it their mission to tease me and then laugh at me when I cried. Your granddaddy called it having a hissy fit." Lucy turned her attention back to cleaning out the garage, but Hank continued to question her about the incident.

"Why did you play with them if they were so mean to you?" One of his favorite things to do was to listen to his mama talk about her childhood.

"They were the only young'uns living out this far from Willow Creek. That's why. Now, set your book satchel down, help me out here, and I'll tell you more. If I can talk and work, you can do the same. Please move all the tools out so I can sweep."

"Yes m'am," answered Hank, picking up a shovel and rake and dragging them out of the shed. He loaded the wheelbarrow and started to move it outside but hesitated. "But why isn't J.D. doing this?"

"Lord Jesus, son. You ask a lot of questions. We are doing this because I fired J.D. today. I caught the sorry son-of-a-you-know-what stealing. He's a damn thief and a dishonest piece of manure."

Hank laughed, "A dishonest piece of manure," but the loud clatter of pots and pans coming from the kitchen got Lucy's attention. She looked up and saw her mother, Genevieve, staring out the open window above the sink, an angry look of disapproval on her face.

Lucy knew that expression well, and, lately, she had seen it more than usual. Genevieve had never shied away from delivering mild admonishments to Lucy, but now it felt more like a heated scolding. It was as if her mother could think of very little except her daughter's perceived failures. Ignoring her mother's scowl, Lucy turned her back on Gen and continued to sweep.

"So, back to the Sims boys," she continued. "Their daddy Jake was supposed to work every day for your granddaddy—some days he showed up and some days he didn't—and the boys usually tagged along when he did.

"On that summer day, Billy Joe told me I could be in their club if I passed a test...one he made up, of course. He dared me to shimmy across a sapling that had fallen over the creek where the cows drank. I'm not sure why it was so

8

important to me to be in their stupid, damn club, but I jumped right up on that skinny tree trunk.

"When I was halfway there, Billy Joe reached down, grabbed the sapling, and shook me off. It was about a 5-foot drop, and I landed in enough mud, manure, and water to soak me from head to toe. They all ran off and left me there but not before Billy Joe yelled, 'First thing you gotta learn is to never trust a damn thing I say.'"

Hank threw his head back and laughed. "That was a funny trick."

"Depends on if it happened to you or not," said Lucy. "I didn't think it was too funny at the time. I was so ashamed. Your granddaddy had warned me many times about letting those boys get my goat. I just couldn't face him after I let that happen, and I certainly didn't want to deal with—" Lucy lowered her voice to a whisper, "your grand-mother."

Lucy opened her eyes wide, her mouth mimicking a silent scream. Hank covered his face with his hands and smothered his laughter. "Mama, you're so funny. But if you didn't go home, where did you go?"

"I started walking up to the ridge—which is something I was forbidden to do. Your granddaddy told me if I ever did, I'd be in the worse trouble I'd ever been in."

"How long did you stay up there?"

"Until I got scared—which wasn't very long. I heard the sound of a truck and men's voices. I couldn't get to Nettie's house fast enough."

The suspense mesmerized Hank. The scene played out in his mind, but he knew there was more to this story.

"I thought Nettie was going to throttle me when I told her where I'd been. Come to think of it, I had never seen her so agitated. It kind of scared me. She told me never to tell your granddaddy."

"Did you tell him?"

9

"Nope. I promised Nettie not to say anything and I didn't. And to this day, I don't understand why there was all of the excitement."

"What did she tell Granddaddy and Grandma Gen?" asked Hank.

"That I fell in the creek...which is the truth, but—as you now know—not all of the truth."

The little boy's eyes grew wide. "So, I am part of the secret now," he said, with pride.

"Yeah, I guess you are...one you better keep," answered Lucy, not so sure she was comfortable with the cover-up.

She motioned to Hank to come help her move a wooden tool box so she could sweep under it.

"Did Billy Joe and his brothers get in trouble?"

"They were always in trouble whether they did anything bad or not. Their daddy beat the daylights out of them if they looked at him sideways. He wasn't a nice man—drank a lot of moonshine every day."

"Was their mama mean, too?"

"Oh no, she was pitiful," said Lucy, shaking her head. "Her name was Etta Mae. She had Billy Joe when she was 14. By the time she was 18, she looked like a bedraggled old woman. She never smiled. Whenever anyone drove by the shack where they lived, she slunk away like a stray dog. One time, your granddaddy and I went to their house to see if Jake was coming to work. I saw Etta Mae peeking out from behind a bed sheet that hung over the broken window. Her eyes were so sad and scared. I never forgot the look on the poor woman's face."

"Is that all to the story?" asked Hank.

"Not really, but it's not a happy ending. Are you sure you want to hear?"

Hank nodded.

"One night, it got really bad. Jake was laying into Etta Mae with his fists, and I guess Billy Joe had taken it as much as he could. He was only 12, but he got a shovel and hit Jake over the head to make it stop. After that, Billy Joe was shipped off to the Macon Reform School, his brothers went to the Baptist Children's Home in Milledgeville, and poor Etta Mae never recovered from the beating. We haven't heard from any of the Sims since then. It's all very sad because the boys were innocent but suffered so much.

"Some folks have it way worse than we can imagine, Hank...way worse."

Hank thought about what his mama had just told him as he pulled the aluminum can down next to the fence. He walked back toward the garage and the only place he had ever called home—the sprawling farmhouse where both his mama and grandmother grew up. Located in the middle of Kings County, Georgia, the surrounding acreage was known as some of the finest farmland around.

Oak trees and sugar maples made a canopy over the white, wood-frame house and provided relief from the summer heat. Geraniums, phlox, and day lilies filled the flower beds that bordered the wraparound porch. Large ferns in planters were on either side of the front door, and four high-back rockers and a porch swing made it look as comfortable as it was pretty.

It was hard for Hank to imagine the kind of pain his mama had just described. His life was, and had always been, comfortable and safe.

When he got back to the garage, Lucy was leaning on a push broom, with one hand on her hip.

"Now that's what a clean garage looks like," she said. "You can't say I never taught you how to do that. Lord knows you've seen me do it enough times."

"You sure know how to get rid of the trash, Mama—all kinds," Hank added with a grin, proud that he cracked a joke.

"Oh, lord," she answered with a chuckle. "We've been talking so much; I haven't given you a hug since you got home from school."

When his mother wrapped her arms around him, Hank realized even though he was only a couple of months away from being eight years old, he was almost as tall as she was.

"Thanks, son. I needed that. It's hard taking care of everything myself and also being what you need me to be. That's hard on both of us. I'm really sorry you don't have a daddy."

"It's okay, Mama. I can't miss what I ain't never had."

"Don't say 'ain't', Hank. It makes you sound ignorant, and you are not ignorant. I know J.D. talked that way, but it isn't correct. It's a bad habit and one I do not want you to cultivate. You have good sense, and that will take you further than anything. Remember what I always told you: 'When somebody pushes you in a corner, try to out talk them first. And if that fails, run like hell. Don't do them the honor of whipping their ass.'"

"But, Mama, you cuss. Why can't I say, 'ain't'?"

"You're right, Hank. I do cuss. But I use good grammar when I do."

Lucy and Hank let out a laugh that Luke Tanner heard as he made his way across the road from the barn, his cow dog, Jenny, following close behind. He saw his daughter and grandson, standing in front of the shed. "What are y'all up to?" he asked. "Cleaning out the garage again, Lulu?"

"We sure are, Granddaddy," said Hank. "You know she can't stand a lazy son-of-a—"

"Son, go help your grandmama set the table," interrupted Lucy, "and tell her your granddaddy and I will be there in about 10 minutes."

Hank grabbed his book satchel and ran around to the front of the house. He listened to see if his grandmama was still banging the pots and pans, but all was quiet at the moment. He took a deep breath and smelled the familiar scent of hardwood floors and home-cooked food. The furniture was a hodgepodge of what Grandma Gen had inherited. It wasn't fancy but was always polished and arranged beautifully.

12

The living room was at the front of the house and had shelves on two walls that went from the floor all the way up to the 12-foot ceilings. They were packed with books collected by Gen's father and grandmother, who were both educators. To reach the higher shelves, you had to use a ladder that was kept in the corner between them. Hank learned at a young age how to maneuver it and get to the books that took him thousands of miles away and years into the past. It was, by far, his favorite room in the house.

Gen's voice suddenly broke the silence. "Hank," she yelled. "I heard you come in that front door. Please go wash your hands and come to the kitchen."

"Yes m'am," he called.

After Hank went inside, Lucy turned and faced her father. "Daddy, I know what you're going to say — that good help is hard to find and that I should be more patient, but —"

"That is not at all what I was going to say," answered Luke. "I was going to say that I agree with what you did. J.D. is a thief. I've been suspecting it for a while. No telling who he works for. I heard hootin' and hollerin' up on the ridge the other night. I think things are worse up there than they were when you were a kid. You've made it clear to Hank that it's off limits unless an adult is with him, right?"

"Well, yeah, but why? What's the problem? Are you ever going to tell me? Unlike you, I don't tell Hank 'Because I told you so.' I try to tell him the truth."

Luke turned around and went to feed Jenny without saying a word.

Supper

Lucy walked in the kitchen door.

"Hurry up," said Genevieve, without looking up. "I didn't fix this food for it to get cold."

"Okay, Mama. Daddy is on his way." She started to wash her hands in the kitchen sink, but her mother told her to go to the back. Hank stared at his plate, trying not to laugh at the face Lucy made when she walked by.

When everyone was seated at the table, Luke Tanner extended his arms to the side and the rest followed suit, holding hands with one another. "Bless this food to the nourishment of our bodies and to the goodness of our souls. In Jesus' name, Amen."

It was obvious to Lucy that Gen was still in one of her not–so–congenial moods...the one in which she had been the better part of the day.

There was little conversation for the next few minutes.

"Lucy," said her mother. "The Willow Creek Woman's Club meets tomorrow afternoon. Why don't you go with me?" It pained her when the other women brought their daughters to the meetings.

Being Lucy's mama wasn't always easy for Gen. Her daughter had an independent streak that bordered on stubbornness and a restlessness in her soul that her mother never understood. Lucy's main concern was how to make the farm more profitable which pleased Luke. Gen wouldn't admit it, but she was jealous of the relationship the two of them had.

"Mama, I can't." she said without looking up from her plate. "I have to help Nettie get the gardens ready for a fall planting. I had to let J.D. go today." She looked up and saw her mother was disappointed. Lucy was on the verge of feeling guilty until Gen quickly assumed that sour look her daughter knew so well.

"I know what you did," Genevieve answered sarcastically. "I heard you telling Hank all about it and cussing the whole time."

"I'm sorry, but if that's the worst thing I do—given everything else I could be doing—then I'd say we're all very lucky, wouldn't you, Mother? After all, he is my son and I decide what's best for him."

"What other things could you be doing, Mama?" asked Hank, trying to diffuse the tension.

"Smoking cigarettes, drinking liquor, and gambling, Hank," Lucy answered with a grin.

"It's okay, Grandmama Gen," laughed Hank. "At least Mama uses good grammar when she cusses, and she tells really good stories, too. She told me all about Billy Joe Sims. His daddy got drunk every day. Isn't that right, Granddaddy?"

Luke cleared his throat and sheepishly shook his head. "That's right son. Moonshine made him do things he shouldn't and not do things he should. Now, you keep that in mind when you get older."

Gen interrupted in a louder than normal voice, "Is this really an appropriate conversation to be having now?"

Hank gulped the last bite of his pie. "Can I please be excused?" He knew when it was time to leave.

"You're excused," said Luke, hoping this conversation was over.

When Hank was out of the room, Gen started in again on her husband. "You're not helping one bit, Luke Tanner…talking about moonshine and getting drunk. For heaven's sake. What are you two thinking?"

Luke didn't say a word and started clearing the dishes from the table. "I'll take care of this," said Lucy. "I know you want to read the paper." Lucy stood up, wanting to avoid any further conversation with her mother but Gen would not be deterred.

"Lucy, I do not think it is prudent for you to use bad language in front of Hank or tell him about unpleasantries. What if he goes to school and repeats what he hears?"

"Mama, he and I have talked about this so many times. In fact, we did this afternoon. Can we please leave it there?"

"I just want you to be happy, Lucy," said her mother, wiping her tears. "And when you cuss, you don't sound happy to me."

"Mama, please don't cry. I'm doing the best I can, and for Heaven's sake, stop worrying about my swearing. I'm

15

not going to Hell for it." She wrung out the dish rag, folded it over the edge of the sink and gave Gen a quick hug.

When Lucy got to the back of the house, Hank was in his room with his pajamas on. "Go tell your grandparents good night. I'll be here when you get back."

Lucy stretched out across Hank's bed and looked out at the black, country night. The windows were open and a little breeze ruffled the curtains, bringing with it the smell of a distant fire…which wasn't unusual. *Someone must be up on the ridge, checking out the deer*, she thought.

She replayed the conversation she had just had with her mother, a conversation they had far too often these days. *Something is out of kilter with Mama. I know I drive her crazy, but it's too late for me to change.*

"I am who I am," she said aloud.

"What did you say, Mama?" asked Hank, who had just walked back into the room and climbed up on his bed.

"There you go…sneaking up on me again. I said, 'I am who I am,'" Lucy answered as she stood up and pulled the covers over her son. "The sooner you accept what you can't change, the better. Remember that." She leaned over and kissed her son's cheek. "Sleep tight. See you in the morning."

Lucy closed the door to Hank's room and walked down the hall toward the front of the house. She opened the front door and saw her parents sitting there. "Good night, y'all," she said.

"Night, Lulu," said her father.

Genevieve mumbled something and nodded her head, but when she could no longer hear the sound of her daughter's footsteps, Genevieve started again. "She could lighten her load if she would only turn to the Lord."

"Lucy has to figure out things her own way—not yours," said Luke, with a sigh.

"You always take up for her. That's the problem. We both need to hold her to a higher Christian standard, which is what my family ingrained in me. And when you married me, you benefitted from their hard work and unwavering faith. Now is the time to stand with me, not against me."

"Gen, I'm tired. I don't want to fight with you. You go on to bed. I left the lights on when I fed Jenny. I'll be in shortly."

Lucy walked down the hall, went to her room across from Hank's and shut the door behind her. She glanced out the window and saw Luke in the garage, wiping his mouth on his shirt sleeve. *What's that about?* She thought. Before she saw anymore, he turned out the lights. She undressed and crawled into bed, feeling exhaustion in every bone of her body.

The solitude exposed her reality, and the loneliness crept over her...the same empty feeling she had when her mother forced her to marry Hank's father when she got pregnant...the same empty feeling she had every time her husband left and didn't return for days...the same empty feeling she had when she walked in and found him in bed with another woman.

Lucy had created a veneer to hide her sadness, a defense to keep her from feeling the pain in her heart. She figured that if the world thought she was fine, she would believe it, too.

But she knew the truth. The demands of being so independent were a tough row to hoe, and pain didn't discriminate. The strong felt it just like the weak did...as did the Christian and the heathen.

Believing in God didn't insulate a person from sadness, nor did not believing in God result in punishment.

Life isn't about doing what others think you should do or trying to be good so bad things wouldn't happen.

It was more like riding a wave and holding on as hard as you could while it took you where it would.

And Lucy Tanner was ready to take that trip.

CHAPTER Two

The Dream

She couldn't see a face, but Lucy felt a warm body
pressing against her.
The faceless lover caressed her neck. Her torso
arched, begging for more.
Lucy tried to speak but couldn't make a sound.

A loud knocking sound shattered the image. "Mama, mama...you ok?" shouted Hank.

Lucy sat up in a panic, expecting someone to be in the bed next to her. She reached for the alarm clock that was going off, knocking it to the floor.

"Yes, yes. I'm fine," answered Lucy. "You go in the bathroom first. I'll be out in a minute."

She closed her eyes and let out a deep breath, trying to recover from the dream that felt real. Lucy looked at her reflection in the dresser mirror and could still feel the passion she had imagined. There was no denying it. She liked it.

After putting on a pair of overalls and shirt, she got a sweater out of the cedar chest at the foot of her bed and walked out of her room. Hank was still in the bathroom at the end of the hallway, trying to comb his wet curls straight.

"What's the occasion?" asked Lucy.

"It's picture day at school. Miss Johnson said to wear clean clothes and comb our hair."

"Oh, okay. Why don't you wear one of your Sunday shirts?" She went into Hank's room and got a pressed one out of his closet.

After he put it on, he turned and at looked at her. "How do I look?"

"Very handsome, son. You look very handsome." Hank had Lucy's curls and blue eyes and he was built like his grandfather—tall and athletic. He had his father's dark hair, but Genevieve said it came from her side of the family. She knew her mama wouldn't admit that Hank resembled his other DNA donor. In Genevieve's mind, her grandson was conceived by immaculate conception.

"Get to the kitchen, son. I can smell the bacon cooking, and I'm sure Nettie is here. She's the boss, you know."

Lucy went to the bathroom and stared at her reflection in the mirror. She dampened her hands and worked her fingers through her hair. *Desire is like these curls,* she thought, *you can press it down into the depths of your soul, deny it exists, and curse it to hell, but it always springs back stronger than ever.*

***

"Well, look at you," said Nettie when Hank walked into the kitchen. "Are you going to school or to preach somewhere?"

"You know I'm going to school," laughed Hank. "It's picture day, so I'm wearing a Sunday shirt."

Nettie fixed a plate and handed it to the little boy she considered her own.

"Nettie," said Hank. "Mama told me a story yesterday about the time Billy Joe Sims threw her in the creek and she ran away to your house. Do you remember that?"

"I certainly do, Hank. She was as mad as wet hen, but she calmed down. Speaking of your mama, where is she?" asked Nettie.

"Still in the bathroom, staring in the mirror. She slept late…woke me up talking in her sleep…well, not really talking—just making a lot of gruntin' noises. And her alarm clock was ringing its head off."

Lucy walked in just in time to hear Hank telling Nettie how the day started. The wise, older woman's lips parted in a slight smile. "Hmmm," she said, acting like she didn't know what she knew.

"It was nothing. I was just in a very deep sleep." Lucy looked at the woman who was like her older sister with wide eyes that said, *"You can drop the subject. Now, please."* Nettie smiled and poured herself a cup of coffee from the pot on the stove and sat down at the table.

Lucy fixed two more cups of coffee, just as Gen and Luke walked in. "Morning," said Luke as he sat down. "What's today, Hank?"

"Friday...best school lunch of the week—chili dogs and chocolate milk," said Hank, taking his last bite of toast.

"Well, there's certainly nothing wrong with your appetite," laughed Gen, as she served plates for Luke and herself.

"Go brush your teeth and grab your books, but don't piddle around back there," said Lucy. "We need to head down to the road in five minutes." Lucy walked down the hall and out the front door. She felt a shift—not only in the seasons but in life, too. She read in the paper yesterday that the United States had officially entered a war in southeast Asia. A Catholic was running for president, and a new drug was on the market—the birth control pill. Change was coming, and she wanted to be a part of it, not a bystander.

The screen door's creak interrupted her thoughts, and Hank walked out with Luke's old WWI knapsack, hanging on one shoulder. "I don't think my hair is gonna lie flat," he said.

"Probably not," laughed Lucy, "but you'll learn to live with it." The school bus stopped at the foot of the driveway. "Morning, Clyde," Lucy said when the door opened. Hank hopped up the steps and sat down in the second row next to the little Tucker girl. He flashed a smile at his seat mate that would make many a heart melt in the years to come.

Lucy walked up the drive, stopping by the two-acre garden next to the house. There was another batch of peas to pick before they could plow and plant the cool weather vegetables.

She heard her father on the front porch tell her mother goodbye, saw him give her a kiss, and head to the barn right on time...just like she'd seen him do since she was a little girl. *I'm still a part of that routine*, she thought, *a routine that feels so stifling sometimes.*

She was restless and wanted to leave this time and place, but she knew she couldn't or was it that she wouldn't? The truth was that she was scared...scared of going out on her own again and having to come back a failure.

The past crept into her thoughts just like a slow-moving fog. *Too bad there wasn't a pill back when she dated David Moretti and couldn't resist having sex* she thought. It was fun, but she got pregnant with Hank. And according to her mother—who was relentless—the only option was marriage...a marriage neither she nor David wanted. She tried to adjust and enjoy the wealth that came with being his wife but finding him in their bed with another woman was something she couldn't accept. David's father paid her off to avoid the scandal, and she came home. It was months before she left the Tanner farm, but when she did, she did so with her head held high and Hank in her arms. She vowed never again to allow anyone's social moirés to pressure her into being or doing anything she knew was not her choice.

"Oh, to hell with it," she muttered. "The past is the past and I fucked it up. But. I'd take that damn pill now if there was a good reason to. And lord knows I wish there was."

Bus #54

"Your mama sho is pretty," said Susie Tucker, looking out the window at Lucy, as the bus pulled away.

"Thanks," said Hank. "She's sweet, too, unless you aggravate her. Then you better look out."

"Where's your daddy?" asked the little girl.

"Not here," answered Hank. "Mama divorced him before I was born. Do you have a daddy?"

"Yep. But he's sorry and yells at my mama."

The old school bus ran over a washed out place in the road, and Hank and Susie almost bounced out of their seat. They were used to it, though. Mr. Clyde never swerved to miss the bumps. He only knew one speed: slow. The veteran bus driver smoked Prince Albert roll-your-owns and sang hymns in a low voice, except for the chorus of "Bringing in the Sheaves," which he belted out as loud as he could.

The 12-mile trip to the Willow Creek School took almost an hour. Mr. Clyde picked up every child who lived out in the country, east of town, which meant he had to go down several dirt roads. His route also went through the Rosedale area, which was where the rich families lived.

The last home at the end of Ivy Street was the biggest and looked like a new version of an old plantation mansion. John Jackson Cooper IV — better known as Bo — lived there and he loved telling everybody in school how much money he had. His buddies, who had homes in the same neighborhood, all met at his house and got on the bus together.

Hank stared straight ahead. This bunch of boys had tried their best to pick a fight with him since the first day of school, but he remembered what his mama said: "Don't do a fool the honor of whipping their ass."

Bo got on the bus first and stopped next to Hank's seat. "Hey sissy britches," he said in a taunting voice.

Hank didn't say a word.

"I said—"

"Take a seat, boy," interrupted Mr. Clyde.

Hank and Bo

Bus #54 pulled up in front of the Willow Creek School just as the bell rang.

Hank knew the school's history well. His great-grandfather, Henry Dobson, founded the original wood frame building in the early 1900s. His Grandma Gen taught there when she was a young woman, too. In the hallway directly inside the main entrance, there were faded photographs of the distinguished Professor Dobson, the original building, and several of the teachers and classes. Until it became a public school and the population grew, there were seldom more than 25 students enrolled.

During Roosevelt's Works Progress Administration program in the 1930s, the original building was restored. Two brick wings were added on either side of the four-room school. Arches, made from locally mined granite, framed the heavy wooden doorways, with flagstone porches at each entrance. A long hallway ran from one end of the school to the other. A state-of-the-art auditorium was built on the back of one of the additions, and a gymnasium was added on the other. Both had red oak hardwood floors, milled from the mountain ridge.

Kings County had a history of prosperity, and good schools were as important to that legacy as the rich farmland was.

Hank was the first to get off the bus and run in to the building. He headed straight to his classroom and sat down at his desk. As soon as the other dozen students filed in, Miss Johnson led the Pledge of Allegiance and the morning lessons began.

At 10 o'clock, the recess bell rang and everyone lined up at the door to go outside.

Hank ran to the sliding board and slid down on his stomach, knowing his shirt was as good as a piece of wax paper on the metal surface. He ran around the slide to go up the ladder again. But when he got there, Bo Cooper and his buddies surrounded him.

"Hey, you," said Bo. "You think you're something, don't you? But I think you're a chicken, and that's why you won't sit with the boys in the back of the bus. What are you afraid of?" Bo interrogated. And with each question he got closer and closer to Hank's face, who turned his head to the side.

"See what I mean," he taunted. "You're so scared you can't even look me in the eye."

"I'm not scared," Hank answered, holding his nose. "I don't want to smell your stinky breath. And I don't want to sit in the back of the bus with y'all, because you fart all the time."

The other kids on the playground stood in a circle around them, hoping they were about to see a good fight. But when they heard what Hank said, they howled with laughter. Even Bo's buddies doubled over when Hank said the word "fart."

Bo's face turned purple with embarrassment. "I'll get you for this. I'm gonna tell my daddy, and my daddy will take care of you," he screamed, poking Hank in the chest.

Just as Hank was about to respond, the bell rang for them to come inside, and everyone lined up at the door, except for Bo. When Miss Johnson walked out, she looked at him and said, "You heard that bell. Get in line now."

After lunch, it was time to have their pictures made. "Walk slowly please, and no talking," said Miss Johnson.

When they got to the auditorium, Hank saw several men in business suits out in the hallway with Mr. Pritchett, the principal. One of them was Bo's father, Jack Cooper, who was president of the First National Bank of Kings County. He shook the principal's hand and said in a loud, boisterous voice, "Everything looks good here, Pritchett. As chairman of the school board, I can say we're proud of the job you're doing."

Miss Johnson told the class to wait at the entrance to the auditorium, and she went to see if the photographer was ready. As soon as she was gone, Bo went over to where his father was and said something to him. Jack bent down and listened. He laughed, whispered in Bo's ear, straightened up, and stared straight through Hank like he wasn't even there.

When the picture taking was over, Miss Johnson let the class go out on the playground again. It was Friday, and she knew the chance of teaching them anything was over for that week. She went outside, too, and put a chair under the oak tree in front of the school where some of the other teachers sat. They watched the children divide up into teams and play kickball, intervening only when a referee was needed to prevent bloodshed.

When the bell rang, the classes lined up at the front door. Hank felt a tap on his shoulder and turned around to see Bo.

"Hey, big shot. You're real proud of yourself, ain't cha? Well, I told my daddy all about it and you know what he told me? He told me not to worry about anything you said 'cause you're a bastard. And bastards can't say nothin' about nobody 'cause they're the lowest of the low. Now. Whatcha got to say for yourself?"

"Bo," said Miss Johnson in a loud voice. "No talking."

Bastard

Lucy settled up the farm books every Friday afternoon. After itemizing the expenses and income for the week, she'd run the numbers and determined the bottom line. She, Nettie, and Luke reviewed everything and decided how much money to leave in the checking account and how much to put in savings, including a college account for Hank. Each of them—including Gen—drew a very modest monthly salary.

In addition to the garden and orchard sales, there was substantial interest and dividend income from the money Luke made when he sold the entire milk herd a few

25

years back. He struck a very lucrative deal with a large dairy group in Wisconsin after his prize cows and sires earned a national reputation. Although he loved his Holsteins, it was an offer he couldn't refuse. He still raised steers but his milking days were over.

Few were aware of how successful Luke was. His philosophy was that if you had money, the last thing you wanted to do was bring attention to yourself. "Most folks who brag about what they have probably don't own their toothbrushes" was one his favorite sayings. He preferred to keep a low profile and a high bank balance.

"Looks like we're going to end this growing season making a profit," said Luke, as he looked over the balance sheet Lucy had just finished. They were in the front of the dairy barn in what was once the room where the milking equipment was sanitized. He sat at one desk and Lucy at another beside his. Nettie sat in a chair between the two. Luke handed her the ledger and said, "What kind of apple harvest do you see us having this year?"

"The best one ever," answered Nettie. "I just checked the orchard on the backside of the farm — those trees are loaded and the fruit is sweet."

"So, let's leave the minimum needed for operating and put the rest in savings when we go into town tomorrow," said Luke, "but for now, time to start putting out the hay. You drive, Lucy, and I'll throw the bales out. See you tomorrow, Nettie." He stood up and started to walk out of the office.

"Wait a minute, Daddy. I need to talk to you about something."

Luke turned around and looked at his daughter, a slight frown on his face. "What is it?"

"I'm worried about Mama. One minute, she's angry enough to spit rusty nails and then, seconds later, she's crying like a baby."

"I've noticed that, too," added Nettie.

Luke chuckled. "Y'all…she's been like that since the day I met her…a sharp tongue with a sweet, tender heart."

26

"But this is different," pleaded Lucy. "It's way out of proportion, and she constantly obsesses about stuff that she can't change. I mean, do we really need to bring up my divorce over and over again? That happened eight years ago."

"Well, I've always heard that the older folks get, the more so they are," said Luke. "I believe that's just what we have going on here."

"Luke, I'm not so sure that's the case," Nettie said, leaning forward in her chair.

"I said she's okay, you two—just a little ornery. Lucy, I'll meet you at the truck."

The women watched him walk out the door and knew full well the conversation was going no further. Lucy shook her head and let out a deep sigh. "He's not going to admit anything is wrong until it's so wrong it can't be ignored," she said. "Jesus, if I still drank, I'd be looking for the bottle right now."

"I have one at my house if you want come over later," said Nettie with a chuckle. "Speaking of which, I'm heading home…see you in the morning."

Lucy got in the driver's seat of the Chevy pickup truck and Luke climbed in the back, just as the old yellow school bus stopped at the driveway across the road. "Good timing," Lucy yelled out the window to her dad. "You know he'll be down here in a minute to help."

When Hank got off the bus, he waved goodbye to Susie and ran up the front steps. "I'm home, Grandma Gen," he shouted as he hurried down the hall to his room.

"I would have never known if you hadn't told me," answered Gen, as she stirred the spaghetti sauce in a stock pot on the stove.

Hank put his knapsack in his room and grabbed an apple from a bowl on the kitchen table. "Headed across the road now," he said to Gen. "It's Friday, and I don't have any homework to do until Sunday."

When he got to the barn, he saw Luke in the back of the truck, putting out bales of hay in the pasture, while Lucy drove very slowly.

"Hey, Hank," called his grandfather. "You're just in time to help me bust these up and put in the troughs."

Lucy looked out the window and smiled, as the truck rolled forward to the last trough. "How did your day go?"

"It was okay. Bo Cooper picked on me during the morning recess again...like he does every day. He said I was a sissy since I wouldn't sit in the back of the bus with the other boys."

"What did you say back to him?" Lucy asked.

"I told him I wasn't scared to sit in the back...that I sit in the front because he farted too much. After lunch, we got our pictures made, but then Bo called me a bastard at recess."

Lucy put the gear shift in neutral, pulled on the emergency brake, and got out of the truck. Luke stopped what he was doing and stared at Hank and then at his daughter.

"What did you say?" she asked.

"Bo Cooper said his daddy told him I was a bastard, and that bastards were the lowest of the lows and that nothing I say matters. But I don't know what a bastard is, Mama."

Lucy straightened her back and looked down at the ground for what seemed like a long time. When she finally looked up, she said very softly, "Well, Hank. Let's go ask Jack Cooper what a bastard is since he called you one."

Hank knew his mama was always quick to act and speak...seldom to his grandmama's liking. But he loved the way she took charge of things and stood up for herself. He also knew his mama was at her fiercest when she was the quietest.

"Lucy," said Luke. "Don't go and do something you'll regret." He knew that look on his daughter's face. She wasn't about to back down—even to Jack. He feared that one day she'd push back a little too hard against that man and feel his wrath.

"I know exactly what I'm doing. And I assure you, I won't regret it. In fact, I'm going to enjoy it. Get in the truck, Hank." She turned and winked at Luke. "We'll be back in less time than it takes to spot a sanctimonious hypocrite at church."

Luke had a sinking feeling in his gut. He no longer owed money to the Coopers, but he was always looking over his shoulder. They could not be trusted or their ruthlessness, underestimated. Luke had witnessed firsthand many years ago.

Lucy followed the dirt road out of the pasture and turned onto the highway, heading in the direction of Willow Creek.

"Where are we going, Mama?" Hank asked innocently.

"To the bank, sugar. To the bank."

The Bank

Lucy didn't say much during the 15-minute ride to Willow Creek. And when she didn't say much, Hank didn't either.

Willow Creek, Georgia, was a typical small town. There was one grocery—Riley and McDaniel Foods. Davis Brothers Drug Store was across the street and had a soda fountain and lunch counter, where the Tanners ate almost every Saturday.

Kittsee King owned the beauty shop, and her brother Laney had a barber shop next door. Buck's BBQ House was the only place to get anything to eat other than the drug store. The largest building in town, though, was Tate Brothers Feed and Seed.

Lucy stopped at the first and only red light in town, then took a left onto Main Street. She drove two blocks and parked right in front of the First National Bank of Kings County.

She turned and looked at Hank. "Don't say anything unless I ask you a question. Not a word. Let me do the talking. Understand?"

"Yes ma'am," he answered. Hank wasn't sure what was about to happen, but he had a feeling he'd never forget it.

Lucy looked in the rearview mirror, smoothed her tousled hair, and wiped the dirt from her face. "Okay. Come on. Let's set this straight with Mr. Cooper."

They got out of the truck and walked toward the building that looked like it belonged in Atlanta, but Jack Cooper was all about making sure everybody knew he had the money to spend on gaudy Greek columns if he wanted. His daddy — JJ Cooper Jr. — was notorious in Kings County back in the 1920s and made a lot of money selling moonshine. He bought up a large part of the county during the Depression, including most of the buildings in the town.

JJ Cooper was a violent man, so the stories went, who had no remorse for anything he did. It was whispered that he killed several men and took whatever woman he wanted when he wanted. Lucy had heard it all, but wrote it off. Legends always get better with time, and she wasn't dealing with ol' man Cooper. She had a bone to pick with his son, Jack. He owned the bank, most of Willow Creek, and the First Baptist Church. But Lucy wasn't afraid of him. She knew she was much smarter than he was.

Lucy opened the ornate mahogany doors and stepped inside. There was one teller working behind the counter and a couple of customers were in line. George Mason, the branch manager, was talking to Kittsee King, as she sat across from him at his desk in the front office.

Hank's and Lucy's footsteps echoed as they walked across the shiny marble floors. Kittsee turned and stared at the pair just like everyone else did.

Since she was who she was and looked the way she did, Lucy always turned heads.

She was a natural beauty, with blue eyes that shot fire, a head full of blonde curls, and a petite frame that was all muscle. Since she worked outside, her olive skin had a constant rosiness to it, and her perfect teeth were as white as snow.

And today was no different. Since she had on overalls, a plaid shirt, and work boots, the heads turned and the eyes lingered even longer.

She walked straight toward the door with a brass plate on it that read "Mr. John Jackson Cooper III, President."

Marge McDaniel sat at a desk outside Jack's office. When she quit her job at the grocery store, Lucy told her it was a mistake…that she was a natural when it came to retail merchandising and that in a few years, she could own the family business. Her advice fell on deaf ears though, and Lucy feared Jack had an ulterior motive. Marge was easy prey. She was young, voluptuous, and bored.

Lucy noticed that her very large bosoms strained the buttons on her pink cardigan. Hank stared, too, with wide eyes. The image made him feel like he was on the Ferris wheel.

Marge looked up from her typewriter. "Hello, Lucy. Do you have an appointment with Mr. Cooper?"

"I do," answered Lucy. "He just doesn't know about it."

"Well, you can't go in without an appointment," Marge said in a low voice. She wasn't sure who she dreaded facing the most right now — Jack or Lucy.

"Really now?" answered Lucy. "Jack Cooper," she said loud enough to make sure every ear in the bank heard and every eye stared. "Come out here. My son has a question for you. And I'm not leaving until you answer it."

Hank heard footsteps inside the office. When the door opened, Jack smiled at them as if nothing was wrong. "Well, hello, Lucy…Hank. Please, come in," he said. The feigned courtesy was obvious even to someone as young as Hank.

He closed the door behind them and turned to face Lucy. "You sure do have a way, don't you? Your mama is nothing like the other women in Willow Creek, Hank. I wanted to date her when she was a teenager, but your Uncle Henry would have none of that."

"That's enough, Jack. Leave my late brother out of this." Seven years her senior, Jack had cornered her when she was leaving basketball practice late one afternoon when she was only 13. Henry was home from college for the weekend and came to pick her up at the gym. He got there in time to see Cooper trying to kiss his little sister and proceeded to beat his ass. Lucy recalled what he said to Jack as they walked away, "You ever try that shit again, and I won't be as kind."

Lucy put her arm around her son's shoulders and pulled him toward her. "Jack, we didn't come here to reminisce with you. Hank has a question."

"Is that right now?" asked Jack, amused. He bent down until his red, puffy face was only a few inches from Hank's. His shirt and vest looked way too small for his rotund body. Hank realized he had bad breath just like Bo's, only worse.

Backing up a bit, Hank said, "Mr. Cooper, today at school Bo said you told him that nothing I say matters because I'm a bastard, but I don't know what that is. My mama said to ask you since you said it. So, what's a bastard?" he asked with innocent, yet unwavering directness.

Jack looked at Lucy—his red face getting even redder. "Ahh, ahh," he stuttered.

"Spit it out, Jack," she said. "Tell the boy what a bastard is."

"A bastard is someone who is conceived out of wedlock—to a woman who isn't nor ever has been married," he answered. His mouth barely opened, and his chin stuck out as far as a braying ass's snout.

Hank looked at his mama who was staring at Jack Cooper with icy eyes. "Hank, tell Mr. Cooper why you aren't a bastard."

"Mr. Cooper, you're right. My mama wasn't married when I was born, because she divorced my daddy on October 31, 1952. That's why Halloween is her favorite holiday."

"Hank, go out there and wait for me," said Lucy. "I won't be long."

After Hank closed the door behind him, Lucy turned and glared at Jack Cooper. "You see, Jack. What's different about me is that I had the guts to get rid of a cheating son-of-a-bitch — unlike your wife and so many other women in this town who turn a blind eye just so they can collect their monthly checks.

"And I suggest that you tell your boy not to say that again unless you want his mother to know about Marge." Jack's jaw dropped and he stared at Lucy with cold dislike. "Oh, how do I know about your little indiscretion, you ask?" She continued, "Because I saw you two in Cantrell City at the Gold Star Inn. I was there, delivering some produce when y'all drove up and snuck in the back entrance. I don't miss a damn thing, Jack Cooper. And don't think I won't tell your wife and everybody else. Years ago, you tried to mess with me, and Henry saw to it that you didn't. So, if you try to fuck with my kid, I'll do the same. Now. Tell Bo you were wrong and set the record straight. Got it?"

Jack looked at Lucy like he wanted to choke her. But he knew that she meant every word she said. "I'm going to get Hank back in here and I want you to apologize."

Lucy opened the door and motioned for Hank to come back in the office.

"I'm sorry, Hank," Jack said. "I shouldn't have repeated what I heard from others. I'll make sure that Bo knows I was wrong."

And with that, Lucy turned around, opened the door, and walked out, leaving him standing there looking like he just swallowed something that tasted really bad.

When Hank and his mama got in front of Marge's desk, Lucy stopped, leaned forward, and whispered, "If you know what's good for you, you'll stay away from that asshole. I saw y'all at the Gold Star Inn. He's using you and nothing more."

The Ride Home

Hank and his mama exited the bank the same way they walked in—looking straight ahead, with everyone staring at them, especially Kittsee.

When they got in the truck, Hank immediately started talking. "Boy howdy, Mama, you sure put Mr. Jack Cooper in his place. What did you say to him after I left his office? Miss McDaniel sure does have big bosoms, doesn't she?"

Lucy slowed down and pulled off on the side of the road. "Hank," she said. "Listen to what I am about to say and listen very carefully. I used an ace I've held in my hand for a long time...an ace nobody knew I had. Life is like poker—you can't let anybody see your cards. Smart people keep what they know to themselves. Stupid ones run their mouths. Remember that."

She put the gear shift in first and pulled back on the road. As she shifted to second, and third gear, Hank thought about what she just said. "Mama," he said quietly. "Can I ask you a question?"

"You can ask. But you know the rest: I may choose not to answer," she said.

"How did you get so smart?"

"By making mistakes and learning from them."

Hank was very proud to be a Tanner that day. He had stood up to a bully and he saw his mother do the same. He felt certain there was no one or anything she wouldn't take on.

"When I grow up, I want to be just like you, Mama," Hank said.

"Sweet boy, I want you to be better than I am."

Lucy and Hank didn't say much for the rest of the ride home. She looked straight ahead at the road, and he watched the Georgia landscape pass by. The truck window was open, and the early fall breeze filled the cab with the promise of cooler temperatures to come.

Hank knew every curve in the highway and every landmark between Willow Creek and the Tanner farm. When they passed the mill on Dobson Creek, he knew they were close. There was an old store building on the right about 100 yards before their house, and as soon as they drove by it, he could see the place he called home. Tanner land was on both sides of the road, the bulk of the 150 acres being on the barn side. Behind the farmhouse, the terrain changed from pasture to forest-covered mountains.

The land was rich, black dirt, fed by numerous creeks and springs. Luke always said a farm in a mountain valley was worth three in the flatlands.

Lucy drove to the barn first so they could help Luke finish. When he saw them pull in, he stopped what he was doing and leaned on the pitchfork. Although Luke was in his 60s, his tall body was still strong, he had a head full of greying blonde hair, and his blue eyes were as clear as a baby's.

"So, did you do what you set out to do, Lulu?" he asked.

"We did," said Lucy. "Jack Cooper told Hank what a bastard is, and Hank set the record straight regarding the fact that he's not a bastard. All in all, I'd say our meeting was quite productive, right, Hank?" she winked.

"It sure was," he answered. "My mama knows how to keep her cards a secret and when to play them."

Supper

Every Friday night, the Tanners had spaghetti, which was the most exotic cuisine Gen served.

When everybody sat down, Luke said, "Hank, why don't you say the blessing tonight?"

They joined hands, bowed their heads, and Hank cleared his throat. "Dear God. Thank you for mama,

35

Granddaddy, Grandma Gen, and Nettie. Thank you for the farm and this plate full of spaghetti. And thank you so much for not making Jack Cooper my daddy. Amen."

Lucy and Luke smiled through their "amens," but Gen was not amused. "What brought that on?" she asked.

"Lucy and Hank went into town and had a little talk with Jack this afternoon," said Luke. "Seems his son Bo said his daddy told him that Hank was a bastard."

"Dear heavens, Luke…not at the supper table."

"You asked, Gen," her husband answered. "It's fine, though. I believe your grandson got a good lesson on how to handle rumors, and he learned what kind of man he doesn't want to be. Right, Hank?"

"Yes sir," the boy answered. "I saw Miss Marge, too, Grandmama Gen. She has really red lips and great big—"

"That's okay, son," interrupted Lucy. She knew if Hank continued his description of Marge's buxom build, her mama might have a stroke. "Your grandmama knows Miss McDaniel."

The plate full of spaghetti had already gotten Hank's attention though. He stuck his fork into the pasta, covered with Gen's homemade meat sauce, and tried to wrap as many noodles around it as possible…completely forgetting about bastards and bosoms for the time being.

The sound of the phone ringing pierced the silence, startling everyone except Hank. "That's odd," said Luke. "No one calls here at this time of night unless something is wrong."

He got up, walked into the hallway, and picked up the receiver. "Hello? Why, good evening, Sue Ellen. Yes, we are in the middle of supper. Can I have her call you as soon as we're done? Okay. I'll tell her.

"Gen, that was Sue Ellen Riley. She wants you to give her a call when we've finished eating."

"What on Earth could she want on a Friday evening?" wondered Gen aloud. "The only time she calls is to gossip. Something must have happened today worth sharing."

36

Lucy looked at Hank, who was completely absorbed in his spaghetti. *I have a feeling I know exactly why Sue Ellen Riley is calling*, she thought. *Damn. It didn't take long for the know-it-alls to start talking. Jesus, this day just won't end.*

CHAPTER Three

Kittsee King's Tale

After Lucy and Hank left the bank, Kittsee looked at George Mason, the bank manager, as if nothing had happened. "Now, where were we?" she asked.

Trying to appear equally as disinterested, he answered, "It's true that you and your brother, Laney, have enough money in your savings account to remodel your shops and your house. However, leaving some in savings and financing part of the bill at a very low rate would be beneficial. You'll be earning more interest on a certificate of deposit than you'll be paying on a small loan. You'll actually make money owing money." He straightened his paisley bow tie for emphasis and smiled confidently at Kittsee.

"I see," she said, paying no attention whatsoever to what George was saying. She was listening to the voices coming from the back of the bank. Turning her head, she saw Jack and Marge arguing in his office. His sweat-stained shirt and clenched fists left no doubt as to the level of his agitation. He started to say something until he realized he had an audience. Staring straight at Kittsee, he closed the door. "That's Interesting," she commented.

"Indeed, it is," answered George, standing up from his desk and motioning for his customer to do the same. "Why don't you go over this with your brother and we'll discuss it again next week? I am certain we can have everything ready to go immediately."

The bank manager was by no means a fan of Jack Cooper—who happened to be his brother-in-law—but he would do whatever was necessary to keep his sister, Anita, from hearing any salacious gossip. He knew the faster Miss King wasn't privy to whatever was going on, the better.

Kittsee thanked George, left the bank, and walked down the sidewalk at a pace as fast as her brain worked: *What business did Lucy have with Jack that made her yell at him in front of God and everybody?* She thought. *Why did Jack look like he wanted to explode? And Marge was in such a stew. Oh, I can't wait to tell Laney.*

Ruby Thompson, who worked at the drug store, was cleaning the windows on either side of the front door, when she saw Kittsee hurrying down the sidewalk. "Hey Kittsee. Everything okay? You look like you're headed to put out a fire."

"Oh, hi, Ruby. Yes, I'm fine…just need to get to the shop and tell Laney what George and I talked about at the bank…and what I saw Lucy Tanner—oh, never mind." She made a dismissive motion with her hand and started to walk on.

"What about Lucy Tanner?" asked Ruby, following close behind Kittsee.

Kittsee stopped and turned to face Ruby. "I really shouldn't, but honestly, that little woman will stand up to anybody. I'm not sure what was stuck in her craw, but she yelled at Jack through his office door and got him to let her and Hank in. I couldn't hear what they said, but when they came out, Jack looked like he wanted to kill somebody, Lucy was smiling like a Cheshire cat, and Marge was as pale as a ghost. Now, don't you say a word to anyone about this until I find out more."

"Oh, of course. You can trust me," answered Ruby, who couldn't wait to tell the first person she saw.

Miss K's Kut and Kurl was just a few doors down from the drug store. Kittsee got out her keys to unlock the door but looked in and saw her brother, Laney, sitting in her styling chair, reading a magazine. "Hey, sistah. How did it go?" he asked when she opened the door.

"It went well, but, first, I've got to tell you what Lucy Tanner did at the bank while I was there."

"Tell, please. Lord knows I need some entertainment."

"Well, she absolutely took over and did or said something to Jack Cooper that made him shake in his boots." Laney held up his hand and opened his mouth to speak, but Kittsee didn't stop to look at him or take a breath. She just kept on talking. "And Marge looked like she didn't know whether to cry or scream. But Lucy? She was as cool as a cucumber and smiling from ear to ear."

Suddenly, the bathroom door opened and out stepped Jack Cooper's wife, Anita, with a towel wrapped around her head. The look on her face said she had heard every word but did not want to hear anymore.

"Why, Anita," gasped Kittsee. "I didn't know you had an appointment."

"She needed a quick wash and set for a dinner party tonight," said Laney. "I knew I could do it if you didn't make it back in time. But since you're here, I'll just take my magazine and go to my side of the shop. Bye Anita." He couldn't have gotten out of there any faster.

"Have a seat, dear," said Kittsee nervously. "I'll have you set, dried, and styled in no time. So, are you and Jack having a get together at your house?"

"No," said Anita in an emotionless voice. "We're going to Cantrell City for a dinner at the Country Club...if he doesn't have to work late—which happens a lot."

"Oh, that sounds like fun," said Kittsee, struggling to ease the tension in the room. "Let's get you especially pretty then. Want a French twist?"

Anita Cooper didn't answer but nodded slightly and withdrew into her well-defined shell that most people perceived as a rich lady's prerogative. But in reality, it protected a broken spirit and a heart that felt nothing.

She knew everyone in town would talk about whatever happened today until the story took on a life of its own. Asking Jack to explain would be wasted energy. He wouldn't tell her the truth, and she wasn't so sure she wanted to know anyway. Denial is so much easier than facing reality, she thought, as she reached into her purse and took out a pillbox. "Can I have some water please, Kittsee?" she asked in a robotic voice.

"Of course. Here you go."

Anita took the cup and washed down a couple of pills. "Migraines," she said. "I get terrible migraines."

Marge McDaniel's Nightmare

"If you know what's good for you, you'll stay away from that asshole. I saw y'all at the Gold Star Inn. He's using you and nothing more," whispered Lucy.

Marge froze and stared straight ahead until she heard Lucy say goodbye to George and Kittsee. She turned and saw Jack standing in the doorway to his office, red-faced and sweating.

"Do you know what she said to me?" Marge asked Jack in a loud whisper, as she quickly walked into his office. "She told me she saw us at the Gold Star Inn. For heaven's sake, what did she say to you? Oh lord, if my mama and daddy hear about this, I don't know what I will do."

"What will *you* do? For starters, you can calm the hell down," said Jack. "You're the one who looks as guilty as a whore in church."

"How dare you call me a whore," Marge said in a stunned, quivering voice.

"Goddamn it," said Jack through clenched teeth. "Get control of yourself. You're making this worse." He looked up and saw Kittsee King staring at them like a 12-year-old boy at a peep show. Nodding his head slightly, he said in an officious voice loud enough for everyone to hear, "I need you to take a letter, please, Miss McDaniel." He closed his office door, and the look of impatient rage returned to his face as he glowered at his secretary.

"You're worried about your mama and daddy finding out? For god's sake, all you have to lose is your stupid reputation. Who are you anyway? Just a small-town bitch who went to a two-bit business school, got dumped at the altar by a con man, and still lives with her parents. I have a lot more at stake than my fucking virginity. My wife's brother and father will have my head for humiliating her publicly. And since her daddy is the best attorney in the entire Great Valley, I'd probably lose everything. So, shut the hell up about this and get out there and act like nothing happened."

"But, what about us, Jack?" wailed Marge. "You said you loved me and that you were going to divorce Anita. I trusted you."

"And you were stupid enough to believe me," he snapped. "I'm warning you. Don't say a goddamn word about me to anyone. Forget we ever slept together. And for god's sake, start wearing blouses and sweaters that are big enough for those teats of yours. Now, do as I say or I'll make up a story about you that makes the Gold Star Inn look like a fucking prayer meeting. Do you understand me?"

Marge opened the door, looking down at her stenographer's pad like she was reading something written on it, but the pages were as empty as Jack's words. She sat down at her desk and tried to focus, but all she could hear was: *"And you were stupid enough to believe me."*

"Marge. Marge." George's voice snapped her out of the daze. "Here is a draft of an agreement with Kittsee and her brother, Laney, regarding a loan and the terms. Would you please type it up and make two copies?"

"Of course. When do you need it?" Marge asked in a quiet, listless voice.

"By Monday morning. I imagine they'll be here early to finalize things."

Suddenly the door to Jack's office opened. He had on his plaid sports coat, his Stetson hat and was carrying his briefcase. "George, I just got a call from Sandy at The Lodge. He needs some cash for the bar since it's Friday. So, I'm heading out now. Can you close up, please?"

"Yes. Of course," answered George with a smile. *Don't I always close, you arrogant excuse for a man*, he thought. *My sister deserves so much better than you.*

42

"Miss McDaniel, make a cash ticket for $100 and get it in twenties, tens, fives and ones," Jack ordered in a dismissive tone. After Marge went to the teller line, Jack looked at George with a stony glare. "You'll open in the morning for first Saturday, right?"

"Yes. I'll be here," George answered, showing as little emotion as he could muster. "Lucy told me she and Luke are coming in tomorrow to make a deposit and discuss interest rates. She's one smart woman, isn't she, Jack?" George took advantage of every opportunity he had to make his brother-in-law feel uncomfortable. It gave him a great deal of pleasure.

"If you say so," he answered curtly. "I'll see you Monday."

"Oh, I'll see you and my sister in Cantrell City this evening," said George with polite sarcasm. "Our parents and I are going to the Country Club for the Newcomer's Dinner, too. I'm sure my father will love seeing you."

Jack nodded, grunted something inaudible, and took the money from Marge. He never looked her in the eye, nor did he say thank you or goodbye. He walked out the front door.

"Marge, don't worry about typing up the documents for Kittsee," said George quietly, pretending not to know she was extremely upset. "You can do it Monday morning. It's fine if you leave now."

"Thank you," the young woman answered. Still in shock, she cleaned off her desk like she wasn't coming back, collected her things and started walking toward the front door. The teller was staring. The customers in line were staring. George was staring. *I feel naked and ashamed*, she thought, barely holding back the tears.

She walked out of the bank in time to see Jack driving away, smiling big like he had just swindled somebody out of something.

Marge crossed the street to the vacant lot where the bank employees parked and got into her car. She looked at her reflection in the rearview mirror and saw a face that made her sick with guilt. The red lipstick Jack asked her to wear looked ridiculously cheap now. She took a Kleenex from her purse and wiped her mouth until it burned. At least she didn't dye her light brown hair platinum blonde like he wanted. Her emerald green eyes filled with tears as reality stuck its teeth into her heart and ripped it apart. She had been having an affair with a married man who lied to her. And she was foolish enough to believe him.

"I can't go home," she said aloud to herself. "I don't want to listen to Mama and Daddy now."

She pulled out of the parking lot, drove to the red light and turned onto the highway that went to Cantrell City, not sure where she was going or why.

Jack Cooper's Escape

"Thank god I'm out of there," Jack said aloud, as he got into his black Cadillac that was parked in a reserved spot in front of the bank. "I'm not sure who was pissing me off more...that stupid piece of ass of a secretary or Anita's queer brother."

He took out his handkerchief and wiped the sweat from his face, pausing to flip down the visor and look into the mirror hidden there.

Jack Cooper was an incredibly vain man who fancied himself as a Hollywood type, handsome and sexy. In reality, he was barrel-chested and medium height, his mousy brown hair was already thinning, and his physique was sagging even though he was only in his early 40s. His complexion was a ruddy red—the result of a lifetime of excessive alcohol and tobacco use. And since he had never really worked a day in his life, his hands were lily white and soft as a baby's.

The truth was that Jack Cooper wasn't handsome or very masculine looking. He simply had enough money to dress well and was able to control people with fear—something his father did and that he felt entitled to do, also.

44

He fed his ego by taking frequent trips to Atlanta or Chattanooga on legitimate business but with clandestine intentions involving whatever girl or woman he could woo with his lavish spending habits. His favorite thing to do was drink a lot, get his companion drunk, order room service and have sex until he passed out...which on more than one occasion, didn't take very long.

Jack Cooper had no empathy for anybody, was allegiant to no one but himself, and considered people his property to use and throw away. He had more enemies than anyone in Willow Creek or Cantrell City.

He loosened his tie, took off his jacket and hat, and backed out of his parking place, confident that he had put that little fire out. Marge would never tell anyone she had fucked him, and Lucy Tanner didn't gossip. He smiled at the thought that once again, he was the winner.

Like most of rural Georgia, Kings County was dry, so private clubs like The Lodge were very popular with folks who liked to drink, white folks, that was. Segregation was strictly enforced in the South in the 1960s, and people like Jack Cooper had no intentions of ever letting that change. A large "Members Only" sign hung on the wall next to the club entrance.

Alcohol was bought legally in wet counties and hauled to the clubs in plain view of law enforcement. Since many, if not all, of the sheriffs liked to imbibe, there was seldom an issue. Even when the booze was transported over state lines, it didn't matter...which was often the case at The Lodge in Willow Creek. The closest place to buy alcohol was Chattanooga, Tennessee.

Founded in the 1930s by Jack's father, The Lodge was a place to drink, dance, and play a little poker. Only men patronized it during the week, but on Friday and Saturday nights, the wives and girlfriends could come.

Heavy curtains covered the windows, blocking out the light and any curious eyes from seeing inside. The bar, tables, and chairs were made from local oak trees, as were

45

the hardwood floors. The mirrors behind the bar were antique fixtures from England, a bit fancy for the rest of the décor but showy and opulent just like the Coopers.

Photographs of former and current members—all men—lined the walls. Overhead fans whirred slowly, and a jukebox in the corner played a continuous stream of Big Band tunes and more current songs by Frankie Avalon, The Everly Brothers, and Elvis.

"Hey, Sandy," called Jack, as he opened the front door to the club. "I have your change, and I need a drink."

Sandy came out from the kitchen, smiling and wiping his hands on a dish towel. "Hey there, Mr. Jack. Whadda ya have?" The lanky, tattooed ex-sailor had a cigarette hanging out of his mouth, and he squinted as the smoke curled into his eyes.

"Scotch on the rocks…a double," said Jack, putting the change order and a pack of Marlboros on the bar. He took a cigarette out, and Sandy reached across the bar and lit it for him. The bartender set the drink down on a white napkin and filled a bowl with salted peanuts. "Rough day, boss?"

"Shit," snorted Jack. "They're all rough. I deal with stupid people who couldn't survive if it weren't for me. I have to listen to them whine and bitch, knowing all along they'd like nothing better than to see me in the ditch. They don't have enough sense to realize they'd be lost without my money."

Jack finished off the drink in three gulps, tapping the bar for another. "I have to go to dinner with my wife at the Country Club in Cantrell City tonight, so I need one more before I go home…my wife. That's a fucking joke. She never was good in bed, but after she lost that baby five years ago, her legs closed up as tight as a tick. All she does is drink coffee and take pills for her migraines. That's another fucking joke. If she has migraines, then I'm pregnant." It was a story Sandy had heard more times than he cared to remember.

The swinging door to the kitchen opened and Daisy walked out, carrying a tray full of clean glasses. She was Sandy's girlfriend and waited tables at the club. "Hey Mr. Cooper," she said. "Need something from the kitchen?"

"You. I need you," snarled Jack. "You wouldn't mind, would you, Sandy?"

"Now, now, Mr. Jack. You know how I am about my girl," he said with a nervous laugh.

"Well, you be sure and let me know if you change your mind," Jack said as he spanked Daisy's behind. She gasped and quickly disappeared into the kitchen. "But now, I have to go home. Time to get dressed up and act like I want to be someplace I don't want to be with someone I can't stand. No wonder I drink so much." He drained the second Scotch and slapped the bar with his hand. "On the house, right, Sandy?"

"Right, boss…on the house."

Sandy watched Jack weave his way out the door, not minding one bit if he crashed his Cadillac into a tree, or better yet, the Sand River.

The Rumor

Nettie Andrews grew up down the road from the Tanners and had worked with them since she was a teenager. She could drive a tractor as well as anyone and had a natural instinct for farming, but her strongest suit was her thriftiness—which was the main reason the Tanner farm was so successful.

One of her earliest memories was seeing JJ Cooper riding a horse down the road to their house the first day of every month to collect rent. He was always drunk and loud. As soon as her grandmother saw him, she would take Nettie out in the backyard to do some chores so her mama and Mr. Cooper could "talk business."

After he left, her mama always heated some water on the wood stove and took a sponge bath. Once Nettie asked

47

her why she did that and her mama answered that Mr. Cooper smelled like moonshine and made her feel nasty. "Don't ever let anyone make you feel like that, Nettie. That's why I wash his smell off. If I could bathe the whole house, I would."

When the little girl asked her mama why she let him come inside, she answered that she had no choice…that Mr. Cooper owned the house. It was then that Nettie decided when she grew up, she'd figure out a way to stop him from coming inside her home and making her mama feel bad.

There was a history between the Cooper men and Andrews women. Jack tried once to have the same arrangement with Nettie that his father and grandfather had enjoyed with Nettie's grandmother and mother, but Nettie remembered what her mother told her when she was a little girl. She politely told him she was not interested and warned him that if he ever came to her home, she had no reservations to use whatever force necessary to thwart his advances.

Her refusal did not go without repercussions though. Cooper put the house up for sale, so Nettie went to Luke for advice. She told him she had enough money saved up to buy it; but since a woman's property rights were determined by her husband's approval and Nettie was single, she needed some help.

The Tanners were not as prejudiced as their Caucasian counterparts, and Nettie was more than someone who worked for Luke — she was a business partner. So, he didn't give it a second thought and said he would put the deed in his name.

She was never late paying her property taxes and kept the house and surrounding yard in immaculate condition. She even built a small garage for the 1952 Bel Air that Luke sold her when he bought his '59 Impala.

Nettie was respected, successful, and independent, but she, like all of the Negroes who lived in the Great Valley, and the rest of the South, lived in a segregated, discriminatory world.

White folks were perfectly fine with letting Colored women raise their children and suckle them at their breast. They had no problem with Coloreds preparing their food, cleaning their homes, and working their fields. But to sit down at the same table with a Black person was prohibited.

Although restaurants, lunch counters, churches, schools, and hotels were strictly segregated in the South, white store owners gladly accepted Negro money. They just didn't want to eat in the same room with them. And while claiming to be defenders of Christianity and advocates of The Golden Rule, they refused to worship with their neighbors who were people of color.

Even though they could shop in most stores, Coloreds knew there was a certain decorum to follow. You always let a white person ahead of you in line, and you never congregated with other Black folks in public. You went in, got what you needed and left, seldom saying anything but "thank you."

On more than one occasion, Nettie was humiliated because of the color of her skin. She knew the pain that prejudice caused. Like her peers, she had to learn to navigate the waters and how to socialize to survive. But Nettie Andrews never accepted the fact that the hypocritical injustices were just. She had an unwavering faith that right would win over wrong.

As she drove the 12 miles into Willow Creek, Nettie thought about how proud her mama would be. *I'm in my own car, going to town on this fine Friday afternoon, and I have enough money to get whatever I need,* she thought. *We have a long way to go, but we're further ahead than we were yesterday.*

When she was a few miles from town, she spotted a familiar pickup truck going in the opposite direction. When the two vehicles passed one another, she saw Lucy and Hank and waved at them. "That's odd. I wonder what those two are up to?" she said aloud. "She never goes into town on Friday afternoon."

49

Her first stop was the drug store. She parked on a side street and walked down the dirt alley to the back door, which had a "Colored Entrance" sign on it…black letters on white tin. Ruby Thompson was outside in front of the store, but the druggist, Mr. Davis, was in the back, filling prescriptions.

Nettie spoke to him and made sure he knew she was there before she started shopping. Her mama warned her early on about white suspicion, telling her to "always speak to the store owner. That way he knows you are there and that you won't steal anything 'cause you're not trying to sneak around."

Soon after she began putting things in her basket, she heard Ruby come in the front door, talking a mile a minute. Nettie was close enough to hear but down an aisle far enough from the front so as not to be seen.

"Come on in Dancy," chattered Ruby. "I'll check on your package in a minute. Several things came in on the morning Greyhound. But first, you won't believe what Kittsee just told me happened at the bank." She looked toward the back to make sure Mr. Davis wasn't listening. "Evidently Lucy Tanner came in and stirred up things as bad as scooting a hose pipe on a wasp nest." At the mention of Lucy's name, Nettie's ears perked up but she kept her head down, pretending to look for the items on her list.

"What did she do?" asked Dancy Riley, who was married to Joe Riley Jr., a partner in the grocery store with his father and Marge's father, Ed.

"Well, she ignored Marge, walked right past her, and yelled at Jack through his closed office door. Her boy Hank was with her, and the two of them went in together, but Hank came out by himself. By the time Lucy left, Jack was as red as a fire cracker, Marge was a mess, but Lucy was just fine. Then Marge and Jack got into it, but they closed the office door and Kittsee couldn't hear what they were saying. And then, just a minute or two after Kittsee told me what happened, I saw Marge driving down the street. I could tell she was crying and very upset."

50

"What do you think it was all about?" asked Dancy, eager to find out something she could pass on to whomever needed to know.

"Well, everybody knows that poor Anita Cooper is miserable, and that Jack has the reputation of being a cheater. I figure he was sneaking around with both Marge and Lucy," Ruby speculated. "Lucy found out and had a fit. I guess Jack listened to her because they say she and her family have quite a bit of money in his bank. And poor Marge wouldn't stand up to a fly. She's as meek as milk toast. But whatever happened, I guarantee you it involves Jack Cooper and at least two women. Now, let me go to the back and check on that package."

After she heard Ruby leave the front of the store, Nettie quickly took her basket up to the counter where Mr. Davis was working. "Is that it for today, Nettie?" he asked.

"Yes sir," she answered, handing him a five dollar bill.

He gave her some change, and she was out the side door before Ruby returned with Dancy's package.

"Here you go," said Ruby, as she walked back to the front counter. "Rich's in Atlanta, huh?"

"Yes. It's a new winter coat. Joe and I are going to Chicago for a grocers' convention, and my old duster simply isn't warm enough...but back to Lucy and Marge. Corinthians teaches us to 'flee from sexual immorality. All other sins a person commits are outside the body, but whoever sins sexually, sins against their own body.' Ruby, our sisters have wandered from the righteous path and only the love of Jesus Christ can bring them back into the fold. Make sure you pray for their souls tonight, just as I will."

As Dancy was leaving, another customer walked through the front door. Ruby greeted her with a warm hello and whispered a request for her sworn secrecy if she wanted to hear what happened earlier at The First National Bank of Kings County. And, of course, the anxious listener agreed.

51

Nettie left the drug store, still thinking about what Ruby said, and drove over to Riley and McDaniel Foods. She always cooked a big meal on Saturday to share with whomever might come visiting after church on Sunday, which was often as many as a half dozen or more. Nettie loved hearing the Word and praising the Lord with song, but the fellowship afterwards was perhaps even more spiritually uplifting. There were plenty of vegetables in her refrigerator, but she needed some staples and a good roasting hen.

She got what she needed quickly, thanked the checkout clerk, and walked out the front door just in time to see Dancy Riley standing on the sidewalk and talking to her husband Joe. When she saw Nettie, Dancy paused and nodded. "Well, hello, Nettie," she said a voice that dripped with sarcastic sweetness. "Thanks for shopping at Riley and McDaniel. Please give my best to the Tanners."

"Good day to y'all, too. I'll be sure and tell Lucy I saw you," answered Nettie, looking at Dancy with eyes that said a lot more than the words she spoke. She put her groceries on the back seat of her car, climbed in the driver's seat and headed toward the Tanner side of town.

Nettie didn't hear what Dancy was saying to her husband, but since she had just been privy to the exchange between her and Ruby at the drug store, it was pretty clear why the young woman was so animated. *I know Lucy went to town with Hank; I saw them going home,* she thought. *But Lord Jesus, there is no telling what the truth will become when it's shared by wagging tongues.* She drove slowly, taking her time to sort out what she heard at the drug store and saw at the grocery. She was certain Ruby had it all wrong.

Lucy Tanner couldn't stand Jack Cooper. There was more to this story, probably something to do with Hank. She knew that Lucy would straighten things out, but not before coming to her house to talk about it. *There's no reason to throw gasoline on this fire right now*, Nettie thought. *It may be a hot one, but with my help, Lucy Tanner will put it out before it spreads too much.* "This can wait," said Nettie aloud, "For now I'm going to enjoy this drive."

CHAPTER Four

The Bridge

The road between Cantrell City and Willow Creek wound north through the Araquah Ridges, crossing numerous streams and creeks. The foliage had a tint of color to it, and the cool air smelled crisp and clean.

Billy Joe Sims hadn't been home since he was shipped off to the Macon Reform School in 1935, but the landscape hadn't changed. He steered his 1951 Chevy truck around each twist and turn, while the wind blew his auburn-red hair with abandon. His physique was muscular from hard work and emphasized his angular facial features and hazel eyes. He was naturally handsome in a rugged way that movie stars tried to replicate but seldom achieved.

His memories of living here were not good ones. His childhood was a nightmare. It took six years in juvenile custody and 20 years in the army to understand why he did what he did and to forgive himself and others. Now, he was coming home to start a new life and to do something for his late mother. He was going to build the home she had always wanted.

After he crossed the top of Big Bear Ridge and started downhill, he saw the Sand River Iron Bridge, a famous landmark in Kings County. During the Civil War, Confederate soldiers burned the wooden structure that spanned the large river, in hopes of halting Sherman's March to the Sea. It only delayed his trek, however, sending him further east to Seraca, where he found safer crossing. But before he left Kings County, Sherman showed his gratitude by burning every home and farm in the Great Valley.

Now, the Iron Bridge was a place where teenage boys went to drink whatever they stole from their fathers' stashes and fantasize about the teenage girls they wanted to know.

It was also a place of legends…stories about star-crossed lovers and lost souls who hurled themselves into the water below.

When Billy Joe got closer, he saw a car parked on the side of the road, and a young woman was standing dangerously close to the edge of the bridge, staring into the swift current, a good 50 feet below. "This is not good," said Billy Joe to himself. He floored the accelerator and blew the horn.

Marge McDaniel looked up and saw the truck speeding toward her, jolting her out of a hypnotic trance induced by her dark thoughts. She stepped back from the edge, trembling from the anxiety that had gripped her as long as she could remember… a feeling she didn't understand. She only knew that sometimes she fell into a black hole and couldn't escape.

"Hey," shouted Billy Joe, as he jumped from his parked truck and ran toward the middle of the bridge. "You having trouble here?"

"My…my car quit running," stammered Marge, eyeing the stranger with guarded relief.

"Well, I'll be happy to look at it," said Billy Joe. "I'm a pretty good mechanic." He extended his hand and smiled. "I'm Billy Joe Sims. I lived in Willow Creek when I was a kid."

"Why, Billy Joe," gasped Marge. "I'm Marge. Marge McDaniel." Billy Joe felt her shaking hand in his and squeezed it gently.

"Of course. I knew you looked familiar." Billy Joe studied her face carefully, marveling how the little girl he had known so long ago was now such a beautiful woman. "About the car," said a captivated Billy Joe. "Let's go check it out." The Corvair started right up when he turned the key. "Sounds like it's running fine now. You headed to Cantrell City?"

"No. I was…I don't know what I was doing actually," said Marge, who couldn't hide the tears any longer. "Just trying to collect my thoughts."

Billy Joe handed her a clean handkerchief. "Hey, it's okay," he said softly, "I know all about feeling sad. Remember who you're talking to."

"You were always sweet, Billy Joe," said Marge through her sobs and sniffles. "Thanks."

She started to get in her car, but the sound of an approaching vehicle got their attention. Billy Joe pulled her to the side of the road, and they watched as a shiny black Cadillac sped across the bridge.

Jack Cooper looked to his right and saw Billy Joe and Marge. He quickly averted his eyes and reached under the seat for his silver flask. Anita saw the couple, too. She reached in her purse and took out the pillbox.

Neither of them said a word.

Marge and Billy Joe

"Man, that's a nice Cadillac," said Billy Joe. "I bet it cost a pretty penny, being brand new like that. The driver looked familiar, though. Do you know him?"

"Yeah, as a matter of fact, I do," answered Marge. "That was Jack Cooper."

"Jack Cooper," said Billy Joe. "Of course. I should have known. Is he as big a jerk now as he was when we were kids?"

"More so," answered Marge. "He's gotten worse with age."

"Hmmm...figures. His dad was scum, too." Billy Joe's eyes hardened with anger, and the rage he worked so hard to control rose up inside of him. But his well-trained soldier's voice told him that too much anger made him vulnerable. "He sold my ol' man his moonshine for way more than what it was worth, knowing he'd pay any price for his poison." He glared at the Caddy's tail lights, wishing he could shoot them out. "But enough of him and back to you. I bet your dad still owns the grocery store, right?"

"Yes, he does, but he took on Joe Riley and his son as partners, which was a good thing, I guess. They put some money in the business and expanded the size of the store. You'd think Joe Jr.'s wife, Dancy, was married to the founder of the A&P chain though."

"I take it you're not a fan?" laughed Billy Joe.

"No. She walks around town like she's the Virgin Mary, when everybody knows she'd run around on her husband given the chance. I hate hypocrites."

"So, I'm sure someone as pretty as you is taken. Who's the lucky guy?"

"Wrong. I'm single — the only single woman in town besides Hilda Hargett and Miss Angela Mason. It's a pretty boring club."

Billy Joe appreciated her sense of humor and was glad she was available. "Well, if you don't have plans, I'd love it if you'd go out to supper with me. Is there someplace we can eat in Willow Creek?"

"Buck's is the only place open in the evenings," answered Marge, "and he has good BBQ chicken on Friday night. I need to go to my parents' house first and let them know I'm okay. I'm surprised they haven't had the sheriff out looking for me. They mean well, but I really am too old to be living with them. Anyway, after I've checked in, I'll walk over there and meet you."

"Good. I always liked Buck. He didn't put on airs," said Billy Joe. He opened the car door for her and leaned in the open window after she got in. "But don't change your mind now. I want to hear more about what's happened since I've been gone." He gave the car a couple of taps and winked at Marge. "I'll see you at Buck's."

***

When Marge pulled up beside the Victorian-style house she shared with her parents, her mother was out the door and waiting for her before she could turn off the engine.

57

"Marge," said Alice McDaniel. "Where on Earth have you been? You're usually home by 4:30 or 5 on Fridays. Your father and I have been worried. Here he comes now. He's been downtown, asking everyone if they've seen you."

"Please, no. Tell me he didn't do that, Mama," said Marge. "I just wanted to go down to the river and be by myself for a while. Then my car stalled at the Iron Bridge, and guess who stopped to help me? Billy Joe Sims. He just got out of the army and is settling down here in Willow Creek. He asked me to meet him for supper at Buck's."

"Who asked you to meet him for supper?" asked Ed McDaniel, getting out of his car.

"Mama will tell you all about it. I need to go inside and freshen up before I leave."

Marge was up the steps and in the front door before her father could answer. She ran upstairs to her room and took off the pink sweater that Jack said he liked so much — the one he shamed her about wearing earlier. "Son of a bitch," she murmured under her breath, throwing the cardigan on the floor. "I wish he'd fall off the Iron Bridge."

She went into the bathroom to freshen her make-up, but her skin already had a soft blush to it. She put on some light pink lipstick and slammed the tube of "Red Passion" in the trash. *That felt good*, she thought.

The pair of navy blue, pencil leg slacks and the polka dot cotton shirt that she just bought would be perfect for tonight. The outfit showed off her good figure but in a modest way. Marge looked in the mirror at her image and smiled. She liked what she saw. For the first time in a long time, she was proud. *I'm tired of being what other people want me to be. It doesn't matter if it's Jack, my parents, or the preacher. I'm tired of it.*

She started to put on some perfume but stopped and stared at the bottle of "Tabu" which was Jack's favorite. "Hell no. Not tonight," she said aloud. She poured it down the drain, washed off the lingering scent and dabbed a little "Wind Song" behind each ear.

Marge walked back into her bedroom and saw the pink sweater lying on the floor. "Your time is up, too," she said with disgust. She opened her dresser draw and took out the pair of sharp scissors she used to trim her hair. Was it worth ruining the edge of a good pair of shears? *Damn right,* she thought.

She picked up the garment and cut off one of the sleeves, dropping it into a paper bag from Belk's. With exact precision, she slowly amputated the other one, disposing of it in the same way. She looked at the sweater and heard Jack's voice: *"And you were stupid enough to believe me."* Holding the sweater by the neck, she stabbed it in the front and slit it all the way in two pieces. "Now, I am done with you." She stuffed the remains in the bag and put it on the top shelf of her closet.

Knowing it could turn cooler before she got back, she grabbed a cardigan and hurried down the stairs.
Her parents were sitting on the front porch, doing what they always did—nothing. Marge was their only child, and they doted on her. She felt like she was their hobby instead of their daughter.

Even though she was an adult, they still fretted about her—especially since she wasn't married and had shown no interest in dating anyone for several years. When she left for a weekend, she told them she was going to see friends in Chattanooga—women friends. They never suspected she was running off with Jack to spend a few days in a hotel room. He never took her to any restaurants and only ordered room service. He said they had to be discreet until the divorce was final. But now, she knew the truth. He had used her like a whore, and she let him.

"So, you're meeting up with Billy Joe Sims?" asked her father. "Isn't he the one that had to go to Reform School?"

"Yes, he did, Daddy...when he was 12," said Marge, a bit sarcastically. "He's almost 40 now and just spent 20 years in the army." Turning her back, she walked down the front steps before her parents could say anything else.

When Marge got to Buck's, Billy Joe was waiting for her outside. She felt a tremor as she soaked in the image of his tall build, wide shoulders, narrow waist, and that fine shock of hair. His hazel-colored eyes locked with hers. She paused as she held his gaze and enjoyed the feeling.

"Wow," he exhaled, bringing Marge back from her thoughts. "I'll be the luckiest man at Buck's BBQ House tonight." He opened the door for her, and she walked inside, knowing full well that whoever was in there was going to get an eye full.

Buck looked up from behind the serving counter, his eyes widening with surprise. "Well, look who's here. Billy Joe Sims," he said in a very loud voice. "I'd recognize that hair anywhere." He extended his arm across the counter, took Billy Joe's hand and gave it a firm shake. "Hey, Marge. Where did you find him? Or did he find you?"

Billy Joe laughed and answered, "Hey, Buck…good to be back."

"Actually, he found me," said Marge. "My car acted up out at the Iron Bridge, and lucky me, Billy Joe stopped."

"Well, it's mighty good to see you. Y'all take a seat anywhere you want. I'll get Annie to bring you some pickles and bread."

Billy Joe put his hand on the small of Marge's back and guided her toward a booth. The "Theme from A Summer Place" started up on the jukebox, making it feel like July instead of September. She couldn't help but notice that Ruby Thompson, who worked at the drug store, was staring at them like she had seen a ghost. Marge nodded, smiled and slid in the booth opposite Billy Joe.

"How are y'all doing tonight?" said Annie as she sat down a basket of sliced white bread, some of Buck's homemade hot pepper sauce, and a jar of the Tanner Farms sweet pickles. "What do you want to drink?"

"I'll have ice tea," said Marge.

"Me, too," added Billy Joe, "and we'll both have the chicken special."

"I'll be right back," said Annie. She turned to leave but stopped and added, "It's good to see you're doing well, Billy Joe. A lot of us always felt bad about what happened back then."

"Thanks, Annie. I appreciate that."

Marge looked at the other patrons in Buck's—all of whom were obviously curious about who this handsome man was. She leaned across the table and whispered, "We're causing quite a stir, you know. Between my father asking everybody in town this afternoon if they had seen me and my actually going out on a date in public, they just don't know what to think."

"What do you mean?" asked Billy Joe. "I'd think you'd have men lined up just waiting to take you out."

"It's complicated," said Marge softly. "I'll explain later. Right now, I want to hear about you. Where were you stationed?"

"Well, I did my basic training at Ft. Benning. During the war, I was in the trenches in Italy and North Africa." His demeanor changed as he stared at the table. Marge saw it but said nothing and let him keep talking. "I was a mechanic who worked on bombers. Sometimes I went out on missions, which was scary as hell. Other times, my buddies didn't come back. I dealt with death every day. When it was over, I came back to the states for a couple of months, but the Army pressed me to reenlist. I didn't have anything better to do, didn't have a home to come back to, so why not? I did tours in Germany, Austria, fought in the Korean War, and—lucky me—ended up in Hawaii."

"Wow, I would love to see all of those places. I've never been anywhere but Chattanooga, Atlanta, and here. Which was your favorite?"

"Hawaii…hands down."

Annie brought their food, and the couple continued to engage only with one another, oblivious to anything or anyone else.

When they finished, Billy Joe went to the counter to pay, and Marge stepped into the ladies' room. She opened the door and saw Ruby, who immediately pummeled her with questions. "Marge, are you ok? I heard there was a horrible falling out at the bank—something about you, Lucy Tanner, and Jack. Did you quit? They said you left early. Well, Billy Joe sure looks good. How did you meet up with him?"

Marge looked at Ruby with a blank stare. "You ask too many questions, Ruby. Now, if you'll excuse me." She went into a stall and shut the door, leaving Ruby more curious than ever.

Billy Joe was standing at the counter, talking to Buck when Marge came out of the restroom. "Thanks again, Buck. We really enjoyed it, and I appreciate the offer to stay out back in your trailer until I get settled somewhere. I'd like to take you up on that. I'm gonna walk Marge home and be back around closing time."

The couple walked out into the cool September evening. "I forgot how good the changes in the seasons are here," said Billy Joe, as he took a deep breath and closed his eyes. "Nothing in the world compares to it—not even the orchids in Hawaii."

The two strolled in silence for a short while, which wasn't awkward at all. When they got to Marge's Street, she stopped and looked at Billy Joe. "I'm not ready to go home yet. Let's go to the park. It's not far." She felt Billy Joe's arm brush against hers but she didn't pull away. Taking it as a sign that she wanted the contact, he took her hand in his and the two headed down the sidewalk.

When they got to the park, they sat down on a bench and Billy Joe put his arm on the back of it, slightly touching Marge's shoulders. She felt the tremor inside again. "So, what have you been up to all these years?" he asked.

"After I graduated from high school, I went to a small business school in Chattanooga for a couple of years," said Marge. She felt calm when she was with Billy Joe, like she didn't have to pretend. It was something new for her. "The war ended shortly after I got there, and when all the boys came home, there was a party every night. The drinks flowed, and everyone was looking for romance. I dated but never really fell in love. It was so good to be away from the confinement of Willow Creek. I just wanted to spread my wings. It was like I had been in a cage my whole life.

"After about seven years of single life, though, I started feeling desperate. I was 25, and everyone I knew was married. So, I started looking. It didn't take long before I met a guy who knew how to spot a woman who was needy — a woman he could easily woo. And he did. We got engaged, and he even convinced my father to loan him some money so "we" could start a grocery store in Chattanooga. Three days before we were supposed to get married, he disappeared…money and all. Just like a puff of smoke, he was gone.

"I thought I was sad, but after I came back to Willow Creek, I realized I was more ashamed than anything. I never really told anyone about my life in Chattanooga…especially my parents. I thought if I came back here and pretended to be the same quiet, obedient Marge McDaniel who left 10 years ago, I could forget all the pain. But it doesn't work that way. When your insides ache and you don't know why, nothing eases the hurt."

Billy Joe reached out with his hand and gently turned her face toward him. "I recognized how deep in thought you were today. What was that all about?" he asked.

She hesitated. "Do you promise you'll never tell anyone?"

"I do," said Billy Joe.

"I'm serious," she said. "The truth isn't always pretty. Are you sure you want to know?"

"I'm sure. You can trust me. I've been to hell and back, and one thing I learned is that you never forsake a fellow soldier. You have my word."

She took a deep breath and exhaled. "When I came back, I started working for my father in the office at the grocery store and told myself it was all I could expect after failing so miserably. After a couple of years of it, I thought I was going to go crazy. Then one day, I went to the bank to make a deposit, and Jack Cooper came up to me and asked if I was interested in learning about the banking business. Of course, I was very flattered — a little attention goes a long way when you're sad, even if it comes from somebody who is not very pleasant to look at. But he could turn the charm on when he wanted something. He asked me to go to lunch in Cantrell City and talk about employment possibilities. I knew he was interested in more than a working relationship and that he was married, but I enjoyed the compliments and the champagne. I went to work for him and looked forward to each day of harmless flirting. I figured it would stop at that, but he wanted more. I knew it was wrong, but I felt like it was my only way to escape. And I was pretty sure I'd lose my job if I didn't give in to his advances. I couldn't bear another failure. And I was foolish enough to believe he was going to get a divorce and marry me. I feel so damn stupid.

"We've been having an affair for almost four years while he continued to have his trysts in Chattanooga and Atlanta — flings I knew about. Why I let myself be used like that, I'll never know. But today, it ended. Lucy Tanner must have found out and threatened Jack in some way. She came in the bank and made him almost have a heart attack. He told me to forget we ever had a relationship. He called me stupid for believing him. He humiliated me.

"And, now, you know. I'm not the sweet, innocent Marge you had a crush on when we were kids. Plus, who knows what the story around town is by now. Ruby accosted me at Buck's. So, everybody is talking, I'm sure."

"You forget what I did to my father…not to mention my war memories," said Billy Joe quietly. "I know all about pain that eats you from the inside out that makes you want to end it. I know all about folks talking behind your back, but I could never think you're a bad person. I've learned people can beat the demons that haunt them. Shithead Jack Cooper needs a long walk off a short pier into a deep lake."

"I know where there's a reservoir not too far from here," she laughed, "but prison isn't worth killing somebody as sorry as he is. So, when are you going to tell me more about yourself? I've done all the talking up to now."

Billy Joe laughed, leaned in, and gently kissed Marge. "…another time. But right now, I'm gonna get you home before Ed McDaniel comes looking for me."

The Country Club

By the time Jack and Anita Cooper arrived at The Cantrell City Country Club, the parking lot out front was almost full. The Annual Newcomer's Dinner was one of the highlights of the year. The club was only about five years old and modern-looking, unlike the older landmarks in Kings County. The single-story building boasted an all-glass façade, low ceilings, and wall-to-wall carpet. It was fancy for Kings County but to the critical eye, the arches out front resembled one of the fast-food restaurants starting to spring up everywhere.

Belonging to the CCCC was an enviable card to carry by anyone who lived in the Great Valley. Folks drove as far as 35 miles and more, one-way, to be counted among the chosen and to rub elbows with the elite. So, receiving an invitation to this event was a hot ticket. Even though Jack hated socializing with Anita and her family, he basked in his perceived glory as the self-anointed Emperor of Kings County. He was good at pretending if it meant getting what he wanted. Keeping a marriage together just for the sake of appearance was okay if it meant money in his pocket.

He pulled up to the front door, got out of the car, and shouted to the valet, "Jesse, park my car around back—can't risk this beauty getting a dent. The keys are in the ignition."

"Yes sir," said the valet, who was at least 30 years Jack's senior but of the skin color that required his being subordinate. He opened the door for Anita and helped her out of the car, bowing his head and saying softly, "Good evening, Miss Anita. Hope you're well."

"Thank you, Jesse," Anita answered quietly, looking up to see Jack going in the front door, oblivious to where she was. "I appreciate your asking." Alone, she walked up the steps to the front porch, holding her head high, as if she didn't care that her husband was ignoring her. She wondered how she was going to make it through this evening. Her head was still reeling from what she heard and saw today. She was ashamed of participating in the sham with Jack for so long. And for what? So, he could do what he wanted. What she had struggled to keep a secret could no longer be squelched, but Anita knew she had to keep up a front for her parents—which would be difficult. Her dad always saw through the veneer.

As soon as she walked inside, her brother rescued her from her solitary entrance and took her to the table where her parents were already seated. Theodore Mason, her father, was a successful and wealthy attorney, and her mother, Isabelle, was the daughter of William Gaines Bishop—one of the richest men in Chattanooga. It was no wonder Jack wanted to marry her and that he did whatever it took to get her. He was a good actor and courting her was one of the best roles he ever played. He had his eye on her inheritance and was determined to get it.

"Hello, Anita," said her father, standing up from his chair to give her a kiss on the cheek.

"Good to see you, too." Anita leaned down and hugged her mother before taking her seat across from them.

George poured her a glass of champagne. "You look nice this evening, sister. I like your hair up like that."

"Thanks," said Anita, trying to hide her sadness. "Kittsee fixed it today," she said, staring at George with an emotionless face that said everything.

George sat up a little straighter and looked at his sister. He could tell she knew. The depth of sadness in her eyes made him shiver. He looked across the room at Jack, who was back-slapping everybody, puffing on a cigar, and slurping down one scotch right after another.

"I see Jack is making sure everyone knows he's here," said Anita's father, "like a noisy gong or a clanging cymbal. I think I'll go over to the bar and listen firsthand to his loquaciousness. Care to join me, son?"

"That's okay. I'll pass on the offer," answered George. "You forget I see him every day."

Jack looked up and saw his father-in-law approaching the group. "Ah, here comes the most renowned attorney in North Georgia, who also happens to be my wife's father. Theodore, I want you to meet my guest, someone I hope becomes a member of the community and the club. This is Dan Cagle. He owns Cagle Mining up in Raleigh, North Carolina." Reaching for his father-in-law's glass, he asked, "Do you need a refill?"

"No thank you, Jack. I'm fine. I prefer to sip. Then I know what I'm saying and hearing," he said with a nod. "My pleasure, Mr. Cagle. And what brings you to Kings County?"

"Iron ore," interjected Jack. "He's going to make anyone willing to invest in his idea very wealthy."

"That's correct," said Cagle. "We've done our homework and determined these mountains are full of red mountain iron ore—just ripe for the harvesting. If we get the financial backing, we need and the county approves our rezoning request, we'll have a monopoly on the richest iron deposits in the Southeast."

"That's a lot of ifs, isn't it?" asked Theodore.

"It is, but I have confidence that Jack here will be able to put a deal together," answered the mining executive, slapping his new ally on the back.

"Now, this looks like an important meeting," said Michael Gilbert, the owner of the *Kings County Tribune*, joining them after a trip to the bar. "Should I be taking notes for a news story?"

"Not yet," said Jack, "but hopefully soon. Michael, I want you to meet someone who is going to make Kings County wealthier than we can imagine. This is Dan Cagle, the owner of Cagle Mining in Raleigh. Dan, Michael Gilbert, the owner and publisher of the county newspaper and a damn good one at that. So, who is your guest, Michael?"

"Hunter Fox, one of the most promising young men in the journalism industry in our state. Hunter, allow me to introduce Jack Cooper III, the president of the First National Bank of Kings County, and his father-in-law, Theodore Mason. If you ever need an attorney, he's the one to hire."

"It's a pleasure to meet you," said Fox, shaking hands with both of them.

"What's your background?" asked Theodore.

"I started out in Atlanta with the *Journal-Constitution* and then went to Savannah and climbed the ranks to be publisher of the *Savannah Morning News*," said Fox.

"Impressive," said Theodore. "I'm familiar with both publications. You are to be commended."

"Well, welcome to the Cantrell City Country Club," said Jack, taking note of the newcomer's exceptional good looks, with more than just a twinge of jealousy. "Allow me to introduce my guest, Dan Cagle, who owns a mining company in North Carolina."

"Mr. Cagle," said Fox, shaking hands with him.

"So, why did Michael invite you to the event, Mr. Fox?" asked Jack. "Are you tired of the city and looking for some rural relief?"

"Actually, I am buying the *Tribune*," answered Fox. "I have a feeling this area is about to become an enviable place to live and visit. You're going to be the favorite play-ground for people who live in the city."

"What?" asked Theodore. "You wouldn't sell the paper, would you Michael?"

"Indeed, I would. Newspaper work never stops, and I've been at it since I was 16 years old. That's 50 years. I'm ready to play golf and relax in Florida. Mary and I are headed to the Sunshine State. Our children already live there, so it's a logical decision for us. And Hunter is the best person to take over my pride and joy."

"Thank you, Michael. I hope the reading public agrees with you," said Hunter with a grin. "You know I don't shy away from telling the truth, though. Mr. Cagle, did I hear correctly that you own a mining company?"

"Yes—out of North Carolina. We believe some of the richest deposits of iron ore in the Southeast are in these mountains, anyone who invests will become very wealthy."

"If you get the money and the county government's approval," added Theodore.

"Now, Teddy, you know since yours truly is leading the charge, there won't be an issue," said Jack. "Coopers get what they want. You should know that."

The attorney bristled inside at his son-in-law's rude familiarity but didn't show his disgust. "Indeed. Now, if you gentlemen will excuse me, I am going to leave this incredibly inspiring conversation."

"Nice to meet you Mr. Mason," said Hunter, shaking the gentleman's hand. "I look forward to learning about the area from someone as knowledgeable as you. Can I give you a call soon for an appointment?"

"Of course," Theodore answered. "I'm in the phone book." He turned and walked back to his table, feeling as though he might have just met someone who wasn't afraid of Jack Cooper.

"So, Mr. Fox, you really think Kings County is going to be a playground for city folks?" asked Jack.

"I do," answered Hunter. "The scenery is breath-taking, there's a lot of water frontage, and the towns have a quaintness to them that the city is missing. Plus, it's a way for people who like to impress to show off. You know what I mean?"

Jack stared at Hunter, who didn't flinch. He'd been in the newspaper business long enough to know that people of influence needed the press but had to learn that the press was not theirs to control.

"Well, we'll see," added Jack, needing to have the last word. "We may find out that mining iron makes more money than tourists from the city. Now, if you'll excuse me, I need to get this dinner started." He turned and walked toward the podium at the front of the dining room.

"Hmmm," said Hunter. "There's already a power struggle brewing here in Kings County...a journalist's dream—development versus the status quo."

"Beware of Jack Cooper," said the veteran newspaperman, guiding Hunter toward their table. "He's ruthless and will do anything to get what he wants."

"Oh, of course," said Hunter. "I think I know his type. You let them talk as much as they want and say little in return."

Jack's voice bellowed over the PA system, asking everyone to find their seats. "As the president of the Cantrell City Country Club, I want to welcome our members and, most importantly, our guests to the Annual Newcomer's Dinner. Please. Enjoy the drinks, the dinner, and the fellowship." He raised his glass into the air and continued. "Here's to prosperity in Kings County. Let's make more of what we all like to have—money. Cheers."

While waiters in white waistcoats and black trousers served the four-course meal, Jack had yet another drink before joining Anita and her family. By the time he sat down, he was almost too drunk to focus or speak without slurring his words.

"So, what did you think about Mr. Fox?" asked Anita's father, knowing Jack had already decided to dislike

70

him for his good looks. He enjoyed making his son-in-law uncomfortable as much as his son did. In reality, he hated Jack Cooper for the way he treated his daughter. It was his goal to live to see him pay dearly for the pain he had brought to his family.

"Just a pretty face," said Jack. "Did you get a good look Anita? How about you, George?"

"You're drunk," said Theodore. "I'd be careful what you say if I were you. You see, I'm not inebriated. Therefore, I won't forget a word that you utter."

Jack started to say something but stopped when he saw Hunter Fox approaching their table. "Excuse me," Fox said with a cordial bow, "but I am calling it an evening. The drive from Savannah, coupled with negotiations with Michael, mean an early evening for me."

Theodore stood up and extended his hand. "I look forward to your being at the helm of *The Tribune*. Good journalism is important to a growing community. Before you leave, however, allow me to introduce my wife, Isabelle, my daughter, Anita Cooper, and my son, George, who is the bank manager in Willow Creek. And you've already had the honor of making Jack's acquaintance."

"My pleasure," Hunter answered. "I did forget to ask you about someone I knew from my days at the University of Georgia, however...Lucy Tanner. She grew up here, didn't she? I was hoping she would be here this evening."

"Why, of course," said Theodore. "She's Luke Tanner's daughter...really fine people. They own a very successful farm outside of Willow Creek."

"Her daddy doesn't spend a dime on anything but necessities and things that make money," slurred Jack. "So, country club dues don't make the list. And Lucy thinks she's better than everybody else...up on her high horse all the time."

"Jack," said Anita, embarrassed at his boorish behavior. Jack started to speak but Hunter was too quick and too sober for him. "Again, I enjoyed the evening and look forward to learning more about the history of Kings County from you, Mr. Mason."

"Theodore. Please call me Theodore."

"I might be too Southern for that, but perhaps with time."

Hunter left his first event in Kings County, amused at how familiar it was to all of the other country clubs he had visited. He grew up in the plastic world of perceived superiority and knew all about it. The pretentiousness was the same regardless of the amount people paid to be a part of high society. *Shallow is shallow,* he thought, *doesn't matter if it's New York City or here.*

"Know-it-all city boy," Jack muttered with contempt, staring at Fox as he left the club. "I'm going to get another drink." He stood up without saying anything to anyone at the table and walked to the bar, stopping several times to steady himself.

"Anita," said George. "You're riding home with us. If he drives off the mountain, I don't want you to be in the car with him."

"Don't I need to tell him I've left?" she asked.

"Why?" asked George. "Give me one good reason why."

Anita

Anita and her mother stood under the portico at the front of the club, while George and her father went to get the car. Both women stared straight ahead as if the silence could erase reality.

George drove his father's Lincoln from the parking lot up the driveway to the club and stopped. Theodore got out of the front passenger's seat and opened the back door for his wife. Anita walked around to the other side and climbed in beside her mother, while George held the door for her.

The uncomfortable silence that ensued for the first five minutes was deafening. Theodore then cleared his throat and began speaking in a controlled voice that had made many a jury eat out of his hand.

"There's something terribly wrong here, isn't there Annie? This is the worst behavior I've ever seen from Jack, and I've witnessed some pretty despicable performances. Can you shed any light on this for me?"

"I'm so sorry, Dad. I know it's humiliating. I never intended to embarrass my family."

"You are not the embarrassment. He is. To be truthful, I have never liked him, but I thought it was what you wanted."

"Well, I'm the one who said 'yes,' the one who settled, and now the one who is sorry she did." Anita looked out the window and saw nothing…which was as dark and empty as her life.

"You deserve so much more." Theodore paused for a second and exhaled. "Tell me something. Has he ever struck you?"

"No. He has never hit me," said Anita, relieved she was finally able to open up to her family. Shoving it down was eating her from the inside out, and she wanted it to stop.

No one spoke for the rest of the drive back to Willow Creek, but Anita's mind was full of noisy dialogue. The ringing in her head was unbearable. She couldn't wait to get home.

The Masons lived on a country estate a few miles north of town. George drove there first and pulled inside the coach house beside the Tudor-style rock mansion. "Anita, we'll go back into town in my car after we make sure everyone is settled here," he said.

"I appreciate your concern, George, but I think I can take care of myself and your mother," said Theodore. "You take your sister home. She needs you right now. We must be united as one." He placed his hands on Anita's shoulders and spoke with conviction. "We will figure this out. And you will be stronger for the pain you have endured. I promise." He hugged her and whispered in her ear. "I love you, Annie."

Tears welled up in her eyes, and she quickly turned away. "I love you both very much. Very much. George, let's be on our way." They walked to the car in silence and watched as their parents opened the front door. George started the engine and pulled out of the circular drive.

"Anita, I—"

"Please don't say anything yet, George. Just get me home."

When they pulled up in front of her house a few minutes later, Anita turned and looked at her brother. "I need you to come inside, please. Bo is spending the night with one of his friends down the street, and I don't want to be here alone."

When they got inside, Anita took off her heels and loosened her pearl choker. "Fix yourself a drink and pour me a glass of white wine, please. I'll be right back." She went upstairs, undressed, and put on her robe. After loosening her hair, she looked in the mirror. "I don't recognize myself anymore," she said aloud. Anita went back downstairs and found her brother sitting in the sunroom, staring out at the night sky. "I need a cigarette, and I know you have one," she said. But let's go out on the terrace."

George took a pack of Winstons out of his coat pocket and lit one for Anita and then one for himself. After taking a sip of wine, she took a long drag, inhaled and slowly blew out the smoke. The nicotine rush was intoxicating and relaxing. She took another drink, another puff, and closed her eyes.

"I want to know what happened today," she said, staring out into the darkness. "I overheard Kittsee telling Laney about an encounter Jack had with Lucy Tanner at the bank. I want to know why I saw Marge McDaniel standing at the Iron Bridge. I want to know the truth, George. I am done with the lies."

"Anita, I wish I knew all the details, but I don't. Suffice to say, however, that the culprit here is Jack, not Marge.

74

Her part pales in comparison to the motives of the perpetrator. There's no telling what he said to her or promised her. He is an expert at spotting vulnerabilities and capitalizing on them at anyone's expense."

"So, has he been having an affair with her?" asked Anita. "For how long?"

George took a sip of his Scotch and exhaled. "Yes. He has, but I'm not sure for how long. But evidently, Lucy found out about it. Whatever she said to him today sent him reeling, and he took it all out on Marge."

"She's not the only one, is she?" asked Anita, now looking directly at her brother. "Tell me the truth, George. When he goes out of town, he does whatever he chooses with whomever he chooses, doesn't he?"

"I don't have proof, but I have my suspicions. There have been occasions when I mentioned to some of our banking associates in other cities that Jack attended certain meetings or seminars. More times than not, they had not seen him there."

"Does he turn in expense tickets for the trips?" asked Anita, feeling more resilient with each sip of wine and every puff of her cigarette.

"Yes. He does."

Anita took another drag and let the smoke out slowly. "Our father knows nothing about what we know or what we suspect, does he?"

"He does not," answered George, "but it may be time to tell him. And right now, it is very important for Jack to think he got away with everything. Don't confront him. We will come up with a game plan, but deceiving the enemy is very important to winning. I do think we can trust Lucy, though, and she will be on your side."

"I believe you are correct," said Anita softly. "She's a good woman. I have always admired her honesty and fearlessness. I will call her first thing in the morning. She'll tell me what she knows."

Anita reached for her wine and looked at the pills she held in her hand. "What happened to me, George? I have lost my passion for life. There is no joy in my heart, and I cannot function without medicating myself with as many of these as it takes to numb the pain. And the more I take, the more I need. They are as poisonous as Jack." She sat her glass on the coffee table, stood up, walked to the edge of the terrace, and tossed the pills into the shrubbery. She sat back down and sighed. "I have to stop. If I don't, these drugs will kill me, and Jack will win."

George leaned forward in his chair and reached for her hand. "You're correct. I've done some reading about what you're going through. It's not uncommon, especially among well-to-do women with doctors who dole the pills out whenever their patients want them. It's not easy to stop, but I know you have the will and strength to do it. We'll get whatever help you need."

"Well, for right now, I need you to stay here with me. Jack won't make it home, I'm sure. He'll sleep at the club. George, please be honest with me about something else. Tell me. Am I the laughing stock in town? That's what upsets me the most. I really couldn't care less how many women Jack sleeps with. I haven't let him lay a hand on me for quite a long time. The sight of him makes me nauseous."

"No, Anita. I don't think you're the laughing stock at all. When Laney tells me the local gossip he hears at the Kut and Kurl, it's never about you. He thinks you're a wonderful woman, who is married to a pompous ego maniac. And I would guess most folks feel that way. I don't know a soul who likes Jack Cooper but Jack Cooper."

Anita chuckled and looked at her brother. "That's the first time I've laughed in a long time. Thanks. Say, are you hungry? I know I am. Let's go fix an obnoxiously big roast beef sandwich and watch some television. There's usually an old movie on one of the Chattanooga stations. I watch them a lot—alone, but this will be a lot more fun."

She stood up and patted George on the shoulder. "Come on. Let's go be naughty nighttime eaters."

George smiled back at her, feeling for the first time in a while that he might get back the sister he knew.

CHAPTER Five

The Phone Call

Only one thing was on Gen's mind while she finished her supper—why Sue Ellen called her on a Friday evening. She excused herself, sat down in the chair next to the phone table and dialed the number to the Riley residence.

"Hello," said a syrupy voice on the other end of the line.

"Hello, Sue Ellen. Luke said you wanted me to give you a call. Is everything okay?"

Lucy fixed two bowls of cobbler and shooed her father and Hank onto the back porch. She listened for any clue as to what this was all about, but her mother's silence meant Sue Ellen was doing all the talking.

"I know she went to the bank today," said Gen, "but what you are insinuating just can't be true."

Once again, silence from the hallway.

Gen cleared her throat. "I don't know why Marge McDaniel was upset, and I don't know why Jack Cooper was so angry. But I don't believe Lucy has anything to do with it," she said, her voice growing louder. "That's ridiculous. She rarely leaves the farm except to deliver produce, and that's before dark."

Silence again.

"I see. So, everyone you've told believes it. Sounds like you've been busy."

Silence once more.

"Hmmm…of course. Well, I'm going to find out what Lucy has to say about this. I'll talk to you later."

Gen hung up the phone without saying goodbye and walked back into the kitchen. Lucy was sitting at the table, eating some cobbler. "Want me to fix you a bowl?" she asked without looking up.

"No. I do not," answered her mother emphatically. "There's more to the story than what you and your father told me, isn't there?" she asked. "What Sue Ellen and others are saying about you makes me angry at them for talking about my daughter and mad at you for whatever you did — all at the same time. What is going on?"

Lucy sat her spoon down and looked at her mother. "Mama, for starters, please tell me what Sue Ellen said. I can't defend myself unless I know the accusations."

"Everybody in town is saying that you and Marge are both having affairs with Jack Cooper." Gen paused and took a deep breath. "They think you found out about Marge, confronted Jack at the bank today, and made a scene. Is that true?" asked Gen, her voice shaking.

"Mama. For Christ's sake. Think about it for a minute. If I was messing around with Jack and discovered he had another girl on the side, would I really take Hank with me while I raised hell about it? No. And as far as Marge and Jack go, she's scared to death of making him angry. She couldn't stop me from getting into his office. I could tell she was terrified of him. Whoever started this rumor should be ashamed of themselves, just like Sue Ellen should be for peddling it." Lucy had no intentions of telling her mother about Jack's and Marge's relationship. That was a secret she intended to keep.

Gen continued to fret. "Sue Ellen said she and several other women from the church are going to Alice McDaniel's house tomorrow morning to break the news to her and have a prayer circle for Marge."

"Good lord. She is one meddlesome woman," answered Lucy.

"So, what are you going to do about it, Lucy?" asked Gen. "You can't let this get out any more than it already has."

79

"I'm not doing anything tonight. I'll talk to Nettie about it in the morning. She always knows how to help me think through something. But in the meantime, put your mind to rest. There's not a shred of truth to what you just heard, Mama. You know why I went to the bank — to call out Jack for what he said about your grandson. Now, that is the truth. Please, give me some credit for knowing what the hell I'm doing."

"But, what if — "

"Mama. Please. I will deal with Sue Ellen Riley and the rest tomorrow. I promise."

The Plan

Nettie woke before dawn every day, even on Saturdays when she didn't go to the Tanner farm. She perked a pot of coffee on the stove and sat down in the rocker on the front porch.

Whatever happened yesterday at the bank was turning into something it wasn't. Nettie knew all about gossips. They could twist the truth faster than a rabbit could run. *As soon as Lucy tells me what's going on, we can deal with this*, she thought, *and since she's in the middle of it, she'll be showing up here in a few minutes.*

She looked down the drive and almost expected to see Lucy walking toward her house like that morning in November 1944, one day after the army officer showed up at the Tanner place with an envelope. That was a sight no family wanted to see, because the news was never good.

It was about Henry, Lucy's older brother. He had been killed in France during the Alsace Campaign. Nettie would never forget the sound of Gen's screams and Luke's attempts to comfort her. Lucy, who was 19 years old and home from college for the holidays, was inconsolable.

When Nettie went out on her porch the morning after they found out about Henry, Lucy was walking up the drive. For hours, she cried without stopping, and Nettie held her.

Ever since Lucy was a little girl, if she was sad or had a problem she turned to Nettie for help. So, within minutes of settling in on the porch this morning, Nettie saw the green pickup truck slowly come down the driveway and roll to a stop.

"Want a cup?" Nettie asked.

"I do, but I'll get it. You know I love going in your house."

Lucy walked into the home that smelled like a wood fire, regardless of the time of year. The rock hearth welcomed her as it had her entire life. She found comfort in its warmth and ageless strength.

"So, you, Jack Cooper, and Marge, huh? Now, there's a sight, Lulu," said Nettie with a grin. Lucy chuckled and sat down in the other rocker.

"How did you know?" asked Lucy.

Nettie smiled again slightly. "I heard Ruby telling Dancy Riley all about it at the drug store yesterday. They didn't see me. I'm good at being invisible, you know. Evidently, Kittsee King had just told Ruby about seeing you at the bank. Ruby then took it upon herself to tell Dancy that it probably had something to do with Jack Cooper and women."

Lucy took a deep breath. "Well, I went to the bank to confront Jack because he told his kid that Hank was a bastard. I lost my temper, but I got that straightened out, with Hank's help. You should have heard him tell Jack why he wasn't a bastard...right down to the date the divorce was final. You'd be proud."

"I'm always proud of both of you," said Nettie.

"Thanks, but I probably went a little too far. I asked Hank to leave Jack's office. Then I told Cooper I knew about him and Marge. You see, I saw them at the Gold Star Inn a while back. I knew I could shut him up by threatening to tell Anita. Nettie, you know he's an ass. No telling what he said or did to get Marge to sleep with him. She doesn't impress me as the kind to fall for Jack. When I left, I told her she

81

needed to stay away from him, that he was no good. She was horrified when she realized that I knew."

"Hmmm," said Nettie. "It sounds like you got that hornet's nest buzzing real good, which is not something I think you set out to do. But now you have a problem, because Marge is the one who could really suffer here...her and Anita, not you."

"I know. I never meant for this to get so out of hand, but you know how stubborn I can be."

Nettie nodded her head and smiled. "Indeed, I do."
"I was just standing up for Hank. But what we have now is a full-blown circus. Sue Ellen Riley even called last night and got Mama all stirred up. She told her that several of the women from the church are going to see Marge's mama this morning and have a prayer circle. Damn it. This is all my fault, and I don't know how to fix it." Staring at the floor and slowly rocking, Nettie took a couple of sips of coffee. The pause seemed like forever to Lucy.

"Well, the mistake women often make when a man cheats on them is to turn on one another, when they should be mad at the sorry son-of-a-bitch who cheated," said Nettie who had stopped rocking. "My mama taught me that when a couple of her friends were fighting over a good-for-nothing man. I was just a little girl, but I never forgot what she told me. 'Those women shouldn't blame one another for this mess,' she said. 'It's the damn man who lied to them who is in the wrong.' Maybe you should try to talk to Marge and Anita. They have both been used by Jack Cooper. What all three of you can agree upon is that you went to the bank to set Jack straight. Now, that's the truth. That you and Marge are having an affair with Jack is nothing but a rumor. In fact, that's a lie. And really, what is going on between
Jack and Marge or Jack and Anita is nobody's business ...especially some folks who don't have anything better to do than meddle in somebody else's life. If y'all show the busy bodies that you stand together, they won't have a thing to talk about."

82

"You're right, Nettie," said Lucy. "If I can convince Anita and Marge this is the best way to deal with things, we can shut it up. It's a long shot, but it just might work. I need to get in touch with Marge anyway. I could tell she was really upset."

"Whatever you do though, honey, do it quickly," added Nettie. "You know those church women are chomping at the bit to take their religion to Marge."

"I'll head home and call Marge first and then Anita," said Lucy. "Hopefully, we can come to an agreement and get to the McDaniel house before the inquisition arrives. Then we'll pay a visit to the beauty shop and the drug store. Hell, if I have to go to the church tomorrow and make an announcement, I'll do that."

Nettie laughed. "That would really get things to churning. Now get going. It's already 7:30."

Lucy turned the truck around and headed out the drive. About a mile from the Tanner home, Lucy passed the site where the old Sims house used to be. There was a pickup truck parked there, and of all people, Marge was walking around the property with a man. "Jesus Pete," said Lucy aloud. "That looks like Billy Joe Sims. And what the hell is Marge doing out here?" She slowed down, looked in the rear-view mirror and made a hard U-turn and pulled in the dirt drive.

"Am I seeing right?" she asked as she jumped out of the truck. "Billy Joe Sims, is that you?"

"Hey, Lucy. It's me alright," he said with a grin. "Fallen into any creeks lately?"

Lucy laughed and gave him a hug. "Wow. What are you doing here?"

"I just got out of the army. I'm moving back to build the house my mama always dreamed of having, right here where we lived when I was a kid. Just think, Lucy. We'll be neighbors again."

"That's wonderful. And Marge, I'm kind of surprised to see you out here this early on a Saturday morning."

"Well, we sort of ran into one another yesterday," said Marge, smiling and nodding towards Billy Joe, claiming him as hers.

"Actually, I was hoping we could talk, Marge," said Lucy, lowering her voice in an apologetic manner. "I was on my way home to give you a call, but this is much better. Can we please have a minute in private?"

"We can talk right here in front of Billy Joe," answered Marge. "It's okay."

A bit surprised, Lucy nodded her head. "Well, according to Kittsee King, Ruby Thompson, Dancy Riley, Sue Ellen Riley and god knows who else, you and I were both having an affair with Jack. Word is that I found out, came to the bank and raised holy hell. Maybe I raised a little too much hell, but it wasn't about what they think. I came to give Jack a mouthful because he told his kid that Hank was a bastard. Believe me, I am so sorry for causing this misunderstanding. It's completely out of hand now. In fact, Sue Ellen Riley and her church buddies are supposed to go see your mama this morning. Did you know that? Has anyone called her yet?"

"No one had gotten in touch with her by the time I left a few minutes ago. And Lucy, you're not telling me anything I don't already know. You forget that I was at the bank yesterday," said Marge, with a hint of sarcasm. "I saw the way everybody looked at me when I walked out in tears. And the town is buzzing for sure, thanks to Dancy and her mother-in-law. Neither one of them have any scruples when it comes to spreading lies about others. You and I both know that. No telling what secrets they have in their closets though. But they carry the Christian flag like they're spotless. Ruby was full of questions about it at Buck's last night, too, but I told her she needed to ask Jack about his business, not me."

Lucy continued to do her best to smooth things over with Marge. "Well, I know I created this mess, but thanks to Nettie, I have an idea. I planned on talking with Anita after I spoke to you. All three of us have a reason to put Jack in his place. I was thinking if we could get our story straight and tell whoever has been talking the loudest, it may help stop some of the gossip. I say we go see your mama first. I imagine the missionaries will be there around 9 or so. Then we'll check in on the other loose lips in town."

Marge didn't say anything for a minute which seemed like an hour to Lucy.

"The truth is that you came to the bank to confront Jack about what he said," answered Marge. "That's all anybody needs to know. A person's private life shouldn't be of any concern to others. I just hope Anita won't be too angry with me to go along with this."

"Well, I imagine she is more concerned with putting a lid on this than exposing anything about you and Jack. Anita and her family have a reputation to protect, too," said Lucy. "Billy Joe, can I borrow her for a bit, please? We have some work to do."

"Sure," said Billy Joe, fascinated by the two women's candor and grateful for it, too. "Just be sure and bring her back in one piece and tell me all about it." He beamed at Marge, who felt the color rise in her cheeks.

The two young women climbed into Lucy's truck. She started to turn the key but stopped. "Marge, I want you to know my intentions were to help you get out of a bad situation. I never, ever wanted to cause you or Anita any pain."

"I know," said Marge. "It needed to happen though. If it hadn't, I wouldn't have been standing on the edge of the Iron Bridge when that gorgeous man, Billy Joe, was driving to Willow Creek yesterday."

That made Lucy shudder from head to toe. "Jesus, I really upset you, didn't I? You are far too good a woman to let a jerk like Jack get you down."

"Well, Jack Cooper is a master at treating people like dirt and making them feel responsible for his bad behavior. He learned from the best—Mr. JJ. He actually made me believe I didn't deserve better than being used. And then, like

85

a scene out of a movie, Billy Joe showed up. The contrast between those two men couldn't be greater. Lucy, do you think there's such a thing as love at first sight?" asked Marge in a wistful voice.

"Yep. I do," said Lucy. "I've never felt it but I believe it's possible. On another note, are you ready to get Anita on the phone and put some know-it-all women in their places?"

The Pact

Anita woke up to an empty house, but it didn't feel so lonely. Jack had not made it back from the club—or wherever he stayed the night—and Bo was still at TJ Baxter's house. Not hearing Jack's hacking coughs or Bo's whining was a silence she welcomed. She feared that her son was turning into a young Jack. It was as if there was a curse on the Cooper name.

After pouring herself a cup of coffee and lighting one of the cigarettes George had given her, she went out on the terrace. The early morning sun made the smoke she exhaled turn into a vaporous cloud. She thought about what she was going to say to Lucy Tanner, but it was pretty simple. Like she said to her brother the night before, she had denied what she knew was the truth. But now she was ready to face it. What it was didn't really matter now. If Jack and Marge were fooling around, the only thing she felt was sympathy for Marge, knowing Jack the way she did. He was capable of anything. Anita missed affection and intimacy, but not with her husband. The thought of his touching her was as nauseating as the actual event.

She looked up the number to the Tanner home in the phone book and dialed it. Hank answered immediately. "Hello? This is Hank Tanner. Can I help you?"

"Why, hello, Hank. This is Miss Anita—Bo's mother. Is your mama there?"

"Ah, no ma'am, she isn't." He glanced out the window to make sure. "Wait. I think I see her pulling in the driveway now. Hold on. I'll get her." Anita could hear him yelling for his mother. "Mama, Mama. Hurry up. Miss Anita is on the phone for you."

Lucy turned and looked at Marge. "Did you hear what he said? This is crazy. More has happened around here in an hour than usually does in a month of Sundays."

When Hank saw his mother and Marge walking toward the house, his eyes grew wide. *Where had his mama been and why was the pink-sweater lady from the bank with her?*

"Marge, I'll be right back," said Lucy. "Hank, be a good host and keep Miss McDaniel company. By the way, where are your grandparents?"

"Grandmama Gen is in the kitchen, washing her hair, and Granddaddy is checking the cows," answered Hank, who had sat down in the rocker next to Marge.

"Thank you, Jesus," said Lucy under her breath. She walked into the house quickly and picked up the telephone receiver. "Hello? Anita? This is Lucy. I'm glad you called. In fact, I was about to try and get in touch with you."

Anita cleared her throat. "Well, we certainly need to talk, but I would rather not over the phone. Jack could show up here any minute. Is it possible for you to meet me at my brother's house?"

"I'm on my way," answered Lucy, hanging up. When she walked out on the front porch, Hank was in the middle of telling Marge the story about Billy Joe's dumping his mama into the creek.

"Mama, did you know Miss Marge and Billy Joe were friends and that he was moving back here?" asked Hank, excitedly.

"Yes, I do know, but for now, I have a job for you. I need you to tell your grandparents I had to go into town early. I'll be back before 11, and y'all need to be ready to head back into Willow Creek as soon as I get here. Your granddaddy and I have a meeting at the bank and then the two of us—you and I—will get our hair trimmed before we eat lunch at the drug store. Have you got that?"

"Yes ma'am," said Hank. "Can Miss Marge and Billy Joe go to lunch with us, too?"

"Of course. If they want to," answered Lucy, "but first, Marge and I have to do what we need to do."

"What's that?" asked Hank.

"Business," said Lucy. "We have to take care of some unfinished business."

Hank watched his mama and Marge walk quickly to the truck and take off down the road at a brisk clip. He wasn't sure what was happening, but he liked it and knew he was part of it.

As soon as they got in the truck, Marge started talking. "What did she say? Anything about me?"

"We didn't discuss any particulars," answered Lucy. "She just asked me to meet her at George's house."

"Does she know I'm with you?" asked Marge, her mind racing.

"No. She didn't ask, and I didn't tell."

"Oh, Lucy, I sure hope this works. I have to keep what happened between Jack and me a secret. My parents would never forgive me. Mama thinks an unmarried woman who has gone all the way will go to Hell. Sometimes I wonder how I was conceived. She probably made my daddy keep his clothes on and turn the lights off.

"She believes that being a virgin until a woman gets married is as important as joining the church. If this blows up even more than it already has, I can see them making me move away. They wouldn't want the stigma attached to me affecting them or the business. The Riley's would make sure that would happen. They've done it before you know. I'd be labeled the whore and Jack the victim. They'd kiss his ass."

"Hey now, stop. We're not going to let that happen. That's why we're nipping it in the bud right now. And believe me. I know exactly how you feel about your mama. All mine can talk about is the fact that I'm divorced and have a child. You'd think I was a damn criminal or worse. If you only knew the arguments, we've had about that. Of course, neither one of our mothers have a damn thing to say about

88

the men involved. They blame the women if the boys unzip their britches. And you know what, Marge? I'm tired of that shit. Where is it written that men can sow their oats but women can't even have them?"

Marge laughed. "Lucy, you're so funny, but you're right. Why do you think they feel that way?"

"Because they were taught that way in church and had it drilled into them at home, you know, the Puritans and all that strait-laced shit. It was all about the men controlling the women. The scriptures tell wives to be submissive to their husbands — code for 'you will do what I say when I say and how I say.' I'm pretty sure that men know if we had a choice when it came to sex, we'd have an opinion about everything else. And then, there goes their control."

"Huh," said Marge, biting her lip. "That sounds like the perfect description of Jack Cooper. I just hope Anita sees it the way we do."

"I'm pretty sure she will. Don't you believe their marriage was over before it began? Her fight is not with you, Marge. It's with Jack."

Lucy pulled in the drive and parked behind Anita's car. "It's almost 8 o'clock. No time to waste." She jumped out of the truck and quickly walked toward the porch, but Anita opened the front door before she could knock.

"Good morning, Lucy. Ah, Marge? I didn't know you were coming. Come on in," she said, motioning them through the door. "Let's go out back on the patio."

As she and Marge followed Anita through the kitchen, Lucy couldn't help but notice how pristine George's house was. There was not a spec of dirt anywhere nor was anything out of place. It was as though he didn't live there.

"Can I get y'all anything?" asked Anita. "I'm going to have a cigarette and finish this cup."

"I'm fine," said Lucy.

"Me, too," replied Marge timidly, barely looking at Anita.

Anita took a long drag off the cigarette. "I'm going to get right to the point of why I asked you to come here. Lucy, yesterday, while I was at the beauty shop, I overheard Kittsee telling Laney about you, Marge and Jack and some episode at the bank. I want to know every detail."

Lucy took the lead and let out a deep breath. "Okay. Here goes." She then told Anita what happened the previous day—including what Bo called Hank, her conversation with Jack, how Jack treated Marge, right down to who spread the rumors. "Their story goes that both Marge and I are fooling around with Jack," said Lucy.

"I see," said Anita, with absolutely no emotion in her voice. "Is that true?"

"Hell no, Anita...absolutely not," said Lucy adamantly.

"And what about you, Marge?" asked Anita, almost certain she knew the answer.

Marge looked down at her lap, rubbed her hands together for a moment and then lifted her head, meeting Anita's gaze. "I was going to lie, but I'm tired of lying. Since Jack was my boss, I didn't feel like I had a choice in the matter. He put a lot of pressure on me—every day. It always left me feeling dirty and cheap, but I didn't know what to do. I admit I was needy and weak. I tried to convince myself I meant more to him than I did, but he was just using me. If that's an affair, then yes, I had an affair with Jack. To me, it felt more like torture. I am so sorry. If I could—"

"No apologies needed," said Anita, smiling through clenched teeth. "Can you imagine what it's been like living with him? If anyone should be saying, 'I'm sorry,' it's Jack. Truly, he's the bastard, not Hank. I apologize for his bullying behavior, Lucy. And honestly, I am tired of lying too, Marge...to myself, to my family, and to the world. It's painful to hear the truth but lies hurt more. I have no intentions of exposing this to anyone but every intention of exposing Jack for who he is. Your secret is safe with me, Marge. You have my word. So, who else knows?"

"Just you, Lucy, George, and Billy Joe Sims," answered Marge quietly. "And I only suspect George. I never came right out and told him."

"George is a smart man. He's known what Jack was doing here and other places for years. But Billy Joe Sims?" asked Anita. "Why on earth him?"

"That's a long story," interrupted Lucy, "one Marge can tell you when we have time."

"You're right," said Anita. "I'd love for Jack to think he got away with all of it. This road is very familiar to me. He cheated on me with a teenager when I was pregnant with the baby I lost. That's when I grew numb to the pain. There's no telling how many women he's slept with or forced himself on."

Lucy sat forward in her chair. "Marge and I are going to her mama's house before Sue Ellen and her church buddies get there. And if you go with us, I think we could throw some water on this after we tell our story. Seeing all three of us there would send those ladies back to church. How does that sound to you, Anita?"

"I like the idea," answered Anita. "But Lucy, you should do the talking since it was you who confronted Jack. I have a couple of suggestions though." She then laid out a plan that both Lucy and Marge agreed could work. "And I want both of you to know how grateful I am for your honesty," added Anita. "You're helping me find the courage I need to face the facts. Let's do get together soon though. I want to hear more about Billy Joe Sims, Marge. By the way, are you going to keep your job at the bank?"

"No. I'm not. I think I'll call George this afternoon and talk to him about it."

"I'm sure he'll help you do whatever you need. For now, we better go," answered Anita. "Lucy, remember you're doing the explaining." She stood up and started to leave but Marge stopped her.

"Anita, thank you so much for not hating me. You are a brave woman."

"Thanks, Marge. I appreciate that," Anita said. "But for now, let's go break up that damn prayer circle."

The Prayer Circle

"Anita surprises me," said Lucy, as she cranked up the truck. "I like the way she took charge, and I hope to hell she can stand her ground against Jack."

"Well, I couldn't believe she didn't want to humiliate me," said Marge. "I guess Jack's infidelity didn't shock her. What an ass, cheating on her like that while she was pregnant."

"You know I agree with you on that one. Jack is an ass."

The drive from George's to the McDaniel home was a short five minutes for Anita but long enough for her to reflect on what was happening. She was a shell of the strong and confident woman who married Jack. But today, for the first time in a long time, she saw the glimmer of who she once was, someone with excellent managerial skills, a good analytical mind, and a talent for getting people involved in a common goal. She was determined to reclaim that side of herself. In her mind, allowing Jack to cheat and lie was no longer acceptable. "I didn't make him the egotistical bastard he is," she said aloud to herself. "I just pray I can get well and be strong enough to divorce him. There. I said it. Divorce." She saw Lucy turn down the side street and followed, parking right behind her truck.

Anita got out of her car, looking at her watch. "We need to hurry."

"Yep," said Lucy, following Marge, who was already turning the corner and walking toward her house.

As soon as Marge's feet hit the front porch, Alice McDaniel opened the door and saw Anita and Lucy close behind. Alice clutched her chest in surprise. "Marge, what on Earth have—"

"Mama, I need you to go in the parlor. I'll be right there."

"Hello, Miss Alice," said Lucy. "Don't you worry now. We have this under control."

"Mrs. McDaniel," said Anita, nodding her head in graceful deference. "I apologize for barging in unannounced, but when people take it upon themselves to spread gossip, those who know the facts must intercede. By the way, you do have a lovely home."

Alice McDaniel stood speechless, unsure what was about to unfold. All she knew was what Sue Ellen had told her over the phone, and that was not good. Now all three women, who were at the center of the story, were in her home, waiting to confront the pillars of the church. It was enough to give her the vapors.

"Lucy, you and Anita wait across the hall in the music room," said Marge. "Close the double doors and draw the curtains. You'll be able to hear just fine." She took her mother to the parlor, grabbed a Bible from the desk, and gave it to Lucy. "I think I just saw Sue Ellen's car pull up, looks like there are three ladies with her." Marge went into the parlor and sat down next to her mother. "Mama, believe me when I say that Sue Ellen and everyone else who has participated in this will think twice before they gossip again."

A sharp knock made Alice jump. Marge stood up and walked toward the door. She looked out the sidelight and saw Sue Ellen, Dancy, Sara Sanders, and Janet Rogers tightly clutching their Bibles, their noses in the air and determined to save some souls.

"Hello ladies," said Marge as she opened the door. "I believe you are here to see my mother, right?"

Sue Ellen looked surprised but quickly recovered. "Why, yes, Marge. We are."

"She's in the parlor. Right this way," answered Marge with cool civility. "Make yourselves comfortable."

Sue Ellen cleared her throat. "Well, we weren't expecting to see you here, Marge. We figured you would be at the bank…working…with Jack," said Sue Ellen in a suspicious voice.

"Well, you know, sometimes, we just figure wrong, don't we? What brings y'all here?"

"Marge, we are here to protect you and your mother. We're here to pray for you. Jesus never turns His back on true believers—no matter what they do. And He calls upon others to do the same…to forgive and love in spite of people's sins and transgressions."

"Hmmm," said Marge. "Really? Why do we need your protection?"

"Dear, we heard about what happened yesterday," said Sue Ellen in a patronizing voice, "but we believe every sinner can be saved and forgiven. That's why we are here."

"What happened yesterday and who did what to warrant prayers and forgiveness?" asked Marge, defensively and with a confidence she didn't know she had.

Sue Ellen cleared her throat, not expecting this challenge. "Kittsee King told Ruby Thompson—"

"Excuse me," interrupted Marge. "If this is about something Kittsee said to Ruby, then where are they? Why aren't they here?"

Sue Ellen looked flustered but her daughter-in-law, Dancy, came to her rescue. "I'll tell you what this is about, Marge. Kittsee saw Lucy Tanner get into it with Jack Cooper, who in turn, was furious with you. Ruby told me all about it. Apparently, this has something to do with you, Jack, and Lucy. Poor Anita—"

"What do you mean 'poor Anita'?" said a voice, coming from the hallway.

Lucy and Anita walked into the parlor and stood in front of the group of women. The color drained from Dancy's face and Sue Ellen slowly lowered herself into a chair.

"Why, Anita, I—" stammered Dancy.

"You probably need to sit down, too, Dancy," said Lucy, in a quiet, yet authoritative voice. "Since Kittsee did not hear what I said to Jack and since Ruby was not even at the bank when all of this occurred, I should probably enlighten you, especially since it appears you have taken it upon yourselves to arrive at your own erroneous conclusions. Unless, of course, you prefer to address the matter, Anita."

"Oh, please. Continue. You went to the bank, not I."

"Well, we all know how angry mamas can get when somebody picks on our children. Right?" asked Lucy.

The ladies all nodded and stared at Lucy and Anita as if they were hypnotized.

"It seems that Jack told his son, Bo, that my Hank was a bastard. Well, as soon as Hank came home from school yesterday and told me what happened, we drove to Willow Creek and marched right in the bank. I ignored Marge, who tried to keep me from going into Jack's office. I made a fuss until he finally let us in. Hank asked him what a bastard was. Jack told him, and then my son set him straight. And y'all know Hank isn't a bastard. You know the story. I've never tried to hide the truth from anyone here. Why? Because I divorced his cheating ass, and I'm not ashamed. Anyway, when we left, I saw Jack light into Marge with a fierceness that scared me. Why don't you tell them what he said, Marge?"

Marge stood up and faced the group. "She's right. Mr. Cooper was furious with me. He told me I could lose my job for letting Lucy get in his office. He was shaking he was so mad. It upset me so much that I left work early."

"Do you realize the harm you women have caused us?" asked Lucy. "My mother couldn't sleep last night because you called her, Sue Ellen. But y'all couldn't stop at spreading tales about Marge and me. You had to bring Anita's name into it, too, commenting on her private life to anyone who would listen. You should —"

"Excuse me, Lucy. I'd like to say something." Anita took her time and locked eyes with each of the four women who were sitting in front of her. "Dancy, would you like to tell us about yours and Joe Jr.'s intimate life? How long has it been for you and Joe Sr., Sue Ellen? Janet, Sara...do you care to share anything with us about your bedrooms?"

The silence was deafening. The four women looked like they had swallowed something rotten.

Anita continued. "Well, guess what? I also choose to share nothing with any of you about my personal life. Just like yours is none of my business, mine is none of yours. I am certain you understand that."

The church ladies nervously nodded. Dancy started to stand up but Lucy held up her hand and stopped her. "You know you can't leave before we at least share some scripture. I mean, this is a prayer circle, right? I think this is a good passage for today. It's from the Book of Proverbs 11:9: 'With their mouths the godless destroy their neighbors, but through knowledge the righteous escape.' I repeat: 'With their mouths the godless destroy their neighbors, but through knowledge the righteous escape.' Now, sisters, let us pray. Heavenly father, please forgive the godless who spread rumor and innuendo. Open their eyes to their destructive ways. Help them to turn toward truth and righteousness and away from falsehoods and hypocrisy. In the name of Jesus, we say, Amen." Lucy breathed a sigh of relief. "Now, isn't it good to have cleared the air? Do you ladies have anything to add?

CHAPTER Six

Hunter Fox

Hunter smelled bacon cooking and coffee perking as soon as he started down the steps to the hotel lobby. When he walked toward the dining room, the clatter of pots and pans got his attention—just as his presence got that of the waitress who was standing in the doorway to the kitchen, looking at a menu with the chef. She nudged her co-worker and smiled at Fox, a gesture Hunter did not miss and quite enjoyed. He liked attention and always responded to it. To him, flirting was something he did for others, never admitting he liked it, too.

"Care for some coffee, sir?"

"Yes, please," he said, squinting to read her nametag, "Patsy."

"That's me," she answered, smiling, taking her time to fill his cup. "And you are?"

"My name is Hunter Fox," he answered with a crooked grin that made Patsy almost giggle.

"I don't mean to be nosey, but one of the cooks said you are from Savannah. Is that right?" she asked.

"Not really from there. That's just the last place I lived, but I'm moving here. I bought the *Tribune* from Michael Gilbert.

Patsy's eyes widen a bit...*I can't wait to tell Ruby what just landed here.* "Are you looking for a place to live?" she asked motioning to the newspaper on the table.

"Yep. That's what I'm doing now, checking out the classifieds. I'll be staying here at the Gold Star until I find the right place."

"Well, welcome to Kings County. I'll let you get back to your morning."

Hunter smiled, watching her as she all but skipped to the kitchen. He continued to scan the ads. "Guest House available. Completely furnished, with kitchen and maid service. References required. Call 664-7613." He circled the copy, folded the paper, and walked out of the dining room into the hotel lobby.

"Everything meet your satisfaction, Mr. Fox?" asked the clerk at the front desk.

"Sure, Jimmy, just fine."

Fox walked up the wide, marble staircase. The brass handrails on either side had a well-worn luster about them that reflected the light from the crystal chandelier, causing prisms to dance on the walls. He marveled at the quiet beauty and felt lucky to be there.

Dating back to the early 1900s, the Gold Star Inn was still in excellent condition. Built of native fieldstone and mountain timber, the décor was a blend of Southern rustic and fine English antiques. Its original charm was still intact, commanding a significant presence in the center of town.

Hunter's room was the largest in the hotel and had a sitting area with a couch, two chairs, a desk and sideboard, in addition to a spacious bedroom and private bath. The ceiling to floor windows faced east, letting an abundance of early autumn light in. Hunter looked at the scene below that was so different from the cities he had lived before...cities with crowded sidewalks, restaurants, and bars. He was just as happy being alone, but journalists had to mingle. People couldn't wait to share juicy tidbits with a reporter, especially after having a couple of drinks—like last night at the country club. *I met some interesting characters for sure*, he thought, *but I'm not surprised. Lucy Tanner is from here.* He stared out the window and remembered when they met at an orientation for University of Georgia journalism students in 1943. He was an upper classman and a group leader. Her straightforward manner got his attention, not to mention her individual sense of style. He got the impression she was completely unaware of how captivating she was.

The phone in his room rang and interrupted his day-dream.

"Hello, this is Hunter Fox."

"Hello, Hunter Fox. I'm glad to know you made it to wherever it is you are."

"Oh, hello, Lisa…I'm fine… just haven't stopped since I got here. And you know where I am. Obviously. You're calling me."

"Right again. And, yes, I know exactly where you are, and there's only one hotel there. You weren't that difficult to find. How is it in Cantrell City?"

"Well, the name is deceiving. It's not a city. It's a town. It's quaint, relatively quiet, and everything closes at 6 o'clock, except for the country club, a couple of BBQ joints, and a place called the Lodge."

"God, that sounds awful."

"Not really. The people are as interesting here as they are anywhere else. And they make news—just like anywhere else. I'm already working on what I think is going to be a big story."

"I'm sure you are. I know you love your work, and it shows. All of your admirers miss your writing here. Speaking of here, are you coming home anytime soon?"

"Lisa. I am home. I have moved here."

"Well, it sounds like if I'm going to see you, I'll have to head to Cantrell City."

Hunter hesitated long enough to remind himself he didn't need to be with Lisa again. "Pretty sure of that. Give me a couple of weeks to get settled, and maybe you can drive up for a weekend with one of your girlfriends if you want. I'll get you a room at the hotel. Just let me know in advance."

"Okay, Mr. Fox," she said petulantly, her voice taking on an enticing tone again, making Hunter sit up a little straighter and clear his throat. "That doesn't sound like much of a party to me, but if it's the best you can do—"

"I'll talk to you later, Miss Sutton. Gotta go to work." Hunter hung up the receiver and stared at it. For a brief second, he felt a twinge—the one he always felt with Lisa. The attraction between them was intensely physical with no emotional connection. Everything else was a complete mess. They were both very headstrong people who were polar opposites except in the bedroom. She was a free spirit with no interest in settling down and was quite candid about the fact that she could not be monogamous. Hunter tried it her way, but the agitation he felt when he saw her with another man or knew she was sleeping with someone else was too much for him. It completely wrecked his psyche.

He wanted to start fresh somewhere—away from her—which contributed to his decision to move. Hunter was a sensitive guy who wasn't afraid to show his feelings. He was brave enough to be romantic, a rarity. He shook off the thoughts he was having and focused on what he was doing before she called. Reaching for the folded newspaper, he dialed the number in the circled ad.

"Mason residence," answered a woman in a refined Southern accent.

"Hello. I'm calling about the guest house for rent. Did you say Mason residence? Theodore Mason's?"

"No sir. This is Miss Angela Mason's home—Mr. Theodore's sister. I'm her housekeeper. May I ask who is calling, please?"

"Hunter Fox. I met Miss Mason's brother and his family at the country club last evening."

"Just a minute, Mr. Fox. I'll tell Miss Mason you're asking about the guest house."

In a few moments, he heard the same voice on the other end of the line. "Mr. Fox, Miss Angela said she will call you after she speaks to Mr. Theodore."

"Good. I'm staying at the Gold Star. She can leave a message with Jimmy Baker at the front desk if I don't answer the phone in my room. Please tell her I appreciate her consideration and hope to speak with her soon."

Hunter went to the bedroom and got a Harris tweed sports coat out of the closet. Always impeccably dressed, he looked in the mirror, smoothed his light brown hair and adjusted the collar of his starched, white shirt and tightened the Windsor knot of his regimental striped tie. He was excited about owning a publication, even if it was a small one. This was what he had always wanted to do. He tossed the newspaper in his briefcase and headed down to the lobby. Just as he got to the bottom of the stairs, he heard someone calling his name. Hunter stopped and turned his head. "Oh, hi. Dan Cagle, right? Cagle Mining."

"You got it. I guess we're both newcomers who want to make some money here," said Cagle, shaking hands with Hunter.

"Well, if I do right by my readers, my employees, and my advertisers, I will do well."

"Ah, very commendable. Then you'll want to make sure the community gets the facts about our mining venture, won't you?"

"Of course," said Hunter. "In fact, I was hoping you and I could sit down as soon as possible."

"Excellent. Are you headed to the office? I'm meeting Jack at the bank in Willow Creek at 10 but have some time now."

"That works," said Hunter. "I'll see you there." Hunter walked out of the hotel's front double doors onto the wide slate terrace. High back rockers and wrought iron planters gave it a regal yet comfortable look. The view from the front of the hotel looked like a photo in a magazine.

An island of greenspace separated two wide streets that ran east and west for several blocks in each direction. The county courthouse sat directly across the street from the hotel. On either side of the main thoroughfare were a variety of stores, shops, and cafes, and all were open for business. Hunter took note of how many people were already shopping. Hardly a parking space was available. "Saturday come to town" was not an idle phrase.

There were newer commercial areas on the perimeter of town where the more modern stores were: the Piggly Wiggly, a couple of car dealerships, a JC Penny's, several drive-in food joints, and a Sears. Hunter was conflicted when it came to the development of commercial areas away from downtown districts and had witnessed it firsthand. That trend was already devastating small businesses in other parts of the country. But he knew the additional ad revenue meant more money to expand the paper. Impact versus profit was an ongoing dilemma for him but a challenge he enjoyed. He felt his pace quicken and his adrenaline pump — sensations that made Hunter Fox who he was.

The Tribune

Hunter walked up the steps to the entrance of the *Tribune* office building, stopping for a moment to read the words on the bronze marker inlaid in the brick beside the front door. *"The Kings County Tribune, Founded in 1903. 'Our Republic and its press will rise or fall together.' Joseph Pulitzer."* He had always taken his job seriously. Accuracy and truth mattered to him. Without it, there was no accountability and no justice.

The front office looked the same as it did when the publication began. There was one large oak desk and numerous filing cabinets. Several shelves that were as tall as the 12-foot ceilings lined the walls and held stacks of current and former editions of the paper. Large windows and a single doorway on the back wall separated the front from the newsroom, where several desks sat in two rows. Anyone who came in the front office could see exactly what was going on there. The layout perpetuated the idea that transparency was the rule and secrecy was not.

The rest of the building, including a modest employee lounge and a press room, was added in the 1940s. The equipment had been updated, but the smell of ink was the same as it had been decades prior. It permeated the entire space, a constant reminder to everyone that there was a deadline to make. A quiet hum from the press room said the newsprint was loaded and sample sheets were printing.

The assistant editor, Pete Carson, was talking to the receptionist but looked up when he saw his new boss. "Good morning, Mr. Fox...checking in with Betsy before I finish up the copy for tomorrow's paper. We have a deadline in about three hours."

"Morning, Pete, Betsy. Yep. I know we need to sign off on the Sunday edition, but I'd like to get a story in about my buying the paper, so folks will know who I am when I start making calls next week. The first thing on the list, though, is a meeting with Dan Cagle from Cagle Mining Company. I met him at the country club last night. He's interested in getting a zoning permit for commercial mining in Kings County."

"Depending on where he's looking at doing it, that could cause a stink," said Pete. "The farms here are mostly family-owned. They won't take too kindly to be having mines in these mountains — we're talking virgin forests that have never been touched."

"I figured as much," said Hunter, "which is why I want to know what Cagle's plan is, seems Jack Cooper is behind it."

"Of course, he is," said Pete, under his breath.

The bell on the front door jingled and Michael Gilbert walked in. "I knew you'd be here first thing," he said, smiling at Hunter. "I just wanted to stop by before we leave tomorrow and wish you the best of luck with everything. Call me anytime you need to some advice or just want to raise hell."

Hunter knew how difficult it was for a seasoned newspaper guy to hang it up and wanted to ease the transition a bit. "Before you let go of the reins, how about sitting in on one last interview with me? I ran into Dan Cagle at the hotel. He'll be here shortly. I need your ears in on this. And

Pete, I want you there, too. Leave whenever you need to get back to your deadlines. Betsy, please bring Mr. Cagle back when he gets here."

They walked back to the conference room, and each took out a legal pad and started writing. Thinking aloud, Huter began. "We need to know what he wants to do and where he's going to do it. I'm pretty sure he and Jack already have some property in mind."

"What about his other mines?" asked Michael. "Where are they? I wonder if they brought in enough jobs to make it worth losing the land."

"Good point. But I'm pretty sure we'll have to dig to find out if there are any negatives. Dan Cagle won't come in with an unbiased presentation. I need to know the details regarding how he intends to get the product out of the mountain's core." Both men looked up when they heard the door to the front office open.

"Right this way, Mr. Cagle," said Betsy. "They're in the conference room."

"Hey Dan," said Hunter, standing up and extending his hand. "You remember Michael Gilbert."

"Yes," answered Cagle. "Good to see you again."

"Same here."

"And this is Pete Carson, my assistant editor," said Hunter, taking his seat. "So, you want to bring iron ore mining to Kings County, huh?"

"That's our intention," answered Cagle, pushing a folder across the table. "Here's a portfolio that gives a good synopsis of our company — what we do, where we operate mines, and how we've benefitted each community we've invested in."

"Thanks," said Hunter, "nice presentation for sure." He flipped through a couple of glossy pages and stopped at a picture of a surface mine, a deep crater carved into a mountain. "How do you get the ore out of the ground?"

"First we drill. Then we blast."

"Hmmm…. So, where are you looking to blast?"

"We believe the deposits are in a ridge located in the northeast quadrant of the county. It's a perfect location because the railroad runs along the base of the mountain on the other side. One thing that makes iron ore more profitable is easy transportation from the mine to the processing plant, and there's one due north of here outside Chattanooga, right on the rail line. It's a perfect set up for smart investors to make some money. Plus, the Sand River will supply us with all the water we need."

"You're talking about what we locals call The Ridge, right? So, who plans to sell you that land?" asked Gilbert.

"Jack Cooper, but he just has to clear up a few details. You know, some people own so much they can't keep up with it."

"I see," said Hunter, "interesting." Hunter's expression and tone didn't reveal his suspicion. "So, are you telling me that Jack doesn't have a clear title to that land?"

"Now, I didn't say that" said Cagle defensively. "You know what? Let's just consider those last comments off the record," said Cagle. "This not my information to tell. That's Jack's business."

Hunter looked across the table at him. "Well, nothing is ever really off the record, but I'll be sure and mention it to Mr. Cooper. So, what is your target date for bringing it before the county commission?"

"The September meeting was last Monday, and there won't be another one until October. In the meantime, we are holding several public seminars, at least one here and one in Willow Creek. We'll give a first-class presentation of what we do, how we do it, and what the benefits to the community will be. I should know the dates and places for the public meetings by Monday or Tuesday; that's very important to publicize. I'll get with you as soon as I can on that."

"You said the land in question is in the northeast quadrant of the county. That's near Willow Creek and includes all the property on the Valley Road," said Gilbert.

"That's right. Nothing but farmland butts up to the ridge, no development to speak of and very few people, not much to disturb," answered Cagle in a dismissive tone. "The jobs we create will counter any negative impact on the land."

"Well, I guess you have that going for you," said Hunter, looking at the folder once again, thinking what an ass Cagle was.

Pete picked up the notepad on which he had been writing the entire time and stood up. "Hate to bow out, but I have a deadline for tomorrow's paper. How much space do I need to reserve on the front page for the story about you, Mr. Fox?"

"About a quarter of a page—bottom of the fold. And I want to look at getting in a short piece about this," Hunter added, motioning toward the folder Cagle gave him. "I'll get with you on both as soon as we wrap up here."

"When can I proof the article about the mine?" asked Cagle.

"I'm afraid there isn't a time you can. I may run a quote or two by you to make sure they are accurate, but other than that, we sign off on our articles." Hunter stood up slowly, and the other two men followed suit. He reached across the table and shook hands with Cagle. "Thanks for taking the time to come in, Dan. I'll see you out." Opening the door to the conference room, Hunter motioned for Cagle to go first. "I'll need the particulars for the public meetings and ownership of the property as soon as you can get them to me. Our copy deadline for Tuesday's paper is after lunch on Monday around 2."

"I see," said Cagle. "I'll be in touch."

"Betsy, will you please give Mr. Cagle a business card? Tell Jack hello, Dan. I'll look to hear from you soon." Hunter walked back into the conference room where Michael had a map of Kings County spread out on the table.

"I'm going to give you a little history lesson about the geography around here," Gilbert said. "This entire ridge that runs parallel to the Valley Road—the one Cagle and

Cooper say is rich in iron ore—has never been used for anything but hunting, fishing, spooning, and moonshine making. Locals assume Jack's granddaddy owned it, since he started running stills up there before the turn of the century. There are plenty of places on that ridge that are so dense that it can only be used for making shine. As long as everybody left one another alone though, things just rocked along. Of course, moonshining isn't the industry it once was, but I can't imagine Jack kicking out the bootleggers. Evidently, there's enough money involved to make him do just that though. But this mine threatens the natural buffer for the property owners along the Valley Road. The Ridge is what makes the land out there so unique. One of the most beautiful farms on that road belongs to Luke Tanner, and I can tell you right now that he and his neighbors won't take too kindly to Mr. Cagle's assessment of low impact."

"Did you say Tanner?" asked Hunter.

"Yes. Actually, the original farm was his wife's family—the Dobsons. They settled in these parts back in the 1800s. Luke bought more land when he and Gen married. He's a helluva of a farmer."

"By any chance, is that Lucy's father?"

"Yeah. How do you know Lucy?"

"College – Georgia."

"Excuse me, Mr. Fox," interrupted Pete. "Can we get that piece on you ready? That's all we're missing on the front page. I saved about a quarter of a page on page three for the mine piece."

"Sure. My resume and photo are in a manila envelope on my desk. You go ahead and put something together. It doesn't have to be long. Michael and I will work on this mine thing."

Hunter turned his attention back to the map. "Something doesn't sound right to me. Cagle was very evasive about the ownership of the property."

"I agree," answered Gilbert. "You heard him say Jack Cooper was working on that part of the deal. Talk about hitting the ground running. The first week you're here and we have the biggest rezoning issue Kings County has ever seen. I look forward to reading all about it — in Florida."

Hunter went to his office and began typing. Within 15 minutes, he finished a story outlining the rezoning request, the principals involved, the location of the proposed mine, and the plan for several public meetings sponsored by Cagle Mining Company and the First National Bank of Willow Creek. The headline read,

"North Carolina Mining Company Seeks Permit in Kings County."

By 1 p.m., the paper was ready to print and the presses were humming. Hunter finished a few things in his office, locked the front door and exited through the press room. He waved goodbye to the production editor and grabbed the first copy of the first newspaper he had ever owned. And like a new father holding his baby, he was in love.

A Saturday Drive

Hunter let the top down on his MG B, a car made for mountain roads.

As soon as he was out of the city limits, he gave it the gas. The sun warmed his back, while the smooth sound of the engine made his endorphins rage. He loved speed which was why he was in the newspaper business. It was fast-paced, spontaneous, and fluid as hell.

When he topped the hill before the Iron Bridge, he accelerated and saw the speedometer break 80 in less than a minute. *Better slow down*, he thought. He pulled over on the side of the road so he could read the historical marker and take some photos. Hunter never went anywhere without his Nikon.

The water below the bridge and was clean and clear, very deep in places but flowing over large rocks in others, creating swirling pools and small rapids. He took several shots and then focused his camera on the hills that surrounded him, snapping one picture after another. Hunter loved the mountain air. It reminded him of his home in the Blue Ridge Mountains near Blacksburg, Virginia. His family was wealthy and commanded blue-blood status, complete with debutantes and parties, a lifestyle that he considered shallow and boring. Being a certain way because it was expected was something he could not do. He wanted substance, passion, and love.

It had been five years since his parents died in the accident, and he hadn't been back. His sister and her family lived on the Fox estate now. He talked to her every month but hadn't had the time, or perhaps taken the time, to go see her and that needed to change.

He knew that remaining neutral about this mining issue was very important, but he could not imagine dynamite blasts echoing through the virgin forests and toxic run off draining into the streams and poisoning the ground-water. The only way to defeat a development was with cold-hard facts: why it should not take place and how it failed to comply with zoning laws. It also takes public disapproval and lots of it. But most importantly, the owner of the land has to be a willing seller. Without that, there is no deal.

Checking the time, he got in his car and headed toward Willow Creek. It was almost three, so there was time to meet a few merchants before he headed out to see where the Tanner place was. He just wanted to know where Lucy lived. Lucy Tanner. There was something about her that had always caught his eye, but their paths just never coincided. He graduated a year after she entered the University.

He saw her for the first time since college at a friend's wedding at the Piedmont Driving Club in Atlanta. She was there with David Moretti, whom he had also known in school. He was the kind of bad boy girls loved, good looking and just wild enough to be appealing but harmless. His family had a lot of money and bought their way into the old Atlanta social scene. Nobody was really clear what his father's business was, but one thing was certain: it made money.

Hunter couldn't understand the attraction Lucy had for Moretti, given her independent spirit. He was jealous of Moretti and somewhat disappointed in Lucy but very attracted to her at the same time.

She looked so different from the other bejeweled women. She had on a navy-blue silk sheath that accentuated her athletic, sexy body. And her blonde curls were everywhere but in a style. He remembered that when she looked across the room and locked eyes with him, he couldn't stop smiling, imagining how soft to the touch her hair probably was.

The thought of seeing her again made him take a deep breath and exhale. He heard through mutual friends that she had moved back to her hometown and had a son. So, when *The Tribune* went up for sale, he was pleasantly surprised it was such a good publication, with a sound balance sheet and excellent potential for growth. He liked to think that concrete financial reasons justified his decision to buy the paper, not the pursuit of someone who had always haunted his dreams.

"Welcome to Willow Creek. Founded in 1815." The wooden sign set in stone got Hunter's attention, so he slowed down, shifting to second gear. He drove to the center of town and parked in front of the feed and seed store, one of the most reliable and oldest advertising accounts with paper. There were at least a dozen customers shopping and several at the counter in the back. It wasn't long before a teenage boy came up to him and asked if he needed help finding anything.

"No, thank you. I'm new to town, just taking some time to meet who I can on a Saturday afternoon. Hunter Fox, here. What's your name?"

"Ben. Ben Tate."

"Nice to meet you. Are you one of the Tate Brothers?"

The boy grinned. "No. But my dad is. Charlie Tate. Are you selling something?"

Hunter laughed. "Not today. I just wanted to introduce myself. I bought the *Tribune*."

"Oh, okay. Well, dad's filling an order. Come on. He's almost finished."

Hunter followed the youngster to the back of the store. Charlie Tate was putting a roll of chicken wire on top of a stack of lumber on a dolly. "There you go, Billy Joe. Glad you're back. Good luck getting your old home like you want it."

"Thanks, Charlie. I'll see you on Monday for some more supplies." Billy Joe turned and tipped his hat at Hunter, who smiled and nodded in return.

"Dad, this is Mr. Hunter Fox. He bought the news-paper from Mr. Gilbert."

"Well, Michael finally decided to retire. As soon as Ben is ready to take the reins, I'm going to do the same. Charlie Tate," he said, extending his hand.

Hunter shook his hand and smiled. "Well, you have a good one in training. I can tell he's a natural business man."

"So, you're gonna be hounding me now to get our ad copy ready, right?"

"I imagine I will be, but I promise not to hound you—just remind you. And since you're county commission chair, I imagine I'll look to you to make sure I have the local government news correct. Speaking of which, have you heard about the mining outfit that wants to set up shop here?"

"Yeah. I wasn't at the club last night, but my brother went. I'll let you know how I feel about that when I know the facts, could be a little controversial. We'll see."

"Well, I know you're busy and ready to have some time away from the store. Thanks for your time. I'll check with you Tuesday or Wednesday. Ben, I'm sure I'll be hearing good things about you."

Hunter was a newspaper man, but he was a politician first—never meeting a stranger and making sure folks felt like he had their best interest at heart. When he walked out of Tate Brothers, the young man he had just seen buying chicken wire and lumber was standing next to his MG B, eyeing the controls and the interior.

"She's a beauty, huh?" asked Hunter.

"For sure," answered Billy Joe. "Right off the 1960 assembly line. How fast can she go?"

"The speedometer says 125, but I've only pushed her to 90, best to take that speed slowly. I'm Hunter Fox. Billy Joe, right?"

"Yep. Billy Joe Sims," he answered. "And I heard you tell Charlie that you bought the newspaper."

"That's right. I've only been here a little over 24 hours, but I already feel at home. I was raised in the Virginia mountains, very similar."

"Well, welcome to Kings County. These mountains might be a little different from yours, though. Not too many people have a MG B around here. Hope to see you later."

Hunter checked his watch and decided to walk around town a little longer. He met one of the owners of the grocery store and bought a milkshake at the drug store.
He knew he was going to like living in a small town. It just felt right.

Michael said the Tanner place was about 10-15 miles east of town, so Hunter drove to the red light and took a right. He checked the odometer and made a mental note of when to start looking for Lucy's home.

Cold Beer, Hot Fire

Billy Joe stopped by the trailer behind Buck's BBQ and grabbed a metal cooler from the shed. He put a couple of six-packs in it and covered them with ice. Saturday nights were made for a cold beer and a good fire, good thing he brought some brew from Atlanta.

He thought it was crazy that almost everybody snuck booze into a dry county, hid and drank it, and then voted against legalizing it. But it was all about the money. People like Jack Cooper made more if it was against the law to sell booze. They could charge anything they wanted for white lightning. Their customers couldn't live without it.

He stopped by the McDaniel home and knocked on the front door. Marge's mother opened it while his fist was still midair.

"Hello, Billy Joe. Come in. Marge is in the kitchen. She said y'all are going out to where you lived when you were a boy. Will it be just the two of you?"

"No ma'am. Lucy is coming, too." Billy Joe stepped inside and stood in the foyer, with his hat in his hand.

"I see. So, you're planning to build a house on the property where you grew up. Are you sure that's a good idea given everything that happened there?"
Alice McDaniel was insensitive to the fact that she was not entitled to comment on someone's personal choices. She really believed it was her duty to save others from making bad decisions.

Marge came out of the kitchen and walked quickly down the hallway to rescue Billy Joe. "Mama, you probably need to check whatever you have in the oven. I'll see you in the morning."

"Goodbye, Mrs. McDaniel," said Billy Joe. He took the basket of food from Marge and held her hand as they walked down the steps. When they got in his truck, Marge exhaled. "I apologize for my mama. She's not a bad person, but she's so nosey."

"Oh, that's okay. If I had a daughter like you, I'd want to know where she was going and who was gonna be there." He leaned over and gave her a kiss. "Great outfit, by the way, you look good in hunting britches and boots."

Marge smiled and edged a little closer to Billy Joe. She couldn't wait for him to wrap those strong arms around her.

By the time they got to his home site, the sun was starting to set. It wasn't long before Lucy showed up on Hank's bicycle.

"You look like a little girl on that thing," laughed Marge.

"Where's Hank?" asked Billy Joe.

"I figured he'd want to come along, too."

"Well, he is a bit star struck by both of y'all, but there's very little that can compete with Saturday night *Bonanza*. He and daddy will be glued to the television." Lucy reached in the basket on the front of the bike and took out a bowl. "Here, Marge. I made some slaw. Hey Billy Joe, I'm ready for that cold Bud."

"Coming right up," he answered. "First, I want to light this fire." Billy Joe had put several logs around the fire ring and motioned for his guests to have a seat. After the blaze was going, he grabbed three bottles out of the cooler. "A toast to new beginnings with old friends." They raised their beers into the air and each took a drink.

"Oh my, that is so good," said Lucy. "I forgot how tasty that first swig is. Since I had Hank, I hadn't had that much to drink."

There wasn't a breeze, so the smoke from the fire rose straight into the dusky sky. There was little if any traffic this late in the day, so being less than 100 feet from the road did not interfere with the serenity of the moment. The Sims home had burned years ago, but a small grove of oak trees remained.

Hunter checked the mileage on the odometer and slowed down a bit. Lucy's home should be in another mile or two. He felt his hands sweat—he was nervous just driving to her house. He almost stopped and headed back to town when he saw the plume of smoke coming from the trees ahead. He sped up a bit and rounded the curve that kept the clearing from sight. "Oh, that's good. Nothing is burning, just some folks enjoying a bonfire."

Billy Joe's ears perked up when he heard the sound of the MG B's engine. "Wait a minute. I recognize that car. That's the guy I met in town this afternoon. I wonder what he's doing out here." He stood up and waved his hands to get Hunter's attention.

Hunter saw him and waved back. Then he slowed almost to a stop and stared. There was no mistaking Lucy Tanner. He didn't think twice about what to do next.

"Looks like he's turning around and heading here," said Billy Joe.

"Who is *he* anyway?" asked Lucy.

"Hunter Fox...he bought the newspaper."

"Oh, sweet Jesus," said Lucy, almost choking on her beer. "You're kidding. Shit."

"What's wrong?" asked Marge. "Your cheeks just turned hot pink."

"I know him from when I was at Georgia. The last time I saw him I was in Atlanta at a party with Hank's dad. Hunter Fox is the last person I'd expect to see in Kings County. What in the hell is he doing here?" Lucy felt the panic grip her insides just like it did every time she was around him when they were younger. He was so self-assured and refined that she barely said anything at all to him for fear of sounding silly.

"You know that guy? That's crazy, Lucy," said Billy Joe.

Hunter turned off the engine and climbed out of his car. His heart was racing but his demeanor was calm. "Hi again, Billy Joe. Ok if I crash this party?"

"You're not crashing at all. This is Marge McDaniel and Lucy—"

"How in the world are you doing, Lucy? It's been way too long."

Lucy stood up, as Hunter moved in and gave her a good, long hug. Lucy hugged him back, surprised and delighted at the affection she felt in his caress. She didn't feel like a silly schoolgirl around this Hunter Fox. She felt like a woman whose passion button just got pushed...hard. He locked eyes with her before turning his attention to the others.

115

"Nice to meet you, Marge. I met a Mr. McDaniel at the grocery store before coming out here. Was that your father?"

"Yeah," answered Marge. "I hope he was polite. He can be a bit gruff sometimes."

"Oh, he was nothing but nice."

"How about a beer?" asked Billy Joe, handing him one before he got an answer.

"Thanks," said Hunter, "but I don't want to intrude. Are you expecting someone else?" Hunter looked at Lucy, hoping she didn't have a date.

"Nope. It's just us," said Billy Joe.

The cold beer went down easy, and the hot fire was mesmerizing. Billy Joe got a couple of blankets out of his truck and gave one to Lucy and one to Marge. "Almost snuggling weather," he said with a grin.

Hunter felt home for the first time in a very long time — perhaps since he was a kid. He had always wanted to find the place where he belonged, where he felt like he and the people there were connected in an unspoken yet tangible way.

"So, you knew Lucy when she was 18," said Marge. "Did y'all date?"

"Nope," answered Hunter. "I had a huge crush on her, but she wouldn't give me the time of day."

"That's not true, Hunter Fox," said Lucy, blushing again. "I always spoke when I saw you."

"Yeah. You'd speak and keep right on walking in the opposite direction," said Hunter, laughing.

"I was shy," said Lucy, laughing in a flirtatious way.

"Lucy Tanner, shy?" laughed Marge, "...my ass, I find that hard to believe. I've seen you stand up to the biggest bully in Kings County." Feeling relaxed by the fire and the beer, Marge continued. "If you haven't met him, you will meet him soon, Hunter — Jack Cooper aka Biggest Asshole in the World. And when you do, remember she put him in his place."

"Oh, Marge, it wasn't that big a deal," said Lucy, "nothing worth talking about."

"Oh, I've met him," said Hunter, "and now I'm more interested than I was five minutes ago." The look in his eyes almost made Lucy stop breathing.

After serving another round of beers, Billy Joe raised a small glass bottle into air. I think we all need a sip of shine to warm our insides up," he said with a smile. "I only bring this out on special occasions, and I'd say today is just that— the first fire of what I hope are many more to come." The look he gave Marge raised her temperature faster than any whiskey could. He took a sip out of the bottle, wiped it with his shirt sleeve and passed it to Marge. "Don't worry if this is pure or not. You'll know it is when it hits your throat."

The moonshine made Lucy feel warm all over, despite the chill in the air. Feeling no restraints, she offered some of the blanket to Hunter and felt the heat from his body. After a while, she leaned into him even more. She'd forgotten how good it felt to be close to a man. At the same time, she was a bit scared at just how inviting he felt. *Better put some distance between me and whatever this is,* she thought. "This has been a lot of fun," she said, "but I should probably head home." She stood up and lost her balance, falling right back down into Hunter's lap.

"I'm not sure you should be behind the handlebars right now," laughed Hunter. "How about if I give you a ride?"

"That's a good idea," said Billy Joe, with a wink at Hunter, glad they were leaving. "We'll have to do this again real soon."

Hunter said his goodbyes and helped Lucy to the car. "Hey, I'm okay. I'm not drunk," she giggled, "just a little over-stimulated."

117

CHAPTER Seven

The Day After

A pounding headache woke Lucy up around dawn. She had the same clothes on she wore the night before—boots and all. She crept out the back door, walked over to the barn and cranked the pickup truck. Within a couple of minutes, she was at Nettie's.

"Looks like you need more than coffee this morning," said Nettie. "You feel okay?"

"No. I feel like shit."

Lucy went into the kitchen and poured herself a cup of the chicory-laced coffee, taking several sips and letting out a long sigh between each one.

When she went back to the front porch, Nate Johnson was wiping his hands on his handkerchief and talking with Nettie. "I think I have that engine problem fixed—probably some trash in the fuel line. Morning, Lucy."

"Morning, Nate."

"I'll take my mug inside and be on my way," he said, tipping his hat slightly. "I have some things to do at the farm before church."

They heard the backdoor close and his truck start up. As he drove by the house, he waved and smiled before heading slowly down the drive to the main road.

Nate Johnson's grandmama raised him down the road a piece from Nettie in the same house where he lived now. His mama died in childbirth and just like Nettie, he never knew his father. Both of them had very strong women in their lives who taught them never to accept less than what they wanted and to be proud of their heritage.

The difference was that Nettie had Cherokee blood but he didn't. Other than that, their backgrounds were similar.

Nate owned his old homeplace and had done so since 1946. When he served in the Army during WWII, he sent every paycheck to his grandmama who gave it to Luke Tanner to put in the bank for her. When Nate got home, he had enough money to buy the house and farm. His grandmama only lived a couple of months after he returned, but it was long enough to see her grandson do what she thought was impossible for a black man to do. And it was all because of Luke Tanner.

"Does Nate fix your engine often?" asked Lucy, smiling slightly.

"When it won't start," said Nettie with a grin." And, I enjoy his company. He's the only man I've allowed to even think about getting close to me. But I have some pretty high walls around my heart. I've seen hurt I don't want anywhere near my insides."

"Hmmm," answered Lucy, wondering what her friend was hiding from her. "So, is Nate more than a friend? Is he really your very close, secret friend?"

"Nothing secret about it. If I want company, I will have company. But you didn't come here to talk about Nate Johnson. What did you do last night? And don't lie to me. I know you have a hangover."

"Marge and Billy Joe had a cookout, and that guy was there," she said pointing to the newspaper on the table. Hunter's photo was on the front page, making her feel as giddy as she did the night before.

"Well, isn't he a fine-looking man?" said Nettie, with a grin. "Reminds me of Cary Grant. Tell me all about it. I wanna know everything, about time somebody rang your bell, Baby Cakes. I figured it was broken."

"This isn't funny, Nettie," pouted Lucy. "I'm too hungover to laugh."

"I didn't mean to poke fun at you, sugah," Nettie chuckled. "You're just so easy to tease. Finish your story."

"Anyway, we drank beer and sipped a little shine. I got really tipsy and very, ah—"

"Stirred up?" Nettie said, already knowing the answer.

"Yes...very stirred up."

"Well, Lucy, I can see why. I can tell that man is full of feelings. How'd he find his way out here?"

"I knew him when I was in college, and Billy Joe ran into him in town Saturday afternoon. He has a sports car, so I guess the two of them hit it off. He was driving out this way yesterday evening, they saw one another, and he stopped."

"Well, he must have wanted to run into you if he was driving on this road—no other reason. So, then what?" asked Nettie.

"I told you. I got so drunk I could barely walk, I fell in his lap, and he took me home. I remember asking him to drive around for a few minutes, so I could sober up. That made him laugh, but he did it anyway. It was a beautiful night. The top was down on his car, and those leather car seats are very close to each other. He smelled really good, too. All I wanted to do was kiss on his neck, but thank goodness, he wanted to talk—about me. God only knows what I told him."

Nettie laughed, "Well, I bet he remembers every blessed-word you uttered, so I hope it was good."

"It was after 1 when I told him it was time for me to go home. I asked him to park over at the dairy barn, so his car wouldn't wake anyone up. I sure didn't need Genevieve to see me in the state I was in.

"He had his arm around me, helping me walk. He felt good—really good. His shoulders were so broad, Nettie. As soon as we got across the road and to the back of the house, I looked up in those eyes of his, told him thanks for the ride, but that he couldn't come inside. He laughed and kissed me—a lot—and I kissed him back. I finally told him I had to go to bed, that my presence at the church was expected in the morning. And now, I can't wait to see him again. What the hell am I doing, Nettie?"

Lucy was reluctant to trust men. For her, getting close meant getting hurt and disappointed, used and discarded. But right now, this felt good…however scary it was.

"By the looks of that whisker burn, I'd say you're having some fun."

"Oh no, really?" asked Lucy touching her chin and realizing it was raw.

"Hey, now, there's nothing wrong with putting some spice in the stew," said Nettie. She laughed, reached over and patted Lucy's hand. "How's that headache now?"

"It's getting there," sighed Lucy. "Guess I better get going…everybody will want to know where I've been when I get home. Hank is as curious as his grandmother."
Lucy stood up to leave, glancing again at Hunter's photo.

"Go in the kitchen and look in the cabinet next to the sink," said Nettie. "Dissolve a couple of those Alka-Seltzers in a glass of water and chug it. You'll be in fine shape by church time."

"You have Alka-Seltzer?" asked Lucy, with a grin.

"I do…for when I get too stirred up," answered Nettie.

Church

Hunter rolled over and opened his eyes. He felt like did when he first met Lucy almost 20 years ago and woke up wishing she was next to him. And what he imagined back then, he confirmed last night. The curves of her body meshed perfectly with his, leaving no doubt as to how much fire was there. He wanted her—in a slow, gentle way that took all the time she needed to feel safe. He had never felt as turned on without skin-to-skin contact in his entire life.

Why was it that she didn't fancy him when they were in college? Every other girl did. But she was different and totally unpredictable. Once he saw her take on a guy who

121

was harassing her in the student union. She took him out with a right hook and a kick to the groin. Her tenacity excited him and her strength was amazing. She was dangerous, and he loved being scared.

He couldn't wait to see her again, and he knew exactly where she would be this morning, whether she wanted to be or not. The scene from last night played out in his head:

They were in the middle of some heavy kissing, and she pulled him as close as she could – pressing his hips against hers. He cupped his hands around her bottom, lifting lightly, and whispered, "Oh my, look at that…the perfect handful." She suddenly pulled away and told him she couldn't stay up any later, because she went to church on Sunday morning…the First Presbyterian Church. Then she kissed him long and hard before heading inside the house. She was absolutely irresistible.

"Huh," Hunter said aloud. "Church sounds good to me." He thought about Lucy a little longer before getting out of bed.

***

"Where you been, Mama, and where's my bike?"

"Morning to you, too, son. I was at Nettie's, having coffee with her, and your bike is at Billy Joe's. We'll get it later."

"If you left my bike there, how did you get home last night?"

"A friend gave me a ride. It was too dark to be out on the highway without lights."

"What friend?" asked Gen who walked in the kitchen in time to hear the conversation.

"That friend," said Lucy, pointing to Hunter's picture, irritated at the interrogation.

"Hmmm," said Gen slowly. "I just read the article. And what…?"

"Do y'all mind? It's no big deal. I'm going to get ready for church."

122

After Lucy left, Gen picked up the paper and looked at the photo. "A friend, huh? Well, that's good. I guess as long as—" Gen stopped, realizing her grandson was listening to everything she said. "Hank, are you finished with your breakfast?"

"Yes m'am."

"Good. How about we study the Sunday School lesson together? I like to hear you read. Your mama used to do that when she was a little girl. She was sweet then, just like you are now."

***

"There's my bicycle," said Hank, as they drove by Billy Joe's. A thin cloud of smoke drifted from the ashes, reminiscent of a fire that burned the night before.

"What's it doing there?" asked Luke.

"Mama rode it over here yesterday afternoon, but—"

"Hank, that's for me to answer," Lucy snapped. "Billy Joe had a little bonfire, cookout thing for Marge and invited me, too. A mutual friend joined us and gave me a ride home since it was dark."

"Who would that be?" asked Luke, thinking he knew every friend Lucy had.

"The one whose picture is on the front page of the paper," answered Gen matter-of-factly.

"Thank you, Mama," said Lucy. "What would I ever do without you to speak for me?"

"Lulu," said Luke. "That's no way to talk to your mother."

"I'm sorry, but everybody has been far too concerned with what I did last night. Drop it." Lucy's reaction was met with total silence. And no one said anything for the remainder of the trip—even Hank.

Hunter walked to the Presbyterian Church. It wasn't far from the hotel, and the morning sun was warm enough to compete with the autumn chill. He didn't want to look like a showoff driving a sports car either. Buying a company car from Buddy Tatum who owned the largest car dealership in town and bought a lot of advertising space in the paper was top of his list.

Luke parked in the same spot at the church he used every Sunday. Hank spotted one of his friends from school and asked if he could sit with him.

"Yes," said Lucy, "but if you start talking, I swear I will come get you and make you sit with us. Understand?"

Hank knew his mama was not in the mood for him or anyone else to challenge her. "Yes m'am. I understand." He opened the door and sprinted to meet up with his buddy.

Lucy stepped out of the car without saying a thing to her parents and started toward the church but stopped when she spotted Hunter walking up the sidewalk from downtown. *Oh, Christ*, she thought, blushing. *What the hell am I going to do now?* Just as he saw her, Theodore Mason pulled in the parking lot and stopped right in front of him. Lucy avoided his stare and walked quickly inside the church.

She sat down in the pew the Tanners had occupied for as long as she could remember, right across the aisle from the Masons. Lucy looked straight ahead, trying to avoid eye contact with everyone. Her parents hadn't made it inside yet, and she breathed a sigh of relief when the organist began playing, signaling to the congregation that social time was over.

Turning her head slightly when Luke and Gen slid in the pew, she caught Hunter's eye who was right behind them. He nodded, smiled and mouthed "Good morning," before joining the Masons. *Oh, Jesus, I know it's written all over my face*, she thought. *I might as well be carrying a sign that says, "I made out with this guy last night and I want to do it again."*

Lucy stared at the minister, resisting the urge to look across the aisle at Hunter. She avoided her mother's curious glances, too. She tried to focus on the sermon but only heard Hunter whispering in her ear the night before. She tried to concentrate on the lesson but could only think about his lips, his smell, and the hardness of every inch of his body.

"May the words of our mouths and the meditations of our hearts be pleasing in thy sight, Lord. And we pray in the name of Jesus Christ. Amen," said the minister.

Lucy had never welcomed the closing prayer as much as she did that Sunday morning. She wanted to get out of there as quickly as she could but she was trapped by her parents who stood in front of her, greeting the Masons.

"Good morning, Luke. You've probably already read about the *Tribune's* new owner, Hunter Fox, but allow me to introduce him formally. This is Luke and Gen Tanner, and I believe you already know Lucy."

"A pleasure," said Hunter, "and, yes, Lucy and I are old acquaintances, and we ran into one another accidentally — or may I say luckily — last night. She told me what a fine cattleman you are, Mr. Tanner. I hope to see your operation soon. And Mrs. Tanner, you're obviously where Lucy gets her beauty." He smiled at Lucy, who felt her insides tremble. There was no way out now.

"Hey, you're my mama's friend who brought her home, aren't ya?" asked Hank, who had just made his way to the Tanner pew.

"Hank," said Lucy, embarrassed beyond words.

"That's right. And you must be Hank. I'm Hunter," he said, extending his hand. "Your mama told me all about you."

Hank grinned and gave his mama an approving look.

Dismissing what everyone else saw, Luke took over the conversation. "Theodore, are you and Isabelle going to the hotel for dinner?"

"Yes, we are. We'll meet you there. Hunter, you'll join us, too, I hope," answered Theodore. "Would you like a ride?"

"No, I think I'll walk. Lucy, care to join me?"

125

"Well...I...okay." She took a deep breath, afraid that she couldn't be around him without letting him know what she wanted to do with him.

"Can I come, too?" asked Hank, tugging on Lucy's sleeve.

"That's fine with me, if it's okay with your mama," said Hunter.

"Sure," said Lucy, letting out a sigh of relief. "Of course, you can. We'll see all of you there."

Luke watched his daughter and grandson walk away with a stranger who acted like he knew them all. "He's more than a friend," said Luke. "I hope she has her head on straight. I can't handle seeing her hurt again. 'Fox' is the right name for that fella, and he's gonna have a lot to prove to me."

Lucy's parents were oblivious to the fact that by forcing her to get married when she got pregnant that they were equally responsible for the divorce and her subsequent pain. They blamed Lucy and never really forgave her.

"What was it you told me just a few nights ago ...something about she had to figure things out on her own and that I needed to have confidence in her? Perhaps you need to take your own advice," Gen answered, looking straight ahead and not at her husband.

The hotel dining room was almost full when Hunter, Lucy, and Hank walked in. The Tanners and Masons were already serving their plates at the buffet table. "Let's get in line before the fried chicken is gone," said Hank.

"Okay, you lead the way," said Hunter. "I bet the desserts are good, too."

"Sure are," said Hank, "especially the cobbler."

When they joined the others at the table, Lucy's father and Theodore were already deep in conversation.

"Ah, here's Hunter. He can probably enlighten us a bit more," said Theodore.

"I read your article about the mining company," said Luke, eyeing Hunter closely. "I don't like the sound of it—especially where they're proposing to drill. It would forever change the Valley Road. Do you know any particulars other than what you printed?"

"Not really. I'm supposed to find out from Cagle tomorrow around noon. We just know it impacts the entire northeast quadrant where your property, the Ridge, and the rest of the valley are located."

"I know my property is in the northeast quadrant, Mr. Fox," answered Luke.

"What are y'all talking about?" asked Lucy, taken aback at her father's contentious answer.

Theodore put the paper on the table and pushed it across to Lucy. "That...an iron ore company wants to come into Kings County. Jack Cooper is behind it."

Lucy stared at the headline. "If that's the case, we're in trouble."

Theodore started to say something but stopped and looked toward the door to the lobby. "Speak of the devil."

"Well, well...it's the Presbyterians," said Jack, "and the new man in town. Why am I not surprised?"

Hunter nodded and started to speak, but Jack kept talking, not caring what anybody else had to say. Motioning to the newspaper, lying on the table, he continued. "Glad to see you wrote a piece about the mine, Fox. It's gonna change things for the better around here."

"I guess that depends on what happens," said Lucy. "Not everybody wants what you do, Jack. Haven't you figured that out yet?"

Theodore and Luke stared at her, surprised by her bold response. Gen was mortified, Isabelle sipped her tea, and Hunter looked amused. *She's more so than she was when she was 18 years old*, thought Hunter.

Jack glared at her with controlled contempt but managed to keep his temper in check. "As I have said before, Lucy, you sure do have a way, don't you?"

Lucy stared right back at him but smiled slightly. "I think we've established that fact, Jack."

"Well, I'll let y'all get back to your meal. I'm picking up a couple of to-go-plates, so Bo and I can watch a little football." He turned around without saying goodbye and walked to the head of the line, cutting in front of everyone.

Theodore cleared his throat. "Why don't you come to my office around 7:30 in the morning, Hunter? I'll try to give you some pointers about the courthouse—where to find what and whom to ask for help. But we really should talk about this someplace else, where Jackass Cooper can't intrude?"

"Theodore," admonished his wife, Isabelle "not in front of—"

"Oh, that's okay, Mrs. Mason," Hank chimed in. "My mama called—"

"That's a good idea, Mr. Mason," interrupted Lucy, not wanting Hank to comment on their recent trip to the bank. "Why don't you come out to the house this afternoon? It sounds like we need to deal with this immediately. Don't you agree, Daddy?"

"Yes, I do. I'll see you around 2, Theodore."

"I think Hunter should come, too," said Theodore. "He probably has some experience with zoning issues that we don't. I know the law, but this is a first for Kings County."

"Well, with all due respect, I have to remain objective about this, so the coverage is fair." He looked across the table at Lucy and immediately added. "But, hey, I can certainly give you some pointers. I'll be there."

Lucy smiled at him, and Luke noticed. He didn't think they needed Fox's advice, but he was outvoted.

"Excellent," said Theodore. "I'll see you all then."

When they got in the car to head home, Gen turned and looked at Lucy. "You barely touched your food?"

"Don't start, Mama. I'm fine," answered Lucy, "just concerned about this mining thing."

"Well, you need to leave that up to Theodore and me," interjected Luke. "I want you to know everything

128

that's going on, but you don't need to be in the middle of the conversation."

"Since when am I not a partner in the farm?" asked Lucy. "You and I talk about everything that affects our property and our family."

"Yes, I know, but this is different. There are other folks involved. People don't want to hear a woman talking like a man."

"You mean men don't want to listen to a woman talk, especially when she's right. If Henry were alive, you'd want him in the meeting."

"Enough," said Luke. "We'll discuss this later."

"Mama, is it okay if I go to Billy Joe's when we get home?" asked Hank, wanting to escape the tension he felt between his mama and grandfather.

"I'll let you know when it's time to go," said Lucy.

The Lay of the Land

Lucy opened the car door before it came to a complete stop. Luke rarely questioned her input when it came to the family business, but now that she wanted to be a part of something he didn't control, he balked.

She loved her father, but this was not about love. It was about her heritage and her life, doing what she felt compelled to do to protect her family's legacy and being with whomever she wanted. She wanted to live the way she wanted to live. Lucy was beginning to understand that choice was not always a matter of choice…it was destiny. And she intended to recognize hers.

"Hank, hang up your Sunday clothes. I'll run you down to Billy Joe's to get your bike. Give me a few minutes to change, too." She walked into the house without saying a word to her parents and went straight to her room. Her clothes from the night before were still on the floor. *Good thing Hank didn't see this mess*, she thought. Everything smelled like wood smoke, so she got out a pair of clean khakis and a white blouse which she tucked in. She started to take off her pearls but decided to leave them on after she looked in the mirror. Her reflection made her feel confident and strong. Stretching one's style does that. She turned up the back of her shirt collar a bit, adding an even more modern look.

"Mama, I'm ready," yelled Hank, as he ran down the hall.

"Head over to the barn," said Lucy. "I'm right behind you."

When they pulled in at Billy Joe's, he and Marge were already busy marking and cutting lumber.

"Hey, Billy Joe," shouted Hank. "Hi, Miss McDaniel. What are y'all building?"

"A chicken coup," answered Billy Joe. "Did you come to help?"

"I'm afraid we can't stay," said Lucy. "Mr. Mason and Hunter are coming out to talk to Daddy about that mine they want to build, and I need to be there. Did you read about it in the paper?"

"Yeah," said Marge. "We were just talking about it, and not in a favorable way."

"You know what?" said Lucy. "You should be there, too. It sounds like this could impact anyone who lives on the Valley Road. I really think you should come."

"Don't know if that's a good idea," said Billy Joe, "I don't know Mr. Mason, and I'm sure he's aware of my past."

"That doesn't matter," replied Lucy. "This is your home, and what happens here is as important to you as to anyone else. And Mr. Mason is very nice. Folks like him who have a lot of money and have always had money also have class — unlike the Jack Coopers of the world. It'll be fine."

"She's right," said Marge. "We should go."

"All right then," said Billy Joe.

"Mama, can I stay and ride home with them?" asked Hank.

"If they don't mind," said Lucy.

"We'd be happy to have him. We'll bring him and his bicycle." Billy Joe winked at Lucy, and Marge giggled.

"Thanks," said Lucy. "Hank, don't ask too many questions. See you shortly."

By the time Lucy got home, Gen had some coffee ready and had put three cups on a tray, along with a plate of shortbread cookies.

"Mama, we're short on cups. I am going to be in on that conversation, and I asked Billy Joe and Marge to join us."

"Why would you do a thing like that?" asked Gen. "Your father doesn't want you involved and now you've gone and invited more people."

"I heard what Daddy said, but I don't care. This is my home and our farm. Billy Joe also owns land that butts up to the ridge. Believe me, if Nettie was home from church, she'd be here, too." She looked directly into her mother's eyes, not

131

flinching. "This conversation is over. I'm going to pick a few flowers to put in the living room."

Gen watched her daughter almost skip down the back steps. *Luke was right*, she thought. *She is definitely thinking about something other than the lay of the land.* But unlike Luke, Gen wasn't convinced it was a bad thing.

The Strategy

Lucy put the tray on the coffee table and moved a vase of zinnias to the sideboard that sat between the two large windows facing the front yard. She looked in the mirror hanging in front of her and saw her father, standing in the hallway behind her.

"This is turning into a regular social event, isn't it?" Luke asked, not hiding his displeasure.

"Daddy, you know this mine affects everyone on this road, not to mention the rest of the county. I know what I'm doing."

"Listen to me, Lucy, and listen good. When it comes to—"

The sound of cars coming in the driveway cut his lecture short, much to Lucy's relief. She was in no mood to hear him say he was right and she was wrong.

"I believe we have company," she said, turning her back on her father and opening the front door. She walked out on the porch and stood at the top of the steps. "Hey. y'all. Come on inside."

Hunter was wearing a denim shirt, khaki pants, and hunting boots. He looked as handsome as he did the night before. "Good afternoon, Mr. Tanner," he said.

"Looks like you're ready to do some real work," answered Luke, without smiling.

"Well, I try to do real work every day," he said with a grin, "but I do take advantage of the times I don't have to wear a shirt and tie. Shall I sit anywhere?"

"Of course," interjected Lucy. She was anxious to begin before her father made another rude comment.

Gen came down the hall, carrying a pot of coffee. Hank was right behind her, eager to see who was in the living room. "Hey y'all," he said with a grin. He liked having company.

"Make yourselves comfortable." said Gen. "Hank and I are going to the pond and feed the fish."

"Have fun," said Lucy, "and Hank, don't forget that you have some spelling homework for tomorrow." She sat down on the sofa next to Billy Joe and Marge and picked up a notepad and pen. "So, tell us what we need to know."

"Why don't you go over the legal aspects first, Mr. Mason?" asked Hunter. "Why is an application for rezoning approved and why wouldn't one be?"

"Obviously, the most important thing is having a willing seller with a deed, and that seems to be the most pressing thing at hand for Jack Cooper," said Theodore.

"Cagle said a rail line ran at the base of the northern ridge and that made it a perfect location for the mine. Who actually owns property that backs up to those mountains?" asked Hunter.

"Let's start about five miles down the road," said Luke. "First, there's all the Tate land that goes for about a mile. Then there's the Davis land that Nate Johnson leases. Next is Nate's own property, which brings us to you, Billy Joe. Between you and Tanner, land is Judge Whitaker's family place. On the other side of us is Dave Wisdom's home, and then Nettie's. The elevation increases at that point and it's all mountains."

"A zoning request must also be in compliance with existing zoning in the area," continued Theodore. "This entire quadrant is agricultural, which is why they must apply to rezone the land in question. In order to deny the request, the governing body — which in our case is the county commission — must determine the development would cause a negative impact on the land and the people who live not only near the property but in the surrounding area. Since most of the property in Kings County is rural farmland, the entire population is affected. And that works in our favor – the more people impacted the better. Hunter, what can you add regarding the public objections? Tell us the best way to organize."

"A petition," said Hunter. "There's something about a list of signatures that brings it home. It's a tangible piece of evidence that gives commissioners grounds to vote against a rezoning request based on public disapproval. That takes a lot of leg work, though...going door-to-door, talking to folks, giving them information, and convincing them to sign, but it is very necessary. The other thing that really helps is hiring someone who is an expert in environmental impact to look at the situation and objectively determine if the effects on the land and streams are significant enough to deny the rezoning. That will take some cash, though, because scientists don't work for free. The last time I covered a similar controversy near Savannah, it cost the citizens fighting it a lot of money. It was worth all the effort and every penny they spent, though, because they won."

"We can raise the cash we need," said Lucy. "I bet there are going to be enough people willing to pitch in."

"If someone who is passionate about defeating this takes the reins, it is very possible," said Hunter, looking straight into Lucy's eyes. *Someone passionate like you*, he thought. "It's also wise to accept the fact that some people are going to be in favor of the development. The integrity of the land doesn't mean as much to them as the money they could make. Greed is aggressive, so be ready for a fight."

Luke listened to every word Hunter said and wished he wasn't so damn smart and articulate. Wanting to take attention away from him, he turned to Theodore. "Wouldn't it be best for an attorney to be in charge of this? I think we need someone who knows the law. Is that something you're willing to do?"

"Actually, you need both," said Theodore. "I will be more than happy to do the legal work and present the case to the commissioners, but you need a private citizen to get the public on your side, someone who knows the county and the people, and who has an ability to get a message across, and isn't afraid. I think I know the perfect person to do that, too. You, Lucy."

"What do you say, Lucy?" asked Hunter, already knowing the answer.

"Sure," said Lucy without hesitation, not looking at her father. "Hunter, can you get me the names of some environmental experts?"

"Of course. I'll get with you tomorrow."

Luke watched his control of the meeting and his daughter dissipate. Neither pleased him. "So, I guess that is decided. Anything else? I need to go over to the barn."

Hunter looked up from his notes. "Yes, there is. When I meet with Cagle tomorrow, I'm going to tell him I want to visit some of his working mines. I think it would be a good idea for at least one of the commissioners and several private citizens to go, too. I am very interested in getting feedback from the folks who live near the mines and work there, not just the investors."

"Excellent idea," said Theodore. "Count me in on that trip."

"I was hoping to get a look at the Ridge today, too," said Hunter. "Is that possible?"

"I'll be glad to show you," said Lucy quickly.

"Anyone else interested?"

"You young people go right ahead," said Theodore, "but I need to head home." He stood up and bowed slightly at the others who followed his lead. "Luke, thanks for having us in your home. Please tell Gen for me, too."

"We have to get back, too," said Billy Joe. "I already know how special the Ridge is; I spent a lot of time up there when I was a kid."

"I'll walk out with y'all," said Hunter. "I need to get my camera."

Luke looked at his daughter. She had the expression on her face she always had when her mind was made up about something. "I hope you have your wits about you,

135

Lucy. You have to be cautious not only about walking in the woods but with whom you choose to walk."

Ignoring his comment, Lucy got an old leather jacket out of the hall closet and turned to face her father. "Pease remind Hank to do his homework. Tell him I'll check it when I get back." She opened the front door just as Hunter was about to come up the steps. He stopped and smiled at her, holding out his hand.

What Luke saw made his heart race. He was not ready for this much change in such a short time. Lucy and Hunter walked through the gate at the back of the house and started across the meadow on a well-worn path that led to the edge of the forest.

"So, did you spend a lot of time up here when you were a kid?" asked Hunter.

"Yeah, I wasn't supposed to. It was off limits for some reason. I never knew why but I didn't care. This is where I went when I 'ran away from home'," answered Lucy, "and I ran away a lot."

Hunter laughed and took her hand in his. "Why did you do that, Lucy Tanner?"

"Because my mama wouldn't let me do what I wanted to or Billy Joe and his brothers teased me, but I told you all about them last night, didn't I?"

"Oh yes, you did," said Hunter with a grin.

When they got to the edge of the woods, Lucy picked up two small tree limbs to use as walking sticks. "We'll need these to get up the steep parts of the trail. I'll go first since I know the way."

Hunter followed her, taking a lot of pleasure in being right behind her and watching her muscles work like she was a teenager. His mind went places he knew it shouldn't go, so he tried to focus on something else. "This is an incredibly beautiful forest," he said. "Is it like this the entire ridge?'

"Pretty much," said Lucy. "There are little creeks everywhere, and all of them run into the Sand River. Hear that gurgling sound? There's one right over this next hill."

Hunter paused when he saw the mountain stream tumbling over smooth stones, creating mini waterfalls. The sound was soothing, and both of them stared at the pristine scene with a reverent silence.

Lucy sat down on one of the larger rocks. "I always stopped here for a while when I was a kid. It calmed me down," she said.

"Do you need calming down now?" asked Hunter, sitting as close to her as he could.

"Yeah, you could say that. This mine thing is very upsetting, and my father is, too. I apologize for his being rude to you, but it's not because of you. It's me. He thinks I am incapable of making any wise personal choices...one mistake and I'm forever a failure in his eyes."

"I don't believe that," answered Hunter, putting his arm around her. "He's just protective of you. I am quite certain it's obvious how much I like being around you." He leaned over and kissed Lucy's cheek. She turned her head slightly and their lips found one another, which is exactly what she had been wanting to happen since she woke up that morning.

"Well, I never did that when I walked up to the ridge when I was a kid," she said with a mischievous smile. "We better keep going, so we can make it back before dark. You would certainly be on Luke Tanner's bad side if we didn't."

Hunter stood up, pulled her to her feet, and wrapped his arms around her. "Well, we don't want that to be the case," he said, as he hugged her close. When they got to the top, Hunter was struck by how far he could see. "This is amazing," he said.

"Yeah, I know," answered Lucy. "See that wide path that follows the ridge and goes in either direction? They say that's one of the roads the Indians and early settlers used. There are lots of legends about these woods, too, especially among the Negroes in Kings County. Jack Cooper's family terrorized them. The story goes that anybody who wasn't white wouldn't make it home at night if they were caught up here after dark. Even Nettie, who is educated, a partner in our farm, and like a member of our family, gets quiet when anybody brings up the mountain behind our land. There's something about all of this that I don't understand."

Hunter took the lens cover off his camera and started taking pictures. Lucy watched every move he made, taking note of his tall, lean build. Suddenly, he turned around, aimed the camera at her, and snapped her picture before she knew what was happening.

"You're not going to put that in the paper, are you?"

"No," answered Hunter. "That one's for me." He took her face in his hands and kissed her again. "I'm pretty sure we need to get back," he said with eyes that paralyzed Lucy, "but I want to see you again very soon...for a real date...dinner—just you and me at the hotel. How does that sound?"

"I'd like that very much," said Lucy, almost in a whisper.

"I am going to convince Luke Tanner I mean no harm to his Lucy." He gave her another good, long kiss before they started to walk down the mountain. He had his arm around her and caressed her shoulder. "This jacket you have on...it was your brother's, wasn't it?"

"How did you know?" asked Lucy, turning to face him.

"I recognize army-issued clothing, and I saw his picture in the living room. And I knew of him. I mean who didn't know the legend...a star quarterback at Georgia and a Rhodes Scholar. I wrote a piece about him for the *Atlanta Journal* when he was killed. He was a real hero, a doctor who volunteered for the front lines."

"You wrote that? I remember it was very good, but I don't recall seeing your byline."

"We didn't have bylines. Everything we published was a U.S. Armed Forces release. I should have written you a letter, but I didn't know what to say. I felt very close and very distant, all at the same time. I apologize."

"Why, thank you. I appreciate that. I idolized Henry, and my parents have never recovered from their loss. I often thought it should have been me, not him. He had so much to give."

"Lucy…no. If your brother could say something to you now, he would tell you to stop judging yourself like that. I am sure he was very proud of his little sister. But for now, we better get down this mountain before Luke Tanner sends the sheriff looking for us."

Hunter's words hugged her heart as tightly as his arms held her. It was the first time a man had ever stood up for her. When they got to the edge of the woods, Lucy was not surprised to see Hank sitting on the back steps.

"Hey Mama, did you make it to the top of the ridge? See any bears?" he shouted as he ran across the meadow.

"Yes and no," answered Lucy. "Did you finish your homework?"

"Yes ma'am, ready for you to check. Are you going to stay for supper, Mr. Hunter?"

"Not this time, Hank. And call me Hunter, if that's okay with your mama. I'm about the same age as Billy Joe."

Hank looked at his mother who nodded her okay.

"That's fine, but for now, you need to go ahead and get your bath. I'll be in after Hunter leaves."

"I'd like to tell your parents goodbye if I could," said Hunter.

"Sure. My mother is probably in the kitchen." Lucy opened the back door and Hunter poked his head inside. Gen was at the stove, frying ham, the smell of which filled the room.

"Goodbye, Mrs. Tanner. Thank you for the hospitality and for letting Lucy be my tour guide this afternoon. Is Mr. Tanner around?"

"No. He's on the phone with Charlie Tate about the mine. I'll tell him you send your regards," Gen answered, managing a little smile.

Lucy and Hunter walked around to the front of the house and sat down on the steps. "Do you think we really can defeat this?" Lucy asked. "The county commission has never voted against anything a Cooper wanted."

"There's always a first," Hunter answered, feeling like Lucy was a first for him. He started to lean toward her, when the porch light suddenly came on. "I bet that's a signal from Luke Tanner," he said with a grin. "I'll give you a call later."

"Okay, around 8:30 will be fine. Hank will be in bed by then. Thanks so much for everything."

"Of course," said Hunter, standing up and reaching for her hand. He kissed the back of it and smiled. "That's the proper way to give a lady a kiss."

CHAPTER Eight

The Puzzle

Monday morning started for Hunter before the sun came up. By 8 o'clock, the *Tribune* staff meeting was over, and he was waiting for the courthouse to open. He sat on one of the wrought iron benches on either side of the massive double doors. The building faced west, as most Southern court-houses did, with large white columns that supported an upstairs balcony with a white railing around it. It could have passed for any one of the Georgia plantations that dotted the countryside 100 hundred years prior.

The minute Hunter checked his watch and saw it was 8 'clock, a woman unlocked the front doors from the inside. She looked at him briefly and turned around. By the time Hunter walked inside, the woman was halfway up the wide staircase. Theodore had told him the county clerk's office and the records room were on the second floor, so he followed her after speaking to the receptionist at the front desk.

The entrance to the courtroom was at the top of the stairs, and a door, with an etched glass window in it, was to the far right. A black and white metal sign that read "County Clerk" was attached to the plaster wall. Hunter opened the door, and the same woman he saw earlier was sitting behind a large desk. There were filing cabinets lining the walls, a couple of smaller desks, and another room was directly behind the clerk's desk.

"May I help you," she asked in a quiet voice.

"Thank you. I'm Hunter Fox from *The Tribune*, and you are?"

"The County Clerk, Hilda Hargett. What can I do for you today, Mr. Fox?"

"I'd like to go over some land ledgers if I could, those records for the Valley Road properties."

"Of course, they are kept in the records room. I'll put them on the table in there."

Hunter spent an hour looking at the ledgers and came up with nothing. Every single plat description on the north side of the Valley Road read, "Bordered on the northern property line by undeveloped forestland and mountains." There were no coordinates given for the land, nor an owner. It was as if the Ridge possessed itself. He walked back into the main office space and cleared his throat.

The county clerk looked up. "Yes?" she asked.

"Miss Hargett, do you know why there are no deeds for any of this tract of land behind these properties out on the Valley Road? Are the records kept someplace else?"

"If the recorded deeds aren't there, then I don't have them," she answered, looking back at the ledger in front of her. "Best to let it go."

"Well, all right. That's odd though. Don't you think so?"

"I don't really think about it," she answered, looking up at Hunter.

"Hmmm...okay, well, thanks for your time," he answered. He left the courthouse, still not knowing who owned that land. It was also obvious that Miss Hargett did not want to discuss it either. As soon as he got to the office, he called Theodore.

"Morning. I just got back from the courthouse. There's nothing recorded, and Miss Hargett had no interest in helping me. In fact, she told me to let it go."

"That doesn't surprise me," answered Theodore. "A Hargett has been clerk of records in Kings County since the beginning of time. She probably knows the truth and is scared of the Coopers."

"How have they managed to control an entire county?" asked Hunter.

"Money, fear tactics, blackmail, threats, and supplying all of the liquor folks could drink — not only around here but in Chattanooga, too. Jack comes from a long line of ruthless con men. I should know. He lured my only daughter into marrying him."

"What about Sheriff Wilkes and all of his prede-cessors?" Hunter inquired.

"Maybe you should pay him a visit," replied Theodore.

"Yep, you're right. Guess I'll call on the sheriff sooner than later. Wish me luck." Hunter hung up and looked at his watch. He called the hotel and asked for Cagle's room.

"Hello. Dan Cagle, here."

"Hey, Dan. It's Hunter. Do you have that information for me yet?"

"Some of it. The first public information session will be next Tuesday, a week from tomorrow, in Cantrell City at 6:30 at the library. The next one will be the following Thursday in Willow Creek, same time, at the depot. As far as the actual deed goes, Jack is taking care of that. He's sure he will have it recorded in time to file for the rezoning application for the October commission meeting."

"Any idea why he or his father or grandfather never took care of that little detail?"

"You'll have to ask him that yourself," snapped Cagle.

"Will do. On another note, I forgot to mention to you that I'd like to visit your mining sites in the Copper Basin. I imagine one or more commissioners and a couple of citizens would like to go, too. Can we arrange that for, say, this Friday?"

"Ah, I think that's possible," said Cagle slowly, 'but why the Copper Basin?"

"It's the closest and the oldest."

"I see. I'll set that up and get back with you."

"Sounds good...talk to you later."

Hunter put a piece of paper in his typewriter and started putting together the story for Tuesday's paper. He wanted to finish it before Lucy came for lunch so he'd have

143

more time with her. He left no details out, right down to the fact that the Ridge was believed to be Cooper land but that no deed was recorded so far. He called and got a quote from Jack, who said, "Old deeds have a way of getting tucked away sometimes, but I'm not concerned about it." Within a few minutes of doing his final edit, he heard the bell on the front door ring.

"Hey, Lucy. What brings you to Cantrell City?" asked the receptionist.

"Hi, Betsy. I'm here to—"

"Lucy, good to see you," said Hunter, walking in from the back. "Betsy, I'll be out of the office for about an hour or so. Pete, I put the mining story on your desk. I'll be back to help you proof everything before we go to press." Putting on his sports coat, he opened the door for Lucy. Catching a whiff of her perfume, he commented, "You smell wonderful. What is that?"

"Something Marge sprayed on me. I was at her house, going through the phone book and making a list of people to go see about the petition before I came here. She insisted I wear it."

Hunter smiled and whispered in her ear. "Tell Marge, thanks." He reached for her hand but she pulled it away and admonished him in a playful, coquettish voice.

"Listen now, Mr. Fox. We are not in Savannah or Atlanta. We are in Cantrell City, where everyone's business is on full display. Folks love to watch what others do, come up with their own conclusions, and then talk about what's going on in someone else's life, as if they knew. Actually, I don't care if people around here are aware that you and I are getting to know one another again, but I don't want that fact to distract from the fight in front of us. Folks need to see us as professionals, working together to get to the bottom of a mystery. Our personal shows of affection must be reserved for when we are alone or with friends we trust."

"You are absolutely correct, smart lady. So, I guess having lunch in my room at the hotel is out of the question, right?"

"I would say so," answered Lucy with a laugh.

"All right. We'll eat in the dining room, but I'm going to figure out how to get you alone again very soon." Hunter opened the front door of the hotel for Lucy and heard Jimmy's voice from across the lobby.

"Wait, wait, Miss Mason. Here he is now. I'll have him on the line in just a minute. Mr. Fox, Miss Angela Mason is on the phone for you. You can take it here at my desk."

"Thanks, Jimmy." Hunter walked behind the counter and picked up the receiver. "Hello. This is Hunter Fox."

Lucy watched him talking and almost smiled but realized Jimmy was staring a hole through her.

"Hey, Lucy," said Jimmy. "What brings you to the Gold Star Inn? I don't think I've ever seen you here except to deliver produce."

"You're right, Jimmy. I usually show up in a pickup truck, right out of the garden, but I'm here on business. I'm trying to find out as much as I can about the mining operation that's proposed for here, and Hunter offered to share what he knows about zoning controversies. We knew one another briefly in college and just reconnected this weekend at church."

Hunter hung up the phone and joined Lucy in front of the lobby desk. "That was good news. Miss Mason has agreed to rent me her guest house. I can move in this weekend. Shall we go in for lunch now, Lucy?"

She nodded and spoke to the desk clerk, keeping a respectable distance from Hunter, a distance that did nothing to negate the heat between the two.

"How did I do? Formal enough?" asked Hunter, pulling out the chair at the table for Lucy.

"Very good," she said. "I passed the test, too. I told him we reconnected at church."

"Well, we did, but that wasn't the first connection I recall," answered Hunter softly.

Lucy smiled slightly but quickly reminded Hunter why she was there.

"Do you have the names of the environmental experts for me?"

"I sure do. Right here," he said, patting his jacket pocket. "I need some advice from you, too. I think the best way to uncover the truth about who owns the Ridge is to talk to people who have lived here a long time or whose families have. I ran into a dead end at the courthouse, and we don't have much time. Cooper and Cagle intend to bring this before the commission at the October meeting just a couple of weeks away. So, tell me where to start."

"Probably with my mama. She was born here, but Nettie would be the best source of information. Her family has been on the Valley Road since way before the Civil War. I've tried many times to get her to talk to me about her past, but she just clams up or brushes me off when I start asking questions. I think this time will be different though. Our way of life is threatened. I'll do my best to get through to her."

"Good. Also, I was hoping that after lunch, you could go to the library with me. We need to read up on the history of the county when it was Cherokee territory."

"Sure, just so I'm at the house by the time the bus runs. I try to be there when Hank gets home. I think that makes him feel secure, and I've always worried about that since he's grown up without a father." Lucy was secretly thrilled to be away from the farm although she felt a bit guilty, too. But doing something in the outside world that didn't pertain to house and garden was fun, even if it is just going to the library.

"As far as I can tell, Hank Tanner oozes confidence, Lucy. You've done a fine job raising him."

"Thanks. I appreciate that. It hasn't been easy, but we've made it so far." Lucy hesitated for a second to collect herself. The thought of opening up to Hunter made her want to cry. She cleared her throat and continued. "So, changing the subject—congratulations on finding a place to live." She was inwardly excited at the prospect of there being somewhere they could get to know one another better—away from public scrutiny.

"Yes, I need to get my things from Savannah though. The house is furnished, but I want my stereo, my TV, books, and so on. I'll probably use a couple of pieces of furniture, too. I'm going over after work to check things out and get a key from Miss Mason."

"Will you have to drive to Savannah to get your stuff?" asked Lucy, hoping Hunter wasn't going to be away for the weekend.

"No. It's in storage at a moving company there. I'll call them today and ask them to deliver everything Saturday morning. I won't be able to move in until after this week is over, too much going on. I want to check out the Cagle operations in the Copper Basin on Friday. I cleared that with Dan this morning. I figure you, Theodore, and at least Charlie Tate will want to go. What about your dad?"

"Well, we'll have to see about that. He's not in a very good mood right now."

"Is it me that has him out of sorts?"

"No, he told me a woman's voice has no place in these matters. But, of course, I choose to ignore him. It's me. Not you."

"Well, I know better than to come between a father and his daughter. I want him to understand that you and I are professionals who are trying to solve a mystery, actually several mysteries: who really owns the Ridge and why I can't stop thinking about you."

"Well, Mr. Fox, if you want to do the former, you better put your mind on your business," said Lucy.

***

Lucy left Cantrell City and headed toward Willow Creek, hoping to get to Hank's school before his bus left. She loved surprising him with a ride home whenever she could.

147

Bus #54 was in front of the school, so she parked the car and walked over to speak to the driver. "Afternoon, Clyde. I'm picking up Hank, so he won't be giving you a rundown of the day; think you can do without that?"

"Oh, Lucy, he's not a bother. His stories make me laugh, and that's a good thing for an old man. You raised quite a jokester."

Before Lucy could answer, the bell rang and the front doors to the school opened. A tidal wave of children's voices and scampering feet swooped down the walkway. Leading the pack was Hank, who ran even faster when he saw her.

"Mama, are you here to give me a ride home?"

"No. I'm here because the principal called me."

When Hank's face changed from ecstatic to horrified, Lucy laughed and told him she was just kidding.

"I can see where he gets it from," Clyde grinned.

"See you tomorrow, Mr. Clyde. Bye, Josie." Hank got in the car and pummeled Lucy with questions before she had a chance to crank the engine. "Where have you been, Mama? I can't believe Granddaddy let you drive his car. And why do you have on a dress? It's not Sunday."

"I had a meeting with Hunter in Cantrell City about the mine, your grandfather needed the truck at the farm, and I have on a dress because it looks more professional than khaki work pants and brogans. Any more questions?"

"Do you like him?"

"Do I like who?"

"You know who, Mama. Hunter."

"Of course. Don't you?"

"You know what I mean, Mama."

"What would you say if I told you, 'Yes'?"

"I'd say, 'good.' I think you need a boyfriend."

"Who told you that?"

"Nobody. I'm smart enough to figure it out. I hear you in your room at night sometimes. I hear you crying. My daddy made you sad, didn't he?"

"Oh, sweet Hank. What happened between him and me was a long time ago. I don't want you to worry about

148

that. Folks just need to let the tears go sometimes. There's seldom just one reason we cry. Most of the time it's lots of things—disappointment, sadness, and even anger. But we all have to learn how to feel what we feel and move on. As far as Hunter goes, I wouldn't call him my boyfriend yet. We're still getting reacquainted. Why don't we just call him my special friend right now?"

"Okay. Did Hunter know my daddy?"

"Yes. They were what you call acquaintances, not really friends, but they knew of one another."

"Huh…okay."

Hank was unusually quiet for the rest of the ride home, making Lucy wonder if the inevitable was here—his wanting to meet his father. She had dreaded this happening, but always knew it would. The two rode the rest of the way home without saying another word.

*****

As soon as Lucy got Hank settled with a snack and his homework, she sat down at the table with him and started reading the material she and Hunter had checked out from the library.

"What are those books about, Mama? Aren't you going over to the barn to help Granddaddy?"

"These are history books about Kings County. And I'm not going over to the barn because we hired Billy Joe."

"Really? Can I go over and see him?"

"When you finish your work," chimed in Gen, who was at the stove, pretending not to listen.

In less than 15 minutes, Hank showed his finished work to Lucy and headed across the road to the barn.

Gen wiped her hands on the dish towel and sat down at the table across from Lucy. "Your father was not happy this morning when he found out where you went and why," she said quietly, "but I told him he should be proud of what you're doing."

149

Lucy looked at her mother with wide eyes. "You took up for me?"

"I did. I think you're doing what you should do, and Hunter seems like a nice man. He is well-mannered, smart, and, well, very handsome."

"Mama," exclaimed Lucy, giggling at the color in her mother's cheeks. "You've always been a good judge of men. Just look at who you managed to marry." Lucy stood up and walked over to where her mother sat. Leaning down, she gave her a hug. "Genevieve Tanner, you'll never know how much I appreciate you right now. I want to be happy, and I want Hank to be okay, but I don't want to upset you or Daddy."

"Don't you worry about your daddy. I'll take care of him. And Hank is fine, isn't he?"

"He asked me about his dad again. This time he wanted to know if Hunter knew him. Mama, he's going to ask to see him one day. You know that, don't you?"

"Yes. I do, and if David agrees, you will oblige. He is the boy's father, and if Hank is asking questions, he's curious. Don't worry. It will be okay. Just love your boy through it like you've always loved him. Sons are special to their mamas."

Lucy looked at her mother and saw the tears welling up in her eyes. "Oh, Mama. You've had a hole in your heart ever since Henry died. We all have, but for you, I know it's worse." Lucy hugged her mother again and felt like something had changed between them...something very good.

Wanting to change the subject, she sat down in the chair next to Gen and motioned toward the books. "So, help me, Mama, you've lived here your whole life. What stories did you hear about the Ridge when you were growing up?"

"What everybody else heard—that Jack Cooper's grandfather, Mr. Jack as they called him, claimed the land. That was before I was born. Nobody talks about who owned it before he did. I asked my father about it one time. He told me never to mention it again and not to go up on there alone. All I know is that Mr. Jack put the fear of God in folks and threatened anyone who questioned what he did on the mountain. That fear is still here."

"I bet Nettie knows something," said Lucy. "Her family has lived in that house for generations, haven't they?"

"They have, but getting her to talk about it won't be easy. She has some bad memories of the Coopers."

"Like what?"

"That's for her to tell you if she chooses to do so." Gen stood up and went back to the stove. It was clear to Lucy that her mother had some fear deep inside her, too. The phone rang, and Lucy went into the hall to answer it.

"Hey, Lucy. Any luck yet?" asked Hunter.

"No. I asked my mama, but she doesn't know anything we don't already know. I'm going to try to get Nettie to talk to me as soon as I can. That's gonna take some work though. The Negro community around here are especially terrified of anything to do with the Ridge. Of course, I've never known Nettie Andrews to be scared of much, so I may have a chance."

"All right, good luck to you. Hey, Pete just came in my office. Can I call you later?"

"Sure," answered Lucy. She hung up and went back into the kitchen. The back door was open and her mother was gone. Lucy looked out the window and saw her standing in the backyard, staring at nothing.

"Mama, what's wrong?" she asked, walking up behind Gen.

"I don't know, Lucy. I don't know. I just get so scared sometimes."

Lucy took her mother's trembling hands in hers and gently held them until the shaking subsided. "It's okay, Mama. There's just a lot of change happening right now. That's all." But Lucy knew better. That wasn't all there was.

Cagle and Cooper

The phone in Jack Cooper's office rang three times before he remembered he didn't have a secretary. "God-damn it," he said, "not having a broad to answer my calls is a fucking nuisance. Hello? Jack Cooper, here."

"Sounds like your Monday was a pile of shit, too," said Dan Cagle on the other end.

"Yeah, my dimwit secretary quit, and the phone has been ringing all day...people asking questions about the mine. I'm glad this day is almost over. What or who got your goat?"

"Fox was at the courthouse when they opened the doors this morning. I saw him out my hotel window. And then, a little later, he called and asked me a lot of questions that made me nervous. He's printing another article in to-morrow's paper. I think you and I need to talk very soon."

"Son-of-a-bitch," hissed Jack. "Of all the places in Georgia he could have picked to be a big shot, why the hell did he have to land here? He's poking his nose in places it shouldn't go. If he doesn't watch out, he's gonna smell more than he can handle. Let's see. It's almost 4. Why don't you meet me at the Lodge? It's closed on Monday, so there won't be anybody around. Park in the back and come in through the side entrance. I'll see you around 6."

Jack opened the bottom drawer of his desk and picked up a clear bottle. He unscrewed the top and took a drink, grimacing at the sting.

He loved the taste of whiskey but sometimes, noth-ing smoothed the edges like moonshine, and he had some mighty ragged edges today.

***

Daisy was finishing up in the kitchen at the Lodge when she heard someone pull in the parking lot. *Oh, good. Sandy is back*, she thought. When he went up on the Ridge to get liquor, she worried the entire time he was gone. He assured her the law looked the other way, but she was afraid he had become too comfortable with what he did and that was dangerous. She looked out the window, expecting to see Sandy's blue truck but it was Jack driving around to the back of the building.

The thought of being alone with him sent a shiver down her spine. She was terrified of Jack Cooper and rightfully so. Every girl who lived on her side of town knew his reputation for taking whomever he wanted whenever he wanted.

She knew she had to hide, and the pantry would be the least likely place he'd go. All the booze was at the bar. She quickly grabbed her sweater and purse and opened the storeroom door just as she heard Jack's footsteps. It was pitch black dark in the closet and quiet except for her pounding heart.

He went behind the bar and filled a shot glass with whiskey. Only a wall separated Daisy from him, so she could hear every sound including his smacking lips and the sound of his pouring another. Before he finished the second drink, she heard him shout, "Come in, Dan. Welcome to the only watering hole in Kings County. There's a drink on the bar for you. No one is here so we are free to talk. What did Fox say that got you going?"

Cagle threw back his drink and poured another. "He won't let it go about the land…who owns it and if there's a deed. Evidently, he did a thorough search at the courthouse and there's nothing on the ledger about the ridge."

"Yeah, I know. The county clerk called me today and said he was there, asking questions. He called me too for a quote for the story. I just put him off. You can't tell anybody what I told you that my granddaddy took that land back in the1800s after the War. He made moonshine up there until he died, and my daddy carried on the tradition. That's how we made our money and bought so much land during the 1920s. I'm sure if there was a deed, he got rid of it. My granddaddy never left any bodies after a fight. But that doesn't matter. Ever heard of squatter's rights?"

"Well, yeah. When it comes to houses, but does that apply to land, too?"

"I don't see why not, and we've been squatting up there for almost 100 years. Dan, the county commission has never voted against a Cooper request in a century. They're not going to start now."

"But Fox..."

"Fuck Fox," shouted Jack, slamming his glass down on the counter. "He's nothing. I own this county and get what I want. There are no legal records in the courthouse about the Ridge. My granddaddy saw to that. That two-bit reporter won't find anything until there's something there I want him to find.

"Stop worrying, Cagle. It makes you look suspicious. We already have one commissioner on the hook. I went to see Buddy Tatum at his car dealership today and promised him a nice little cut from the mine. Plus, I threw some cash his way. I only have to convince a couple more and we're home safe."

Daisy stood in the pantry, hearing every word and wishing she hadn't. Almost feeling faint, she reached out to steady herself, accidentally knocking a bottle from the shelves to the floor.

"What the hell?" shouted Jack. "Who's there?" He opened the kitchen door and turned on the lights. Seeing no one, he glanced at the door to the storage closet. "Must be a rat in the pantry," he called out, "but I ain't dealing with it." He cut the light off and walked back in the dining room just as Sandy came in the front door.

"Hi, Mr. Cooper. I didn't know you were coming by this evening." Trying to hide his worry at not seeing Daisy anywhere, he continued, "got a good haul of home brew to-day to go with the legal stuff."

"Good, Sandy. We're gonna need every drop you can buy or steal. Things around here are getting a little nerve racking. By the way, this is Dan Cagle, the owner of the mining company we're bringing to Kings County. Make sure he has whatever he needs when he comes in here. Sandy's a damn good bartender who knows all the hot girls in town. Speaking of, where's your little number? Wait to you see her, Dan, she's got a rack out to here and an ass to match."

"She's at home," said Sandy, bristling at Jack's crude remarks, "and she's not just my little number. We're getting married."

"Now, why do you want to go and fuck a good thing up, Sandy? Women forget how to spread their legs once they hook you." Jack laughed and slapped Cagle on the back, "Right, Dan?"

"If you say so, Jack," answered Cagle, who was beginning to feel the effects of the booze. "I'm ready to call it a day. I'll talk to you tomorrow."

"All right, Danny Boy. Now, stop worrying, and if the law pulls you over before you get to Cantrell City, just tell them who you are, where you've been, and who served you a drink."

After Cagle left, Sandy put the empty glasses on a tray and wiped the bar. "I need to unload the liquor, Mr. Cooper. Do you need anything else?"

"Naw, I'm drunk, and that's what I like to be. I'm heading home. Anita is still out of town, Bo is at her parents' house, and I'm expecting a visitor soon—a visitor I paid to come here from Chattanooga."

As soon as Sandy heard Jack crank his car and pull around the building, he started calling for Daisy. He threw open the kitchen door just as she came out of the pantry. "Are you alright?"

"I'm okay...scared but okay. I heard way more than I wanna know. Jack Cooper is up to no good."

"What did he say?" asked Sandy.

"It's about the Ridge and that mine he's pushing. He said his granddaddy stole the land and took the legal records from the courthouse. He told that Cagle guy not to worry about anything, because he's already bribed Buddy Tatum and won't have a problem paying off two or three more commissioners. If he knew I heard what he said, he'd kill me."

"Stop, Daisy. Nobody is going to kill you. I'd take care of Jack with one swat, just like a housefly, but I won't have to. I know exactly what to do to put a wrench in his plan. He's not the tough guy he thinks he is."

"No, please don't. He's dangerous, Sandy. He'd—"

"Hey, don't worry. I'm not going to do anything. I'm just going to let the right people know what's happening."

"Who? Sandy, tell me what's going on."

"No. I don't want you to know who, what, or where. You just have to trust me. Isn't that what married folks are supposed to do? Trust and love one another?" He gave Daisy a good, long kiss and held her close. "Speaking of loving one another, let's get out of this joint and go home. Okay?"

The Forgotten Cherokees

As soon as Hank was asleep, Lucy put on her pajamas, fluffed up her pillows so she could lean against the headboard, and started reading "*The Forgotten Cherokees*." It was in a box of books the librarian found at the front door a few days prior. They hadn't been catalogued yet, but she agreed to let Lucy go through them and pick out a few. The title got her attention since she felt like that's what they were doing—trying to find a missing link about the Ridge. She opened the thin, faded blue journal and read the title page:

"The Forgotten Cherokees"
A Memoir by Lita Davidson
1870
 Dedicated to The Original Inhabitants of The Great Valley and Their Descendants.

Lucy sat up straight, staring at the words. *This is about here*, she thought. She couldn't start reading fast enough:

Haroldo Tsalegi (translated Harold Ridge) was a Cherokee chief who led his people before the White men settled the Indian territories.

He was considered a powerful and successful chief in the Cherokee Nation East during The Early Times...before any treaties were signed with the United States Government.

His lands included the entire Great Valley in North Georgia. He was known for his leadership qualities, peaceful ways, and success as a business-man. He controlled one of the main routes through the mountains in Georgia all the way to the North Carolina border. Used by both Cherokee and White traders, the flow of goods was prolific. Chief Tsalegi protected those who used the trails in exchange for cloth, skins, dried meats, vegetables, livestock, and tools.

In keeping with many of the early Cherokee chiefs, Tsalegi was a Christian and literate — thanks to George Gist's (Sequoyah) invention of an Indian al-phabet. He was an avid teetotaler and enforced strict rules among his people regarding the use of intoxi-cants.

Education was very important to him, so much that he financed the building of schools through-out his territory.

In the Cherokee culture, people with his first name are considered powerful, who possess abun-dant leadership qualities. Chief Haroldo Tsalegi was such a man.

His personal life was marred by sadness when his young wife died in childbirth. The baby girl whom he named Tablita (meaning 'crown') survived and was the subject of his constant attention and af-fection. He never took another wife and trained his daughter to take over his duties as chief upon his death.

To prepare her to rule in an area that was becoming increasingly settled by White people, he sent her to the Valley Union Seminary for Girls in Roanoke, Virginia. It was there that she met Andrew Davidson, the White son of a prominent landowner. When Tablita traveled home after the fall session, Andrew accompanied her along with a chaperone. Tablita had already sent a message to her father about the visitor.

Upon arriving in the modest, yet very advanced settlement where she was born, Chief Tsalegi welcomed his daughter, excused her to go rest from the journey, and instructed his guest to meet with him in the governing hall, located near the chief's home.

A nervous Davidson did so and waited for the chief to speak first. When he asked the young man what his intentions were, Andrew replied that he was in love with Tablita and she with him. With the chief's blessing, he intended to marry her when she finished her education at the end of the year. He said that Tablita expressed the desire to live among her people and that he gladly concurred. He told the chief that he would work as hard as a real son to ensure their lands and people flourished.

Chief Tsalegi sent for his daughter and asked her if what Davidson said was accurate. She affirmed their love, their desire to marry, and their intentions to live in the Great Valley.

Her father agreed, blessed the union, and called for a great feast and celebration to be held that evening. It was whispered that he planned the event as soon as he received his daughter's message, knowing he could not refuse her wishes.

I know this intimate account of Chief Tsalegi, Tablita, and Andrew Davidson because I am Tablita or 'Lita', as my husband called me. My father treated my husband like a son and embraced our children.

Lucy was intrigued, hoping she had found a clue to solving the mystery. The phone rang, interrupting her thoughts. She heard Luke answer it and then tap on her door.

"It's for you," he said in a flat voice.

Lucy's heart jumped, hoping it was Hunter. When she heard his voice on the other end of the line, she smiled and sat down in the chair next to the phone table. "Hunter, you won't believe what I found at the library a few days ago. It's a memoir, from 1870 and written by the daughter of a Cherokee chief whose territory included all of the Great Valley. It might lead us to what we're looking for."

Luke opened the door to her parents' bedroom, startling her. "I know this is important to you, but going to sleep is important to me. Can you finish this in the morning, please?"

Lucy turned her eyes away from Luke's condescending stare and whispered into the receiver. "Hey, I—"

"It's all right. I heard. Why don't you come into town tomorrow? Say, around the same time you did today," asked Hunter, "no reason to upset your dad."

"Okay. I'll see you then. Good night."

"Good night, Lucy Tanner."

She hung up the phone, resenting her father more than ever, but she was far too curious about the Cherokee narrative to dwell on his rude behavior. She walked quietly back to her room and continued reading.

Chief Tsalegi listened to Andrew, who was aware of the White encroachment on Cherokee territory. He feared we would lose our lands, so he convinced my father to certify his ownership of the property in the Great Valley and put a legitimate deed in his name. He knew a White man had a better chance of holding

159

on to the property than an Indian descendant, especially a woman.

He also helped my father draw up a will, in which he gave full governing authority of our lands and businesses to Andrew and me.

Sadness came into our lives, however, when our great chief's day to die came, and he walked on into his next journey. But there was little time to grieve.

As White settlers increased in numbers, the demand for the agricultural commodities and non-perishable goods we produced increased significantly. So, my husband decided to farm all of the land in the valley between the great mountain ranges. He bought slaves, something my father would have opposed, and was very successful producing corn and other staples he traded for money and goods. We had four children—three boys and one girl.

When my dear Andrew died from the fever, my heart was broken, and the challenges of running the farm, the territory, and the trading business were too much for me.

My oldest son Nathaniel took charge of the lands and married the daughter of his Black foreman. After the War, he freed all of the slaves but most remained and continued to work on the farms. My daughter married a prominent white settler, and my other two sons entered the seminary.

It seemed my late husband had done a good job making sure our lands were protected, but what he did not plan for, however, was the prejudice that ensued against the Cherokees and half-breeds. Not only were my children the result of a Caucasian and Cherokee union, but now my son's children had a Black mother.

As I write this, my heart is filled with fear about their futures. I have heard the stories about families with Indian heritage having their lands stolen. I know about the harsh treatment of Black people, even though slavery has been abolished. They say that nothing is as powerful as the White man's greed.

My son assures me he has taken care of everything and that he has a will which states that all he owns shall pass to his wife, but I fear Nathaniel is too trusting. As a Cherokee, I know that White influence and control grow every day.

As I write this, I watch my oldest granddaughter Annette play in the stream near the traders' route. Will her daughters and sons be able to breathe the sweet air and drink from the cool creeks that have sustained our people since the beginning of time?

I'm afraid I won't live to know the answer to these questions. With each passing day, I feel closer to the time my next journey will begin. When it does, will I walk on as a bird, as my father always said I would? Will I be the majestic eagle that flies over the valleys and mountains once filled with my ancestors?

My father told me my spirit would rise above everything—that Cherokee princesses never die. They just got wiser and stronger.

I want to believe him, but he did not live to see what was happening to our tribal lands. He did not live in his human form long enough to understand how ruthless men can be. I fear the Great Valley will become the land of *"The Forgotten Cherokees."*

Lucy breathed for the first time since she started reading. She put the journal on her nightstand. Unanswered questions flooded her mind. What happened after the Cherokee matriarch passed away? Did the US government take their lands? What happened to the deed and the will?

Time was of the essence if they wanted to stop Jack Cooper. Tomorrow morning, she would begin unraveling a haunted past that needed to be exposed…one that would require courage on the parts of those who knew the truth.

Sid

The Chattanooga Food Company truck backed up to the side door of the Lodge right on time Tuesday morning. The driver was already opening the back doors and pulling down the steps when Sandy walked out to help. "Hey Joey," he said. "I need you to give this to the boss as soon as you get back to the office. After he sees it, I bet you'll be driving right back here."

"What is it?" asked Joey.

"Today's newspaper," answered Sandy. "Cooper is about to fuck up the Ridge."

"That's why he has you here, Sandy, to keep an eye on everything and everybody. I'll make sure he gets it as soon as I get back."

Within 15 minutes, the grocery order was unloaded. Sandy looked at his watch when Joey left and figured he'd be hearing something from his real boss—Sid Ramsey—in about an hour or so. He owned the largest grocery supply business and distillery in Chattanooga, but one of his most profitable ventures was the liquor he smuggled to dry counties in North Georgia and Tennessee.

Ramsey depended on the Ridge. His main supply of moonshine was made there, which was as popular as the distilled whiskey he smuggled.

When alcohol sales were legalized, he started a distributorship in Tennessee and had the biggest share of the legitimate liquor trade in several states. He stored the booze destined for thirsty but dry Georgia counties in small sheds, hidden in the thickest, most secluded parts of the Ridge. Sandy hauled the liquor to the Lodge where Sid's food company trucks picked it up and delivered it along with grocery orders to private clubs like The Lodge—the only places that served liquor in dry counties in Georgia. He pretty much had the corner on the grocery supply business in North Georgia, too.

Sid Ramsey was a very wealthy and powerful man. His family had been doing business with the Coopers since the early 1900s, an arrangement that had made a lot of money for both parties. His father was a wealthy Mexican landowner and businessman who migrated from Texas to New Orleans to capitalize on the booming business along the Mississippi River. Given the prejudices against Hispanics, he changed his name from Ramirez to Ramsey and married a woman from a wealthy Creole family. Since he was a devout Catholic, he had no problem fitting into his wife's social class.

He had a keen eye for economic opportunity and believed there was more money to be made in parts of the South that were beginning to experience growth from the railroad. He eventually moved his family to Tennessee and started the Chattanooga Food Company, which quickly morphed into more than just groceries. When he died, his son, Sid, took over the business.

Sid Ramsey hired Sandy right after WWII. He was immediately impressed with the young man's work ethic, his stony silence, and his loyalty. When his guy at the Lodge passed away, Sandy was a logical choice to put there. His job was to get an inventory of how much shine was made, make sure Ramsey got his take, and see that it was safely delivered to Chattanooga when needed.

He also funneled cash from Ramsey to Cooper and vice versa. Sandy's most important job, however, was to keep an eye on Jack and make sure he wasn't cheating Sid out of anything. He had to pretend to be loyal to Jack, and that was the hardest part of his job because he hated him.

About an hour after Joey left, the phone rang. "Hello," said Sandy. "You've reached the Lodge. Can I help you?"

"Expect another delivery in one hour, and Jack Cooper needs to be there," said Joey.

"Sure thing," answered Sandy. He hung up and called Jack's office at the bank.

"Jack Cooper, here," said a hoarse voice.

"Mr. Cooper, the man from Chattanooga will be here in about an hour. He expects you to be here."

"Shit. Why can't he give more notice?"

"'Cause he doesn't have to," said Sandy.

"I'm supposed to meet some folks about this mine thing then," said Jack. "Damn it. Okay. I'll be there." He hung up the phone and leaned back in his chair. *Relax*, he said to himself. *When Ramsey realizes how much money the mine could make, he'll be ok. Nothing spoke to that spic like the American dollar.*

He made a couple of calls, rescheduled the meeting, and unfolded the newspaper lying on his desk. Hunter's story about the mine was on the front page. The headline read: **"Amid Questions Regarding the Ridge, Developers for the Proposed Mine Plan Public Meetings."**

"Goddamn it," sputtered Jack. "I've got to come up with a deed before that son-of-bitch Fox fucks everything up." He got out his address book and turned to the "A's" and looked for attorneys.

"There he is; just who I need. I know Sid uses him…must be good." He called the number and left a message with Skip Jones' secretary. He was confident he'd have something to pass for a legitimate document soon. Jack fortified his nerves with a couple of pops of vodka and left out the back entrance to the bank.

***

Sid Ramsey put on a driver's uniform and a baseball hat he kept in his penthouse office. He seldom left Chattanooga to call on his clients but when he did, he made sure he didn't bring attention to himself.

Showing up in Cantrell City in a limousine would. Arriving in a Chattanooga Grocery truck wouldn't. He took his private elevator down to the basement garage of the

164

office building he owned. Joey was waiting for him, standing next to the truck and holding the door open.

"Thanks, Joey. I'm going to catch a nap while you drive. Wake me up when we get to the rat hole."

He closed his eyes and drifted off to sleep but not before reflecting on just how much he detested doing business with Jack Cooper. He embodied everything Sid abhorred: gluttony, crudeness, an over-inflated ego, un-deserved success, disregard for others, greed, and — last but not least — an unawareness of just how ignorant he was. Cooper's demise was something Sid would not mourn. In fact, it would please him a great deal.

Nettie's Secret

As soon as Hank got on the bus Tuesday morning, Lucy hurried back to the house. By the time she got to the kitchen, Gen was at the sink, peeling apples.

"Where's Nettie?" asked Lucy.

"She's out in the canning shed, getting the jars we need for these apples. She could use your help."

"Okay, but I'm heading to Cantrell City around 11 to tell Hunter what I've found out. I'm sure you heard us trying to have a phone conversation last evening."

"I did, but face-to-face would be more fun for you two, wouldn't it?" asked Gen, smiling slightly.

"Mama, this is business."

"Oh, of course, of course. By the way, the Women's Club is having a special meeting Thursday to discuss the toy drive for Christmas. Why don't you come and talk about the mine and encourage the members to attend one of those meetings I read about in today's paper."

"That's a great idea. I may even go to Belk and shop for a couple of new outfits today. Khakis and overalls don't work all the time." She winked at her mother and walked out the back door.

***

165

When Lucy opened the door to the canning shed, Nettie was about to climb a ladder leaning against the shelves where the last empty jars were stored.

"You know better than that," said Lucy.

"Why? Because your great-grandfather fell off one almost a hundred years ago?" asked Nettie.

"No," answered Lucy, ignoring her sarcasm, "because it's dangerous. Why don't you let me climb up there and hand the jars to you?"

"I am perfectly capable of getting up and down this ladder without hurting myself, but if that will stop your fussing, go right ahead."

Nettie was not in a particularly congenial mood this morning, causing Lucy to wonder if she should bring up a subject that was taboo. But given the urgency of the matter, she dove right in.

"I know you've been following the story about the mine," she said, as she climbed up the ladder. "Mama told me y'all had talked about it. So, I am sure you understand how important it is that we stop it."

"I do, but I don't see how we can. Jack Cooper gets what Jack Cooper wants. You know that. I know that."

"But it's not right, Nettie. Hunter said there's no deed in the courthouse."

"Hunter, huh? Your mama told me you went into town yesterday to meet with him. I'm glad. You're in a better mood since he showed up."

"Stop changing the subject, Nettie. Your family has lived out here for generations." Lucy reached for another jar and handed it to Nettie. "Think please, and try to remember if your mother or grandmother ever said anything about a Chief Haroldo Ridge." The sound of the jar crashing to the cement floor almost made Lucy lose her balance. She looked down and saw Nettie, staring at the jar.

"How do you know that name?" she asked in a quiet, yet husky voice.

Startled by her reaction, Lucy quickly climbed down from the ladder and put her hands on Nettie's shoulders. "I read about it in this book—a journal really—that I found in the library yesterday. Nettie, I didn't mean to upset you. What is it? Tell me."

"You didn't upset me," said Nettie, trying to hide her anxiety. "I just haven't heard his name mentioned since I was a little girl when my grandmama was telling me a story about him. Mama heard her, got really mad, and yelled at both of us. It was terrible. I thought they were going to get in a fight. My mama told me to go outside but I heard what they said. I crouched down beneath the open window. Mama told my grandmama that she knew what their story was supposed to be—that Mr. JJ Cooper owned that land and our house and that telling some crazy tale about a Cherokee chief whose descendants did could get a body killed, or in the case of a woman, worse than dead. She told my grandmama that even if it was true, what good would it do some colored women, with no husbands? What was lost was gone and what is done is over. After she finished, she called me back inside and told me never to mention what I heard to another soul, and I haven't until now."

"What was your grandmama's name?" asked Lucy.
"Annette," said Nettie softly, "...just like me."

The Boss

Jack parked next to the Chattanooga Grocery Company truck at the back of The Lodge. He wiped his face with his handkerchief and loosened his shirt collar. "Jesus, it's too hot for September," he said aloud.

As soon as Jack opened the side door, Sandy stood up from behind the bar. "He's in the back office."

"Do I get a drink first?" asked Cooper.

"No. He said not to give you one."

167

Jack hated the way Ramsey threw his weight around, but he had no choice but to stomach it...for now anyway. He knocked on the closed office door. "It's me."

"It better be," answered Sid.

"What brings you to town?" asked Jack, opening the door and knowing exactly why Ramsey was there.

"I heard a rumor that you were behind bringing a mine to Kings County, but I just couldn't believe that you would do something like that without telling me first. I mean, a mine up on the Ridge just wouldn't serve our interests, would it?"

"I was going to tell you when things were settled, Sid...a surprise, you know. We're going to make a lot of money, more than we make now. I just have to tie up a couple of loose legal ends."

"I bet you do," answered Sid. "Selling land, when ownership is questionable is a problem, and when somebody backs out of a deal, that's a problem, too."

"Now, Sid. You know I wouldn't jeopardize our business dealings. We can still operate like we always have ...just with a few modifications."

"Like what?" asked Ramsey.

"Well, we won't have the run of the entire mountain ridge but we can still store the booze where we do and make the same amount of shine. We'll just have to change the trails we use to go up there and come down. But I guarantee you that the money we make from the mine will offset any inconvenience."

"How do you suppose that we are going to make money from the mine? I only see one person cashing in on this deal, and that's you if you sell that property."

"True, but we can both make money by investing in the mine."

"Hmmm. That sounds risky. I don't usually bank on what other people manage or promise."

"I am aware of that," said Jack, "but more counties are passing alcohol ordinances. The days of making money from illegal liquor are dying."

Sid hid his agitation with Jack's presumptuous attitude and pretended to agree. "You're probably right about that. I guess I'm just sentimental about the changing times. My father always said liquor tasted better when you had to hide it. So, what's my share of the land sale and per-centage of the profits from the mine? The fact that my business is affected is my investment."

Jack cleared his throat and nervously loosened his tie. "Cagle and I are still working out the deal in terms of the mine, but I should know more by the end of the week. As far as the land goes, what do you think is fair?"

"I want half."

"Half?" sputtered Jack.

"That's what I said. Half. We're 50/50 on everything else, why change now?"

Jack knew he had no choice but to agree. Otherwise, Sid could throw cold water on the deal with Cagle. "You're right. Half it is."

"Good," said Sid standing up. "I expect to hear from you by Friday about my cut from the mine. On your way out, ask Sandy to bring me a glass of water. Deal making always makes me thirsty. You look like you need a little cooling off yourself."

Cooper nodded and left the office, barely making eye contact with Sandy. "He wants a glass of water." Jack got in his car and left, not feeling like the big shot he envisioned himself to be. "I'm not going to let that spic undercut me," he said aloud. Looking in the rearview mirror, he spoke directly to his reflection. "I'll figure something out. Jack Cooper always wins."

Before Sid left, he told Sandy to find out everything he could about who in the county was in favor of the mine and who was against it. "And be careful. I trust Jack Cooper less than I ever have. If he catches wind you're working for me, I wouldn't put anything past him. He's desperate to make this deal happen. Any ideas why?"

"No, boss, I don't have any ideas, but it wouldn't surprise me if he was running low on cash. I heard his wife — who really has more money than he does — left town this weekend. Daisy said the talk is that somebody caught him cheating and told her. Word is that she's gonna kick him to the curb when she gets back. He'll have a helluva alimony bill if that happens."

"That's true. Keep me posted, Sandy, and be careful. Desperate men are dangerous."

CHAPTER Nine

Deceiving the Deceitful

Three days had passed since George drove his sister to Chattanooga to see Dr. Susan Hightower, a psychiatrist and Anita's best friend from college. She was a pioneer in the field of mental health and treated it differently. She was of the opinion that too many of her peers handed out pills to their patients without discussing the cause for their unhappiness. She believed no amount of medication could heal emotional pain.

The doctor talked honestly with her friend about what was going on, down to every sordid detail. After assuring Anita that the problem was one that could be addressed, she gave her a regimen that included a healthy diet, moderate exercise, no tobacco or alcohol, and a slow reduction of the medication she was taking. Because Anita had the desire to change her habits, Dr. Hightower told her to go home with George and start the hard work of healing.

By Monday she was better. But more importantly, she felt the relief from not being around Jack. George told his brother-in-law that she stayed in Chattanooga, when, in fact, she had been secretly recuperating at her brother's home since Saturday evening. Her father knew what was going on, and, hopefully, no one else did.

It was George's idea to give Jack free reign. A divorce —especially if the wife was seeking one—was almost impossible to get unless the suing party could prove adultery or physical abuse, and George was sure Jack would be on the prowl. While Anita was meeting with Dr. Hightower, he went to see a private investigator whom he hired to watch the

Cooper residence and follow Jack wherever he went. George told him he wanted pictures to prove infidelity.

And that didn't take long. On Tuesday morning, the investigator called and said he would have photos from the night before developed by the end of the day. Evidently, Jack had a visitor at his house, but George told him to continue the surveillance. They wanted as much ammunition as possible.

Anita thought about seeing the evidence while she was doing her exercises, but she wasn't sure she wanted to. Not because of the pain they would cause but because of the disgust she knew she'd feel. It was as if Jack Cooper was already part of a past that she wanted to forget.

The phone rang twice and stopped — a signal that George wanted to talk to her. She called him at the bank, and he immediately picked up the receiver. "Hey. I'm sure Jack will be here for the rest of the morning. He has meetings until 1. Do you want me to get Dad to stop by and take you over to your house? I heard Jack say he was heading up to the cabin at the lake as soon as he could, and I saw his suitcase in his office. So, I believe you'll have most of the day to start packing up some more of his things. I've already called the investigator and told him where to go. He's renting a place nearby the lake house and will be staked out when Jack arrives."

"Okay. Tell Dad I'll be ready in about 30 minutes."

Anita climbed in her dad's car and slumped down in the seat so she couldn't be seen. Theodore drove to the back of the house she shared with Jack to avoid the stares of any curious neighbors.

"Be careful, please," he said to Anita, "and call me as soon as you're ready to head back to George's. I'll feel better if you were only here for a little while."

"I'll be fine," said Anita. "I started cleaning out some closets last week — a premonition, I guess. Jack has so much stuff crammed in his closet that he won't miss what I'm throwing out."

Within an hour, she had filled the boxes with clothes Jack hadn't worn in 10 years and would never be able to fit in again. The outdated suits and shirts were like trophies he kept around to remind himself of his youth.

She carried everything downstairs and waited for her father to come pick her up. Surveying the surroundings, she made mental notes of the furniture she wanted to get rid of, anything that reminded her of Jack. She couldn't wait to put his recliner on the curb and break all of his favorite whiskey glasses. For now, however, it was paramount that he not suspect a thing.

"Looks like you made a lot of progress today," said Theodore as he helped her load the car.

"I did, and I can't wait to throw out the rest as soon as you serve the bastard with the papers. When will that be?"

Her dad chuckled. "Anita, I must say that alluding to him in those terms is uncharacteristic for you but quite appropriate. He'll get the papers just as soon as we've gotten all the evidence we need. According to what George told me, that could be as soon as the next couple of days. I already have the restraining order, a notice to vacate the premises, and the divorce papers ready to go. Your copies are in that envelope on the back seat. After I'm done, Jack will leave with nothing but the clothes on his back."

"Sounds like you've been ready for this day for a while."

"I have, but pulling the plug had to be your idea. It's your divorce, but we're here to support you."

"Thanks, Dad. I appreciate it so much. Is Bo okay? He said he was when I talked to him on the phone, but you never know."

"Oh, Bo is fine. It seems he and Hank have forged a friendship and have been playing football at recess. His comment was something akin to 'I didn't like that he skipped a grade, but once I got to know him, he's really cool.'"

"Cool?" laughed Anita. "Where did he get that?"

173

"Probably watching *'Leave It to Beaver'*," chuckled Theodore. "Anyway, he misses you, but y'all will be back together soon, without the real bully."

"Back to this mine business," said Anita. "What's happening with it?"

"Other than Fox, the person who knows the most at the newspaper is Lucy. She's really taken this on and is doing a fine job. Why don't you call her?"

"Okay, as soon as we're ready to deliver Jack his surprise. She and Marge stood up to him and a bunch of church ladies and helped me do what I needed to do. I want them to be the first to know I'm divorcing him."

"Honey, I want to make very sure you are ready for all of this. There's no turning back once we take Jack on."

"Oh, I am very certain," she answered. "I never knew that deceiving the deceitful could be so satisfying."

***

Jack made it easy for the private investigator who had a clear view inside the cabin, no curtains drawn and no precautions taken.

Shortly after Cooper arrived, a taxi pulled up and the same woman from the night before got out. She paid the driver, who kept his eyes straight ahead and slowly drove away.

The front door opened and out came her host, champagne, and glasses in hand. He greeted her with a kiss and a slap on the bottom, all of which the investigator photographed.

The two went inside, leaving the door wide open. After downing the entire bottle and opening another, Jack turned the radio on and motioned for his guest to dance. The investigator quickly switched to his home movie camera and filmed everything, from her slowly taking her clothes off right down to the deed done on the couch.

When Jack passed out, his companion wiggled out from under his comatose body. She stood up, half-dressed, and paused at the front door for a moment, looking out into the darkness. Since the lights were on inside, the investigator had a perfect shot, but he lowered the viewer enough to prevent filming her face. He figured she had been de-graded enough for one night.

Satisfied with the results, he quietly slipped back to his cabin, packed up and headed back to Chattanooga. The Mason men would have their proof by noon the next day.

Thursday...The Women's Club

Lucy looked in the mirror and took in the wide belt around her new silk dress one more notch. Between how busy she and Marge had been the last few days and the "love" butterflies in her stomach, her already petite waist was a little smaller.

She adjusted her stockings and put on the new leather pumps that matched her bronze-colored sheath and bolero. The skinny stiletto heel was the latest rage, and Marge insisted she get them. She said that plain, black pumps with a chunky heel just didn't do the ensemble justice, and she was right. For a second, Lucy remembered that in the past, she always styled like this. "All of the time doesn't work now, but some of the time does, especially since Hunter will be at the meeting," she said aloud.

"And to think that just last week, you wouldn't have been caught dead dressed like that or going to a club meeting with your mama," said Nettie, who was peering in her room from the hallway. "You got it bad, sistah."

"I am doing this for one reason...to save our valley and the ridge," answered Lucy indignantly.

"Uh-huh...and I'm gonna turn white tomorrow," said Nettie, walking away.

Lucy laughed, but she knew what Nettie said was true. For the last eight years she had isolated herself on the farm, swearing she would never let another man into her life. The relationship with Hank's father was a disaster.

Although it was fun at first, the sex turned everything up-side down. He told her not to worry, that he knew exactly what he was doing. And she trusted him. But when she got pregnant, her parents told her she didn't have a choice, that she had to marry him.

David's deceit and her parents' inflexibility de-stroyed her confidence. The range of emotions swung from being angry at all of them to blaming herself. And after she caught him cheating, she believed it was because she was unworthy and insufficient sexually. She blamed herself for his weakness and felt responsible for her son not having a father.

The guilt consumed her and the pain was so intense she felt like she was dying. But she was beginning to realize that her behavior sent the wrong message to Hank. If he was going to grow up to be the strong, confident person she wanted him to be, he needed to see her in the same light, and not just around the farm. He needed to see her brave enough to love, and the clock ticked along every day. Living doesn't stop when a person puts their life on pause.

The phone rang and Lucy made a beeline into the hallway before Nettie could answer it.

"Hello, Lucy. Are you free to talk?"

"Anita, I am so glad to hear from you. Are you okay? I heard you've been in Chattanooga since everything hap-pened last weekend."

"I am fine, but I'm not in Chattanooga. I've been at George's. We've had a private investigator tracking Jack, and you know as well as I do what he discovered. I've de-cided to get a divorce. I wanted you to know before he's served at the bank this afternoon."

"I'm sorry you and Bo are going through this, but I confess it's the best news I've heard in a long time. You de-serve a better life than living with that asshole."

"Speaking of Bo, I am so glad he and Hank are get-ting along. Dad told me they were playing football at recess. That's good. Bo is going to need as much normalcy as pos-sible. On another note, Dad said you were doing a good job commandeering the opposition to the mine. I'd like to hear more about what's going on."

"Well, can you come to the Women's Club meeting this afternoon? I'm going to talk about it then. After it's over, I'll fill you in on what else I've learned, which I won't share with the ladies…it's far too sensitive to proving the Ridge may not for be sale."

"I'll be there."

***

The first thing on Hunter's list that morning was to call the sheriff.

"Hello Sheriff Wilkes. This is Hunter Fox. I—"

"I know who you are, son. When ya coming by to introduce yaself?"

"I was hoping that now works," said Fox.

"I'll see you in five minutes. That's how long it will take you to walk to the jail. It's behind the courthouse." The sheriff hung up without saying goodbye, which wasn't a surprise to Hunter. A lot of folks from that generation did the same thing.

When Hunter walked into the jail, he saw Sheriff Wilkes sitting in his office, with his feet propped up on the desk. "Come in, Fox. I'd say make yourself at home, but that don't make sense when you're talking about jail, does it? Have a seat."

Hunter chuckled and extended his hand.

"I'll consider that after I hear you talk about why you're here," said the sheriff in a gruff voice, changing his tone dramatically.

"Well, I'm here to see if there is anything I need to put in this week's county police report and to ask you a few questions about the Ridge."

The sheriff took his feet down and looked through the papers on his desk. "Nothing for you so far. There ain't been any drunks passed out on the park bench, no reckless-

177

driving teenagers, or any fights on the colored side of town. That's about all we have to deal with around here. And we don't interfere with the coloreds unless it gets too noisy. That's my motto: If it ain't making noise, it ain't a problem. And the Ridge...it don't make a peep."

"I see. But once the mine cranks up—if it's approved —there will be some noise then," said Hunter in a neutral voice. "What do you think about that?"

"I'm not sure yet. It depends on what we hear next week. Things are rocking along as usual up there ...no trouble from any hunters or anybody else. Why fix something that works? I ain't too fond of change." Sheriff Wilkes had been around a long time and seen a lot of bad things happen. He had learned to choose his battles wisely, know when to put the hammer down, and when to ignore things that did no one any harm. A boring day was a good day as far as he was concerned.

"I completely understand that, but if you're interested in finding out more, there's a group of citizens and a couple of commissioners heading to the Copper Basin tomorrow to see the Cagle operation there. No better way to find out the facts than to see firsthand what goes on in one of their mines."

"You know, that sounds like a good idea. My deputy can handle things for one day. Want me to drive?"
"Sure. Between you and me, we'll have enough seats for anyone who wants to go."

The sheriff stood up and held his hand out. "For a city boy, you might be okay," he said, with a grin, "...not too uppity."

Hunter smiled and shook the old cop's hand. "And I promise not to make too much noise, unless the news is loud."

He left the sheriff's office not really sure who Wilkes really was. But there was one thing for sure: This was his county and he protected it the way he wanted. Glancing at his watch, he quickened his pace so he wouldn't be too late to the Woman's Club meeting. Slipping in quietly, he sat down in the empty back row, before anyone knew he was there — except Lucy, who was already at the podium.

Hunter listened to her give the presentation to the ladies of Willow Creek and Cantrell City, never taking his eyes off of her. Not only was she sexy as hell, but she was damn smart. In closing, she asked if there were any questions. He raised his hand.

"Go ahead, Mr. Fox," she said in a steady voice.

"This really isn't a question but an offer," he said, standing up and smiling at Lucy, knowing she knew exactly what he meant. Every head turned and every eye stared. "I have arranged for a tour of the Cagle operation about an hour north of here. If any of you are interested, either let Miss Tanner or myself know. Sheriff Wilkes and I are both taking a car. We're meeting at the Tribune office at 8:30 tomorrow morning and will be home by lunch or a little after. I promise you won't miss the Friday night football game."

He sat down and nodded at his approving and attentive audience. Lucy cleared her throat and told him thanks for the offer, slowly regaining the attention of the club members. "Now, I'll turn things over to my mother who will discuss the Christmas toy drive."

When the meeting was over, the room was buzzing. Hunter was covered up with ladies who wanted to meet him, and Anita was inundated with questions she skillfully avoided. Several women engaged Lucy about what they could do to help with the effort, and Gen watched her daughter handle it all with finesse. When the two of them walked out of the club house, Anita was chatting with Marge and Hunter.

"You did an excellent job, Lucy," said Hunter. "I know you're proud Mrs. Tanner. When strong women decide to take something on, look out. I'd hate to be in Dan Cagle's shoes with this bunch nipping at my heels." He slightly bowed to Gen and turned his attention back to Lucy. "I have to run now though...talk later?" he asked, giving her hand a gentle squeeze.

Feeling quite weak-kneed, Lucy nodded and smiled. "Sure."

"I do believe Mr. Fox is interested in more than your speaking abilities," said Anita.

"Oh, he is," said Marge. "He couldn't..."

"Oh, stop. We have more important things to discuss than Hunter's intentions. Mama, you can go on home if you want. I need to tell Anita what I couldn't tell the ladies. Marge, can you give me a ride?"

"Of course."

"Let's all go to my house," said Anita. "It doesn't matter if Jack knows I'm there, because he's about to find out that he doesn't live with me anymore. And it is my house. Y'all need to be gone before 5, though. Things could get a little dicey when he's served."

***

There were as many lawyers in Chattanooga as there were churches, but Sid Ramsey's favorite was Skip Jones. He kept a low profile, and discretion was his long suit.

Jones looked at the note his secretary had put on his desk a few days prior about calling Jack Cooper. It was the end of the week, and he knew he had kept him waiting long enough. He called Ramsey's private number and Sid answered.

"Skip, if you're calling me, it can't be good. What's up? Is somebody suing me?"

"No, but Jack Cooper called me about doing some deed work for him, and I haven't gotten back with him yet. You said never to do anything he asked without clearing it with you first."

Sid Ramsey kept a tight rein on his businesses. He paid his bills and had the reputation for being honest, even though he made a living breaking the law. People close to him were loyal to him, and he, in turn, was good to them.

He also had a penchant for thinking ahead and knew it was just a matter of time before alcohol would be legal in more places than not. He already had a plan in place that would allow him to step right in and be one of the largest distillers and distributors in the Southeast.

Being successful for him had more to do with respect than money. He was already very wealthy. Having a reputation for producing quality products that people wanted is what he wished to achieve. And scum like Jack Cooper had no place in his scheme.

His father used the Coopers. Sid knew that but he felt no guilt whatsoever. They were paid handsomely for making and supplying moonshine, but the time had come to cut the ties. He simply didn't need a Cooper anymore.

"Huh, I'm not surprised. He's up to no good, but if he wants to carry out this ruse, he'll have to do it without my help or anyone who works for me. Call him back and tell him your caseload is too much to take on another job right now. Let him figure it out on his own."

"Done," said Jones.

***

Jack had a headache from drinking too much the night before and wanted to go back to the lake, but he had one more call to make.

"Skip Jones, here," said the voice on the other end of the line.

"Hey, Skip. Where you been? I expected to hear from you by now. It's already Thursday."

"Actually, I was just about to give you a call. I can't take on another case right now—I'm completely covered up."

"What the hell?" barked Jack. "Do I need to call Ramsey?"

"I'm not sure what he has to do with this, but..."

"Oh, fuck it," snarled Jack, slamming down the receiver. He closed his eyes and put his face in his hands. His heart pounded and the noise in his head was deafening. *This damn deal has to go through,* he thought. *I'm in debt and can't dip into the bank's reserves anymore without raising alarms. The line of credit I got from Sid includes a mortgage on my home, the title to my car, and my stock in the bank as collateral. Without the cash from the sale of the land, I could lose everything. Shit. Shit. Shit. I could lose everything. No, that ain't gonna happen because I'm not going to fucking let it happen.*

He called the tax office at the courthouse and Miss Hargett answered.

"Is anyone in your office?"

"No. I'm alone. Why?" Hilda asked nervously.

"I need you to come up with a deed for the Ridge," he said, the sweat pouring down his face.

"What did you say?"

"You heard me, goddamn it."

"How do you expect me to do that, Mr. Cooper?" she asked, her voice shaking.

"I don't give a fuck how you do it but know this and know it right now. Get it done by tomorrow or you might not have a job. How are your cats doing by the way? I don't like cats very much. I used them for target practice when I was a kid. Now, draw up a goddamn deed and a transfer of ownership from my grandfather, John Jackson Cooper Sr., to my father, John Jackson Cooper Jr. Date it 1920, and make it look real. And don't say a fucking word about this to anyone. Do you understand?"

He hung up without waiting for an answer and opened the bottom drawer of his desk, but a knock on the door interrupted his vodka time.

"Yeah, come in," he snapped, expecting to see George. "Hello, Jack," said Sheriff Wilkes. "You okay? Ya don't look so good. I hate to make it worse, but I have some papers for you."

"What kind of papers? Let me see."

"Sign here first," said the sheriff.

Jack scribbled his name and opened the manila envelope, his hands still shaking as he took out the documents.

What the hell could happen now, he thought. He read the first sentence and felt like he was suffocating.

> *You are hereby given a notice of divorce proceedings filed by Mrs. Anita Mason Cooper. In addition, you will find a notice to vacate the premises shared by you and the plaintiff and a restraining order prohibiting you from getting in touch with or going near said plaintiff and your juvenile son, John Jackson Cooper, IV.*
> *Your copies of all of the appropriate papers are enclosed. Failure to comply with any of these orders will result in your arrest and confinement in the county jail."*
> *Theodore Mason, Esquire.*

"Jesus, she can't do this." Jack's face turned purple with anger. He stared at the documents and threw them on his desk. "Wait until I get my hands on that bitch. I'll—"

"Jack, you need to listen and listen good," said the sheriff. "This ain't a game. If you're smart, you'll go by the house with me right now, get your things from the front porch, and take your ass up to the lake. And don't do anything stupid like getting drunk and showing up at Miss Anita's banging on the door like an idiot. If you do, I'll arrest you. Got it? And, Jack, you ain't got no business with a damn gun in your drawer either. Leave that here."

"Goddamn it, but I promise—"

"You need to shut the fuck up and do as I say."

When Jack turned on Ivy Street, with Sheriff Wilkes close behind, Marge and Lucy were just pulling up to the stop sign. He made eye contact with them, thought about running into them head on, but yelled out the window. "Fucking women. Y'all need to go back to your goddamn club meeting."

The two women looked straight ahead and didn't say a word.

***

The telephone repair truck was parked in front of the Tanner home when Marge and Lucy pulled in the driveway. Hank was in the front yard tossing sticks for the dog, Jenny. "Hey, y'all," he said, as he ran to meet them, with Jenny on his heels. "I sure like your car, Miss Marge. Does it go fast?"

"If you want it to," she laughed, "but I usually stick to the speed limit."

"As you will when you start driving young man. Thanks for the ride," said Lucy, waving goodbye. "I'll see you in the morning." She put her arm around Hank as they walked toward the house. "Are we having trouble with the phone lines?"

"No m'am. It's a surprise." Hank felt all grown up, being in on the secret.

The phone man was coming down the hall when Lucy opened the front door. "Everything is up and running just fine," he said.

"What's up and running?" asked Lucy.

"Come to your room and see," said Hank. He ran ahead and opened the door. "Look."

There on Lucy's bedside table was a brand-new phone, one of the modern trimline styles in light blue.

Lucy gasped. "What...whose idea was this?"

"Mine," said Gen. Lucy turned around to see her mother standing there, smiling. "You need to be able to talk without everyone in the house listening." Gen's constant impatience with Lucy stemmed from her concern for her daughter. She had watched Lucy build a wall around her feelings and deny herself any interaction with another person outside of the immediate family. When a child hurts, a mother hurts, often deeper. Gen wanted Lucy to heal, and she believed Hunter was a good start.

"Mama, thank you so much. Was it expensive?"

"More expensive than it was worth," said Luke as he slammed the kitchen door and went in the backyard.

"Why must he act like that?" said Gen, looking as though she was about to cry.

Before Lucy could say anything, Hank left the room and followed his grandfather outside.

"Granddaddy, don't say mean things to Mama and Grandmama Gen. You sound like Jack Cooper. Why are you mad all the time now?"

"Because I don't like change, and your mama has turned on a dime."

"She hasn't done anything but make some new friends. Bo called me a bastard, so I could really be mad at him. But he told me he was sorry, and that he knew his dad was wrong. Now we're friends. But you say something mean to Mama every day. That's wrong, Granddaddy."

Luke watched his grandson run around the house, calling for Jenny. He knew the boy was right. He'd been a real ass.

At suppertime, Luke asked Hank to say the blessing, who ended with, "and please help my family be happy like it used to be. Amen."

Luke cleared his throat. "I owe everyone an apology —especially you, Lulu. There's no excuse…only reasons. To think that I could or should keep you from doing what you want is wrong of me. I'm just so grateful to have you here again and never want it to change—unless, of course, that's something you want. It's just hard for old men to adjust, but I promise that I will do better. Protecting my family is my job, but maybe I take it a little too far. Hank, thanks for setting your ol' granddaddy straight."

"You're welcome," said Hank, "…anytime."

***

Lucy's phone rang right on time at 8:30. She told Hunter about her dad's apology and her mama's surprise. "Do I sound different? She got one of the new style phones."

Hunter laughed. "No. You sound the same—Southern and sexy."

185

"Oh, stop it," said Lucy, loving every bit of his flirting and wanting him to do anything but stop. "And guess what? Anita is divorcing Jack. They hired a private investigator who has pictures of his shenanigans this week. Evidently, he's been busy. Plus, I finally figured out where the journal came from. Anita found it when she started cleaning out Cooper's closet last week and getting rid of his shit. That means it has been in his family's possession. All this time. He knows he doesn't own that damn property."

"Damn...talk about walking into a beehive. I've been in Kings County less than a week, and things are turned up-side down. We have a major rezoning issue, the little bully who thinks he's a big man is about to find out that judges don't play his game, and I am smitten with you. I love the pace. How about you?"

Ignoring Hunter's comment about his feelings, Lucy dove into the business at hand. "Well, I'd like it better if we could find what we need. The hearing is the week after next. That doesn't give us much time. I know you said we needed to wait until after those meetings next week before we get signatures on the petition, but Marge and I have already got-ten about 50 between us."

"Go ahead and do what you can. Just save some time for me this weekend, okay? Didn't you hear me say I was smitten?"

"I did. But are you sure you're not just in-fatu-ated...you know, trying to relive your days as a college guy?"

"No, not at all. I'm a grown man who likes you. Period."

"Well, I'll consider a date if you behave yourself to-morrow. Dancy Riley called and wants to go to the Copper Ba-sin, and I'm quite certain her motive is not her interest in learning about Cagle Mining. She loves to spread stuff she knows isn't true and is hurtful. I know. She's tried to cut my throat a few times. I can't stand the bitch."

"Lucy, I'm shocked at your language."

"No, you aren't. And you know exactly what she was doing at the club this afternoon—batting those fake eye lashes at you and acting so coy. She's a married woman for god's sake."

"That is completely your imagination at work."

"And you, Mr. Fox, are obviously playing the innocent, but that doesn't work with me...which is why we get along. I'm not going to bullshit you, and you better not try anything with me—unless I want you to." Lucy lowered her voice almost to a whisper. "And so far, the things you've tried I like. I'll see you in the morning."

"Whatever you say, Miss Tanner. Whatever you say. Sweet dreams and good night."

Lucy hung up the phone and hugged her pillow close. *No problem with those dreams,* she thought.

CHAPTER Ten

Friday

Lucy hurried back to the house after putting Hank on the bus. The mantle clock chimed seven times, which meant she had an hour to get ready. She quickly straightened up Hank's room, made her bed, and chose another new outfit for the trip to the Copper Basin. She could hear her mother and Nettie in the kitchen, planning the day and deciding what to do first. After putting on the black and white, gingham-checked pants that hugged her ankles, a white sleeveless shirt and short black jacket, she opened her door and walked down the hall.

"Do y'all think this looks okay?" Lucy asked.

"Oh, Lucy. You look like a teenager," said Gen, smiling.

"Looks real good to me," said Nettie, "especially those bare feet."

"Oh, for heaven's sake, let me go put on the new shoes I bought." She went back to her room and took the red leather flats out of the box. She slipped her feet into them and went back into the kitchen.

"Red shoes, huh?" asked Nettie. "Aren't you the saucy one?"

"This has nothing to do with sauce and everything with looking professional," said Lucy, knowing full well she was telling a white lie.

"Well, it works," said Gen.

Lucy grabbed her purse and walked to the front of the house. Luke was standing on the front porch and turned around when Lucy opened the door. "Lulu, you sure look nice."

"And you're mighty dressed up for farm work, aren't you?"

"I'm going with you," answered Luke. "We'll take the truck, so your mama has the car here."

Lucy put her arms around her father's neck and gave him a hug. "Thank you, Daddy. Thank you so much."

Gen watched her daughter and husband out the bedroom window and sighed with relief. "Nettie, this is a good end to a hard week, but I've always loved Fridays."

***

Sheriff Wilkes and Hunter were in front of the newspaper office when Lucy and Luke got there. Lucy seethed when she saw that Dancy was sitting in the front seat of the *Tribune* company car, but she didn't let on how perturbed she was.

Luke got in the sheriff's car, but Lucy chose to ride with the Masons. She was afraid she'd throw up if she had to watch Dancy making a fool of herself.

They were just about to leave when Nate Johnson drove up. Lucy rolled down the window. "Hey, Nate. Are you going with us?"

"I sure am—if you have room."

Sheriff Wilkes nodded at Nate. "Here. Ride with us. Charlie can sit in the back seat. You ride up front with me. You need the leg room. No offense, Tater."

Nate chuckled. "This is a sight now. A black man in the front seat with the sheriff, and I'm not even under arrest."

Hunter got out of his car quickly. "I want a photo of this," he said.

***

Hilda Hargett got to her office at the courthouse before the doors opened to the public. It was Friday, and she'd probably be busy later—no time to waste.

She slept very little the night before. Jack Cooper's threatening voice played over and over in her head. She was terrified of what he could do, and she knew he meant every word he said. Hilda wished she knew how to break out of the prison in which so many before her had served life sentences because of the Cooper family.

Her hands shook nervously as she unlocked the records room. She quickly went through the old deeds and found one that had an extra piece of paper with the county seal on it. After verifying the coordinates for the ridge, she sat down at the desk where the first typewriter ever used at the courthouse was on display. Putting the piece of yellowed paper in it, she typed out what looked and read very official. Since the keys stuck and the ribbon was old, the document appeared authentic.

When she was done, she put the fake deed in the appropriate file and called Jack Cooper at the bank.

"It's done," she said.

"Good. You still have a job," barked Jack.

She hung up the phone, hating what she had done but detesting him even more.

***

The visitors to the Copper Basin saw all they needed to see in a couple of hours. The land was stripped and barren. Dan Cagle attempted to whitewash the scene, saying they mined there before the strict federal oversights were in place. But the Kings County contingency was not impressed. Hunter took photos the entire time, and the others pummeled Cagle with questions. It was not a particularly warm day, but he sweated profusely.

After leaving the mining site, the group went to the nearest town for lunch. When Hunter questioned the owner about the Cagle operation, he spared no words. "It's never brought anything here but dust, noise, and runoff to the creeks. They bragged about how it was going to make business better, but that was a lie. Those folks who work up there just make enough to feed their families. I'm glad for them, but it ain't done nothing for the town. There's a rumor going around that the federal government is about to shut them down. That's probably why they want to come to your neck of the woods."

Hunter was writing the entire time the man talked, who stopped and looked at him. "You a newspaper man?" he asked.

"I am," answered Hunter.

"Well, don't put my name in there. I don't need no trouble from Dan Cagle."

"Deal," said Hunter.

When Lucy finished eating, she excused herself to wash her hands and hurried outside. She climbed in the front seat of Hunter's car and smiled at Dancy, who rolled her eyes and got in the back seat next to Marge.

"You don't mind if I sit up here, do you, Dancy?" asked Lucy, not turning around. "Back seats make me car sick."

***

When the caravan made it back to Cantrell City, Jack Cooper was just coming out of the newspaper office.

"Well, well...just in time, Fox. The deed is filed and at the courthouse...y'all coming to the game tonight? It ought to be a good one." He walked away without waiting for an answer from anyone.

Lucy looked at Hunter. "Well, I guess I better get to the courthouse and check that out," he said. "Anyway, thanks to everyone for coming along today. This is your home, and you should decide what's best for it."

Theodore motioned to Hunter, who walked over to his car and leaned down to look in the window. "I have known the Coopers for a long time," he said. "You can't

191

trust when they say what day it is. George, I want to go with Hunter. You two go ahead."

"Okay," said Hunter, "but let me check in with Pete before we head over there. You're welcome to wait inside." He turned and walked to where Lucy and Marge were.

"Dad had to get back," said Lucy, "but Marge and I are going to visit a few merchants before we leave town. Will you get a copy of whatever Jack filed? I would love to see it."

"I will. Why don't you meet me back here in about 30 minutes?" answered Hunter.

Theodore and Hunter walked to the courthouse and climbed the wide stairs up to the second floor. When they walked into the tax office, Hilda Hargett looked up from her desk and nervously cleared her throat. "May I help you?"

"Hello, Hilda," said Theodore. "I trust you are well."

She tried to avoid eye contact, but his grey eyes were sharp as a knife and made the woman exhale before answering. "Yes, I am, Theodore. What can I do for you?" she answered, as if she didn't know.

"We would like to see the deed for the ridge property. Jack Cooper told us it had been filed."

The clerk stood up and opened a cabinet behind her desk. She took out a folder and handed it to Theodore, who gave it to Hunter, never averting his stare from Hilda.

"May we go in the archive room to look at this?" Theodore asked. "And, of course, we'll want a couple of copies. So warm up that mimeograph machine."

***

"Something's not right here," said Theodore, as he and Hunter left the courthouse. "Hilda was not herself. The deed looked okay, but I have my suspicions."

The town was busy and many of the folks they met stopped them to talk about the mine. Every comment was negative, and the concerns far outweighed positive opinions.

People were aware of the problems that mining created in Tennessee and Alabama. They knew that entire towns had been swallowed up by the companies and left with little to show but devastation after the resources were gutted. No one wanted to see that happen here.

Both men retained their quiet objectivity and encouraged people to attend one or both of the public hearings and to read the story in Sunday's paper about the visit to the mine in the Copper Basin.

When they got to the *Tribune* building, Lucy and Marge were waiting in the conference room.

"So, let us see it," said Lucy.

Hunter put the file on the table and opened it. "There it is. It looks real, and without proof that it isn't, we have a problem."

Lucy looked at Theodore. "What do you think, Mr. Mason?" she asked him.

"Well, unfortunately, we don't have the evidence to refute Jack's deed."

"But what about the diary Anita found?" asked Lucy.

"That's nothing without concrete proof. The opposition would call it a fairytale. For now, keep collecting all the signatures you can on that petition and make sure there is vocal turnout at the meetings next week," said Theodore. "By the way, have we heard back from the environmental expert yet?"

"He's supposed to call me Monday afternoon," said Lucy. "I'm hoping he will drive here from Atlanta to survey the location and give us his assessment."

Hunter glanced at his watch. "Y'all are welcome to keep talking, but I have to excuse myself—time to get tomorrow's paper done except for the sports page."

"We need to head back, too," said Lucy. "...school bus time."

"We'll give you a ride, Mr. Mason," said Marge.

"Lucky me," said Theodore, winking at Hunter.

"Hello…the Lodge. This is Sandy," the bartender said into the receiver.

"Is anyone around?" asked Sid.

"Nope. The Friday night fools aren't here yet."

"Good. So, tell me how the mine thing is going."

"It's heating up, Sid. I mean it's really heating up. Daisy got a job at the beauty shop and said she overheard a couple of ladies saying their husbands thought it would be good for business…seems Jack has a problem, though. The last article in the paper said there was no deed filed at the courthouse."

"Yeah, I read that," said Sid, not letting on he knew what Cooper was up to.

Before Sid could say anything else, Jack came in the side door, interrupting the call. "It's time to celebrate, Sandy. I got that damn deed filed today. Those mother fuckers are dead in the water. I don't care how many signatures that little bitch, Lucy Tanner, gets on her fucking petition. I'm selling that land and gonna make some money. I don't need Theodore and his piss ant of a daughter. I'll have my own fortune. Now pour me a stiff drink."

Sandy started to say something but Sid whispered, "I heard the bastard. Call me after he stumbles away."

Jack threw back a couple of shots. "I'll see you after the game…think I'll get a room at the Gold Star tonight …don't feel like driving back and forth to the cabin. Too bad that fucking divorce isn't final. I'd love to have a couple of cheerleaders join me." Jack laughed at his own joke, but Sandy just nodded his head and pretended to agree.

"How about putting a bottle or two in a bag for me?" Jack asked. I want to be drunk when I see that bitch who tricked me into marrying her frigid ass. By the way, where's your piece? I hadn't seen her around all week."

"Kittsee hired her. She wants to get her hair-cuttin' license so she can have her own shop. I'm gonna build her one at the house, so she can work from home. That way, we can have a baby or two." Sandy didn't let on the real reason Daisy quit working at The Lodge nor how much he hated Jack.

"Jesus, I thought you were smarter than that," said Jack, as he burped and left without saying goodbye.

When Sandy was sure Jack was gone, he picked up the phone and called Sid, who answered immediately.

"Hey, Sandy...yeah, I heard what he said. His worst enemy is himself and that incessantly moving mouth of his. My mother always said the biggest fools are the ones who don't realize they are foolish. That description fits Cooper perfectly. He thinks he's smart but he's an idiot. So, who is this Lucy Tanner he referred to? Since he doesn't like her, she must be smart."

"The Tanners own a farm on the Valley Road. Her family has been there since before the Civil War. She's sort of leading the fight against the mine—you know, getting folks to sign a petition."

"Hmmm...maybe she and I should put our heads together. I do have a vested interest in seeing the Ridge stay the same—purely sentimental, you know. How about looking up her telephone number for me?"

"Sure, said Sandy. "Let's see...Luke Tanner...Valley-8643."

"Thanks, now sell as much booze as you can tonight."

***

The school bus was leaving when Marge pulled in the driveway. "Call me if you and Hank want to go to the game with Billy Joe and me," she said. "Otherwise, I'll look to hear from you tomorrow."

Lucy waved goodbye and greeted Hank with a hug.

"Are you as happy it's Friday as I am?" he asked.

"Almost," laughed Lucy.

Gen opened the front door and called to her daughter. "The phone's for you."

Lucy hurried inside, with Hank close behind. "Hello?" she said, expecting a call from one of the merchants she had left her phone number with earlier.

"Is this Miss Tanner?"

"Yes. This is Lucy Tanner. And who is calling please?"

"Sid Ramsey in Chattanooga. I own the Chattanooga Food Company and often drive through Kings County on my way to Florida. I even take the *Tribune*. My family has done business there for a very long time."

"Hello, Mr. Ramsey. But why are you calling me? We grow groceries. We don't buy them."

Sid laughed at her quick response. "Actually, I am calling you in regards to the proposed mine there. I'd hate to see that happen. That is some of the prettiest land in North Georgia. I read you were organizing an effort to fight it and was hoping we could meet next week. I may be able to offer some advice and help."

"Oh, certainly. We need all we can get. Would Monday work? What time and where?"

"Let's say 10 in the morning at my office in Chattanooga. The address is 1300 Water Street. I have a tight schedule, but I would like to discuss this. Just go to the lobby on the first floor and give your name to the girl at the desk."

"Okay, Mr. Ramsey. I'll see you then."

"Good, Lucy. And please call me Sid."

Lucy hung up the phone and stared at it. She realized she had just agreed to go to Chattanooga and meet with a man she didn't know. But there was something about his voice that made her believe he meant what he said. The phone rang again, startling her. "Hello?"

"Hey," said Hunter. "Were you sitting on top of the receiver?"

"No," laughed Lucy, "I just had the craziest phone call from Chattanooga. It seems—"

"Why don't you tell me on the way to the game?" interrupted Hunter.

"What game?" Lucy asked, distracted by the previous call.

"Lucy…the Kings County High football game. I want to take you and Hank. I'll have to take pictures and do a couple of interviews, but it will still be fun. I'll be there to pick y'all up in an hour."

"Okay. That sounds great. Hank will love it. See you then."

"I'll love what?" her son asked, tugging at her sleeve.

"Going to the football game with Hunter," said Lucy.

"Really, Mama?"

"Yes, really. I'll put some clean clothes out on your bed. You'll need to wash that nasty face, too."

***

The high school football field was the place to be on a Friday night. The Kings County Wild Cats were usually one of the top teams in the state in their class, and this year promised to be one of the best ever, with the state championship clearly within reach. Last year's team came in second statewide, and the entire first string returned for their senior year. The local heroes in these parts were the high school football players. The little kids idolized them and put them on a pedestal. Business owners gave them gifts and favors. And tonight, the stands were full, and the noise was deafening.

"I'll grab something for us to eat, while you two find a seat," Hunter whispered in Lucy's ear, making sure his lips brushed against her cheek.

"Mama, I see Miss Marge and Billy Joe down toward the front," shouted Hank. "Let's go sit next to them."

"You got that?" said Lucy to Hunter, who gave a thumbs up.

Hank traversed the bleachers with the nimbleness of a goat and waved at Billy Joe and Marge, who looked toward Lucy and motioned for her to join them. Within a couple of minutes, Hunter came down the aisle, carrying a box full of food.

When the teams finished warming up, Hunter gulped down the last bit of his hot dog and stood up. "Time for me to start taking some photos. Hank, do you want to go down on the sideline with me until the game starts?"

"Mama, can I?"

"Sure, son."

"I'll bring him back before kickoff," said Hunter, giving Lucy's shoulder a squeeze. She knew curious eyes were taking it all in, and she didn't care because she loved it.

"Marge filled me in on the trip today," said Billy Joe, "and Jack Cooper's welcome home surprise."

"Yep...not what we wanted to hear from him," said Lucy, "but I got a phone call today that might change things for ol' Jack. Sid Ramsey, who owns Chattanooga Grocery Company, asked me to come visit him at his office. He said he thought he could help us. I'm driving up Monday."

"Sid Ramsey?" asked Marge, her eyes wide open.

"Yeah, why?"

"Honey, he is one of the richest men in Chattanooga, single, and very good-looking. Does Hunter know about this?"

"I haven't had time to tell him, but why should it matter? It isn't a date, and Hunter doesn't have a claim on me."

Billy Joe looked sideways at Lucy and grinned. "Keep telling yourself that, Lucy."

She waved him off but looked down at the field and saw Hunter leaning down and letting Hank look through the view finder on his camera. That man felt so right it terrified her. She heard someone calling her name, looked up and saw Anita walking down the aisle toward them.

"Anita, what a surprise," Lucy said. "Is Bo with you?"

"He is, but he saw Hank on the sidelines and ran down there. The game is about to start, though, and it looks like Hunter is bringing them back up here. Are you two conducting business tonight, Lucy?" she asked, with a grin and a wink.

The Wild Cats kicked off, forced a fumble and scored within the first minute. It looked like it was going to be a long night for the visiting team. By halftime, the score was 35-0. Hunter came back to where Lucy was sitting, while the boys went to the open area next to the playing field with a flock of other kids, who were choosing sides for a quick game of their own.

"You know, that happens at every high school game in the country I bet," said Hunter. "Look at Hank go. Damn, Lucy, he's a natural."

Suddenly Anita gasped. "Oh, no. There's Jack. I can tell he's drunk and he's heading toward the boys." She started to stand up, but Hunter stopped her.

"Don't worry. There's Sheriff Wilkes cutting him off at the pass."

Jack didn't stand a chance. Before any of the kids saw him, the sheriff had grabbed his arm and practically lifted him off his feet, escorting him away from the crowd. They disappeared into the parking lot, and Anita let out a sigh.

Lucy reached over and patted her hand. "Hey...it's gonna be okay."

***

The final score was 63-6. Hunter took pictures of the entire team, with as many of the kids he could round up. Hank and Bo ran up the steps toward Lucy and Anita, with Hunter close behind.

"I am so glad those two are getting along," said Anita. "Hank is a good influence on Bo."

The boys' faces were red and sweating from playing more football than they watched.

"Looks like you two had a grand time," said Anita.

"Oh, we did, Mama," said Bo. "When can we play again?"

"Well, we're going to your grandparents' house tomorrow and spending the night. Grandpa Teddy is going to take you

199

fishing and let you swing a golf club or two. Why don't we take Hank? We'll bring him to church on Sunday."

"Please, Mama," begged Hank.

"Sure," said Lucy. "That sounds like fun."
"Why don't you drop him off at the house around 10?" said Anita.

"Okay, see you then," answered Lucy.

The boys waved goodbye to one another and Hunter smiled. He liked the sound of that plan. It meant Lucy was free to be with him. "All right you two…time for y'all to see firsthand what it takes to get a newspaper on the presses," he said. "Let's get some ice cream and go see Pete."

"I can't believe it," said Hank. "This has been the best day of my life, and tomorrow will be even better.

After Hunter started processing the film, he told Pete he'd help finish up after taking Lucy and Hank home. "I'll be back in about an hour. The photos should be done by then and we can get this baby on the presses. Folks are gonna love all the shots of the crowd, especially those of the kids."

***

By the time they had driven less than a mile out of Cantrell City, Lucy realized it was very quiet. She looked in the back seat and saw Hank fast asleep.

"Hunter, thanks so much. He had a blast."

"Of course, but I'm the one who should thank you." He stretched out his arm on the back of the seat and pulled her toward him. "And. If you're free tomorrow, as I know you are, why don't we see each other again? We can christen my new home with dinner and a good bottle of wine. How does that sound?"

"Wonderful. What time?"

"I'm going to take some photos in Cantrell City and Willow Creek first thing in the morning and meet the movers at my house around one o'clock. Why don't I pick you up when I'm done with them? Say around 4?"

"Okay, but do you want some help tomorrow afternoon?" asked Lucy in a seductive voice. "I'd love to if you're interested."

"Hell yeah, I'm interested. I'll pick you up at noon."

She leaned her head against his shoulder and watched the landscape through the window. Everything that was familiar felt so incredibly new. And everything new felt so incredibly familiar.

When they pulled up in front of Lucy's home, she chuckled. "Looks like Luke Tanner is warming up to you. I know that because he left the light on."

Hunter opened the car door and picked Hank up. The boy never stirred, even when they put him in his bed and Lucy took his shoes off. Hunter watched as she pulled the covers over him and kissed his forehead. The things in life he thought he could never embrace suddenly were right in front of him, and he wanted to wrap his arms around it all.

"So, I'll see you tomorrow at noon?" Hunter whispered when they walked out on the porch.

"Yes. You will." She put her arms around him and kissed him, feeling the tremors in her body and his. He picked her up gently and held her close, his eyes melting her heart.

"I can't wait," he answered, as he let her slide gently down until their bodies found that place where the fit was perfect.

Saturday

Lucy dropped Hank off at Anita's and drove over to the McDaniel's. She knocked on the screen door and heard Marge calling from upstairs. "Come on in...I'm up here." It was quiet in the house, except for the sound of the radio coming from Marge's room. Lucy ran up the stairs and found her friend painting her toenails and sipping on a Coke.

"You look exactly like you did when we were in high school," laughed Lucy. "Are you and Billy Joe going out tonight?"

"Better than that. We're going away to Chattanooga for the night."

"Really? What are you telling your parents?"

"That I'm going away for the night. We have an understanding now. They don't ask and I don't tell. But I don't think I'm going to be single too long. Billy Joe is building that house faster than Noah did his ark. And as soon as it's ready, we're getting married."

"Marge, that's wonderful. Has he already proposed?"

"Yep, and neither one of us want to wait. We know it's right."

"Speaking of waiting, that's why I'm here," said Lucy. "Do y'all, I mean…you know…."

"You mean do we have sex?" asked Marge. "Yeah, of course."

"What do you use for birth control?"

"He doesn't come in me," said Marge matter-of-factly. "Of course, they say an errant sperm can still find its way to an egg, but that's the chance you take. You forget I lived in Chattanooga when the war ended. I heard other girls talk more than I actually did anything, but I was engaged and had a fling or two. But, hey, you're the one who had a husband. What did you use then?"

"I know all about errant sperms. I was a virgin when I met Hank's dad and not prepared for what I was getting into. I knew nothing about birth control. When I told him that we should be careful since I wasn't protected, he told me not to worry…that he was a pro. Shit, I should have known then what a dog he was. I did get pregnant though, and we had to get married. You know there wasn't and still isn't a choice for women. Men get to do whatever they choose and say, 'Oh well', and we're left to deal with it…which is what he did. I have to admit that I was relieved when I caught him cheating though. His touch me made me sick. He only cared about two things: getting laid the way he wanted and when he wanted it."

"Does Hunter know about all of this?"

"Oh, no. Not yet. We're just in the kissing stage, but Hank is spending the night with Bo, and Hunter asked me to come to his house for supper. He's moving in today. Marge, I'm scared as hell of intimacy, but when it comes to having sex with Hunter, I'm anything but nervous. It feels so good to feel that way."

"It's okay, Lucy," said Marge. "Times are changing, and women are starting to do what men have been doing all along."

"I know, but my track record is pretty bad."

"Hey...Hunter is crazy about you. He's not going to ask you to do anything you don't want to do. Just enjoy yourself, but tell him you are very fertile and not on birth control. That will make him pull the reins in and put a cover on his 'Hi Ho Silver.'"

***

Lucy called the Tribune office around 11 and Hunter answered. "Hello, Kings County Tribune."

"Hey, it's me."

"Hello, me. Don't tell me you're calling to break our date."

"Oh no, not at all. I was calling to see if you wanted to eat some lunch with us. Mama fixed spaghetti last night, and there's a lot left over."

"I never turn down a home-cooked meal. I'll be there in 30 minutes. We're almost done laying out tomorrow's paper."

***

When Hunter got to the Tanner home, Gen had lunch ready to serve. Luke was very cordial, and Lucy was beyond relieved. When the plates were empty, she stood up and started clearing the dishes. "I'll do that, Lulu," said Luke. "Y'all need to get going if you're going to make it to Cantrell City by 1. Hunter, we enjoyed having you. Come again when you can." He shook hands with Hunter and gave Lucy a hug. "Be careful now. That's a mighty sporty car you have, and even though she's all grown up, she's the only little girl I have."

"I will," said Hunter. "Thanks for that delicious meal, Mrs. Tanner. I've been living off sandwiches and coffee for the last week."

"Lulu?" asked Hunter with a smile when they got in his car and pulled out of the driveway.

"Damn it. I knew as soon as Daddy said that, your antennae went up. Yes. Lulu. He has called me that since I was a little girl, because he knows it makes me mad."

"Why does it make you mad?"

"Because it isn't my name, and it sounded babyish. I had a hard enough time with Billy Joe and his brothers teasing me, and being called Lulu only made it worse."

"Well, I think it's precious, just like you." He pulled off the road, leaned over, and gave her a kiss. "By the way, I like those khaki britches you have on...reminds me of when you took me up on the Ridge."

***

The movers were right on time. While Hunter was directing where to put everything, Lucy went to the main house to speak to Miss Angela Mason...no reason for conjecture. She was there to help an old friend from college unpack...nothing more.

Theodore's sister was as clever as her brother. However, she knew the young women of today were cut from a different cloth—something she admired. Her generation allowed the world and the men who ran it to keep them on a string. Of course, Angela Mason was not one of them. She had been active in the National Union of Women's Societies and applauded any woman who stood up for herself.

Within an hour, the movers had left and the furniture was in place. While Hunter set up his stereo, Lucy started unpacking boxes in the kitchen. "Where do you want me to put these plates and bowls?" she called out.

"Wherever you think they need to go," answered Hunter.

She stood on the small step stool so she could reach the higher shelves. The sound of a record dropping onto the turntable got her attention, and Sam Cooke's honey-laden voice cut the silence: *Darling, you-ou-ou send me. I know you-ou-ou send me. Darling, you-ou-ou send me, honest you do, honest you do, honest you do, whoa-oh-oh...*

Hunter walked into the kitchen and lifted her off the stool, holding her close and swaying in perfect time with the music. They danced without saying a word until the song ended. Lucy looked up at Hunter and whispered, "I'm thirsty."

"Well, then, how about a cold beer?" Hunter asked, opening the refrigerator door.

"Billy Joe must have gotten you a supply when he went to Atlanta last week," Lucy commented.

"Yep, and some wine, too. I don't care if you get tipsy."

"Why? So, you can take advantage of me?"

"No. So *you* can take advantage of me."

By five, they were done and the empty boxes were stacked outside. Hunter's furniture blended well with those pieces already in the small house, and the rugs he added warmed up the hardwood floors nicely. He had an extensive collection of books that filled the built-in shelves, along with an assortment of framed photographs. Lucy picked up one of what she assumed was Hunter's family. "How old were you in this?"

"I was about 20 I think. Those are my parents and my sister."

"Is that your home? Geez, it's a mansion."

"Yeah, it is. I come from a long line of successful lawyers and doctors. The fact that I chose journalism as a profession was always a disappointment to my father. He tried not to let on, but I knew."

"Do they still live there in Virginia?"

"No. They were killed in an automobile accident a couple of years ago. The state troopers said black ice was the cause. My sister and her family live in the house now."

"Oh, Hunter, I'm sorry. I didn't mean to…"

"Hey, it's okay. I want you to know all about me. As soon as we get this mine thing settled and catch a break, we should go up there. I'd like for you to meet what's left of my family."

They had just sat down on the couch and opened another beer when someone knocked on the door.

"That must be Jimmy," said Hunter. "I asked him to bring some dinner over from the hotel when he got off work."

"Hello, Hunter. Here's your food. Oh, hi, Lucy."

"Hey, Jimmy."

Hunter came back from putting the food in the kitchen. He reached in his pocket and took out some money. "Keep the change, buddy. I appreciate your making the trip over here."

"Thanks. Oh, I almost forgot. You got a couple of calls this afternoon. Mr. Gilbert told me to tell you he asked how you were holding up after your first week at the paper, and a Miss Sutton called from Savannah. I gave both of them your number here like you asked."

"Thanks. Have a nice evening." Hunter closed the door, picked up his beer and took a long sip. "I've been working all day and need a shower to get the moving dirt off," he said, walking out of the room quickly. "I won't be long. Want another beer?"

"Not yet," said Lucy. "I'm fine." But she was not fine. Inside, she was quaking. *Why do I feel like he's hiding something?*

Shortly after Lucy heard the water come on, the phone rang. She stared at it, wondering if it were Michael Gilbert or Lisa Sutton — whoever she was. Five minutes later Hunter came out of the bathroom, wearing a pair of Bermuda shorts and an old football jersey.

"Ah, that feels better. You're welcome to do the same."

"No thanks, but I would like to wash my hands."

When she came back in the living room, Hunter was sitting on the couch. There was a tray on the coffee table with a bowl of boiled shrimp, saltine crackers, cocktail sauce, and a bottle of chilled white wine. He filled two glasses and gave one to Lucy. "To my new home and my new friend, Lulu." Lucy started to say something, but he put his finger to her lips. "No reason to object. It won't do you any good."

"I was going to tell you that you had a phone call while you were in the shower."

"Well, if it's important they'll call back."

As soon as the words were out of his mouth, it rang again.

"Hello," said Hunter. "Oh, hi. It's going good...very busy...yeah, you're right...I have a friend here who helped me get unpacked...sure...talk later."

"So, I take it that wasn't Michael Gilbert," said Lucy.

"No, it wasn't," answered Hunter, "just a friend from Savannah."

"Lisa?" asked Lucy.

"Yes. Lisa. She was part of a group of writers, artists, actors who got together socially in Savannah."

"Which is she — writer, artist, actress or musician?"

"Actress."

"Hmmm...I see."

"Lucy, she's a friend. Eat some shrimp with your wine...you know how fast alcohol goes to your head... you're short."

"Well, you called me your friend. Does that make us the same thing to you?"

"No, of course not, but what should I call you?"

"I don't know…Lulu, maybe?"

Hunter laughed nervously and refilled her glass. "Hey, you never told me about the phone call you got yesterday."

"You're right. I didn't. It was Sid Ramsey who owns the Chattanooga Food Company. According to Marge, he's one of the richest men in that city. He wants to meet with me at his office to discuss how he can help with the mining issue. Evidently, he has a soft spot for Kings County. I'm driving up there Monday morning."

"By yourself?"

"Of course, by myself. Why not?"

"Well, I don't know. I mean—"

"Mr. Fox, are you jealous?"

"No more than you are," said Hunter, setting his glass down and taking hers. "Come here." He cradled Lucy's face in his hands and kissed her gently. "I just don't like the idea of some wealthy, powerful man having you in his office. That's all."

Lucy felt better, smiled, looked down for a second, and then whispered in his ear. "Are you ready for dessert?"

CHAPTER Eleven

1300 Water Street

Lucy loved the drive from Kings County to Chattanooga.
The two-lane highway wound through the Chattahoochee
National Forest, where the slightly changing leaves hinted
at fall.

The mountains were old, well-rounded by time, and,
in their silence, spoke volumes to her. Their history is what
drove her to protect her home and the ridge. Losing the an-
cient backbone of the valley meant losing the valley, and she
knew it.

*"I have one straight off the presses," said the voice from the
radio. "Georgia's own, Ray Charles, singing his version of
Hoagie Carmichael's hit, Georgia on my Mind."*
The music stirred her and made her think about Hunter. He
was an excellent dancer and kept the records spinning Saturday night, making the romance come easy...maybe too
easy. As much as she wanted to lose all restraint, Lucy was
hesitant to trust herself or anyone else.

A deer loped across the road, causing her to brake
slightly. "Get your mind on your business," she said aloud
to herself. "Think about who you're going to see and why."

Marge filled her in on Sid Ramsey's Hispanic heritage and his reputation as a businessman but nothing about
him personally. Sid seemed incredibly private; he kept to
himself and rarely went out in public.

Lucy found her way to 1300 Water Street, parked in
the garage attached to the multi-storied office building, and
went in the front door. The modern décor resembled what

one would see in Manhattan, not in a mid-size city in the South.

After checking in with the receptionist, she took the elevator to the top floor and stepped out into what looked like a penthouse at a luxury hotel. As soon as she did, the double doors at the end of the hallway opened, and a tall, dark-haired man walked down the hall towards her, smiling.

"Lucy...welcome," said Sid, bowing slightly. "Please come in." He extended his well-manicured hand and shook hers, pausing to take in every feature of her face. His eyes were as dark as night and as calm as a lake.

How on Earth has he managed to stay single? she thought. *He's as smooth as churned butter.*

"I sure do appreciate your taking the time to meet with me," she said, almost blushing.

Sid continued to stare at her, transfixed. "Excuse me," he said. "I know I appear rude, but you remind me of someone I once knew. Please, come in and make yourself comfortable." He motioned toward a velveteen-covered armchair that sat in front of his ornate mahogany desk. After taking a seat in the leather office chair directly opposite her, he leaned forward, resting his arms on the clean surface. "So, tell me what's going on down there in Kings County."

"As you know from reading the paper, there's a proposal to rezone the ridge so a mining company can locate there. I don't have to tell you how devastating that would be to our livelihoods and our homes. I'm sure you're aware of the havoc caused by iron ore mines."

"I do, and I'd hate to see that happen there. My father loved that area. It was one of his favorite hunting and fishing spots."

Lucy exhaled, relieved he was an ally. "I see. But can you assure me this conversation is confidential?" asked Lucy. "Some of what I know isn't public knowledge."

"I promise you. Discretion is the most important thing in the world to me." He smiled slightly and gave her a look that told her she could confide in him.

"All right then. You probably know that Jack Cooper, the president of the bank, is behind the mine. Do you know him?" asked Lucy.

"Only by name," said Ramsey, bending the truth, "but he has a reputation around here for being an unsavory fellow, who thinks he's god's gift to women."

Lucy laughed. "Well, you might not know him, but you know what he is. His grandfather made a bunch of money bootlegging and bought a lot of the land in the county. Jack gets what he wants no matter who or what he hurts in the process."

"So, how do you intend to stop this?"

"Find out who really owns the property, because I don't believe Jack does."

"Why is that?" asked Sid, eager to hear what stories were circulating and if they were true.

"I found this in the donation box at the library. Jack's wife, Anita, discovered it while cleaning out his closet." Lucy handed the thin book to Sid, who opened it and read it intently.

"So, you think the Coopers stole the Ridge, which explains why he doesn't have a deed. Lucy, he can't sell a piece of property without one though. It's not possible."

"Which brings me to the next detail," added Lucy. "He filed one on Friday, and we have no proof it isn't the real thing. That's why we need as much vocal opposition as possible. We're also hiring an environmental expert to make an assessment of the potential damage a strip mine would do to the waterways and the soil. I'll admit that I'm worried though. We only have a week until the commission meeting."

Sid listened to Lucy as best he could, but his determination to see Cooper go down occupied his thoughts. He cleared his throat and tapped the desk with his finger.

"I can't help you with the deed, Lucy, but I can help with any expenses you're incurring. What is it going to cost to hire the expert you mentioned?"

"A lot," said Lucy. "We're asking for donations from anyone who is willing to chip in."

Sid got up out of his chair, opened a safe in the credenza behind his desk, took out some money, put it in an envelope, and handed it to Lucy. "That should help," he said.

Lucy stood up and smiled. "I can't thank you enough and I'm certain everyone opposing this will appreciate it, too."

"There's one condition, though," said Sid, staring at her again with those deep, dark eyes. "Actually two: First, this donation must remain anonymous, and, secondly, promise me you'll come visit me again."

Lucy felt her cheeks warm. "I can assure you your request for secrecy will be honored. As far as the other goes, though, I just started seeing someone... I think."

"You think?"

"Well, it's too early to tell."

"I see," answered Sid with a chuckle. "Well, the invitation stands if you determine you're not seeing someone, okay?"

"Okay," said Lucy, almost feeling like she was cheating on Hunter. "I should get back now, though. I'm expecting a call this afternoon from Atlanta about the environmental assessment." She turned to leave but a photograph of a young woman on the cabinet behind Sid's desk got her attention. She stared at it as if she had seen a ghost.

"Now, you know why I couldn't take my eyes off of you," said Sid. "That's my late wife. I miss her every day.

Jealousy

Hunter found it hard to concentrate, knowing where Lucy was. He looked at his watch, figuring she should be back by now. It was 12:30.

The phone rang, interrupting his thoughts. *Maybe this is her.*

"Hello...Hunter Fox, here."

"Hey, Hunter. This is Charlie Tate. I'm afraid I have some bad news. Judge Whitaker called me a little while ago. Since I own land on the Valley Road, I have to recuse myself from the vote next week...conflict of interest. That puts everything in a different light. I thought I could sway some of the other commissioners, but now, Buddy Tatum is ramping up his support. I'm pretty sure he has Pritchett on board. He only needs one more to side with him, and the deal is done."

"Folks are not going to be happy about this," said Hunter. "Have you told anyone else?"

"No, but I won't have to. Buddy called me not long after the judge did, asking me if it was true, and he has a mouth on him. The other three commissioners have already gotten in touch with me, too. I'll preside over the hearing, but I can't vote."

"Okay, I'll call Whitaker for an official statement and ask who complained about it, but of course, we know who that is."

"I'm sure your hunch is the same as mine. As much as I hate to admit it, I'm really worried about this."

Hunter hung up the phone and called the judge. He verified what Charlie said and their suspicions that Jack Cooper filed the complaint, which he included in the article for Tuesday's paper. He gave the story to Pete and dialed Lucy's number. It was busy. He waited a couple of minutes and tried again. No luck.

"Pete, I'll be back in about an hour or so. I have some business to take care of."

In 20 minutes, he was at the Tanner home, knocking on the front door. He heard footsteps coming down the hall, and he knew it was Lucy. He let out a deep breath when he saw her standing in the open doorway.

"What's the matter with you?" she asked. "You look agitated."

"That's because I am," said Hunter, snapping his gum. "

213

I was worried because I haven't heard from you, and Charlie Tate just gave me some bad news."

"I have been on the phone taking care of business since I got home," answered Lucy, somewhat defensively, but at the same time, pleased he was obviously perplexed. "Come in and calm down. Do you want my good news first or do you want to give me the bad?"

"I'll go." Hunter sat down on the edge of the sofa, turning to face Lucy. "Charlie Tate has to recuse himself ...conflict of interest since he lives out here and has property that could be impacted. I talked to the county judge, and I'll give you one guess who filed the complaint."

"The asshole."

"Yep. Charlie is really worried. He's pretty sure Buddy has convinced one commissioner to side with him, so he only has to lure another one for the deal to go through."

"Maybe my dad needs to talk to the preacher and Mr. Riley," said Lucy. "They're old fashioned and will respond to a man better than a woman."

"That's a good idea. In the meantime, give me some good news. I need it."

"The environmental study will be ready by tomorrow and delivered by noon. It is not a good report for Cooper and Cagle. And...I have the money to pay for it. Look." She reached in her pocket, took out the envelope and handed it to Hunter.

He opened it and gasped. "Where the hell did you get $500?"

"Sid Ramsey, but you can't tell a soul. He made me swear to secrecy."

"You must have really made an impression on him. What was he like?"

Like you haven't already quizzed Marge," thought Lucy. "Mr. Ramsey is very successful, secretive, and quite sentimental about the ridge. He's also a widower and still in love with his late wife. Her picture was on his desk. We kind of look alike."

"It sounds like you two really got to know one another. How long were you in his office?"

"You sure are asking a lot of questions, Hunter. Why's that? Don't you trust me?" asked Lucy, not sharing the fact that Sid asked her to come visit him again.

"Yes, I trust you, but I don't trust other men. Were you fascinated with him?"

Lucy took Hunter's hand in hers and kissed it. "Listen. I have managed to keep other men at bay for quite some time. Although your jealousy flatters me, you can relax. I am fascinated with you, silly man. Go back to work. I need to find dad and talk to him about reaching out to the commissioners. I'll answer the phone at 8:30 if you call."

Hunter kissed her softly. "And you know I will."

The Cooper and Cagle Show

There were capacity crowds at both public meetings held that week. Many of the same people attended the one in Cantrell City and Willow Creek. Lucy had come up with good questions to ask and gave them to key people in the audience. They drilled Cagle about the noise, the runoff, and the desecration of the forests. He deftly danced around the issue with slick, carefully crafted answers.

Lucy pointed out that there was very low unemployment in the area. "Who are you going to hire?" she asked Cagle.

"The county will probably experience some growth in population with folks moving in who want to work for us," Dan answered, "and some people who already live here may leave the jobs they have now for a better one."

"There's not a lot of available housing. If people move here, where will they live?" she asked.

"I'm sure ol' Jack here will be glad to make them a loan, and Tater — isn't that your nickname, Charlie? — will be more than happy to sell them some lumber." Only he and Jack laughed at his feeble attempt at local humor.

215

Commissioners Pritchett and Riley squirmed in their seats, while Charlie Tate's expression remained a stony stare.

Cagle continued his brazen attempt to sound like he knew what was best for the people who lived in Kings County. "Y'all deserve to benefit from the industrial growth the rest of the country is experiencing. Why stay stuck in an agrarian economy when modernization offers a better life?"

Lucy seethed at his suggestion that farming was an inferior occupation, but she kept a straight face. She saw Dancy Riley staring at her, with that smug smile on her face. Her father-in-law, who was a commissioner, was acting mighty cozy with Cagle before the meeting. Lucy just knew it was all Dancy's doing. She was a spiteful, jealous woman who would do anything to hurt those she resented. And she had always hated Lucy.

The meeting adjourned around 8:30, but a crowd lingered outside, talking among themselves. Hunter left quickly so he could get a story done for the next day's paper, waving at Lucy from a distance. After a few more minutes, Luke motioned at his daughter that it was time to go. No one said much on the drive home.

When they arrived, the phone was ringing and Hank ran inside to answer it. "It's for you, Mama…Mr. Mason."

"Hello," she said. "Are you as worried as we are?"

"I am, but I honestly don't know what to do. Keep trying to find out whatever you can. Is Luke available? I want to speak to him, if I may."

Lucy handed the phone to her dad and got Hank settled in bed. He fell asleep quickly, and she walked out on the back porch. Progress threatened the silence that she had always taken for granted. The quiet, wild forests could turn into a noisy wasteland. What would happen to their way of life if Cooper got his way? The routine she thought would never change had suddenly turned upside down.

Jealousy, Part Two

Even though she had a restless night, Lucy woke up early Friday morning. She felt determined and confident. After getting Hank off to school, she went to the barn to go over the books with Luke and Nettie as she did every week. Billy Joe was already on the tractor mowing the pastures.

"You must have had trouble sleeping, too," said Lucy. "You look tired, Daddy."

"I guess I'm worried," he answered, "just couldn't get comfortable. I'll be okay. Us Tanners are tough, right?"

Lucy nodded. "Yep, we are, and I have a feeling we're going to need all the toughness we can muster. But in spite of everything going on, the farm had a good week monetarily. Interest rates are up, and the steers brought a good price at market," she said looking at the statements and receipts. "Plus, Billy Joe is worth every penny we pay him."

"He's a good man," said Nettie, "never seen anybody build a house as fast as he has either."

"I'd say he's anxious to make Miss Marge his wife," laughed Luke. "Reminds me of myself after Gen hit me upside the head with those pretty green eyes of hers. I know I've told y'all the story hundreds of times, but when I came to pay my respect after her daddy died, she looked at me in a way that made me want to stay around forever. During that visit, she told me she wanted to finish the new school rooms he had just started building. The next day I showed up with my tools and didn't stop working until it was done. I asked her to marry me the day The Willow Creek School was dedicated...good thing for you she said, 'yes', Lulu.'"

"I love that story. Have you ever told it to Hank?" asked Lucy.

"I have. His response was that he wished someone would hit you upside the head," laughed Luke. "Speaking of, you and Hunter still getting along?"

"I'd say they are," chimed in Nettie.

217

"Well, there's your answer from the expert," said Lucy with a grin. "In fact, I'm going to surprise him at lunch with a plate of what you're having."

"Good. That's what it should all be about, you know...doing things for the people you love and making them feel appreciated."

"I never said anything about love," said Lucy, with conviction that neither Nettie or Luke believed.

"Of course," said Luke. "Of course, you didn't." He stood up, kissed his daughter on top of the head, and winked at her. "Then you better wear a helmet to town so it won't hurt when you get hit upside that pretty noggin of yours."

**

Lucy daydreamed about how pleased Hunter would be when she surprised him at the office. She loved the way his face lit up when he saw her. It was like everything and everybody else disappeared. She looked in the rearview mirror and realized she was beaming. Maybe she did love him.

It was a beautiful early fall day, and the drive to Cantrell City didn't disappoint. By the time Lucy got to the Tribune office, she was so excited, her hands trembled when she picked up the box lunch she had packed for Hunter. She opened the door to the building and put her finger to her lips, signaling Betsy not to say anything. She wanted to surprise Hunter, but when she opened the door to the press room, she was the one who got the surprise.

She saw a very stylish, sophisticated woman, with auburn-colored hair in a perfect French twist, balancing on high stiletto heels, with her arms wrapped around Hunter, giving him a big hug. And he was hugging her back. Hunter looked up, saw Lucy, and the color drained from his face. Quickly pushing his visitor away, he exclaimed, "Lucy, hi. What a surprise."

The woman turned around and smiled. "Oh, hello. I'm Lisa Sutton. And you are Lucy who?"

"Of course, you are," said Lucy. She sat the box of food down on Pete's desk, who was staring at the scene in horror. "I brought this for Mr. Fox, but there's not enough for his guest. So, why don't you enjoy it?" She turned and walked out as fast she could, with Hunter in pursuit, but she was out the door and getting in her car before he had a chance to say anything.

"Lucy, please. Let me explain," he said, grabbing her arm.

"Let me go," she said, feeling the hot tears roll down her face. She jerked her arm away and got in the car, still not looking at him. "So, that's your friend, Miss Sutton. Hunter, you've slept with her, haven't you?" She turned her head and stared at him with eyes on fire.

"Not lately," blurted Hunter. "I mean...damn it. It didn't and doesn't mean anything."

"Funny. That's what Hank's dad said when I caught him in bed with the carhop from Burger World. And to think you were questioning me after a business meeting and doubting Mr. Ramsey, knowing all along you and Miss Sutton were bed buddies. And, oh, by the way, Sid was quite impressed with me. I failed to mention that he asked me to come see him again. Sounds like a good idea to me now."

"Lucy, please, don't—"

"You know what, Hunter? I don't want to hear your damn voice right now." She cranked the car and backed out too fast, almost hitting the person driving down the street.

Hunter watched her leave, a defiant and angry look on her face. "Shit," he said, turning around to see Lisa coming out the *Tribune* building.

"Hmmm. So, why didn't you tell me about Miss Lucy?" she asked. "It's obvious you're crazy about her."

"I am crazy about her, but she's mad as hell at me now. She was at my house when you called last Saturday. I

219

told her you were a friend and nothing more. She's not going to understand this...not at all."

"Well, you probably should have been more honest with her and with me," said Lisa, "but that has always been your tragic flaw—afraid to tell the same truths in your personal life as you do in your professional one. Don't you get that facts matter in real life just like they do in a news story? Jesus, Hunter. People won't know how you feel unless you tell them. Anyway, I'm going now...no reason to make any more scenes. I need to get to Nashville anyway. My audition is tomorrow afternoon. Good luck with this. By the way, what's her last name?"

"Tanner," answered Hunter quietly. "Lucy Tanner is her name."

***

"Son of a bitch," said Lucy, hitting the steering wheel with the palm of her hand. She looked at the speedometer and took her foot off the accelerator. She was driving way too fast, but she continued to rant aloud. "And to think he was quizzing me about being in Sid's office. Goddamn it. Why did I trust him? And furthermore, why do I care?" she wailed.

She pulled over at the Iron Bridge to collect herself, but the tears wouldn't stop. "I let myself fall in love, damn it. Damn him." She leaned her head against the steering wheel and sobbed.

By the time she got home, her grief had turned to full-fledged indignant anger. She walked in the back door, hoping to avoid her mother and went straight to her room. After changing into her work clothes, she threw the dress she wore to town on the closet floor. "I can't believe I was so stupid that I actually started dressing for him."

"Lucy? That you?" called her mother from the living room.

"No. It's the Virgin Mary," shouted Lucy, who immediately felt bad for speaking to her mother that way. "I'm

220

sorry, mama," she said, walking down the hall. Her eyes filled up with tears again, "I just…."

"What's wrong?" asked Gen, looking up from the book she was reading.

"I walked in the newspaper office and Hunter was hugging on a woman from Savannah…an actress he told me was just a friend—you know the kind of friend you, you—oh, Mama, why do I fall for lying cheaters?"

"Oh, honey. I'm sure there's an explanation for this. Did you give Hunter a chance to tell you what's going on, or did you jump to a conclusion? You know you are prone to do that."

I don't want to hear his damn excuses. I'm furious with him and angry at myself." She looked out the window and saw the school bus pulling in the driveway. "Did school get out early today?'

"Yes. Hank told you this morning. Don't you remember?"

"See, I was so caught up in that damn Mr. Fox that I didn't pay attention to what I should be focusing on. I need to go wash my face. I don't want Hank to see me upset."

Good luck with that, thought Gen. She opened the front door and waved at Clyde. Her grandson ran up the front walk, gave her a hug, and began calling for Lucy. "Mama, mama. What time is Hunter picking us up for the game tonight?"

Lucy came out of the bathroom, with a towel in her hand. "We're not going," she answered flatly.

"Whadda ya mean we're not going? Why?"

"Because I'm not feeling well, and Hunter has company."

"Which one is it? That you're not feeling good or Hunter has company? Granddaddy says that if somebody gives more than one reason for not doing something, they're making excuses."

"Hank. We're not going, and that's all I have to say about it right now." Her voice cracked and she felt the lump in her throat. "I'm going to lie down."

"But, Mama—"

"I said that's all I have to say about it right now."

"This isn't fair," Hank whined. "You get to decide everything. I like being around Hunter. Why can't you just be happy for once?"

"Because he likes someone else. That's why. Now, please. I need to—" The phone rang, saving her from the awkward conversation with her son.

"It's Anita for you," said Gen, handing the phone to Lucy.

"I'll talk in my room," said Lucy.

"Come on, Hank," said Gen. "Nettie made some sugar cookies today. Let your mama have some privacy."

"Hello?" said Lucy.

"Hey," said Anita. "Bo wants Hank to come home with us after the game tonight. I thought I would take them to my parents again tomorrow.

Dad loved having them around. I think it takes his mind off the commission hearing."

"That's so nice of you, Anita, but we're not going to the game."

"Why not? Are you sick? You don't sound like yourself."

Lucy told Anita about her encounter with Hunter and Lisa, right down to her thorough lashing of him. She even added the bit about Sid Ramsey and that she was considering giving him a call.

"Lucy, don't do anything rash now. Hunter doesn't seem like the cheating kind. I'm sure there's a logical explanation for this. Anybody can see that he's head over heels for you. Give him a chance to set things straight."

"Now is not the time. I'm too upset."

"Well, let me come pick Hank up and take him to the game. He can stay two nights with us. You need some time to sort through all of this."

"That would be really good, Anita. Thanks."

"We'll be there in an hour to get him. Just pack his suitcase and stop worrying. You'll see more clearly in a day or two."

***

As soon as Anita and the boys got to the football game, Hank saw Hunter on the sidelines and called out to him. Fox looked up from his notepad and motioned for him to come down. "I'll be right back," he said to Bo.

"Where's your mama?" asked Hunter.

"She didn't want to come, because you like somebody else now. Is that true?"

Hunter knelt down and put his hand on Hank's shoulder. "No. That's not true. Your mama and I have a little misunderstanding, but I'm hoping we can set things straight. And don't worry. I still like your mama and only her. Go sit in the stands now. The game is about to start. I'll see you at halftime." He waved at Anita, who smiled and nodded like she understood. Hunter looked in the view finder of his camera, focusing on the team lined up on the field, but the only thing he saw was Lucy's face.

Chapter Twelve

Payback

Lucy stared at Sid's business card. She picked up the receiver and dialed slowly, taking a deep breath and exhaling. He answered after one ring.

"Hi, Sid. It's Lucy."

"Well, hello, Lucy. This is a pleasant surprise. Are there new developments there?"

"It doesn't look good for the opposition," said Lucy, pretending to be all business. She told him about the recusal and the apparent coalition between three of the commissioners.

"I wish I could do more," said Sid, who was already thinking about who to call to stop Jack. "I'm curious though. Since you called me on a Friday evening, when people who are dating typically go out, does that mean you decided you're not seeing anyone?"

Lucy hesitated. "I'm mad at him. I don't think he's been honest with me. In fact, I know he hasn't."

"Do you mind if I ask who 'he' is?"

"The guy who writes what you read in the paper."

"Oh, Mr. Fox, the new owner of *The Tribune*."

"Yeah, him," said Lucy.

"Hmmm...well, in light of that, why don't you join me for lunch at my home on Lake Chickamauga tomorrow? You are welcome to bring your son, too. It's perfect weather for boating."

"You know, that sounds like a good idea, but Hank is spending the weekend with Anita Cooper and her boy, Bo. I would like to come up though. A day away from here would do me good."

Lucy wrote down the directions to Sid's house and told him she would see him around noon. She hung up the phone and looked at the clock. *Hunter is probably on his way to the office about now*, she thought. *He'll want to finish up so he can go home and be with Miss Savannah.* The phone rang, saving her from getting lost in the thoughts that made her shake all over. She stared at it, knowing it could be him. She wanted to answer it, but felt determined not to do so.

After five rings, she heard her father say hello. "Oh, hey, Hunter. Just a minute." He tapped on Lucy's door. "Honey, it's for you. Hunter."

"Tell him I'm asleep," said Lucy, turning out her light and pulling the covers over her head. "I'll be damned if I will let him talk me into believing his lies," she said to herself. "He can roast in hell." But Lucy Tanner knew she didn't believe what she was telling herself.

***

Lucy had angry, terrifying dreams all night—she was either screaming at Hunter or being swept away by flood waters. She woke up before dawn and left the house just as the sun was peeking above the horizon.

When she pulled in Nettie's drive, she saw Nate out front, scanning the ground with a long-handled instrument and pausing every few seconds or so.

"Morning, Lucy," he said.

"Hey, Nate. Whatcha got there?"

"A metal detector. I've been reading about folks finding all sorts of coins and artifacts, dating back to the Civil War. I thought I'd give it a shot."

"Hmm…come to our house sometimes. No telling what you might find. Mama's family was a little…you know…" Lucy made the swirling motion with her hand that stood for cuckoo and Nate laughed. "Where's Nettie?" she asked.

"Asleep."

"Is she sick? She'd have to be if she's still in the bed."

"No. She just had a restless night…those nightmares."

"What are you talking about?"

Nate put the metal detector on the front porch and quietly said, "You want some coffee?"

"Of course," answered Lucy. She sat down in one of the chairs under a massive hickory tree and anxiously waited for Nate. He came out of the house, holding two cups. After giving one to Lucy, he sat down.

"Nettie has always had nightmares," he started, staring at the ground, "but they're worse now that all of this has come up about the Ridge. Since she started trying to put the pieces together about her grandmama, her mama, and the Cooper men, she's been talking out of her head and waking up in a sweat, scared to death."

"Oh, Nate. This is my fault," said Lucy, almost in tears.

"Naw. That ain't right," said Nate. "It's the fault of the men who terrorized her. She needs to get this out. It's like there's a demon living inside her, but that bastard needs to leave. But Lucy, this has to be between you and me. Nettie would be so embarrassed if she knew we talked. She is mighty scared and weak right now. I'm afraid if she found out I told you, she'd run like hell back to that place that's a prison for her."

"I won't say a word." Lucy stood up to leave but stopped. She turned to face the man who had just shared his heartfelt story with her. "Nate, do you love Nettie?" asked Lucy.

He looked at her with eyes that gave it away. "Yes ma'am, I sure do."

***

Lucy got back to the house just as Luke was heading out the front door. "You been at Nettie's?" he asked.

"I have, but she was in no mood to talk," said Lucy, bending the truth a bit and not telling the whole story. "I'm afraid we've lost this one, Daddy."

226

"You're probably right, but in the meantime, let's take our minds off that damn mine and plant some fall vegetables. Digging in the dirt will be good for us."

"I can't, Daddy," said Lucy, seeing the disappointment in his eyes. "I have some important business to take care of. I need to collect more signatures on the petition," she said, feeling guilty about straight out lying to him.

"Oh, Lulu, I was looking forward to working with you today, just like old times. I guess Billy Joe will have to suffice. Well, be careful."

She went inside and got ready to head out to Chattanooga. After telling Gen the same story she told Luke, she left before anyone could ask too many questions.

When Lucy got to Billy Joe's, she saw Marge taking boxes out of her car and putting them inside the house. *Maybe I should tell her where I'm going,* she thought. She slowed down and turned in the driveway. Marge looked up and waved.

"Where are you headed all dolled up on a Saturday?" asked Marge. "I hope you're going to see Hunter so he can explain. I've never seen a man so torn up over a woman. He was pitiful last night."

"I hate to disappoint you, but I'm headed to Chattanooga to see Sid. I called him, and he invited me to lunch. My parents think I'm getting signatures on the petition, but I wanted you to know the truth."

Marge shook her head. "I don't believe you really want to see Sid Ramsey. You're trying to convince yourself you don't care about Hunter."

"No. That's not true. I'm trying not to make a mistake — again. I am simply exploring my options. Your house is looking great by the way."

"Thanks. We're staying here tonight. We don't have much furniture yet or running water, but I don't care. Billy Joe bought a mattress — gonna christen it," Marge said with a wink.

"I'm happy for y'all," said Lucy, wishing she was going to be on a mattress with Hunter—a thought she quickly erased from her mind. "I'll toot the horn when I pass by on my way home later."

"Okay, Lucy. Listen to your heart, and don't do something you'll regret."

"Don't worry," Lucy answered. "Sid Ramsey is a very proper gentleman...you know, the bowing kind."

***

Hunter waited as long as he could to call the Tanner home but gave in well before noon.

"Hello," said Gen. "Tanner residence."

"Good morning, Mrs. Tanner. This is Hunter. May I please speak to Lucy?"

"Hello, Hunter. I'm afraid she isn't here. She said she needed to get more signatures on the petition. I would imagine she'll be in town though. Maybe you'll run into her there."

"Okay. Thanks...hope to see you soon."

"Yes. That would be nice. Goodbye."

Gen hung up the phone and stared at a photograph of Lucy and Hank she took on Easter Sunday. It was one of her favorites, because she could see so much of Henry in her grandson. "Lord, please guide her to do the right thing," she prayed a loud. "Help her lose some of that stubbornness and see what's in front of her. Amen."

***

Hunter grabbed his camera, a notepad and pen. "Pete, I'm going out to do a street poll about the mine. I'll be back in plenty of time to put tomorrow's paper on the presses."

He walked out on the sidewalk, looking in both directions, hoping to see Lucy. He found lots of folks who were willing to have their photo taken and give their

228

opinion. Not one person was in favor of the mine coming to Kings County.

But there was no sign of Lucy Tanner in Cantrell City. So, he got in the company car and left for Willow Creek.

When he got into town, he parked in front of the hardware store and had several photos taken and opinions recorded in no time. As he walking down the sidewalk toward the beauty shop, he saw Marge's car parked in front of it and his pace quickened. *Maybe she's with Lucy*, he thought.

"Hey, Marge," he called when he saw her coming out of the drug store. She stopped and waved back.

"Is Lucy with you?" he asked as soon as he caught up with her. "I called her house and her mother said she was out getting more signatures."

Marge hesitated, not really knowing what to say. "No, she's not with me."

Hunter sensed her uneasiness. "Then where is she?" He was desperate—something he was not accustomed to feeling.

Marge let out a sigh. "She's gone to Chattanooga."

"What? Why? Oh, wait. She went to see the Ramsey guy, didn't she?"

"Yes. She did, but she's upset. If she didn't care, it wouldn't matter to her if you were hugging on Lisa Sutton."

"Damn it. I wasn't really hugging on her in that way. It was like I'd hug you if I hadn't seen you in a while. Lisa and I are friends who—"

"You don't have to explain. I understand, and, hopefully, in time, Lucy will. Just leave her be for a while."

"Shit. I've really screwed up this time."

"Don't give up yet. Hey, why don't you come out to the house after you finish at the office? You know Billy Joe will have some beer, and I think you could use a couple of drinks."

"I don't want to impose."

229

"Don't worry. We'll tell you when it's time to leave," Marge said with a laugh.

Hunter chuckled. "Thanks. I look forward to it... don't really want to be alone tonight. I thought I'd never hear myself say that."

Lake Chickamauga

The directions Sid gave Lucy were as flawless as he was. She stopped at the secured entrance to his estate and pressed the button on the intercom box.

"May I help you?" said a voice coming from some place on the other side of the rock wall.

"Yes. I'm Lucy Tanner, and I have an appointment with Mr. Ramsey."

"Of course, he's expecting you. Come in."

The ornate gate slowly opened, revealing a long drive, bordered by oaks, maples, and boxwoods. She drove slowly, taking in every detail of the immaculate landscape. In a couple of hundred yards, she saw the rambling rock house, very modern with windows everywhere. Surrounded by a wide terrace on all sides, it looked more like a resort than a private home. When she got closer, she saw Sid, standing at the foot of the wide steps that led to the front entrance. The driveway made a circle, around a rose garden that had a large fountain in the center.

"Hello, Lucy. How was your trip?" said Sid, opening the car door for her.

"It was fine, thank you. Your home is beautiful."

"I'm glad you like it. I'll give you a quick tour."

The double glass front doors opened into a massive great room, with a sunken sitting area. The entire back wall was windows, allowing a panoramic view of the lake. An open dining area was on the upper level, and original paintings graced the walls. Fresh flowers in crystal vases were everywhere.

"The kitchen is around that corner, and there are four bedrooms on that wing, and the master and my office are on the other," said Sid, "but the best part of the property is the outside area and the lake."

They walked out the sliding glass doors on to a slate terrace, decorated with large urns and outdoor seating. "Oh my," exclaimed Lucy, when she saw the expansive lake beneath them. "This is gorgeous. I bet you spend a lot of time in this spot."

"I do. In fact, I thought we'd have our lunch out here." He pulled out one of the chairs at a table, covered with a white tablecloth. A vase of roses from the front garden sat in the middle. Within seconds, a young woman in a black uniform and white apron brought a plate of fresh fruit and cheese to the table.

"Rosa, this is Lucy Tanner."

"Nice to meet you, Miss Tanner. What can I get you to drink?"

"What are you going to have, Sid?" asked Lucy, hoping champagne was on the list.

"Tea."

"I'll take the same," Lucy said.

"I took you for a sparkling wine lady. I don't drink, but feel free to sample what I picked out if you wish."

"That's okay. Tea is fine," answered Lucy, trying not to think about how much fun she and Hunter had sipping together.

After they finished lunch, Sid stood up. "Ready for a boat ride?" he asked, briefly taking her hand. They walked down to the dock, but Lucy felt nothing from his touch. No spark. No tingling. It had nothing to do with who he was and everything to do with who he wasn't.

Sid backed the cruiser out of the slip and drove slowly out into the middle of the lake. "There's not much traffic this time of year…looks like we have the entire lake to ourselves." He hit the accelerator, and the boat's speed terrified Lucy. It was the first thing her host had done that wasn't slow and methodical. She gripped the side of the boat, not really sure if she was enjoying it or not.

"I'm sorry," shouted Sid above the roar of the engine. "Did I scare you? I'll slow down."

"Thanks. I'm used to a fishing boat and paddles…no way near this fast."

"My apologies," said Sid. And just like that, he was unflappable again.

The silence that ensued told Sid everything he needed to know. He drove just a bit more and returned to the dock.

"Thanks. This was really nice," said Lucy, as they walked up the steps to the house. "I'm sorry I wasn't an enthusiastic boating mate."

"Hey, no apologies needed. I should have used a bit more restraint."

"You are the picture of restraint and the perfect gentleman, but I should probably get going. I haven't spent much time on the farm lately."

Sid walked her around to the front and opened her car door. He leaned in and kissed her on the cheek. "Be careful driving back. I'll be in touch soon about how to stop Jack Cooper. That's still very important to me."

Lucy thanked him and drove away, not feeling a thing but sadness.

***

After Lucy left, Sid went back down to the boat house. Santos, his caretaker, was cleaning and tying off the cruiser. "Are you going out again, Mr. Ramsey?"

"Yes. I am." He needed to think but not about Lucy; there was a connection with her, but it wasn't romantic …more like that of a younger sister. Their love for the land was akin to a familial tie.

Lucy was not on his mind now but how to expose Jack Cooper without revealing himself was.

He navigated the boat across the glassy lake, cut off the motor and drifted. Underneath his smooth exterior, Sid was very sentimental. He thought about the Ridge and how often his father took him there when he was a boy. *I learned a lot from him while we were alone in the mountains,* Sid thought...*things that guide me every day. Those hills are like a shrine to me, and I don't want to see them desecrated...especially by Jack Cooper.*

He went over everything he'd heard from Lucy, Jack, Sandy and what he had read in the paper. Maybe his man at the Lodge had more information. Alcohol has a tendency to loosen the lips—one of the reasons he abstained. If anybody has heard anything, it would be Sandy. He took the boat back to the dock where Santos was waiting.

He walked quickly up the steps to the terrace and sat down next to a small table where there was a telephone. He dialed the number to the Lodge.

"Hello. Sandy, here. Can I help you?"

"Hey, Sandy. Are you covered up with Saturday drinkers yet?"

"No, boss," laughed Sandy. "Not yet. What's going on?"

"I want to stop Jack Cooper. Have you heard anything else that might help?"

"No sir. I haven't," said Sandy. "I know most folks are opposed to it, but that won't do any good since he filed a deed. Plus, I heard he has at least one commissioner in his pocket."

"What did you say?" asked Sid, whose antennae went up at the last comment.

Sandy cleared his throat. "Well, it's just a rumor but—"

"Sandy, you forget to whom you're speaking. Why are you nervous all of a sudden?"

"Boss, I'm afraid what might happen if I tell you."

"You know I'm not going to let anything happen to you or anyone else who works for me. What is it?"

Sandy let out a deep breath. He recounted Daisy's story about Cooper and Cagle conspiring, including the story about Jack's grandfather stealing the land and Jack bribing Buddy Tatum."

"Why didn't you tell me this sooner?" asked Sid.

233

"Because Daisy is terrified of Cooper. Who can we trust to tell anyway? If he claims he didn't say it, we have no proof other than Daisy's word. That bastard would hurt her then. I just know it."

By now, Sid's blood was at a boiling point. "Listen. If I get someone from the outside to investigate this, do you think Daisy would help us out?"

"From the outside? What do you mean?"

"Trust me. I know what I'm doing. You convince Daisy to cooperate and get back with me as soon as you can. I need to jump on this."

"Okay, boss. I'll talk to her when I get home tonight."

"Call me after you do. I don't care what time it is."

Sid hung up the phone and went to his office. He unlocked the bottom drawer of his desk and took out a thin black book. The alphabetized pages contained important phone numbers to business associates all over the world, but there was only one he was interested in calling. He flipped over to the O's and found Jigs O'Brien's number. Jigs was a good friend from his childhood, who just happened to be an undercover agent with the Georgia Bureau of Investigation.

The phone rang four times before Jigs answered it. "Hello?"

"Jigs, it's Sid. I have a tip for you. Something is afoul in Kings County."

"Make it quick," said Jigs, who was always leery of long phone conversations.

Sid filled him in on what he suspected Cooper had committed based on Daisy's revelation and the journal Lucy had shown him.

"When is the hearing?" asked Jigs.

"Tuesday evening."

"I'll be in touch."

Sid hung up the phone. Although some of his operations were outside of the law, he had an intense dislike for his fellow criminals who made money from the pain and suffering of others...extortion being one of them. He knew that if anyone was capable of bursting Cooper's bubble, it would be Jigs.

Lost

Hunter drove his MG to Billy Joe's place, with the top down and taking the curves a bit too fast. When he got there, a cold beer and a shot of shine was waiting on him.

"Where's Marge?" he asked.

"She'll be here soon. So, tell me why you're on Lucy's shit list."

"This woman I knew in Savannah stopped by on her way to Nashville. Lucy walked in just as she was giving me a hug. You can imagine how that went over. But she wouldn't let me explain. Lisa is a friend. Sure, we've slept together—a lot—but there's no emotional connection. The relationship didn't and doesn't mean anything."

"To you," said Billy Joe. "But to Lucy, I'm sure it does. And it means something because she's crazy about you. Haven't you been involved with enough women to know how they are?"

"I've had encounters but no long-lasting ones."

"Why not? A good-looking fellow like you?"

"I get bored, but, honestly, Lucy is different. Billy Joe, I'm a goner, and I don't know what to do."

"Let her realize how much she cares by giving her time, bud. Here. Have another shot."

***

On the drive back from Chattanooga, all Lucy could think about was Hunter. She turned on the Valley Road, rounded the corner and saw him and Billy Joe just in time. Lucy looked straight ahead, not knowing if they saw her or not.

But Hunter did. He reached for the moonshine bottle and took another long swig. He'd never gotten shit-faced over a woman before, but he did that evening.

***

When Sid's phone rang at midnight, he knew who it was. "Boss, it's me," said Sandy. "Daisy says she's too scared to talk. I'll keep trying, but I'm not sure I can do anything to change her mind."

"Okay, maybe in time. Thanks for letting me know." Sid hung up the phone and turned the light out. *This isn't over*, he thought. *I won't stop until I see Jack Cooper gone."*

Having an unusual ability to compartmentalize, Ramsey rolled over and went sound asleep.

Pain

Lucy woke up early Sunday morning. When she went out on the porch, Luke was sitting in his favorite rocker.

"Morning, Lulu. We got three acres planted yesterday, but it wore me out. I think I'll pass on church. I need this chair more than I need a sermon."

"Okay. Can I get you something?"

"No. I'm fine…sitting here is all I need." But Luke wasn't fine. He was terrified Cooper was going to get his way, which would mean the end of the lifestyle he and his family knew. The entire county will be impacted in a negative way. *I should have pulled the plug on that crowd a long time ago*, he thought. *I'm to blame for a lot of this.*

Lucy went inside and told her mother she and Luke were staying at home. She wanted some alone time with her father, but more than that, she wasn't ready to see Hunter. And she knew he'd be at church.

After Gen and Hank left, Lucy cooked lunch. When everything was ready, she looked at the clock. *Daddy must*

236

have fallen asleep, she thought. *I haven't heard a peep out of him since mama left.*

She walked out on the front porch and saw Luke holding his chest and gasping for air. Fear froze her in her tracks. "Heart, heart," he whispered, as he slumped over. Lucy snapped to attention, caught him and helped him get back in the chair.

"We have to go to the hospital now," she said in panic-stricken, yet stern voice. "I'll go get the truck."

She started to run across the road, but saw Billy Joe pulling in at the barn. "I think Daddy's having a heart attack," she shouted. "I need you to come help me." She saw that Luke was already turning blue from the lack of oxygen. She ran inside and made a quick call to the hospital to alert them they were headed that way. By the time she ran out the front door, Billy Joe had already gotten her father down the steps and into the truck. As he pushed the truck to speeds Lucy didn't think were possible, she held her daddy's hand.

When they pulled up to the emergency room entrance, two orderlies rushed out to meet them and loaded Luke onto a gurney. "Dr. Stanley is waiting inside. He said for you to sit in the waiting room. He'll let you know something as soon as he can."

"I have to go get Mama," Lucy said to Billy Joe. "You go on in."

Lucy drove as fast as she could to the church. She opened the doors and almost ran down the aisle. Her mother looked up with a shocked expression on her face. "Mama," she whispered. "Daddy's having a heart attack. You and Hank need to come with me to the hospital."

The preacher stopped talking, and the entire congregation stared as the Tanners walked quickly out of the church. The service ended early because everyone, including the reverend, was preoccupied with what had just happened.

"I heard Lucy say Luke was having a heart attack," said Theodore. "I'm going to the hospital. Anita, why don't you come, too? Bo can go to George's with your mother."

Hunter stopped Anita and whispered, "I don't think it's wise for me to go, but, please, let me know how he is." She nodded and quickly followed her father outside.

When they got to the hospital, Lucy was sitting in the waiting room, her face ashen. Gen was staring at the doors that led into the operating room, and Hank had his arms around his mama. Marge was sitting next to Gen, comforting her.

"What can we do to help?" asked Anita.

"Someone go tell Nettie. I need her here with us."

"We can handle that," Anita said. "Hank, do you want to come and wait at our house? Bo is really worried."

"No ma'am. Thank you, but I'm gonna stay with my mama," said the little boy, his eyes filling up with tears.

"Nettie's probably still in church," said Lucy, "the First Harmony Baptist."

"All right," said Theodore. "We'll take care of everything."

The waiting was excruciating, and Hank got restless. "I'm thirsty, Mama."

"Of course, you are, sweet boy. Marge, do you mind going to the snack bar and getting us something to drink...maybe some cheese crackers, too."

When she got back, Hank asked if he could go outside. He sat down on a bench under the huge oak tree and took a sip of the Coca-Cola Marge had gotten him. Even though that was a real treat, it didn't taste good.

"Hey, you," said Hunter, appearing out of nowhere.

Hank looked up, and tears started streaming down his face. "Hunter, my granddaddy is sick."

Hunter sat down next to the little boy and put his arm around him. "It's gonna be okay. My grandmother always said when you get to the end of your rope, you tie a knot and hang on. So that's what we have to do. Hang on as tight as we can."

"But my mama has gone back to being sad, and we might lose the Ridge."

"We're not going to think like that now. I know it seems like the world went from good to bad in a minute, but sometimes that's how life is. It's too early to throw in the towel though."

"Why don't you go talk to my mama then? That would make her feel better."

"Now is not the time. She'll let me know when she's ready to see me. In the meantime, you must be strong for her and for me, too, okay?"

Marge walked out to check on Hank and saw them sitting on the bench.

"How's Mr. Tanner?" Hunter asked.

"We don't know anything yet. They have him in the emergency intensive care. I can call you when we hear something."

"Thanks, but I'll probably still be out here. I'm parked across the street."

Marge and Hank went back inside, and Hunter continued to sit on the bench, lost in his thoughts. He felt a great sense of remorse. Was this his punishment for lying to himself one too many times? His denial of why he made the choices he did was coming back to haunt him. He couldn't remember ever crying, but that afternoon, he did.

***

About three hours later, Dr. Stanley finally came out to the waiting room.

"He's stable," he said, as he sat down across from Gen and Lucy, who both let out sighs of relief but still had tears in their eyes. Nettie was sitting next to Hank who was lying down, with his head in her lap. He sat straight up when the doctor started talking. "He's in an oxygen tent and heavily sedated. I think you got him here in time. I've ordered a private room with 24-hour nursing attendants. You

239

can go in one at a time to see him now, but understand he's asleep and can't respond. I don't want him agitated. He's a strong man, who wants to live. I know this is futile for me to say, but try not to worry. Gen, do you want to go first?"

Lucy watched her mama walk through the heavy doors and felt like her entire life was a shambles. What had seemed so clear was now one giant blur.

***

Hunter kept his vigil at the hospital the entire afternoon. He watched a steady stream of friends and neighbors go in to give their support to Lucy and her family. He had never witnessed a community come together like this. Although he had been in Kings County for only three weeks, he felt a strong sense of loyalty to the people and the place.

When the Tanners left the hospital, he went home to a house that was incredibly empty. Feeling the absence of another person is something he had never experienced.

Loosening his tie, he stared at the telephone. The ache was real, but he knew there was nothing he could do about it. He put a piece of paper in his typewriter and started writing. It was only thing that had ever made sense out of nonsense for him.

CHAPTER Thirteen

Monday Decisions

The phone woke Lucy up before the alarm did. She answered it quickly, fearing the worst.

"Hello, Lucy. This is Dr. Stanley. I just checked on your father. He's awake and doing better. He's not out of the woods yet, but the nurse said he rested well and is ready to see you and your mama."

"Thank you so much."

She hung up the phone and got out of bed, hoping to have a few minutes alone. Her heart ached. *How on earth will I find the strength to get through this*, she thought. There hadn't been an 8:30 phone call from Hunter since Friday night. The silence made the distance insurmountable.

Within minutes, Nettie arrived at the house, and her mama and Hank woke up. Lucy quickly took charge and organized the morning. "Dr. Stanley called. Daddy had a good night, and we can go see him. Hank, I'll take you to school after we go to the hospital. Nettie, can you stay here for now and listen for the phone?"

By 8:00, they were at the hospital and went up to the floor where Luke was. A nurse took them to his room and tapped gently on the door. A private attendant opened it and whispered, "One at a time per doctor's orders, but Lucy, it's okay if you come in with Hank."

Gen went in first and sat down next to the hospital bed. She caressed her husband's hand as he slowly opened his eyes.

"Hello, beautiful," Luke said in a weak voice. "Didn't mean to give you a scare. Are Lucy and Hank with you?"

"They are. I'll step out so they can visit for a minute."

When Hank saw Luke, he cowered and latched onto Lucy as tight as he could. His grandfather looked old and grey, and the oxygen tent frightened him. "It's okay," said Lucy. "Come closer and touch his hand."

Luke smiled at his grandson. "This is some contraption, huh, buddy? Don't let it scare you though. It's helping me breathe until my heart can work on its own. In the meantime, I need you to be the man of the house. And trust me, that's a hard job. Keeping your mama and Grandma Gen in line isn't easy."

Hank felt a little relieved, touched Luke's hand, and gave him a smile.

"Hey, Lulu," said Luke, with as normal a voice as he could muster. "I don't want you to worry now."

"Daddy, I'm so sorry. I should have never left Saturday."

"Hey, that's nonsense. What I need you to do now is concentrate on getting ready for the showdown tomorrow night. Any new developments?"

"No, but we're not going to give up though, even if the commissioners fail us. You rest for now and don't worry. Mama wants to stay here while I take Hank to school." She kissed her father's hand and held it close to her cheek. "Remember what you said? We Tanners are tough."

***

After Lucy returned from taking Hank to school, Gen insisted on staying with Luke.

As soon as she walked in the door, Nettie handed her a piece of paper. "Lots of calls this morning. Most folks were just wanting to know how your daddy was. Only two wanted you to call them back."

"Okay, thanks for taking care of things here." Lucy looked at the two names at the bottom of the list: Lisa Sutton and Sid Ramsey.

She dialed Sid's number first. He answered immediately and was all business. "Any new developments?"

"No, but I've been a bit preoccupied. My father had a heart attack yesterday morning."

"Lucy, I'm so sorry. Is he okay?"

"He's better, but I'm worried about him. We had quite a scare. I do wish I had good news about the Ridge, but I don't. I'll call tomorrow night after the vote."

She hung up and stared at the piece of paper Nettie had given her. *Why had Lisa Sutton called me?* she wondered. Too tired to deal with it, she went into the kitchen where Nettie was stirring a pot of turnip greens on the stove.

"I think I'll go outside and work in the garden some," Lucy said. "I need to collect my thoughts about what I'm going to say tomorrow night."

For the next couple of hours, she hoed weeds and picked peas. Although her mind was still cluttered, she managed to come up with a few things she wanted to say. Wiping the sweat from her face, she picked up the bucket of peas and sat down under a tree. Nettie came out, with a couple of bowls and a glass of cold water. The light breeze was comforting and for a split second, Lucy remembered how many years they had been here, under the oak, shelling whatever the garden produced. The possibility of losing the serenity to a strip mine was unimaginable.

"When we finish these, let's head to the hospital. Maybe Mama will take a break, so you can visit with Daddy for a while. We'll swing by the school and pick up Hank on our way home."

"I know you're sad, Lucy, about a lot of things."

"I am, but you are, too. We're facing the same challenges and different ones of our own. I'm worried about you, Nettie, and I don't know what to do to help. I do know I need you though. You're my rock and always have been."

"Baby Cakes, I love you like the child I never had. I'm worried about myself, too, but there's just so much pain...and it's buried deep."

***

On Monday morning, Jigs O'Brien pulled the files on Jack Cooper as soon as he got to work. He knew that the GBI had long suspected he was up to something other than making moonshine but had never been able to make a tight case against him. He called a buddy who worked in the agency that issued permits for mining in the state and asked him about the Cagle Mining proposal in Kings County. His response was "What proposal?" Evidently, Cagle had failed to apply for a permit which should happen when an application is filed. Jigs' associate said it wasn't necessary because a company could get a permit after local approval, but not applying for one usually raised a red flag.

He walked down the hall to his boss's office and tapped on the open door.

"Whatcha got there, O'Brien?" barked Chief Moody.

"The file on the Cooper family in Kings County. I had a tip come in over the weekend."

Jigs filled in the chief about Jack, the mine and the alleged wrongdoings.

"Then you should probably head up there. What name will you be using?"

"Sam O'Neil."

"Okay. Keep me posted and keep your head down. Even though it's mountain country, the criminals are just as savvy as they are in the city. But you know that already, don't you?" Moody grunted an Illegible response and motioned for Jigs to be on his way.

***

Lucy talked her mother into coming home from the hospital, promising her she would take her back first thing in the morning. When they got to the farm, she sat down at the kitchen table with Hank while he did his homework. Nettie and Gen busied themselves with supper.

"Mama, we started studying about the history of Kings County today. Did you know this was the heart of the Cherokee Nation?"

"Yes, I did," replied Lucy, half listening.

"And did you know that they had to leave their land and move where the United States government made them go?"

"Yes, I knew that, too."

"I think that was mean. The Cherokees who lived here were peaceful. They didn't hurt anybody. They had their own alphabet and started the first newspaper we ever had around here. They tried to be like the white settlers but got nothing for it. Grandma Gen, did you know any Cherokees in the old days?"

"Yes, I did. In fact—"

"In fact, I have Cherokee blood," interrupted Nettie, looking deep into Hank's eyes.

Lucy and Gen stopped and stared at her.

"Really?" exclaimed Hank. "Wow...did you ever meet a full-blooded Indian?"

Nettie chuckled. "No, I didn't. I just know my great-great grandparents were Cherokees. They died long before I was born."

"Wow," said Hank. "Did you know that they buried their dead folks in the exact spot where they died? See. Here's a picture of some graves. So, do you know where your ancestors are buried?"

"I...I don't know," stammered Nettie, looking away. Lucy looked at Nettie and saw her hands trembling. "What else did you learn today?" she asked Hank, changing the subject.

"...That Josie wants me to be her boyfriend."

"So, did you say, yes?" laughed Lucy pushing back her chair and standing up.

"Yep, but I don't really know what that means."

"Just be sweet to her," said Lucy.

"Well, Hunter is sweet to you, but you won't let him be your boyfriend."

"Okay, enough of this. You need to finish your homework. Nettie, can you give me a hand outside for a minute?"

When they were out of earshot, Lucy stopped Nettie and faced her. She had never seen the expression on Nettie's face that she saw now. "What's wrong? Why did you get so scared when Hank asked you about where your ancestors were buried?"

"Because the graves are haunted. My mama told me that haints lived there and if anybody set foot in the graveyard, the ground would swallow them up."

"Nettie, do you believe that's true?"

"I don't know what to believe, but I was warned not to go to those rock mounds."

"What rock mounds?"

"The ones in the deepest woods on the Ridge, where we knew not to go. When I was a little girl, though, I snuck off and found them. It was so scary that I don't remember what happened. I just know I ran home as fast as I could. My mama knew exactly what I had done. I got a bad whipping. Lucy, I can't talk about it anymore right now."

"Okay, I understand. No more questions. Why don't you call it a day and head home?"

Lucy went through the motions of finishing supper and getting Hank in bed. The house seemed empty without Luke's six-foot frame, his sense of humor, and his calm strength. After she was sure her mother was settled, she went to her room. Exhausted, she lay down on the bed and closed her eyes. She was just about to drift off to sleep when the phone rang. She answered it this time, hoping it was Hunter.

"Hello, Lucy. It's Dr. Stanley. I just checked on your father. He's doing okay and resting."

Lucy thanked him and hung up. That made her feel better but not hearing Hunter's voice was disappointing. They'd see one another at the meeting tomorrow night. There was no way around it.

The piece of paper with Lisa's number on it caught her eye. *That's for tomorrow*, she thought. *This day is done.*

Tuesday Dilemmas

Lucy started working on her speech as soon as Hank left for school. Gen and Nettie were at the hospital, so the house was quiet. She started writing down the thoughts that had been in her head for the last few days, but the images of a desecrated Ridge made her stop.

She was haunted by the potential effects. Losing the farm would deal a brutal blow to her family, but they had the means to relocate if it became impossible to live here anymore. But what about Hank's little friend, Susie Tucker, her mama, and the rest of the people who lived on Hogg Road? What about all of the less than fortunate families whose patched-up sharecroppers' houses were everywhere in Kings County? What about the colored folks who lived in town in shacks where you could see the ground through the floor? If the people they worked for left, what would they do? Lucy felt like she was caught in a windstorm she couldn't escape. The life she had just wished would change now seemed lost. The mine would do more than alter life here. The mine would completely destroy it. She started writing again.

"Land is a precious commodity. Wars are fought over land. Families are torn apart over land. And politicians win or lose elections based on how they handle land use controversies."

The phone rang and interrupted her train of thought. She quickly made a few notes before answering it.

"Tanner residence," she said impatiently.

"Hello, may I please speak to Lucy?"

"May I ask who's calling, please?" asked Lucy, knowing exactly who it was.

"Lisa Sutton."

"This is Lucy," she said with an icy voice.

247

"I know you're wondering why I'm calling you."

"I am."

"Listen. I've known Hunter since he moved to Savannah, and what he told you is true. We are friends, and he had no idea I was coming to see him the other day. I stopped by on my way to Nashville for an audition. What you saw was my saying 'hi' to him the way I say 'hi' to everybody. I know him well enough to know that he's crazy about you. We've had our little whatever you want to call them, but he's not in love in me. I'm calling to tell you that he's a good man—a little confused maybe, but a good man."

"Do you love him?" asked Lucy in a flat voice.

Lisa laughed. "Oh, no, Lucy. I love acting. Like so many in my profession, what I do is more important than anything else. Why do you think there are so many divorces In Hollywood?"

"I guess I never thought about it. So, did you get the part?" asked Lucy, a bit envious of Lisa's carefree lifestyle.

"I did. I'm heading to New York this afternoon. I just wanted to call you before it got crazy. Lucy, Hunter loves you. Now what you do with that love is your business, but I care about my friends, and he is one who deserves a chance. And just so you know, Hunter did not put me up to this. He has no idea I'm calling you."

Lisa said goodbye, lit a cigarette and fixed herself a drink. Acting came easy for her but living was another story.

***

Lucy hung up the phone and walked out on the front porch. There was just too much happening at once. She looked across the road and saw the flag was down on the mailbox, giving her an excuse to walk away from everything for a minute.

A letter addressed to her in Hunter's handwriting was on top of the usual stack of bills and junk mail. She anxiously opened it:

To Lucy:
If the space were any wider,
Time would leave me here forever
To miss you and love you from some distant star.
And my light would caress your cheek only
When you raised your eyes to look my way,
And wondered if the soft glow meant more than
Some distant star had just grown a little brighter.
Love, Hunter

She folded the piece of paper, tried to ignore what her heart said to her, and wept anyway.

***

Jigs O'Brien decided to leave for Cantrell City after lunch on Tuesday. His first stop was the courthouse. He went to the records floor and introduced himself to Hilda Hargett as Sam O'Neil. "I'm from Atlanta and interested in investing in mountain property. I heard there was potential development happening here. Is that true?"

"It is," answered Hilda cautiously. "Are you talking about the proposed mine?"

"As a matter of fact, I am," answered Jigs, appreciating her natural, understated beauty. "Can I see what has been filed? I'd like to do some research before I make inquiries with the company."

She nervously handed him the folder and told him he could use the desk in the records room if he wished.

He scanned the deed, looking for any clues that might point to its being fake. But whoever drew it up knew what they were doing. He looked up and saw Miss Hargett, staring at him. He smiled and nodded, causing her to blush slightly and avert her eyes. *Someone who looks at deeds all day — like you, Miss Hargett,* he thought, *but you don't impress me as a criminal. You're someone a criminal would use.*

249

Jigs had always had a sixth sense—the one detectives and cops must have to solve crimes. He had a way of looking through someone rather than at them and hearing their silent secrets.

He then searched the Cagle file for a state permit. Of course, there wasn't one.

"Mrs. Hargett, can I please see the ledger book that has the records for this property and the rest of them on the—let me see—the Valley Road?"

"It's 'Miss' Hargett," Hilda answered, smiling slightly. "Pardon me," apologized Jigs, who already knew what her proper prefix was. "I'll remember that." He bowed slightly, winked, and took the ledger book from her.

Jigs looked at every entry, noticing that none of them specified who owned the land on the ridge. As he was turning the pages, something caught his eye. It was a tiny piece of paper sticking out from the spine of the ledger. *Somebody tore a page out*, he thought. Checking the sequence of the numbered pages still intact, he discovered there was one clearly missing…the one that belonged to that almost invisible clue.

Jigs was smart enough to know he didn't have a case, but it was a start. He asked for copies of the paperwork, thanked her profusely for her help, adding that he hoped their paths crossed again, and left. Once outside, he walked across the street to the Gold Star Inn and got a room.

*****

The courtroom was filled to capacity for the commission meeting. The Tanners, including Hank, sat with Nettie, Nate, Billy Joe, Marge, Anita and Bo. Theodore was on the front row on one side. On the other was Cooper and Cagle. A large table was in front of the platform where the commissioners' desks were.

When Hunter got there, barely on time, he hurried down the center aisle, nodding slightly at Lucy when he passed by. He liked to sit as close to the front as possible so

250

he could hear everything and have a clear shot with his camera.

At 7 p.m. sharp, Charlie Tate hit the gavel and called the meeting to order. He went over the agenda, which stipulated that the applicants presented first, followed by the spokesperson for the opposition. Then the citizens who had signed up spoke next. The applicants could then counter, followed again by the opposition's attorney. At that point, the vote would be taken.

Cagle reiterated what everyone had already heard at the sessions held the prior week. Cooper bragged about what an economic boom the mine would be for the community. Lucy could barely contain herself from jumping up and screaming "liar."

Theodore did an excellent job refuting their claims and going over the environmental impact study that clearly stated the mine would forever change the complexion of Kings County. He reminded the commissioners that almost 200 people had signed the petition in protest.

No one spoke in favor of the application, but Joe Riley Jr., and Dancy smiled like the doting wife she wasn't the entire time.

After the Presbyterian reverend, Dr. Stanley, Miss Angela Mason, and Mr. Davis from the drugstore spoke, it was Lucy's turn.

She walked to the front and stood behind the large table in front of the commissioners, rather than sitting in the chair. She avoided looking at Hunter but her entire body felt the warmth of his stare. She cleared her throat and began:

"My name is Lucy Tanner. I live on Route #3, the Valley Road. I want to thank the commissioners for giving me the opportunity to address you.

Land is a precious commodity. Wars are fought over land. Families are torn apart over land. And politicians win or lose elections based on how they handle land use issues.

And it is no different here in Kings County. Land use is at the center of everything we do and have. And now, it is at the center of a controversy.

*We are an agrarian community. It is true there are two small towns here, but we are primarily farmers who drive the trade there. Furthermore, there are ordinances in place that protect us from development that would impact our livelihoods – the most important one being that **anything** that is incompatible with raising farm animals and growing crops should **not** be allowed.*

Gentlemen, if a mining operation is allowed in Kings County, the Ridge will become a barren wasteland. The natural habitat that it is for wildlife will disappear. The headwaters of the creeks that feed our valley will be polluted. I have seen what a Cagle mine did to the Copper Basin. It is no longer the green, lush forest it once was. It is now the useless remnant of irresponsible greed.

In closing, I will remind you that your first responsibility is to us, the citizens who pay property taxes. I will also remind you that we vote – either for or against you. Please don't turn your backs on the will of the people. Please do what you know is right. Please don't gamble with what we and generations before us worked so hard to preserve. Thank you."

The ensuing applause was so loud that Charlie Tate had to hit the gavel three of four times to quiet the audience down.

Cagle's response was to assure the commissioners that taking care of the land was his foremost concern—a claim that everyone knew was false. He also insisted that mining was really an agrarian venture. It just took things out of the ground instead of putting anything in the ground. His defense could not have been more ludicrous.

Theodore's rebuttal centered once again on the impact report and the unavoidable negative effects on the property adjacent to the ridge.

"If this is allowed, we might as well kiss the prettiest stretch of farmland in the county goodbye. I rest the case of the people."

Charlie hit the gavel again and called for a vote. When he asked for a show of hands in favor of the request, the Baptist preacher was the only commissioner who did not raise his.

Every person in the room stood up and booed. The commission chair gave up on bringing order to the chaos. He stood up and abruptly left. Hunter took one picture after another of the angry audience, while Cooper and Cagle congratulated one another.

Sheriff Wilkes walked to the front of the courtroom, held his massive arms up in the air and shouted, "All right y'all…the votes over and the meeting is, too. Go outside and cool down. My jail ain't big enough for all of you."

Jigs O'Brien watched the scene from the back row but quickly exited before anyone noticed him…except the sheriff. He had the same sixth sense Jigs had.

***

It was quiet on the drive home. Hank was asleep on the back seat and Gen rested her head against the window. Lucy missed her father, the future of the farm was bleak, and she wanted to talk to Hunter so badly, it hurt.

She parked the car in the garage and helped her son and mother into the house. After they both went to bed, Lucy went into her room. She turned out the light and tried to go to sleep but could not stop thinking about Hunter's poem.

Lucy dialed the number to the newspaper office, knowing he was there working on the story for tomorrow's paper.

"Hunter Fox, here."

"Hey, it's me," she whispered.

CHAPTER Fourteen

Unresolved

Jigs called Chief Moody first thing Wednesday morning. "I'm staying up here at least another night. Things are popping. You know where to find me if you need me."

He hung up the phone and scribbled on the notepad he carried at all times. At the top of the list was to get a shave. In his haste to leave Atlanta, he'd forgotten his razor, and before he paid another visit to Miss Hargett, this stubble had to go.

"Front desk. Jimmy speaking. May I help you?"

"Morning, Jimmy. This is Sam O'Neil in Room 204. Can you please point me in the direction of a good barber shop?"

"Why, yessir. My friend Laney King and his sister, Kittsee, have a shop in Willow Creek…men on one side and ladies on the other. You don't need an appointment. Just tell Laney that I sent you."

"Thanks. And can you please book this room for me another night?"

"Of course, Mr. O'Neil. Let me know in the morning if you want to extend your reservation again. Have a nice day."

Perfect, thought Jigs, *what better place to get the skinny than a barber shop.*

He put his cigarette out and grabbed his keys. As he was walking toward the stairway to the lobby, he saw Dan Cagle hanging a "Do Not Disturb" sign on the door to his room.

Jigs tipped his fedora and then looked straight ahead. Now was not the time to introduce himself. He preferred to do that when he knew exactly what he wanted to say.

***

Lucy unfolded the newspaper. Gen sat on one side of her and Nettie was on the other. The headline was larger than usual and in all capital letters: "**COMMISSION VOTES TO APPROVE REZONING FOR MINE.**" The story took up the entire front page. There were also photographs of the crowd protesting and the speakers, including her.

The three women read in silence. When she was done, Lucy stood up. "Now, I'm madder than before. All you have to do is look at the facts to know that our commissioners failed us."

The phone rang and she went to answer it, while her mother and Nettie continued to read the article.

"Tanner residence," Lucy said.

"Lucy. It's Theodore. I know we lost the first round, but I have an idea. I'm going to appeal this ruling to the state ethics board that oversees county governments. At least, it will slow down the process. Nothing can happen until our petition is reviewed."

"Well, at least it's not completely a lost cause," she answered, "but will that cost anything?"

"No. It won't. I'm leaving for Atlanta right now. I have an appointment this morning, but tell me, how's your father?"

"Holding his own. We'll head in to check on him shortly. I'll tell him you asked."

She went back to the kitchen and saw Nettie standing at the sink, looking out the window. "Where's Mama?"

"She said to tell you she was getting dressed for her appointment at the beauty shop."

255

"Oh, that's right. I forgot. But first, I need to check with Billy Joe and go over what's happening around here. Do you want to go with mama and me?"

"No. I think I'll stay here. It's a good day to be quiet."

***

Jigs parked in front of Miss K's Kut n' Kurl. There were two entrances to the small brick building. One door had a woman's silhouette on it, and the other, a man's. As soon as he stepped inside the gentleman's side, he was greeted with, "Hi. I'm Laney. You must be Mr. O'Neil. Jimmy called and said you were on your way."

"How considerate of him," said Jigs, becoming acutely aware of how important it was for him to keep everything on the down low. When you're in a small town, your business is everybody else's. "As you can tell, I need a shave...forgot to pack my razor."

"Have a seat. We can take care of that in no time. And this is Daisy. She's apprenticing with my sister and me."

The young woman acknowledged Jigs with a quiet 'hello.' She placed a warm towel on his face and set the shaving cream mug and brush on the counter behind the chair. "Can I get you anything to drink?" she asked.

"Got a shot of whiskey?" Jigs asked with a grin.

"Ah, no sir, but—"

Jigs laughed. "That's okay. I'm fine...just kidding...too early in the day for me."

"So, what brings you to Kings County?" asked Laney, as he lathered the shaving brush.

"Land...I'm interested in buying some property somewhere in the mountains for when I retire, but I read the morning paper...doesn't look so good for around here, with that mine and all."

"I know," answered Laney. "We're all sick about it— I say 'all' except for Jack Cooper and the guy who owns the mining company. I'm sure you saw their picture on the front page, all smiles. Well, they were the only ones smiling except for that crook, Buddy Tatum, and the two commissioners who voted with him. Cowards." Laney paused for a moment to give instructions to Daisy. "Sweetie, always make sure the lather is warm. I added hot water to it to make it foam. Here, you try putting it on Mr. O'Neil's face. But back to the mine mess...I'm pretty sure Lucy Tanner isn't going to let go of this, and neither will Theodore Mason. He hates Jack Cooper. In fact, his daughter is divorcing the louse. Caught him, you know," Laney lowered his voice to a whisper and turned his head so Daisy couldn't see his expression. "Anyway, I'd bet my mother's pearls they're trying to figure something out at this very moment."

"Huh, so you think there's something not right with this?"

"Oh, I'm very sure, but unfortunately, the Coopers always get what they want—by hook or by crook, if you know what I mean. But if anybody did know that it was all a setup and had proof Cooper was up to no good, they'd probably be afraid to stand up to him."

Jigs felt Daisy's hand shake, as she tried to put the lather on evenly. He stared at her until she made eye contact with him. And at that instant, he knew she was the one Sid was trying to get to talk. "That's too bad," stilling looking at Daisy. "I learned a long time ago that the only way to stop a criminal from hurting folks was to be smarter and braver than he is—I say 'he' because most criminals are men."

"Is that what you do, Mr. O'Neil, chase bad guys?" asked Laney, thirsty for intrigue.

"Oh, no," answered Jigs with a chuckle. "I just enjoy reading crime stories. I'm in sales."

"Well, too bad. We need a good cop to bust Jack Cooper. Thanks, Daisy. I'll take over now. We'll work on how to handle a razor some more before I turn you loose on a customer."

The young woman nodded and mumbled something before straightening up and opening the door to the other side. Laney looked up and saw Lucy coming in with Gen.

"Lucy," he said loud enough for her to hear. "Come over here. I want to give you a hug. You were so good last night."

"Not good enough," she answered, as she walked through the open door. "Want me to shut this?"

"Please. I don't want to hear Kittsee's incessant chattering. Mr. O'Neil, this is the famous Lucy Tanner. Lucy, Mr. O'Neil. He's looking to buy some land in the mountains and liked it here until he read about that damn mine," continued Laney, as he deftly moved the straight razor over Jigs' face with soft, yet incisive strokes.

"I can understand your concern…we're in the same boat," said Lucy, not feeling up to any small talk. "Laney, I'll see you later," she said, giving him a hug. "Gotta go check on Daddy."

"How's he doing, sweetie?"

"Getting a little stronger every day. I'll tell him you asked…nice to meet you, Mr. O'Neil."

"You keep that chin up now, Lucy," said Laney. After she left, he added, "That is one tough girl right there." Jigs then heard Lucy's life story in five minutes right down to the fact that she and Hunter were an item. "Everybody is so happy for her. And lord help me, he is one fine looking man. Speaking of fine looking, take a gander at that clean, smooth face of yours." He turned the barber chair around, smiling at his professionalism. "Smooth as a baby's bottom."

Jigs walked out of the Kut n' Kurl with more information than he got in most formal interrogations. He decided to drive out to the Valley Road to see the land in question. *And when I get back*, he thought, *I'm going to pay a visit to Mr. Cooper himself.*

***

Hilda Hargett saw Jigs leave the hotel earlier that morning, but he didn't see her, so she was able to stare as much as she wanted. He wasn't what you call Hollywood handsome, but there was a ruggedness about him that she

258

found quite appealing. His physique was very fit, and he definitely had a quick gait. With a head full of dark curls, peppered with grey at his temples, and green eyes that shot arrows, Jigs O'Brien definitely caught Hilda's eye. She noticed that he left the hotel without any luggage. And that made her smile.

Miss Hargett had never married. Not because she wasn't interested, but because she had not met her intellectual equal. She loved opera, English literature, and French wine, and no available man in Cantrell City shared the same joie de vivre. She often wondered what her life would have been like if she had left Kings County 15 years ago when she was 25—a choice she never had.

"Taking in the scenery, Hilda?" asked Judge Whitaker, who walked up behind her.

Hilda spun around. "Oh, morning, sir...just getting some fresh air before I go to work. These cool days are wonderful."

"Indeed, they are," answered the judge, eyeing Jigs as he pulled out of the parking lot next to the hotel. "A friend of yours?"

"No, sir. I just met him yesterday. He came to the courthouse. He's interested in buying some land here."

"Hmm. I see." He nodded at the clerk and walked up the steps to the courthouse.

Hilda realized that once again, Jack Cooper was preventing her from being who she wanted to be. His control was suffocating. Her desire for his forgery to come to light was taking over any fear she had of him, but she didn't know how to bring him down without taking herself with him.

***

Lucy tapped on the door to Luke's room and was surprised when her father answered with "Come in."

"Daddy, look at you. Where's your nurse?"

259

"Shift change. My day girl hasn't gotten here yet."

"You sound really good, even though you're still in that plastic tent." Lucy blew him a kiss. "I brought you a copy of the paper, but I see you already have one."

"Hunter came by first thing this morning. He was mighty proud of you last night and wanted me to see your picture and read what you said. The nurse let him in for about five minutes."

"Huh, that was nice of him," said Lucy, smiling.

"So, you're not ready to snatch him bald anymore?"

"I haven't completely decided," said Lucy.

"Well, don't do anything rash. I'd hate to read your name in Sheriff Wilkes' police report."

Lucy laughed. "I miss your jokes, Daddy, and can't wait for you to come home. Has Dr. Stanley given you any idea when that will happen?"

"No...too early for that now. One day at a time. One day at a time."

"Okay, but it can't happen soon enough for me. Have you looked at Hunter's editorial yet?"

"Nope. Why don't you read it to me?"

Lucy turned to page three and smiled inside when she saw his picture next to his column.

Nothing is Stronger than Community
According to Webster's, community *"is a feeling of fellowship with others, as a result of sharing common attitudes, interests, and goals."*

Since relocating to Kings County a mere month ago, I have seen community at its best. I have witnessed a coming together to resist outside intervention that is deemed incompatible with that which is here. I have seen a coming together to protect a heritage that so many have worked to build and maintain. And I have seen neighbors come to-gether to support their friends in time of an emer-gency.

But last night, the commissioners, with the exception of Charlie Tate and Preacher Thomas Adams,

260

failed their community. Those who voted in favor of the rezoning request showed a blatant disregard for the evidence presented by Theodore Mason. More reprehensible, however, is that they turned a deaf ear to their constituents' voices.

More than 200 people signed the petition to deny the request. The entire audience stood up and booed their decision. And still, three elected officials chose to vote in favor of greed instead of what is best for the community.

And no one said it better than Lucy Tanner, who spoke on behalf of the entire county. She spelled out perfectly why the proposal is inconsistent with existing land use in the county and why allowing a mine here would be devastating to the region, and she minced no words in reminding the commissioners to whom they should be accountable.

Today, it feels like we lost the war, but I truly believe the people who live here are a tough lot. I also know your valleys and mountains are sacred to you. This is not over.

I am extremely honored that I now live in Kings County and serve you through the written word.

And I am convinced that nothing is stronger than community.

Lucy's eyes filled with tears and a couple rolled down her cheeks.

"Now, that's what I call some damn good writing," said Luke. He gently caressed Lucy's tiny hand with his work-worn, tanned one, not looking at her and giving her time to wipe her tears. When he heard her clear her throat, he looked up and locked eyes with his daughter. "Lulu, don't run away from this person who has come into your life. I know I was pretty hard on him at first, but I was scared and didn't want to lose you. I know that was wrong of me. When you love somebody, you never leave that person's heart…which means I'll always be in yours, and you, in mine. But. Let yourself love Hunter and let him love you. For me. Now. How about fetching my bride? I want to see those shiny green eyes of hers."

***

The phone was ringing when Sandy walked into the Lodge. He ran to the bar and answered it quickly.

"How did it go last night?" asked Sid.

"As we expected. The commissioners caved. The only one voting against it was the Baptist preacher. The crowd was angry as hell. The sheriff had to calm everybody down."

"Hmmm. I can't say I'm surprised…disappointed but not surprised. What about Daisy? Is she warming up to the idea of talking?"

"Well, maybe. She told me about this guy who came in the barber shop yesterday…said he was in town to look at property. You don't know Laney the barber, but he talks so fast, he don't know what he's saying sometimes…a good person but a mouth that won't shut. Anyway, when he started talking about Cooper and how nobody would stand up to him, she started feeling real guilty. And that guy—the one who said he was looking for property—stared straight through her…made her want to blurt out everything. So, we'll see."

Sid listened to Sandy's description of who he knew was Jigs. He was the best at getting people to trust him. If anybody could break the chains around Kings County, it was him. "Well, that sounds interesting. Just keep your ear to the ground. I imagine Jack and his cronies will turn out in force this evening. Keep me posted."

Sid hung up the phone and lightly tapped his desk. *Give it time*, he thought. *Jigs knows exactly what he's doing.*

***

262

It didn't take long for Jigs to understand why the Valley Road and the Ridge were important to protect. The fertile farmland tucked between the mountain ridges was breathtaking. He felt like he had gone back in time 100 years. It was peaceful and very quiet.

When he got back to Willow Creek, he parked in front of the bank. After letting the window down, he lit a cigarette. Jigs hated the smell but sure loved how tobacco tasted. After a couple of puffs, he put it out and went inside Jack Cooper's hide out.

George stood up from his desk and walked out of his office when he saw Jigs come in the front door of the bank. Fresh faces, which often translated into new business, were always welcome.

"Hello. I'm George Mason, the bank manager. May I help you?"

"Sam O'Neil...from Atlanta. I'm here to discuss potential real estate investment opportunities in Kings County. The talk in my circle is that there is a proposed mining development for here. Is this something you could help me with?"

"Actually, the bank president is the one you need to speak to—Jack Cooper. He is one of the investors and knows firsthand what's going on. Let me buzz him and see if he's available."

While George went in his office and called Jack, Jigs looked around at the opulent marble, brass, and mahogany furnishings. He wasn't surprised.

"Right this way, Mr. O'Neil," said George. Jigs followed him through the lobby toward Jack's office. The bank manager tapped gently on the ornate door and Cooper bellowed, "Come in, come in." George held it open so Jigs could enter. "Welcome," continued Jack, standing up from his desk. "You can close that when you leave," he said dismissively to George. "Can I get you a drink or a cigar?"

"I'd love a good cigar," said Jigs, "but I'll pass on the drink."

Jack opened a fancy wooden box and offered a Cuban to Jigs. "The best I can find. A friend imports them for me." He bent over and flicked his lighter open. As he reached toward Jigs, his massive cuff link caught O'Brien's eye. But who wouldn't take note? It was by far the biggest damn piece of gold he'd ever seen. Jack was all about expensive taste, albeit bad taste. Jigs knew the type—bigger appetites than bank accounts. He inhaled several times until the grey smoke formed a cloud above his head.

"So, tell me why you're interested in Kings County, Sam," said Jack, pouring himself a shot of vodka and sizing up his guest as if he was the detective.

"I hear things are about to pop around here. Some buddies of mine were talking about it at the club a few weeks ago. I've heard you're the top investor and the man who knows the most about Kings County business."

Loving the flattery, Jack took a long pull on his cigar and leaned forward. "Well, you heard right, my friend. The county commission approved the request for rezoning last night. We just have to get a couple of permits and then we can start blasting that iron ore right out of the mountain ridge and making some money. Are you interested in investing in the mine or land?"

"Well, I'd like to hear about both."

"You're here at a good time to buy real estate. I imagine a lot of those folks who live adjacent to the mine's location will be forced to move. What's cheap farmland now will become valuable commercial property—more development to make more money. But if you invest in the mine, you stand to profit from that, too. For every dollar you invest, you could make ten."

"Hmmm. Do you have some information on the company and the terms for investing?"

"I sure do. Here you go."

Jigs scanned the paperwork quickly. "So, it says here that investors pay the money directly to you, as agent for the bank, and you, in turn, transfer the funds to Cagle Mining. Correct?"

"That's it. Pure and simple. When the operation starts producing, you'll receive a share based on how much you've invested. It's like being a silent partner."

"Have you had good luck getting folks to give you money so far?"

"Yes, we have," lied Jack. "I got one really big fish from Chattanooga. He prefers to remain anonymous, but I know for a fact he never backs away from a good deal—legal or otherwise." Jack grinned at Jigs and poured himself another drink.

"How do your investors know they're getting a fair cut?" asked Jigs. "Will you provide balance sheets and profit and loss statements?"

"Eventually, but in the beginning, this will be a handshake-type of deal. Give us the cash, and we'll promise to make it worth your while."

"I see. Let me think on it. It almost sounds too good to be true. In the meantime, please put my name on the list of people who are interested. I think you might have a gold mine that actually sells iron ore." Jigs stood up, ready to take his leave.

"I like you, Sam," laughed Jack, following suit. He gave Jigs a pat on the back and walked with him toward the office door. "I'm pretty sure we'll be doing business together. You're my kinda guy," he said, shaking Jigs' hand.

"Thank you. You'll find out that I'm all about business," answered O'Brien, slightly smiling at Jack.

"Hey, if you're hanging around these parts another day, be my guest at The Lodge tonight. It's about a half mile north of Cantrell City. Say, about six?" offered Jack.

"Okay. Thanks. I guess The Lodge is the only place I can get a drink, right?"

"It sure is, and we have some of the best shine in Georgia."

***

Jigs got in his car, made a few notes, lit a cigarette, and headed back to Cantrell City, so he could pay a visit to Miss Hargett before the courthouse closed.

He parked his car and went up to his room first. Hilda impressed him as a fastidious woman so he smoothed his hair and brushed his teeth. After getting an iced tea to go, he walked across the street and climbed the stairs to the county clerk's office.

"I hope I'm not interrupting your workday, Miss Hargett," he said, "but I needed to look at the land ledger again. I thought you might like something to drink. It is that afternoon slump time, you know."

"Why, thank you, but please call me Hilda," she said, smiling slightly as she beamed inside. "I was just about to go get something at the café next door. Here is the ledger. You can use the same office as you did before."

O'Brien made a list of the property owners on the Valley Road and studied each deed and its coordinates. Every property listed ended at the same northern coordinate. When he examined the topographical map, he discovered that the entire ridge was not a part of any of the properties. It was a lot of land, and Jack Cooper stood to make an enormous amount of money from selling it. The missing page had something to do with it. It just had to. He closed the book and went back to Miss Hargett's desk.

"Thank you again."

"Were you able to find some property you liked?" asked Hilda, wanting to delay his departure.

"Not yet, but I paid a visit to Jack Cooper at the bank today," he said, watching Hilda closely for any adverse reaction. "He seems like a sharp businessman and is keeping his eye out for me. As someone who lives here, what do you think about him?"

Jigs noticed the clerk's good nature suddenly dissipated, and she turned around to put the ledger book back on the shelf. "I don't have much occasion to deal with him. George usually comes in to check on deeds when there's a sale or a purchase. Mr. Cooper's secretary used to run errands for him, but she quit a couple of weeks ago. I don't think Jack works. He just tells other people what to do."

"Huh...that sounds like a good set up. So, do you think it's a good idea for me to do business with him? I trust your opinion, given you are the custodian for the taxpayers' records. I'm certain you're reliable."

Hilda cringed inside. Here was a man who seemed like a good person—a man who had manners and class, telling her he trusted her—the very person who forged the deed for Jack Cooper. "I'm reluctant to say if I think it's a good idea or not...depends on his actions over the next couple of weeks in regards to this mine issue. I stayed out of the fray, but I'm sure you're aware that he has angered most of the people who live in Kings County."

"I understand your hesitancy, but I'd really appreciate it if you could be the eyes and ears for me. Here's my number. If you think of anything you need to share, or just want to talk, please feel free to call." Jigs took out a business card that had "Sam O'Neil" printed on it and jotted down his telephone number. "I only give that to people I want to have it." He started to leave but stopped and turned around. "Oh, I almost forgot. When I was looking at the ledger, I noticed there was a page missing. The numbers are out of sequence. I just thought you might want to be aware of that...hope to see you again soon. And you can call me Sam." He smiled and left Hilda standing there, reeling.

***

The Lodge was busy on Wednesday nights. It was closed Sunday through Tuesday, so the patrons were very thirsty by mid-week. The heathens who didn't go to prayer meeting arrived early, and the hypocrites snuck in later.

Jack drove there as soon as the bank closed. He had been celebrating the win from the night before for most of the day, only sobering up after a huge lunch at Buck's BBQ House and a nap. But by six, he was feeling no pain again.

When Jigs got there around 6:30, the room was filled with cigar smoke, loud voices, and overly robust laughter.

"Sam," shouted Jack. "Glad you made it. Everybody, this is Sam O'Neil from Atlanta…seems even the big money guys have heard about our good fortune and want a piece of the action. Sandy, pour our friend a shot of whiskey, or would you prefer shine?"

"Whiskey is good," answered Jigs, inwardly disgusted at Cooper's distorted familiarity.

Jack handed him the glass and proposed a toast. "To new friends and new fortunes," he slurred.

Jigs took a small sip and gave his approval, even though he preferred a cold beer to hard liquor.

"Buddy, come here," yelled Jack. "I want you to get to know this man. He'll probably turn out to be one of your best car-buying customers. Tell him what a good guy I am and how he can't go wrong investing in Kings County."

Weaving a bit, the automobile dealer walked over and sat down on the stool next to Jigs. He asked Sandy to top off his drink and leaned in far too close to Jigs' face for his comfort. "I've known Jack Cooper for years, and there's no better person for figuring out how to make money. Whenever he tells me about a deal, I just say yes without even knowing much about it. Cooper always delivers…just like he'll do this time. Hell, I don't care what those lame brains at the commission meeting think or want. I vote with the money—every time. They have no power compared to that man over there. And in the end, nobody will buck him. Why? Because they want to be on this side of the ground. If you're smart, you'll invest in this mine. Just like I did."

"So, if you don't mind my asking, how much money did you give him?"

Buddy chuckled. "Oh, I didn't invest money. I invested my vote." He grinned and excused himself, stumbling in the direction of the juke box.

Jack saw him leave and sat down next to Jigs.

"So, was Buddy helpful?"

"Beyond words," answered Jigs, with a crooked smile. "Will you be at the bank on Friday? I need to go to Atlanta tomorrow to speak with my investors. If they are amenable, which I believe they will be, I'd like to bring you some cash then."

"Damn right, I'll be there. I'm always ready to take somebody else's money."

"I bet you are," answered Jigs, setting his glass down. "I bet you are."

***

Nettie was sitting on the porch of her house when Luke phoned her late that afternoon. She was surprised yet pleased to hear his voice.

"Hey. Is there any way you can come to the hospital now?" he asked. The strength in his voice amazed Nettie, but she knew she shouldn't expect anything less. "I have some things I want to discuss with you. I'm sorry to bring this up at the last minute, but you know...business is always on my mind."

"Of course. I'll be there in 20 minutes." She called Nate and told him where she was going but that she would be home by suppertime.

She drove around to the back entrance of the hospital. Dr. Stanley had made arrangements for her to visit Luke whenever she wanted, but she knew it best to use the door that Coloreds always did — the one in back.

A stair well led to the floor where Luke was. His room was only a short distance down the hallway, so she was able to be at his door before anyone saw her. She knocked gently. A nurse opened it, nodded, and left.

"Well, you sure look better than you did yesterday," said Nettie. She sat down in the chair next to Luke's bed and opened a notebook she kept her to-do-list in. "I figured I might need to write down what we talk about so I can go over it with Lucy."

"You won't need to do that, Nettie. This isn't about the farm."

"Well, what in heaven's name is it about?" she asked.

"You, Nettie. And me...what I did, what I didn't do, and what I need to do now." He extended his arm toward her. "Come closer, please. I need to look into your eyes and hold your hand."

Nettie felt like the entire world had stopped spinning. Her heart pounded in her chest, but she did as Luke requested.

"Do you remember anything about what happened up on the Ridge when you were a girl?"

"No, except that I got in a lot of trouble for sneaking up there. What I saw or did there is a memory I can't find, but that was the maddest I'd ever seen my mama. Why are you asking me this?"

"That was my favorite place to go and have a sip. You didn't know I did that, did you? Sip?"

"Of course I knew, Luke. I do, too. I bet if Gen tried it, she'd want to sip, too. But what does that have to do with me?"

"I was up there the afternoon you snuck up there. I saw what happened to you."Hhe gripped her hand tightly but not in a bad way. "Sugah, JJ Cooper raped you."

Nettie gasped and put her hand on her chest. She was certain she was going to have a heart attack right there in the hospital. Everything started caving in but the images became clear in her mind.

"You were stronger than he was, though," Luke said, trying to comfort her as best he could. "You got away and ran down the path toward me. I pulled you in the underbrush where I was until that bastard left. You never looked at me, and I never said a word to you or anyone else, which was a terrible thing on my part. But I was terrified of the Coopers, too." Luke went on to tell Nettie how he had mortgaged the farm and owed them money. "That's no excuse for not coming forth though. I swore from that moment on I'd make sure you were okay. But I should have known you are your best defense. It was your strength that stopped JJ and nothing more, my friend."

Nettie put her other hand on top of Luke's. "Well, I don't feel so strong right now. I feel weak. Now, I know why I tremble at the thought of going up on the Ridge or talking about my childhood. That darkness has lived inside of me far too long." The tears welled up inside of her but Luke's voice stopped them from overflowing.

"There's more," he said. "I found a shovel he left up there. JJ was burying something under the rocks at the edge of one of the graves when you startled him…something you probably need to find."

The nurse opened the door and told Luke and Nettie they only had another minute or two.

"Nettie, I want you to know I love you like a daughter. I always have. And what you have meant to me as a friend and business partner is something I can't express. There are no words."

Nettie bent over and kissed his forehead. "I love you, too, Luke Tanner."

***

Hunter called Lucy right on time that night.

"Hey," she said softly. "Thanks for taking a paper to my father today. He was very proud you did."

"Of course," answered Hunter, relishing the sound of her voice. 'I wanted him to know what a fine job you did."

"I read him your editorial, and he said it was some damn good writing."

"That's a compliment I like hearing. If he's a fan, maybe you'll come back to the club."

"Is Miss Savannah a member?"

"No, and when I have the chance, I will be as honest as you want me to be about my relationship with her. All I ask is that you listen and believe me."

"All right. I'll do that. I want to trust you. I really do."

"Good. I couldn't ask for more…well, maybe a little more," added Hunter.

"Like what?" asked Lucy.

"…To see you again, to talk face-to-face, to laugh like we do when we're around each another, to hold you, to kiss you."

"Huh, is that all?"

"Well, for now."

Lucy snuggled down in the covers and whispered, "I think I can manage that. When?"

Hunter laughed at her quick honesty, "…as soon as possible, Miss Tanner."

Upheaval

Lucy was in a deep sleep around midnight when Jenny's barking and a knock on the back door awakened her. Grabbing her robe, she knew something was wrong for this to be happening in the middle of the night. *The cows across the road must have gotten out*, she thought. *Good thing Billy Joe has a phone now. I'll ring him as soon as I know for sure what's going on.*

She turned on the back porch light and was startled to see Dr. Stanley. Her heart fell to the floor as she opened the door. He was standing there, with his hat in hand, and a somber look on his face.

"No, no, don't say it, Dr. Stanley," she whimpered, opening the door.

"Lucy, I'm so sorry. Come here," said the veteran doctor, taking the young woman in his arms as he would his own daughter. "Your daddy had a massive attack in his sleep. He never knew what hit him or when. He died instantly."

Disbelief flooded Lucy's entire being and inconsolable sobs consumed her. Dr. Stanley held her as she dealt with the worst news she had heard since her brother Henry was killed.

"Dr. Stanley, this is more than I can bear." The doctor felt his shirt grow damp from her tears and had to muster all he had to keep from doing the same.

"I'll help you as best I can. Let's go see Gen first. If Hank doesn't wake up, wait until the morning."

They walked quietly down the hallway, and Lucy motioned for the doctor to have a seat in the living room. She closed the doors separating the back of the house from the front and opened the door to her mother's room, who was still sound asleep. *Thank God she's hard of hearing*, thought Lucy. She went over and sat on the side of the bed and gently touched Gen's hand. Her eyes flickered opened and at first, she was startled.

"What is it, Lucy? What's wrong?"

"Can you please put on your robe and come with me?" asked Lucy, trying hard to keep her voice from shaking. She helped her mother out of bed and took her into the living room. When Gen saw Dr. Stanley, she faltered. He jumped up and helped get her to the sofa. Tears were already streaming down her face when the doctor told her what had happened.

The guttural sound that came out of the grief-stricken woman's soul was something Lucy never forgot. "It can't be," she sobbed. "I was dreaming about him when you woke me up. He was so happy and out in the fields with his cows and Jenny...smiling at me, with those blue eyes shining. Oh Lucy, whatever are we going to do?"

"I don't know, Mama, I just don't know." She held her mother and rocked her gently, feeling every ounce of her pain and more.

"Lucy, I can stay here as long as you need me," said Dr. Stanley. "Can I make any calls for you?"

"Yes, please. Nettie. I need you to call Nettie. Her number is 9611."

***

Billy Joe got out of bed and walked out on the front porch of his new home. The indoor plumbing was complete, but there was something about the freedom of relieving one-self outside that he had never forgotten from his child-hood. Those times were when it was just him and the stars, with no fear of anyone.

He noticed something was different, but it took a moment for him to realize that the lights at the Tanner place pierced the typically black country night.

"That's not right," he said aloud. He quickly dressed, jumped in his pickup truck, and drove down the road.

When he pulled in the driveway, he saw Dr. Stanley's car and feared what he was about to encounter. Mustering all the strength he had accrued from living a hard life, he walked up to the front door and knocked gently.

Dr. Stanley opened it, Lucy looked up, and the tears started pouring down her face again. "Daddy's dead."

"Oh, Lucy, I am so sorry," said Billy Joe, choking back his own grief. "What can I do?"

"Please call Marge and ask her to let Anita know first thing. But tell her not to worry about coming out this evening, but I will need her first thing in the morning if possible. There will be a ton of folks coming to pay their respects and bringing food. Nettie is dealing with her own sadness and will need help. Mama and I will have to go to town and start making arrangements."

Gen sobbed and repeated, "No, I can't," over and over again when she heard Lucy's words.

"Okay," said Billy Joe. "But do you need me to do anything now?"

"Yes. Go out and find Jenny. She knows something is up. She's been pitiful since Daddy got sick."

"I can do that, Lucy. Then I'll go home and call Marge. I'll be back first thing in the morning."

As Billy Joe was leaving, Nate drove up with Nettie, who was already in tears and unable to speak. Her conversation with Luke from the night before played over and over in her mind.

"This is gonna be some pain for these women," said Nate, after Nettie went inside, "even though they're some of the strongest folks I know."

When Billy Joe left, he looked back at the house and saw Nate, sitting in one of the rockers, his head bent down and his shoulders shaking.

***

When Nettie walked in, Lucy stood up and practically fell in her arms. "It's gonna be okay, Baby Cakes. Just let it go," she whispered through her own tears. She then sat down next to Gen and embraced the woman she considered family. "I got you, Gen. We all got each other."

Dr. Stanley, who stood up when Nettie came in, was standing near the door to the hallway. "Lucy, I'll be going now, so you and your family can have some privacy. But I want to leave some medication for y'all. It isn't strong but will just help you relax, so you can get some rest."

"Thank you, Dr. Stanley...for all you have done," said Lucy, squeezing his hand. "We still have to tell Hank, but maybe he will stay asleep for now."

After the doctor left, Nettie went into the kitchen and made some mint tea and brought two cups to Lucy and Gen. "Here," she said. "Sip on this and let your souls feel all the grief they have." She walked out on the front porch where Nate sat. "You can go in if you want to. I'm sure they'd appreciate your comfort. I'm staying here for the night, but can you come get me before sunrise so I can go home and change?" He stood up, held Nettie close while she cried, and then went inside to see Lucy and Gen.

When he left, Lucy helped her mother to her room. "Here. Take this and try to rest some. We have a hard couple of days in front of us. If you need anything, I'm just down the hall, and Nettie is in the guest room." She kissed her mother softly and added, "We'll get through this somehow."

Lucy went into the kitchen, where Nettie was washing the tea cups. "I have to call Hunter," she said, her voice shaking. "I need him right now."

"Then you call him, Baby Cakes. All of us must ask for exactly what we need. As a matter of fact, I'll take one of those relaxing pills, please. My body feels like it's about to jump out of itself. I'll be in the rocker in your mother's room. I need to be close to her."

Lucy gave Nettie a pill and went into her room. She called Hunter and waited on the front porch for him to get there, which didn't take long. He jumped out of his car, ran up the front walk, and wrapped his arms around her. "I need you right now," she said through her tears. "I need you to lie down with me and hold me, please."

CHAPTER Fifteen

Thursday Troubles and Truth

Lucy woke up when she heard Nettie leave out the back door. The flood of grief she experienced when she fell asleep in Hunter's arms engulfed her again. He stirred and kissed the top of her head. "I should get going, unless you want me here when you tell Hank," He whispered.

"Do you mind staying until Nettie gets back? He'll be waking up soon."

"I don't mind at all."

Lucy lit the stove under the pot Nettie had fixed the night before and put some milk and sugar on the table. Her movements were robotic and the lump in her throat was as big as a grapefruit. The sound of Hunter running some water in the bathroom drifted down the hallway—a sound she felt like she had heard a million times.

She opened the cupboard to take out some coffee cups and saw her father's favorite one - the one her mother brought him from Chattanooga before they got married. She started to cry just as Hunter walked in. He wiped the tears from her face and gave her a hug that said everything she needed to hear. They sat down at the kitchen table, and Lucy heard Hank stirring a bit. She braced herself for what she had to do.

Hank walked out of his room and saw his mother's door was already open. *Hmm?* he thought to himself, *I didn't hear the alarm yet.* Rubbing the sleep from his eyes, he walked down the hall to the kitchen.

"Hunter, what are you doing here? Mama, what's wrong? I can tell you've been crying."

277

"Come here, son," said Lucy. She lifted the little boy who was almost as tall as she was into her lap and cradled him close. "Granddaddy fell asleep last night and didn't wake up. He's dead, sweet boy."

Hank felt something he had never felt before—unexpected pain and loss. His tears exploded. "No, Mama. That can't be true. My granddaddy can't be dead. He's supposed to live forever," he wailed.

"I know, son. None of us want to be without him, but I'm afraid we must."

"How can we do that?"

"By being strong, just like he taught us to be. He'd want you to be the man of the house now—for me and Grandma Gen. Remember when he told you that was your job?"

"Yeah, but I don't feel very strong right now. Do I have to go to school?" Hank asked through his sobs.

"No, sugah. You won't go the rest of the week. Hunter, I hear Mama making some noises. Can you take over here, please?"

Hunter picked up Hank and walked out on the back porch. "Let's go outside and watch the sunrise, okay? That always helps me feel better."

Within a few minutes, Nettie drove up. She walked up on the back porch and Hank reached out for her to take him. "Thank you, Hunter," she said. He patted her on the back and went back inside. Gen was sitting at the table, staring at her folded hands.

"Mrs. Tanner, there's nothing I can say right now," Hunter said. "Just know that I am here for you."

Lucy followed him down the hall and out onto the front porch. He took her in his arms and gently hugged her. "Thanks," she said, her voice shaking. "Can you check on me later, please?"

"Of course. I'll try my best to do whatever you need to help you get through this."

"I appreciate it a lot," Lucy said, kissing him gently.

"You don't have to thank me. That's what it should all be about, you know, doing things for people you love."

Lucy smiled through her tears, realizing she just heard what her father said to her the last time she saw him.

***

Jigs was up by dawn and at the front desk about the time Jimmy was getting to work.

"Morning, Mr. O'Neil. You're the first person stirring around here."

"Yeah…wanna get an early start. I'm checking out and heading back to Atlanta."

"Okay, I'll figure up your bill. It'll only take a few minutes."

Jigs sat down on one of the leather armchairs in front of the stone fireplace. He loved the fact that the old hotel still looked like it did when it was built. He had a deep appreciation for anything that transcended time—architecture, furniture, land, people—which was why he found himself feeling an affinity for Kings County as a whole.

"Here you go," said Jimmy from behind the desk.

"I'll probably be back tomorrow," said Jigs. "There will be rooms available, right?"

"Under normal circumstances, yes, but this weekend is unusual. Mr. Luke Tanner passed away unexpectedly last evening. My cousin at the hospital called me in the middle of the night. His funeral could be as early as Saturday, and I imagine there will be quite a few out-of-town guests. You might want to reserve a room now and cancel if you decide not to stay."

"Oh, I hate to hear that. I drove down the Valley Road and noticed his farm…beautiful land. He wasn't that old, was he?"

"No, sir. I think he was in his 60's. This is a terrible shock to our entire community. Everybody loved Mr. Luke."

"That's too bad," said Jigs, "but thanks for the advice. Go ahead and reserve the same room for tomorrow evening. I'll let you know as soon as I decide if I'll need it or not. Here's the key and the cash for my bill. And keep the change."

Jigs went out onto the veranda and saw Hilda walking down the sidewalk toward the courthouse. She glanced his way, and he waved. "Morning," he called out. He walked across the street and bowed slightly. "Looks like it's going to be another beautiful day."

"Yes, but a sad one."

"Jimmy told me about Mr. Tanner.... I'm sorry for the community's loss."

"Thank you. He was an inspiration for a lot of us." Hilda looked at the small duffle bag he carried. "Are you heading back?" she asked.

"I am, but I'm probably coming back into town tomorrow...more business. Maybe I'll see you then." Jigs smiled and started to leave but stopped and turned around. "Hilda, I'll be done by 5 or so. Would you like to have supper with me tomorrow night? Say, around 6:30, at the hotel?"

"Why, yes. I would," stammered Hilda. "That sounds nice."

"Good. I'll see you then."

***

Jigs went by his apartment in downtown Atlanta before heading into work. He called Sid as soon as he had a shower.

"Hey. I have some news for you. Mr. Luke Tanner passed away last night. I found out right before I left Cantrell City."

"That's too bad. Thanks for letting me know. Anything else?"

"Nothing I can share. You know that. But let's say the research has been lucrative so far. I'll talk to you soon."

"You never disappoint, Jigs."

The veteran cop drained his coffee cup, got dressed, and was at the office in less than an hour. After checking the messages left in a neat pile on his desk, he took off his sports coat, loosened his tie and buzzed the chief.

"Moody, here," grunted his boss.

"I'm back, chief. I need to fill you in and go over my plan as soon as possible. Are you busy now?"

"I'm busy all the goddamn time, but come on."

After spending 20 years working with Moody, Jigs knew how to condense a memo full of data into a concise verbal report. Within 15 minutes, he gave him an overview of his suspicions, the overt confessions he heard, and his plan for catching Jack.

"If I give him some cash, and he's skimming — which I would be willing to bet my record collection on that he is — that will add fuel to fire."

"How much?" asked Moody.

"I figure $5,000 will make him feel very special."

"Fuck. It should."

"Yeah, it's a lot, but I want him to think I'm rolling with the big boys. The cockier he is, the more reckless he is."

"Alright. When do you need it?"

"I want to get it to him tomorrow. It's important to ride on this high he's on right now."

"I'll have it by the end of the day."

Jigs turned to leave but Moody stopped him

"O' Brien," he said in a serious, quieter tone. "Don't fuck this up now. You don't have enough years in your solitary life left to pay me back."

"Yes sir. I won't."

***

A steady stream of folks came and went at the Tanner home all day on Thursday. They brought so much food that Nettie started putting some of it in the deep freezer. Marge and Anita were there to help, while Lucy and Gen went to Cantrell City to make arrangements. Hank and the dog stayed close to Billy Joe, never leaving his side.

By the time Lucy and Gen got back, they were both spent beyond words. They had met with the undertaker and the minister, and all of the arrangements had been made. The visitation was going to be Friday night and the funeral Saturday afternoon.

Luke was a simple man, so Lucy made sure the service would be, too: two songs and two scriptures.

He had always told her that he didn't want flowers at his funeral. Instead, request donations to the Chattanooga Boys' Home where he lived until he was 14.

By 6 o'clock, the crowds had stopped coming to the Tanner home. Nettie went to her house to rest, and Gen sat down in her rocker on the front porch. She looked at Luke's empty chair and called her grandson. "Hank, please come out here."

"What is it, Grandma Gen?"

"Sit in your Granddaddy's chair, please. It looks very lonesome."

They rocked silently and looked across at the barn. Hank wished Luke was walking toward the house, with Jenny at his heels, but he didn't say a word. He knew his grandmama was probably thinking the same thing.

Hunter got to the house about dark, and Billy Joe did, too. Lucy and Marge fixed everyone a plate and brought the food out on the front porch. "It's too pretty a night to be inside," said Lucy. But she knew changing the routine might ease the grief somewhat.

After Gen and Hank were settled, Hunter and Lucy sat down at the kitchen table and started working on the obituary for Friday's paper. As the details of Luke's life unfolded, Hunter found himself grieving for a man he had only known for a little over a month.

"Your father was a remarkable man, Lucy. If we all had a tenth of his strength and humility, we'd be much better for it. I promise I will write something deserving of his legacy."

"I have no doubts about that, Hunter. You know our last conversation was about you. He asked me to let you love me and for me to love you. He told me not to walk away from the best thing that had ever come into my life. What did he say to you the morning before he died?"

"…that he knew we loved one another because we both took pleasure in doing things for one another. He said, 'That's what it should all be about, you know…doing things for the people you love.'"

"He gave us his blessing because he knew he wasn't going to make it, Hunter. We can't fuck this up."

Hunter chuckled slightly. He leaned in and kissed her. "I love that mouth of yours, Lulu…for a lot of reasons. I'll be back after I put the paper to bed if you want."

"I'd like that. I'd like that a lot. I'll leave the back porch light on and the door open."

***

After a very long, grief-filled day at the Tanner home, Nettie was relieved to see Nate was already at her house when she pulled in the driveway. He was sitting on the front porch, smoking his pipe. He stood up and reached for her hand when she started to climb up the steps.

"Hey, I have some soup on the stove. Want me to get you a bowl? It's not too chilly out here and it's peaceful."

"What I want is a blanket and a drink," she answered.

"Nettie. It's Thursday…not Saturday.'

"I know what day it is, but I want a drink. You better fix one for yourself, too. I have something to tell you."

Nate went inside and returned with two glasses of whiskey and blanket over his arm. He covered her legs with the blanket, and sat down next to her.

"Luke and I didn't talk about farm business last night like I said we did. He told me about something that happened a long time ago." She took a long drink of the warm liquid and cleared her throat. Nate was wise enough not to ask any questions and let her talk.

"Do you remember that time we were supposed to meet on the Ridge so you could prove to me there weren't any haints up there?" asked Nettie.

"I do," answered Nate, "but like I told you then, my grandmama wouldn't let me leave." He looked away from Nettie, hoping she didn't see into his eyes and know he was lying. He could still remember how Luke looked — the blood on his clothes, the gun, the shovel.

"I told you I didn't go up there, too — that my mama had chores for me to do," said Nettie in almost too-soft a voice to hear. "That wasn't true. I did go. And Mr. JJ Cooper was there. I surprised him, and he…he…he raped me."

Nate almost dropped his glass but set it down before doing so. "Oh lord. No, he didn't. You were so young. Oh, honey — "

"There's more. Luke was up there, a little way down the path." Nettie told Nate the story, which was now crystal clear in her mind. "He said he never said anything to me, and I never looked at him. When I got home, my mama gave me the worst whooping I ever had. Think about that. I got a beating because someone raped me."

The tears Nettie had denied since finding out the truth could no longer be stopped. Nate knelt down beside her chair and took her hands in his. "It's okay. He can't hurt you anymore."

"Oh, I know that," answered Nettie, wiping her face. "These are tears of relief. The faceless demon is gone. I no longer feel beholden to anyone. I saved myself. I am strong because I am strong…not because someone taught me to be. But, Nate, I believe Luke knew his time was nigh. He had to tell me before he died. He carried that guilt and burden his entire life. We ended on a good note, though. I know how much he loved me. And he knows the same about me."

"I have to tell you something, too," said Nate. "I did go up there that day. I was waiting, hoping you'd make it when I heard someone coming up the path. It was Luke. I saw the blood — blood that now I know was yours. He picked up a shovel from the gravesites and left without seeing me. I was scared out of my wits and never told a soul."

"That was JJ's shovel. Luke said he buried something under the rocks at the edge of one of the graves…something he thought I needed to find. And after we lay Luke to rest, you and I will do just that. We will go up on the ridge — without fear — and find whatever JJ Cooper hid there."

Friday

Jigs got to Cantrell City right after lunch on Friday and parked next to the hotel. After checking in with Jimmy, he went upstairs and opened his duffle bag. He took out the cloth bag on top and unwrapped the stack of $100 bills and put them in the inside pocket of his sports coat. Although Jigs had carried out multitudes of undercover stings during his career, the excitement was the same. The adrenaline still pumped. He picked up the brown paper bag he had brought with him and went downstairs.

"Hey, Jimmy. I'm having a guest for dinner here tonight. I'd like to have that table on the far side of the veranda ready at 6:30 if I could. Here's my brown bag. How about storing it in the refrigerator for me," he said with a wink.

"Of course, Mr. O'Neil."

Jigs leaned in and whispered. "I know you want to know who it is…Hilda Hargett, but don't tell anyone."

"Oh, that's wonderful. I love her, and she deserves a date with a sophisticated man like you. Bless her heart. She was about to move to Atlanta a good while back but stayed here to take care of her daddy after her mama died. Mr. Hargett developed hardening of the arteries, though, so temporary turned into 10 years. I guess it was just too hard to make a change by then. Well, I will certainly make this special — fresh flowers, cold champagne, and candlelight."

"Thanks, Jimmy. That sounds delightful. I'll see you later this afternoon. Oh, by the way, is Mr. Tanner's funeral tomorrow?"

"Yes, at 3. The whole county will be there."

"Well, I'll be checking out in the morning in case you need my room."

Jigs lit a cigarette when he got outside and started toward the parking lot. He looked up and saw Sheriff Wilkes coming down the sidewalk toward him. "Good day," he said, tipping his hat and averting his eyes.

"Same to you," said the sheriff, sensing this would not be the last time they spoke.

***

"Hello, Mr. O'Neil," said George, when Jigs walked in the bank. "Jack is expecting you. I'll let him know you're here."

In a few seconds, the door to Cooper's office swung open and Jack spoke loud enough for everyone to hear. "Hey, Sam. Come on in."

When the two men were seated, Jack opened the engraved wooden box and offered a cigar to Jigs. "Business deals require a good smoke, right?" asked Jack. "And I'll have a drink, too. I'm still celebrating."

"Of course, you are. My investors are hoping they will be, too. But before I buy into this deal, assure me one more time that you're going to make good on it, Jack."

"Oh, I'm gonna make good on it. Don't you worry. Money is what drives me, and there's never too much money. This mine is going to give me the cushion I need to live the lifestyle I want. I'm about to be a single man, and you know as well as I do that the broads like the cash."

"I hope you're right. My partners don't take too kindly to failure."

"Failure ain't a possibility. Should I call them and assure them? Who are they?"

"That isn't for you to know." Jigs reached in his coat pocket and took out the stack of bills. "Here's $5,000. We expect a substantial amount in return as soon as the first iron ore comes out of that mountain."

Jack's eyes grew wide and he cleared his throat, trying to mask his surprise and delight. "Don't you worry. Your partners are going to be rolling in it. I'll just put this right here in my little stash box." He turned around with his back to Jigs and opened the middle doors on his credenza. Cooper took out the vodka bottles and lifted up the bottom shelf. After placing the money in the hidden compartment, he put everything back and turned to face Jigs. "Your money is very safe."

O'Brien smiled and nodded, more aware than ever that Jack Cooper considered himself much smarter than he really was. Jigs looked forward to enlightening him as to how misguided he was.

***

Hilda checked her image in the dresser mirror one more time before heading to the hotel, which was only a few blocks from her home. She turned on the porch light and walked down the sidewalk as the streetlights started to come on.

Jigs sat on the hotel veranda, waiting for his date. He felt nervous but wasn't exactly sure why. When he saw Hilda coming down the sidewalk, he stood up and went to meet her. "So good to see you," he said, offering his arm to her. "If I wasn't so hungry, I'd suggest we keep enjoying this time of day and keep on walking."

"I know," said Hilda. "I love the light when it can't decide if it's day or night."

Jigs smiled at her perfect description of dusk. "We can enjoy it without walking, though. I have us a table outside, right off the dining room."

Jimmy had not disappointed. The setting was perfect for a quiet dinner. "I took the liberty of guessing you would enjoy a glass of wine with dinner. I brought a bottle of *Pouilly-Fuisse´* with me from Atlanta."

287

"Oh, yes. As a matter of fact, that's my favorite," said Hilda, beaming.

Jigs poured two glasses, sat down and lifted his into the air. "Here's to being here." Hilda felt her cheeks warm from the attention and the wine.

The setting was perfect, as was everything else, but what was a surprise for both of them was just how much they had in common...down to owning the same record albums and collecting the similar genres of art.

After the dessert and more wine, Jigs reached across the table and took Hilda's hand. "It's a good thing I'm not driving you home, but I'm pretty sure I'm steady enough to walk you there. By the way, you look beautiful tonight." Hilda laughed and squeezed his hand. "Well, if we hold onto to one another, maybe neither one of us will fall down."

CHAPTER Sixteen

Over the Line

It was standing room only inside the church for Luke's service, and the front yard was full of people, too. Practically every person who lived in Kings County was there. Everyone but Jack Cooper. He passed out around sunrise after a raucous night of drinking and didn't wake up until after the funeral had started.

The first thing he did was take an Alka-Seltzer and fix a drink. After another one, a craving for some of Buck's barbecue hit him. He opened his wallet and realized he had spent all of his money the night before. *That's no problem*, he thought. *There's five grand tucked away at the bank, and I have the security key.* He laughed aloud, took a swig of Vodka out of the bottle and drove to Willow Creek.

***

Daisy and Sandy stood outside at Luke's funeral. As soon as the last song began, she whispered in his ear. "I have to go back to the shop. We left in a hurry and didn't have time to straighten up. I'll call you at the Lodge when I get home."

She drove to the small house she and Sandy rented in Willow Creek and left her car there. It was a short walk to the beauty shop, and the late afternoon sun was just setting.

The town was empty and eerily quiet for a Saturday afternoon. She unlocked the front door and took off her sweater. Being a fast worker, it didn't take her long to sweep, gather the dirty towels, and straighten up the waiting room and styling stations. She got all the trash together and carried it out into the alley behind the shop. While dumping it into the large can several businesses shared, some paper cups fell on the ground. Hiking her skirt a bit, she bent over and picked them up.

Jack was coming out of the back door of the bank and saw her firm derriere in the air. He stepped back a bit so she couldn't see him and continued to stare. Her bare legs were flawless. When she stood up, she pulled her skirt down and adjusted her bra. Her ample breasts pressed against the bodice of her blouse, and Jack stared at the silhouettes of her erect nipples. He was obsessed with her and had been since the day Sandy brought her to the Lodge. She oozed sex, without even trying. And now, nothing and nobody stood in his way. He just won the jackpot, and he was ready to claim his prize.

She walked back in the shop and realized she hadn't checked the bathroom. She grabbed the small can and opened the door to the alley. As soon as she stepped out, Jack grabbed her from behind, put his hand over her mouth and started pawing her breasts and pulling up her skirt. His foul breath filled her nostrils, and she could barely breathe.

She bit his hand and tried to run inside but he hit her so hard she fell down. He flipped her over, tore her blouse open and ripped off her bra. He threw his body on her and covered her mouth again. "I'm going to fuck you, bitch," he snarled. He reached between her legs and pulled down her panties. "Whores like you don't wear stockings, do you. Always ready, huh?" He thrusted his fingers into her va-gina, jabbing and pounding her until she started crying in pain. He stopped for a moment, and she thought he was done, but she heard him unzipping his pants. She managed to pull her arm out from under his massive body and grab his wrist, pulling at his shirt sleeve, and trying to stop him from penetrating her. She heard something rip and then everything went black. Jack hit her so hard it knocked her out, but that didn't stop him from doing what he set out to do.

After he finished, he hoisted himself up, leaned over, bit her breast, and stumbled to his car.

***

Nate stopped by the grocery store to pick up some extra rolls for supper at the Tanners. They expected a lot of visitors to come by after the funeral. It was customary in these parts to gather around the family after a service. Nettie was already there, with Marge and Anita, setting the food out.

He pulled out of the parking lot and noticed a light was on at Miss K's. He thought that a bit unusual since town was so deserted. He parked in front of the shop and knocked on the front door. When nobody answered, he turned the door knob and went inside. "Hello," he called. "Kittsee, you here? Laney?" He walked toward the back and opened the curtain that hung between the storage area and the main shop. What he saw made him rock back on his heels. Daisy was lying in the alley, her clothes torn and her nakedness exposed. He immediately took off his jacket and covered her bruised and beaten body. He checked her pulse and was relieved she was still alive. He ran back inside and dialed the sheriff's office.

"Kings County Sheriff Department," said the deputy. "This is Nate Johnson. Something bad happened at the beauty shop. It's Daisy. I need the sheriff and an ambulance as fast as you can get them here. She's in the alley."

He ran back outside and knelt down next to Daisy, who was still unconscious. "Hang in there. Help is on the way. You just hold on to my hand." He looked at her battered face and felt the tears well up in his eyes. "This ain't right," he said aloud. "No one deserves this."

Within 10 minutes, he heard the sirens coming from Cantrell City and breathed for the first time since he found her. The ambulance stopped at the entrance to the alley, with the sheriff close behind. They covered her with a

291

blanket and gently put her on the stretcher. "Get her there fast, boys," said Wilkes. "You okay?" he asked Nate. "I know you were a medic during the war, but this is different. It's home."

"Yeah. This is different," answered Nate quietly. "Have you called Sandy?"

"Yep. I told him to go to the hospital. Tell me what you know."

Nate recounted his story, including the fact that there was no one anywhere around when he found her.

"Well, let's just hope she lives so she can tell us who did this," said the sheriff. "For now, you go on to the Tanners. I know you, Nate, so I'm not worried about your talking about this to just anyone. Folks are going to know soon enough."

After Nate left, the sheriff went inside. Nothing looked out of place. He went back out to the alley and saw the small trash can on its side, with trash spilling out on the ground. He took out a handkerchief and picked it up. And then something caught his eye. Under the garbage was something shiny. He picked it up.

Nobody in Kings County wore a gold cufflink like this but one person. He took out a paper envelope, dropped the evidence inside, licked the flap and sealed it.

He got in his car and started out of town, heading to the lake where Jack was staying. When he passed Buck's, he saw Cooper's Cadillac. "Good. This saves me a trip." He parked his patrol car and went inside. Jack looked up and grinned. "Howdy, sheriff. Come join me. I'm a little tipsy, but there ain't a law against that, is it?"

"That depends on what somebody does when they're a little tipsy." The sheriff slid in the booth opposite Jack. "How about sharing one of those fries with me?" he asked. "I need something before I order."

"Sure. Here you go." Jack reached across the table and set the plate in front of the sheriff. Both men saw the torn shirt sleeve at the same time.

Jack tried to pull the arm of his jacket over it, but the sheriff caught his hand.

"Where's your cuff link, Jack?"

***

Sandy's heartbeat as fast as his pickup truck's cylinders. His hands clenched the steering wheel and his breathing was staggered.

He knew in his gut who did this to Daisy: Jack. The only thing that kept him from tracking down the son-of-a-bitch was that he had to get to his girl.

The ambulance was at the emergency entrance when he came to a screeching halt at the hospital. He ran in the double doors and saw them wheeling her into the examining room. "Stop. That's my fiancé," he shouted. "I need to see her."

Dr. Stanley turned around and blocked Sandy from entering. "Wait, son. Let us tend to her. Just as soon as I can let you in, I will. Right now, we have to get her stable."
He sat down in the waiting room and put his face in his hands. The outside doors opened, and Billy Joe came in. He walked quickly to where Sandy was and knelt down.

"Hey, man. I thought you might need some company."

"How did you know?"

"The sheriff called Hunter. He's on his way to meet Wilkes at his office, so he can get the facts straight. Something like this can get out of hand pretty quick."

"I'm gonna kill him," whispered Sandy.

"Who?" asked Billy Joe.

"That mutha fucker Jack Cooper."

"How do you know it was him?"

"I just know."

"Buddy, I know what you're feeling. But that won't do Daisy any good right now. Let the sheriff handle this. You just send all your strength through those doors to her.

Here. Why don't we go outside and have a smoke? I'll let the nurse know where we are."

***

Jack tried to pull his arm away from the sheriff's grasp but didn't stand a chance against Wilkes' brute strength.

"I said, where's your cufflink, Jack?"

"I don't know. I guess I lost it," sneered Cooper.

"Let me see your other wrist," said the sheriff, not letting go of Jack's hand.

Cooper slowly put his left arm on the table, revealing the missing cuff link's twin.

"Jack, you and I both know what happened to that chunk of gold. You're gonna have to come down to the jail with me. Out of respect for Miss Anita and your boy, I'm going to spare you the embarrassment of making a scene here in Buck's. Walk up to that counter, pay for your meal, and come outside."

"Am I under arrest, sheriff?" slurred Jack.

"I guess you could say that. I'm just not cuffing you in. Give me your car keys and meet me out front. If you try anything, you'll only make this worse."

When the sheriff got inside, he opened the door to Cooper's car. An empty vodka bottle was on the floorboard on the driver's side. He reached down to check if Jack had his handgun under the seat — the place where all good cowboys keep a pistol. He felt around and didn't find a weapon but what he did discover was an envelope with a wad of cash in it. "Jesus Christ," he said. "What the hell is he doing with this kind of money hid under his seat?"

He put it in the evidence bag with everything else and turned to face Jack, who had just walked outside. "Turn around and put your hands on top of the patrol car."

"What the hell, sheriff? What the hell are you doing?"

"Shut the fuck up, Jack. I'm older than you, but I could take you down to the ground in front of all those folks looking out Buck's windows or you can do what I tell your ass to do. Turn around and put your hands where I can see them."

As the sheriff was putting Jack in the cruiser, Hunter drove by on his way to the jail.

"Shit," he said aloud. "This is going to hit this place like an earthquake."

***

The news about Daisy spread as quickly as a brush fire. Nothing like this had happened in Kings County since Billy Joe's childhood tragedy. It shook everybody. Coupled with Luke's death, it sent the entire community into shock. Hunter was at the jail when the sheriff arrived there. The deputy came out to help get Jack inside.

When Jack saw Hunter, he snarled, "You son-of-a-bitch. None of this would have happened if you hadn't stuck your damn nose into Kings County business. Nobody questioned what I did until you started poking around."

"That's enough," snapped the sheriff. He turned and faced Hunter. "There's gonna be a lot of talk about Jack's involvement, but I'd prefer that you simply say it's an on-going investigation. I don't want anything to jeopardize holding him or whoever is responsible accountable. I'll give you the details when I can. I'm just hoping and praying that girl will wake up. In the meantime, I'm holding him here."

***

Sandy sat in a chair, holding Daisy's hand. The room was dark except for a dim light, coming from the lamp on a table next to her hospital bed. She was still unconscious, and the doctor couldn't say if or when she would wake up. The young man stared at her bruised face. The line between his anger and his sadness was non-existent.

295

A tap on the door got his attention and a nurse walked in. "Let her rest now, Sandy. I'll call you the minute anything changes."

Sandy drove to Willow Creek and parked next to Daisy's car in front of their house. *She must have walked to the beauty shop,* he thought...*something she loved about working in town.* When he opened the front door, he saw her slippers sitting next to the doormat. She was always so careful about taking off her street shoes as soon as she walked inside.

He switched on a lamp and sat down in a chair next to the phone table. He picked up the receiver, dialed a number, and the voice on the other end of the line answered quickly. "Hey, Sandy. Everything okay?" asked Sid.

"No, it isn't." His voice cracked, but Sandy managed to tell him about Daisy. "The doc isn't saying much. Boss, one way or another, we're going to tell the truth about Jack. If Daisy wakes up, she will. But if she doesn't," Sandy paused to swallow his tears, "I'll tell the sheriff what she told me."

"Okay, Sandy. Let me make a phone call. And don't do anything you'll regret. Let the law handle this. I'll call you."

Sid hung up the phone and immediately dialed Jigs' number. "Jigs," said Sid when O'Brien answered the phone. "Something bad has happened in Kings County, but because of it, the witnesses we need will talk."

Jigs was about to answer him when the direct line to Moody started ringing. "Hey, my boss is calling, maybe about this. I'll call you right back."

"Yessir?" answered Jigs quickly.

"We have a situation up in Kings County. Meet me at the office as soon as you can get there."

I'm on my way."

He dialed Sid's number. "Whatever happened has already hit Moody's desk. I'm on my way to the office now. Tell your source to sit tight and don't say a word to anyone. I'll let you know when to go see the sheriff."

Jigs lit a cigarette, grabbed his keys and was about to leave when his phone rang. "Hello?" he said quickly.

"Sam, it's Hilda," she said, her voice shaking.

"Hey, what's wrong?" he asked.

"Daisy Culpepper, who works at the beauty shop, was raped. I need to talk to you as soon as I can."

"Oh, no. I met her...sweet, quiet girl. Ah, give me a little bit. I have some things I have to tend to, but I can call you back in about an hour or so."

"I hate to impose, but this is really important. Is there any way you can come here? I don't want to do this over the phone."

"Sure...and it's no imposition. I'll let you know when I leave here."

Jigs hung up the phone and lit a cigarette. What he just heard and felt added yet another stick to the fire...not only to the investigation but to the importance of his cover.

***

As soon as Hunter got to the office, he called Lucy. "Listen. Some bad shit has happened. Daisy was raped in the alley behind the beauty shop. She's—"

"I know about it. It doesn't take long for news to spread."

"Well, you might not know this: Jack Cooper is the main suspect."

"What? Who knows about him?"

"I am guessing Wilkes, the deputy, and me. I'm sure everybody who was at Buck's knew something was up but are just speculating at this point."

Lucy looked down the hall and saw Laney talking a mile a minute to Kittsee and some other ladies. "Oh, no. Laney's out in the yard. He's mighty excited about something and is telling anyone who will listen. I have to go find Anita."

"Okay. I'll be back out there when I finish this story. It has to be in tomorrow's paper."

Lucy hung up the phone and turned around. Anita was standing there, her face ashen. "That was Hunter,

297

wasn't it? So, what Dancy Riley so eagerly pointed out to me is true."

"Hey, don't pay any attention to what that bitch says," said Lucy.

"Go get in your car. I'll find Bo and tell George and your folks so they can follow you home."

After the Masons left, the crowd thinned out until the Tanners were finally alone. Lucy and Nettie were straightening up in the kitchen, and Gen sat on the front porch, staring at the barn.

"Nettie, I have something to tell you," said Lucy, drying her hands on the dish towel. "Hunter called. The sheriff arrested Jack. They believe he was the one who raped Daisy."

Nettie gripped the sink and let out a groan. "Oh, lawd, that poor child. Too bad that dog can't meet up with an accident in the jail. He's a bastard who comes from a long line of bastards. There is no punishment too severe for him."

"Yep. I agree. Hey, it's been a long, hard few days. You and Nate go on home. I can handle everything now, and Hunter will be back here soon."

"Is he spending the night here?" asked Nettie.

"He is." Lucy smiled and hugged her best friend.

***

When Jigs got to Moody's office, Stan Walker—the GBI agent in charge of the North Georgia district—was already there.

"So, here's what we have," said Moody. "Sheriff Wilkes has brought Jack Cooper in on suspicion of rape and public drunkenness. Normally, that would not involve us. But. When he searched his car, he found an envelope with a stack of $100 bills in it. Fill Walker in on what you know."

Jigs lit a cigarette and told Walker everything he had uncovered during his operation.

"When I gave him the money, he hid it in a compartment in the credenza behind his desk. He told me it was where he put stuff he didn't want anyone to find."

"So, what do you suggest?" asked Walker.

Jigs took a drag and let out the smoke slowly. "Does Jack know the sheriff found the cash?"

"No," said Moody. "It's with the other evidence he collected where the assault happened."

"Huh…okay. So, why don't we do this?" Jigs laid out a plan that both Moody and Walker agreed would work. He gave them the number to the Gold Star Inn but told them he preferred getting in touch with them. "My cover is still intact there…don't want to change that. There's a motel between Cantrell City and Willow Creek… the Mountain View. Stan, you stay there and let Moody know the room number. I'll check in with the chief in the morning and give you a call around lunch tomorrow."

O'Brien left the office, went to his apartment and quickly packed his bag. He looked at his watch and he picked up the telephone receiver. It was 7. There was only one ring before Hilda answered. "I'm on my way. I'll be at your house before 8:30."For the entire trip, he rehearsed what he would say to her.

***

Nate fixed two glasses of whiskey and went out to the front porch where Nettie sat.

"How can things go from up to down so fast?" she asked, after taking a long sip from her drink.

"I don't know, Net, but that sure is what has happened here. Mr. Luke and now this. I just pray that she'll be alright. No word, yet?"

"No. Nate, what did he do to her?"

"Beat her, ripped her clothes off, and…" he stopped mid-sentence.

"And, what?"

"He bit her."

"Oh god, no. Where?"

"Her breast, Net. He bit it so hard it was bleeding."

Nettie paused, feeling the pain rise up in her. "He's an animal, Nate…a damn animal. I hope he burns in hell."

***

Jigs tapped on Hilda's door, which she immediately opened.

"Come in," she said. "Thanks so much for coming. I know I look frightful, but I've been very upset. I'm having a glass of sherry, but it looks like you brought something with you."

"Yep…a six-pack of beer. I'd prefer one of those."

"Let's go out on the back porch. I need some fresh air," said Hilda.

So do I, thought Jigs.

They sat down on the glider and Hilda started swinging it gently. "I have to get something out in the open. Eventually, I'll have to go see the sheriff, but I wanted to tell you first. Jack Cooper threatened me. He said if I did not do what he told me do, he would kill my pets and hurt me anyway he could. His family has kept mine paralyzed with fear for generations, starting with my grandfather. It's time for that to end."

Jigs cleared his throat, despite being the veteran he was, he was unsure that he could hear her story without showing outrage. "What did he force you to do?"

"He made me draw up a fake deed in his name for the ridge property. I knew he didn't own that land. I'm not sure who does because, as you know, the original page of the ledger was torn out. He told me his grandfather did that a long time ago. He threatened me, and I feared for my job, my animals, and my life. I knew he meant what he said."

O'Brien took a swig of his beer and sat it down on the table next to the glider. He stopped the swaying and faced Hilda. "I'm no attorney but in cases like this, I believe witnesses can get immunity. I have a buddy who is a cop, and he's told me about such cases. The best thing for you to do is to hire an attorney immediately, confide in him, and do what he says. Is there one here you trust?"

"Yes. Mr. Theodore Mason. He was very good friends with my father. I wonder if it's too late to call him now."
"The lawyer friends I have say it's never too late to interview a potential client. In a case as critical as this—especially since it seems a young woman has been brutalized by the same man—I would think that Mr. Mason would be happy to hear from you. I think you need to go call him right now."

Jigs stayed on the back porch while Hilda went inside. He could hear her muffled voice through the open window but could not make out exactly what she said. It was imperative, however, that he not act upon the desires he had. Until this investigation was over, his relationship with her had to remain platonic.

The screen door opened and Hilda sat back down on the glider. She handed Jigs another beer.

"He's going to meet with me tomorrow before church starts. That's fitting, isn't it? ...confession on a Sunday."

Vindication

Before dawn on Sunday, Nettie and Nate made their way up the steep incline to the top of the ridge. They needed a flashlight since the sun had not risen yet. Once they were at the top, Nettie looked around, acclimating herself to the surroundings. Her memory was clear, and the images, vivid, although what she was reliving had happened long ago. "Aren't the rock mounds over there?" she asked, pointing to a heavily overgrown spot.

"Yep. They are," answered Nate. There was no pathway leading there, which meant he had to use a machete to cut away at the brush and saplings. The sun was just beginning to peek over the Eastern horizon, but it was still dark in the woods. "Watch your step," he said. "Snakes are moving to where they're going to spend the winter."

It was terrifyingly quiet, except for the occasional hoot of an owl, calling it a night, and the howl of a coyote. Neither of them said a word.

After about 15 minutes of slow progress, Nettie stopped. "Look. I recognize that clearing ahead. Don't you?"

What they saw looked surreal...at least a dozen mounds of rocks neatly placed in round piles.

Nettie stared at the graves. She remembered exactly what she saw the day she discovered Jack's father there. "He had his back to me and was digging a hole as close to the rocks as he could, but I don't know which of the graves it was."

"Well, then we'll just check each one," said Nate. "Shine the flashlight where I'm looking with the detector."

The first minutes seemed like hours and revealed nothing. The sun finally made it into the dense forest and Nettie could see the entire graveyard. Suddenly, she saw an image in her mind that made her gasp. "I remember. It's the largest mound in the center. The shape at the bottom is irregular, and the rest of the graves aren't that way. But you know as well as I do that disturbing a grave is forbidden. God forgive me. I don't mean any harm. Move those rocks and let's see if I'm right."

Nate carefully moved each stone, keeping an eye out for rattlers, while Nettie shone the flashlight into each crevice. When he finished, he started moving the metal detector meticulously back and forth. Nettie stared, barely breathing. It only took a couple of minutes before a beeping sound cut the silence. Nate reached for the shovel, but Nettie held onto it. "I'm doing this," she said.

She dug the shovel into the ground. When the hole was about a foot deep, she suddenly hit metal. She dug furiously, throwing the dirt aside. Kneeling down, she started using her hands, clawing at the ground. She lifted the metal box up and tried to pry the top open. "Nate, see if your knife can pop this. It's rusted shut."

Nate sat the box down on the ground and knelt beside it. He put the blade next to the latch, wiggling it back and forth until he felt some movement. "It's loosening," he said. Suddenly, the lid popped open. "Here you go, Net."

She took the box and lifted the lid. There it was. Her grandmama's Bible...the book her mama used to teach her to read. Her hands trembled as she took out the book and opened it. She recognized the page where her ancestors' names were written. She touched it and felt like she was caressing them. For the first time in a very long time, Nettie felt like her family would suffer no longer. She kept turning the pages, finding pressed flowers, pieces of lace, and hand written notes. She turned the bible over and opened the back cover. There it was. What she needed — what everyone needed — proof that the ridge was not for sale.

***

Jigs woke up Sunday morning, thinking about the night before. A brief hug was the only show of affection he allowed himself to show Hilda. He hoped she took it as an act of chivalry and not rejection. Just as soon as this sting was over, he could come clean with her — but not until then. He could not risk jeopardizing the investigation at this point. He was too close to bringing Jack Cooper to justice.

Hilda was supposed to meet Jigs at 9. He figured the two would be paying a visit to Sheriff Wilkes very soon. He dialed Moody's private line at his house.

"What?" growled his boss.

"The clerk is ready to talk. She's meeting with her attorney in a couple of hours and confessing everything." He filled Moody in on what Hilda told him the night before. "I'm guessing you'll be hearing from Wilkes pretty soon. Fraud of this magnitude is state jurisdiction. But listen. I want complete immunity for this woman. She is giving us a big piece of the puzzle."

303

"Hmmm…sure you're not being influenced by 'this woman'?" asked Moody.

"I will admit I like and admire her, but, no, I am not recommending this because of that fact. I am saying this because far too many people—especially women—have suffered at the hands of this guy. It's time to end his reign."

"All right. We'll see. I'll give Walker a call and tell him to pack his bags. What's next on your list?"

"I'm going to sit tight. Tell Walker to call you as soon as he talks to Wilkes and to leave the number at the motel where he's staying. At that point, I'll call him and we'll decide what to do next."

Jigs hung up the phone and lit a cigarette. He called Jimmy at the front desk. "Morning. Can I get some room service…maybe a pot of coffee and some toast?"

"Of course. I'm checking out Mr. Cagle now, but as soon as I'm done, I'll be right up."

"Thanks."

"Huh," said Jigs aloud. I guess the fire's getting a little too hot for ol' Dan."

***

The trip down the mountain was a quick one for Nettie and Nate, and very little was said. Nettie set the box, the bible and the deed on the kitchen table. "Do you realize that you now have the evidence that proves you, in fact, own the ridge?" asked Nate.

"Yes, I do, but it's still sinking in. I've remembered a lot in a short period of time, but I've held it in my entire life. I was taught to keep things to myself—not to whine—but I knew something wasn't right…my soul was so anxious. I didn't really know what I was hiding. I was never sure of anything and doubted everything. Now, my prayers have been answered and not by accident. This was Luke's doing. Through his honesty, I was able to remember the truth."

"I wonder why ol' man Cooper buried this rather than burn it," commented Nate.

304

"I guess even somebody as evil as he knew what curses would fall upon him for burning a bible. I'm ready to take this to the sheriff."

She dialed the number to the jail and Wilkes answered.

"Sheriff, this is Nettie. I need to talk to you. It's very important."

"Alright. I'm expecting someone here soon. Head this way in about 30 minutes."

"I want to tell Lucy before we go," said Nettie. "She worked harder than anyone to save the Ridge. This will ease some of her grief."

***

The headlines said it all. "**THE UNTHINKABLE HAPPENED HERE.**" Lucy stared at the newspaper. She was sitting on the front porch, feeling like she had been running her entire life and finally stopped. For the first time she could remember, she didn't feel guilty for not working or going to church. Her mother was playing the piano, and Hank was doing the schoolwork he'd missed the week before. She promised him they would do something away from the farm when he finished.

"Have you looked at the paper yet?" asked Hunter, who just walked out of the house.

"No."

"…want me to read it to you?" he asked.

Lucy nodded, closed her eyes and listened while he recounted the grim details about what happened the night before. He did an excellent job of letting the public know what they needed to know without being sensational. Of course, Daisy's name was not used nor was the suspect in custody identified.

But every single person in Kings County knew who they were.

"Good lord," said Lucy, letting out a deep breath. "What in god's name could happen next, Hunter?"

305

As soon as the words were out of her mouth, Nate and Nettie pulled in the driveway. Hank heard the car and came outside. Nate got out and opened the car door for Nettie. She started walking toward the porch. "Hey, Baby Cakes. I've got something for you."

When Lucy saw what was in Nettie's hands, she gasped. "Is that...?"

"Yes m'am. It is." Nettie set the metal box in Lucy's lap. "We found it in the burial grounds up on the Ridge. Open it."

"Grandmama Gen," shouted Hank. You need to come out here."

Hunter leaned in to see as Lucy opened the dirty, rusted top. There, on top of a bible was the deed to and what looked like a ledger page. The paper was old, yellowed and fragile. "I'm not going to touch it. It's sacred. But tell me what it says," whispered Lucy.

"It says my great-great-great-grandfather—a Cherokee—owned the ridge and deeded it to his son-in-law, Andrew Davidson, who signed it over to his daughter—my great-grandmother, who bequeathed it to her descendants, and the only living one is me. What you found in that journal is true, Lulu. I own it."

Lucy set the box on the table in front of the chaise and stood up. Her eyes filled with tears and she put her arms around Nettie. "Daddy is smiling big right now, Nettie. He's very proud."

"We're on our way to see the sheriff," said Nate. "Should we let Theodore know since he represented us in the hearing?"

"That's a good idea. Want me to go give him a call?" asked Hunter.

"I'll do it," said Nettie. "I want to be the one to tell everybody."

In a few minutes, Nettie came back outside. "I got Mrs. Mason on the phone. She told me Theodore was at the sheriff's office, so I called him there. He said to bring everything to the sheriff. He'll meet us."

"Did he say why he was with Wilkes?" asked Hunter.

"No. He just said that it was important."

"Huh...sounds like we need a special edition of the Tribune tomorrow morning," said Hunter. "I think I'll pay the sheriff a visit, too. I know we're not supposed to work on Sundays, but I think we'll be forgiven for this. Folks need some good news in the morning after last week."

Within a couple of minutes, Lucy was alone again on the front porch. She wanted to sit a little longer and digest everything. She heard the cows mooing and calling to one another from the pasture across the road. It was peaceful and quiet, like it should be.

She couldn't help but feel like her daddy had a little something to do with this. When everything calmed down, she wanted to hear just how Nettie came to remember where to look for the clue that was going to save the Ridge.

***

When Nate pulled in at the jail, Theodore and Hilda were just leaving. She looked shook up, and Theodore had to help her get in his car. "I wonder what that's all about," said Nettie. She nodded at Theodore, who walked over to Nate's truck. "Let me take Hilda home. I'll be right back."

The sheriff was in his office and on the phone when Nettie and Nate walked in. Although the door was almost closed, they heard what he said.

"Yep, that's correct. She confessed but wants immunity. I need an agent here as soon as possible. Let me know when to expect him." He hung up, saw them, and motioned for them to come in. "It's been a helluva morning on top of a bad night. What can I do for you?"

Nettie set the box down on his desk. "This is my grandmama's. The deed to the Ridge and other documents are inside. It's all here. The land was left to the descendants of my great-grandmother. And I'm the only one left."

***

307

Wilkes looked at his notes from both interviews. He had instructed everyone to keep this to themselves until he told them otherwise. The GBI agent couldn't get there a second too soon for him. The phone rang and he answered it, hoping it was word from Atlanta, but it was Jack's attorney asking that a bond be set.

"You'll have to wait until the judge is available, which could be in the morning." He looked up when he heard the front door open, while the lawyer protested. "I don't give a damn if you like it or not," he snarled. "It's Sunday." He slammed down the phone. "Can I help you?"

"I'm hoping we can help each other. I'm Agent Stan Walker. Wanna fill me in on what's going on here, sheriff?"

"Some real shit. That's what's going on here...some real shit." Wilkes recounted in chronological order the events that had occurred since Saturday night, including Hilda's confession and Nettie's discovery.

"Does Jack know you found the money?" asked Walker.

"No, he doesn't. I have it right here, locked in my desk, and I can't wait for you to take responsibility for it." He handed the envelope to Walker, who opened it and took out the stack of bills. He checked the numbers and said, "This money is hot...stolen in Atlanta and then wound up under the front seat of a car in Kings County. Was that Cooper's attorney on the phone with you when I walked in?"

"...Sure was...asking for bail."

"Well, he can spit in one hand, wish in the other, and see which one fills up first. That's not gonna happen I don't think. Have you counted the money yet?"

"No sir. I couldn't lock that shit up fast enough."

Wilkes chuckled. "I understand." He counted the money as deftly as a seasoned bank teller. "That's odd. $4,900.00. Where did you arrest Jack?"

"At Buck's BBQ joint."

"You said that you found the money before Jack came outside. So, did he pay for his meal?"

"He did. I saw him handing Buck a bill."

"I bet he did. A hundred-dollar bill. Can we get in touch with Mr. Buck?"

"Yeah, he takes the day off on Sunday. I don't think he's much of a church-going man either. Let me give him a call."

The sheriff hung up after a very brief exchange. "You're right. Jack paid with a Ben Franklin. Buck deposited it and the rest of his receipts in the night depository at the bank."

"Okay. Then I need a search warrant for the bank and Cooper's residence. Is that something Judge Whitaker will do for us?"

"I'm pretty sure he will," said the sheriff. "When do you plan to execute the search?"

"We'll do it first thing tomorrow morning. What time is the First National Bank of Willow Creek open for business?"

"Nine."

Good. We'll be there at 8:30. We'll go over the protocol later. After we find what we know we're going to find at the bank, ol' Jack will have a conversation with you and me. I'll be at the Mountain View Motel, compiling the evidence and getting it ready to present to a grand jury. Let me know the status of that warrant when you know. Nice working with you, sheriff. You've done a good job here."

"How about the immunity deal for Miss Hargett?" asked Wilkes.

"Oh, yeah. We agree. I'll take care of getting that. And notify her attorney. I want her confession as part of the indictment."

Both men turned around when they heard the front door open. It was Hunter.

"Fox. Come here," commanded Wilkes. "This is GBI Agent Stan Walker...Hunter Fox, the publisher of the local newspaper. Boy, I'm not even going to ask you why you're showing up here on a Sunday, but I'm certain it's not for casual chit chat."

"No sir. It's not. I have some questions about what's going on with the Ridge, and why a GBI agent is here. You know how quickly word spreads…best to get the facts straight and out there quickly."

"But there's not a paper until Tuesday," said Wilkes, eyeing Fox with a narrow stare.

"You're right, but we're putting out a special edition tomorrow morning. If, in fact, the Ridge really isn't for sale, folks need to know that. I don't have to tell you that this has been a brutal week for the community."

"Walker, how about you telling him what he can print without fucking up the investigation?"

The agent gave Hunter as much information as he could, including the fact that an unnamed witness had confessed to forging the deed. Hunter wrote furiously, asking as many questions as the agent would answer. Walker asked that he also add something in the story, instructing anyone who has any information about the mining proposal to come forward. Every person in Wilkes' office knew that when people are scared of getting caught, they squeal. "I imagine there are a couple of folks Cooper bribed. You can bet your ass that after they read this, they are going to tell anybody who will listen," said Walker.

"Is that it?" asked Fox. "Can you tell me when and where you're going to pop him?"

"Nope, but I can tell you I like to get my banking business taken care of first thing on Mondays."

Fox let out a sigh. "Shit. When things start un-raveling, they sure fray quickly, don't they?"

"Yep. They sure do…especially when what you sew is laced with lies," said Walker.

***

Jigs answered the phone in his room after one ring.

"Walker is ready to talk to you," said Moody im-patiently. Call him at TU4-3969, room 10. Things are moving quickly up there. You two better deliver, or I'm gonna have your asses…fucking up my Sunday like this."

"Don't worry, chief. We —," but Moody slammed down the phone before Jigs could finish his sentence. He dialed the number to Walker's room and he immediately answered.

"Hey. So, what's happening?" asked Jigs.

"A lot," answered Walker. "Not only has your clerk confessed to forging the deed for Cooper but the Tanners' business partner, Nettie Andrews, found the original deed." He filled in Jigs with the details, going all the way back to the Cherokee chief, the original owner of the land.

"My god. That sounds like a novel," said Jigs.

"Yeah, a good one," chuckled Walker. "There's a lot to do before tomorrow though. Sheriff Wilkes is going to call Hargett's attorney this afternoon and ask both of them to come in his office first thing tomorrow. We'll get a signed confession from her and give her complete witness immunity. I've already had a conversation with the prosecutor for this circuit. Wilkes is securing a search warrant for the bank, and we'll execute it before the doors open. I imagine there will be a lot of out-of-town press here. The publisher of the paper here knows folks in the business in Atlanta and Savannah. He interviewed me this afternoon. After we finish there, I'll spend some time with Mr. Cooper. Do you wanna be in on that?"

"Nope. I want my cover to remain intact around here. I'm leaving as soon as I can in the morning."

"Why not today?" asked Walker.

"I have unfinished business to take care of," said Jigs.

"Hey. Don't you fuck this up," snapped Walker.

"I assure you that doing anything to jeopardize bringing Jack Cooper to justice is the last thing I want to do. I'll see you when you get back with that piece of shit in tow."

Jigs immediately called Hilda. The line was busy, so he waited a few minutes and tried again. When she answered, she sounded much better than she had the night before.

"I just got off the phone with Mr. Mason," she said. "The sheriff called. They agreed to give me immunity. I'm signing my confession first thing in the morning."

"Good. I had a feeling they'd cooperate. What time are you going in?"

"We have to be there at 8."

"Okay. Now, this is just some unsolicited advice, but I think you need some time away from here, especially after this news breaks. Why don't you ask for some time off? After you finish at the sheriff's, I'll take you to Atlanta. There are some really nice hotels downtown. The change of scenery will do you good."

"…Only if you'll agree to show me the town," said Hilda in a soft voice.

"That's a deal," answered Jigs with a smile. "Just give me a call when you get back."

CHAPTER Seventeen

Judgement

By the time the stores in Cantrell City and Willow Creek were opening for business Monday, everyone had seen the morning paper. The headlines to the special edition screamed:

October 20, 1960
The Kings County Tribune
Special Edition

Breaking News: The Ridge Is Not For Sale
Rezoning Issue in Jeopardy

The story outlined the forgery, without mentioning Hilda's name, and revealed that Nettie was the rightful owner. It made no mention of Cooper, but everybody knew he was the culprit. What mattered the most, however, was the fact that the commission's decision to rezone the ridge was now null and void. A quote from Judge Whitaker substantiated that fact. In addition, Charlie Tate, the commission chair, announced there would be a called public meeting Tuesday evening to reconsider the motion.

There was a universal feeling of relief for most, except for Buddy Tatum and the other two commissioners who voted in favor of the rezoning. Joe Riley Sr. sent his wife to the grocery store to tell Ed McDaniel he had come down with a stomach virus. Superintendent Pritchett called in sick, and Buddy simply didn't show up at the car lot.

The revelation was the topic of conversation on the school bus and in all the classrooms. Every patron at the diner next to the courthouse was reading the paper and talking about it. But there was no place buzzing like *Miss K's Kut & Kurl*, where Kittsee sat at the front desk, with the paper spread out in front of her. Several folks stood behind her, all reading over her shoulder.

"Lord Jesus," exclaimed Laney. "This sounds like something that would happen in a big city, not a sleepy little place like this."

"Well, I've known it was just a matter of time," said Kittsee. "Jack Cooper is a snake. I, for one, am very happy he got caught. Look what he did to Daisy and how he has made Anita suffer for so long…time for that bastard to get his due."

"Why, Kittsee," said Ruby, who had come over from the drugstore to partake in the morning gossip. "I don't think I've ever heard you cuss."

"Well, this is worth cussing about, and I'll say it again. He's a bastard. And for Nettie to be the one who owns that land is the best news I've heard in a long time. You know the stories about the Cooper men and the women in her family. God has prevailed and will judge the wicked."

Jimmy let out a laugh. "Kittsee, you just called somebody a bastard and invoked the name of God in the same breath. So, tell me this: who do you think forged the deed?"

"Probably some slimy lawyer in Chattanooga," added Laney. "I've heard Cooper does shady dealings with some mighty sketchy characters."

"Well, we don't really know if it's Jack," said Ruby. "It doesn't say it's him."

"Oh, I'm pretty sure that's who it is," said Jimmy, who was looking out the front door. "Y'all. Look. Look down there."

The others walked out on the sidewalk and saw two shiny, black sedans parked in front of the bank, with Sheriff Wilkes' car in between them. Four men in suits and the sheriff were standing at the door to the bank. Walker was holding his badge up to the window, while George stared at it…a slight smile on his face. He opened the door and the five men walked inside.

Within minutes, a crowd had gathered on the side-walk and out in the street. Hunter and Pete were there, along with a couple of television crews and reporters. Lucy and Nettie were front and center, along with others who lived on the Valley Road. There was a low buzz of conver-sation, as everyone watched and waited.

Inside, Walker gave instructions to George, who co-operated to the fullest. Buck's deposit was taken from the night depository, and Jack's office searched thoroughly. The agents emptied the credenza behind Jack's desk and put everything in large boxes, along with all of the files in his desk.

Before they left, Walker looked in Buck's money bag. It was no surprise that the bill they were looking for was right on top of a stack of cash. "Gotcha," the agent said with a grin. "Thank you, Mr. Mason. We have what we came for. Carry on. Have a good day."

Oh, you have no idea what a good day I'm going to have, George thought, *"…simply the best Monday morning ever."*

***

The reporters swooped in and surrounded the agents and Sheriff Wilkes as soon as they came out of the bank. Walker stopped and took a few questions but told them to come to the jail and wait for a formal statement. "I'll take more questions then. We have work to do now."

"Do you know what time that will be?" asked the re-porter from the *Atlanta Journal.*

"Nope. I don't. I suggest you get some breakfast and enjoy the scenery in Cantrell City. When it's time, I'll let you know."

"How will you do that?" asked the guy from the Chattanooga television station.

"I'll go outside and start talking," answered Walker.

***

Lucy and Nettie were the center of attention after the agents and Sheriff Wilkes left. It didn't take long for the reporters to realize they were the Andrews and Tanner women mentioned in the story. Hunter was close by, monopolizing the questioning and making sure no one got too pushy. But he realized quickly Nettie and Lucy did not need him to intervene. They were clever as hell.

After a few minutes, Lucy took charge and announced they were done. "Until the investigation is complete, we have nothing more to say."

"Hey...one more thing," shouted the Atlanta Journal reporter. "What are you going to do with all that land, Miss Andrews...sell it and get rich?"

"I'm not going to do anything with it. I'm already rich." And with that, she got behind the wheel of her Chevrolet. Gen climbed in beside her, while Lucy jumped in the back.

Nettie turned on the radio. Sam Cooke's voice crooned, "That's the sound of the men working on the chain gang...."

All three women laughed aloud.

"And we dedicate this to Jack Cooper," said Nettie, imitating a DJ's voice. She backed out of the parking space and headed toward the Valley Road.

***

Jack had been in jail since Saturday. The withdrawal from alcohol had wrecked his body with nausea and sweats. "Hey," shouted Jack. "How about getting me something for this goddamn puking? Is anybody out there?"

He heard the heavy door to the holding area open and in walked Wilkes.

"There ain't nothing I can give you. Just throw some cold water on your face and come over to the cell door." Jack did as he was told. "Now, turn around and put your hands behind your back. "

"For Christ's sake, Wilkes. This shit ain't necessary."

"That's not for you to decide. Now do the fuck as I say." The sheriff cuffed Cooper and led him out of the cell into a small interrogation room, barely bigger than a closet. Walker sat at a table, facing the door. Files and notes were spread in front of him. Wilkes put Jack in the chair across from the agent and sat down next to Walker.

"Good morning, Mr. Cooper. I'm Agent Walker with the GBI. I'm going to ask you a few questions."

"Wait a minute. I thought my lawyer was ready to bail me out."

"You know, he may be ready to bail you out, but the judge hasn't made a decision yet. There's a process, Jack, and it's just beginning. If you're smart, you'll cooperate with us. By the way, would you like something to drink?"

"Yeah...a glass of vodka."

"I'm sorry. I can't fulfill that request, but I'm sure we have some coffee or water, right, Wilkes?"

"Yep. Whadda ya have?"

"Nothing," snapped Jack.

"All right then. Let's get started."

Walker verified Jack's identity, his residence, and his position at the bank. He then asked him if he was the rightful owner of the Ridge.

"Yes. I am. Just look at the deed I filed."

"You mean this one?" asked the agent.

"Yep. That one."

"Now, tell me. Do you recognize these documents?" Walker placed several pieces of paper collected from Jack's desk at the bank that listed loans made to himself, his wife, The Lodge, and Buddy Tatum.

Jack stared at the evidence and suddenly had the urge to mess in his britches.

"I have to go to the can," he said softly.

"By all means," grunted Walker.

When the sheriff brought him back, Jack's face was past pale. It was ashen.

"Okay," said Walker. "Ah, yes...the documents. Jack?"

"It's a list of loans I personally made."

"Huh...so why aren't these loans you made listed on the bank's balance sheets? And why are there cash outs from petty cash for these amounts on the same day you made the loans?"

"Because I had a stupid cunt for a secretary who was always screwing shit up. That's why."

"Name?"

"Excuse me?" asked Jack.

"What's her name? I'll bring her in and question her."

Jack stared at the agent, not saying a word.

"Marge McDaniel," said the sheriff. "Her name is Marge McDaniel. I'll give her a call." Wilkes walked out and left the other two men alone.

"And finally, Jack. Where did the sheriff arrest you Saturday night?"

"You already know where. Buck's BBQ House."

"And you paid for your meal with $100 dollar bill before you left?"

"Yeah, why?"

Walker stood up. "I'll be right back. Don't go anywhere, Jack."

Cooper's head throbbed and his heart pounded. The room was cold and void of any comfort. The walls closed in on the claustrophobic space. He felt like he was falling down a deep, dark hole.

Walker and Wilkes walked back in the room. The sheriff lifted Jack up by the arm. "Jack Cooper, you are under arrest for alleged fraud, bribery, embezzlement, and theft by taking," said Walker.

"Wait. I'll tell you where I got the money. A guy from Atlanta—Sam O'Neil—gave it to me. He and his partners

318

wanted to invest in the mine. I didn't steal it. I just borrowed it."

"What are his partners' names?" asked Walker.

"He wouldn't tell me."

"Of course, he wouldn't," said Walker. "And I'd be willing to bet he didn't give you a telephone number where he could be reached either did he?"

"No. He didn't."

"Well, I'd say you have a problem then," answered Walker. "You might have borrowed the money, but you borrowed some money with trouble written all over it. But that's not all you have to worry about. Right, sheriff?"

"Yeah. Jack, somebody just filed a formal complaint against you for rape. This is long from over."

Walker got as close to Jack's puffy, sweating face as he could stand. "Pack your bags, Jackie. I sure hope that BBQ sandwich was worth the shit you just stepped in."

***

Jigs parked his car across the street from the Georgian Hotel in downtown Atlanta. He cleared his throat and reached for Hilda's hand.

"There's something I need to tell you," he said quietly, praying she would understand. "My name isn't Sam O'Neil. It's Jigs O'Brien. I'm an undercover cop for the GBI. We've been waiting for Jack Cooper to screw up for a long time. I couldn't be honest with you until we knew we had him, but I'm being truthful now. I was just doing my job, but I didn't plan on meeting someone who made me want to blow my cover. Are you okay or do you want me to take you back to Kings County?"

"Jigs, huh? asked Hilda.

"Yeah...Jigs."

"Hmmm...I like that name better than Sam. It fits you." She leaned over and gave him a kiss. "How about that lunch you promised me?"

***

Resolution

The phone at the Tanner home had been ringing non-stop since the news broke. Lucy finally took it off the hook Monday afternoon, but it started up again first thing Tuesday morning.

"Hello," she said, a bit impatiently. "Tanner residence."

"Lucy, it's Sid. First, I want to tell you how sorry I am about your father."

"Hey, Sid. Thanks. Then, I guess you've heard about everything else, too."

"I've done more than hear about it. I've seen it. You and Nettie made the morning news here in Chattanooga."

"Oh, lord. You're kidding me."

"Not a joke," he answered with a chuckle. "You'd think you were old pros at being filmed. Hey, I'm happy for you and the rest of the people there. On another note, you know Anita Cooper, don't you?"

"Yes, I do."

"I have some very important business to discuss with her. Would you intercede for me...maybe set up a time when the two of you can head up here?"

"Of course. Do you mind telling me what this is about?"

"It has to do with Jack and an agreement we had. I doubt she knows anything about it, but as soon as the GBI digs into his files, she will. I want to make sure we take care of this now. Just tell her you met me during the rezoning controversy and you want her to meet me. Make something up about being a patron of the arts or something."

"All right. I can do that. And Sid, even though that incredibly generous contribution to the Boys' Home in Daddy's honor was anonymous, I have a feeling it was you. Right?"

"That's my middle name — anonymous."

320

"Well, thank you very much. I'll be in touch soon about a visit. Goodbye."

Lucy let out a sigh of relief when Nettie walked in the kitchen door.

"Thank god you're here. I'm tired of talking on the phone. It's time to get back to farming. We have a lot to do to get ready for winter. Mama, if you need us, just come over to the barn."

The two women spent the rest of the day working with Billy Joe, taking only a short time for lunch. Luke's absence was definitely felt, but they knew what to do and how to take care of things. He had taught both of them well and neither had ever shied away from hard work.

The difference was that there wasn't one captain anymore. There were two.

While Billy Joe bushhogged the pastures, Nettie plowed up the gardens that weren't sown with cold weather crops. Lucy weeded the collards, turnip greens, and dug some sweet potatoes.

By the time they checked and watered all of the cows, it was close to quitting time. They sat down under the oak tree next to the barn. Nettie took out a bandana and started wiping off her face.

"That sure felt good. I needed to drive a tractor for a while. Did you check the apple orchard? Nate said the pickers would be here next week."

"Yeah. We're going to have a really good crop this year. Hey, what do you think about fixing up the old store again?" asked Lucy. "Given the publicity Kings County has gotten, we'll probably see some tourist traffic out here. And city slickers love to buy anything made or grown in the country. I think it would prove very profitable."

"I love that idea. We need to save that building anyway. That was one of your daddy's dreams." She paused for a second and cleared her throat. "Lucy, there's something I have to tell you. When I went to see Luke in the hospital, he told me some things he had kept to himself since I was a young girl. Do you remember when I told you that I went to the graveyard and got a bad whooping when my mama found out?"

"Yes. I do."

"Baby Cakes, that's not the whole story. Your daddy knew what really happened. He was up on the Ridge and heard me screaming. By the time he got to me, he said I was running as fast as I could. My dress was torn and blood was running down my legs. Then he heard ol' man Cooper yelling that when he caught me, he was going to do more than bust my cherry. Luke hid me in the brush until Mr. Jack stumbled down the path. He never said a word to me. He just nodded his head and pointed toward my house when it was safe to leave. I was in shock and pushed what happened as far down inside of me as I could. It wasn't until your daddy told me about it that I remembered. That's how I knew where to look for the bible. And that's why I'm your business partner now. Luke Tanner was trying to right a heinous wrong done to me. He felt terrible about it."

Lucy stared at the woman who had taught her how to be strong and independent. Never had she loved and admired her more. "Oh, Nettie. I'm so glad that's over for you," she said, reaching for her hand.

"Sugah, I don't think those stories ever end. You just learn how to keep them from making too much noise in your head."

Neither of them said anything for the next couple of minutes. Billy Joe came back from mowing on the backside and sat down under the tree with them. "Whew. That was a long day on the tractor, but I can't say I minded it. It makes going home to a good meal really nice."

"You and Marge have really set up housekeeping, haven't you?" asked Lucy.

"We have. Wanna know a secret?"

"What do you think?" asked Nettie.

"We're getting married this weekend...heading up to Chattanooga to tie the knot."

"That's wonderful, but I thought Marge wanted a wedding," said Lucy.

"No time for that," said Billy Joe with a broad grin. "She's got something baking in her oven."

Both Lucy and Nettie squealed but stopped just as the school bus pulled in the drive across the road. They knew if Hank heard them that he would not stop until he knew the reason.

"Oh my," said Nettie. "I can't wait. I thought we'd never have another baby around here."

Billy Joe stood up. "Now...not a word. We don't want anybody to know until after the weekend."

"Promise," said Lucy. "We'll see you in the morning." They watched him drive away, pausing to wave at Gen and Hank on the front porch.

"We have a lot to be thankful for, Nettie. Even though Mama calls Hank, Henry, and tells the same story over and over about the outhouse turning over when Judge Whitaker's daddy was in it, we are in good shape."

"Yep. We are. And there goes one good reason why I am a lucky woman." She waved at Nate, who was driving down the road toward her house.

"Does he eat with you every night?"

"He knows his feet better be under my kitchen table at suppertime. What about Hunter? It's about time for him to show up, isn't it?"

"No. As you know, he was here last night for the get together we had. But when it came time to turn in, I told him I really needed to get things back to some kind of routine around here. I'm crazy about him, Nettie. That's no secret to him, you, or anyone else, but what am I going to do with him right now? Marry him and move him in? No. Keep doing what we're doing? Maybe...but not here."

"Is he okay with that?" asked Nettie.

"He's fine with it. He understands," said Lucy. "Losing daddy is not something I can get over in a hurry. And I don't know what's going to happen with mama. But Nettie, for the first time in a while, I do think things might settle down."

"Lulu, I can honestly tell you that will never happen. Life doesn't settle down, and it better keep going. Otherwise, we're dead. Don't fool yourself. There's a lot more to the story here on the Tanner side of town."

THE END